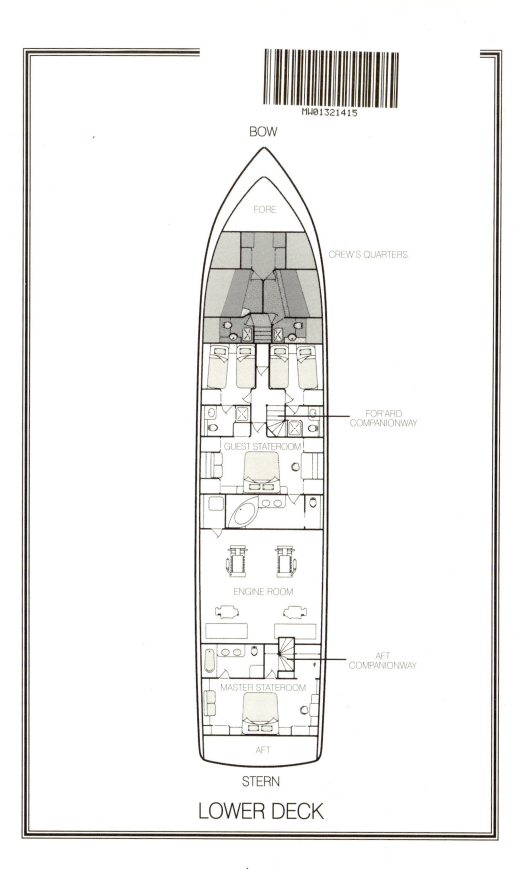

FATAL GREED

Library and Archives Canada Cataloguing in Publication

Landori, Robert, 1934-

    Fatal Greed : a novel

    ISBN 1-55207-090-5

    I. Title

PS8623.A513F37 2006 C813'.6 C2006-940087-3
PS9683.A513F372006

Printed in Canada

FATAL GREED

a novel by

Robert Landori

*To Allysson
Enjoy the read.
Robert Landori
June 3/07*

A STUDIO 9 BOOK

Copyright © Robert Landori-Hoffmann, 2005.
Edited by Robert Davies.

This is a work of fiction, a product of the author's imagination, unrelated to any real persons or actual events. The author affirms moral proprietorship of all characters.

Published by Studio 9 Books
mail@studio9.bz

Ordering information:

USA/Canada:
from the publisher or
Ingram or Baker & Taylor

France/Belgium:
CED-Casteilla
78184 St Quentin Yvelines Cedex France
+33(0)1-3014-1930 43460-3132 info@casteilla.fr

U.K./Euroland/except A-N.Z.
Booksource, 32 Finlas Street, Cowlairs Estate
Glasgow G22 5DU Scotland
+44(0) 141-558-1366 4 557-0189
info@booksource.net

Australia:
Peribo Pty Ltd, 58 Beaumont Rd Mt Kuring-gai NSW 2080
+61 (02) 9457 0011

New Zealand:
Forrester Books N.Z., 10 Tarndale Grove, Albany, Auckland
+64 0-9-415 2080

We wish to thank the Sodec (Québec) for its generous support of our French and English language publishing programs.

Acknowledgement

Writing a well-researched political spy thriller is a formidable undertaking that I could never have managed without the encouragement and help of my family, my friends and the professionals who kindly consented to work on the book with me.

I am particularly indebted to my friend and editor, Robert Davies, who made my prose—especially the dialogues—sparkle, to Pat Hutchins, Elaine Kerner and Marianna Boukas who helped with the editing, to Nicole Pratte and Madeleine Demers who spent countless hours typing and retyping the drafts, and to my friends whose constructive criticism of the early manuscripts made the novel what it is today. To my translators Helene DeSerres, Adele Simon, Eva Olah and Juan-Antonio Juarez—*chapeau*. I must also thank the eagle-eyed Mandy Tendler for her excellent proofreading.

Tom, Irv, Ted, Joe and Buddy, I'm most grateful for your solid and unwavering support.

This said, let me state clearly that I assume full responsibility for any and all shortcomings, errors and omissions in this work.

Last, but not least, thank you my children, Lydia and Paul, for your love and patience and for not losing faith in me.

Montreal, December 2, 2005

To my children, Lydia and Paul

PROLOGUE

At one thirty on a lazy and humid Toronto summer afternoon, Travis McNiff has less than four hours to get fifteen hundred applicator kits assembled, pasteurized, packed and out the door before the workday ends. Shift foreman at Plasmalab, a manufacturer of Plasmacol, a revolutionary surgical glue made from cow blood, Travis leads a team that performed flawlessly throughout the first six months of the year. A few more hours on target during this final week before the company's annual summer shutdown will mean a bonus equal to two weeks' pay for each team member. It's one heck of an incentive, but timing is tight because at five pm all the shift workers are set to close down the line and leave.

Travis has another reason to be keen to get away on time: He has a date at seven sharp for cocktails with Tracy Holland, a coworker and the object of his passionate, but as yet unfulfilled, desires.

Travis loves his job. Hardly twenty-eight, he rides herd over thirty-six women on two assembly lines, and counting another twelve staffing the ancillary equipment and the quality control lab, he has a fluttering pool of forty-eight mostly attractive female employees with whom to flirt incessantly, among them Tracy, a beautiful, and fun-loving, twenty-five-year-old hazel-eyed blonde.

An anxious glance along the assembly line tells Travis that the team is running low on components for the applicator kits, each consisting of two vials (one containing fibrinogen, the other thrombin) the contents of which, when combined by means of a plunger-equipped spraying device, produce a magic-like sterile glue used in surgery involving tissue too fragile and thin for the more common staples or sutures.

Recent demand for Plasmalab's patented applicator and magic glue, manufactured through a process in which cow blood extract is pasteurized, has increased exponentially, and the company is straining to satisfy its customers while respecting its union contract that limits work hours and guarantees the annual shutdown. The company's fortunes ride on its hard-won market share for Plasmacol, its chief moneymaker.

It would be unthinkable to surrender any revenue through failure to deliver product on time.

If Plasmalab's managers are anxious about making target, Travis is doubly concerned, first because of the possibility of losing the bonus, and second because of the imminence of making his own target: bedding Tracy. For two months now he's been pursuing her with shameless single-mindedness, sharing risqué stories, laughing at their bosses' foibles, flirting with gusto and engaging in the occasional fleeting caress, only to have his advances put off, but in a way that seemed to signal Tracy wanted to play him a little longer before giving in. Then, just a week earlier, she suggested that a long weekend at a quiet lodge on a lake in the Laurentian hills near Montreal would be the ideal place to spend time together. "Quality time," as she had put it with a wink.

And Travis had thought of little else since.

"Joe, quick, we need at least another three thousand vials—fifteen hundred of each kind," Travis yells to his assistant, Giuseppe Bucalo, a second generation working class Toronto Italian, whose Neapolitan family had settled in Canada after World War II because no more U.S. immigration visas were available that year. Joe nods, jumps into a lift truck and speeds off in the direction of the inventory processing area. He's soon back, face pale, eyes flashing with anger. "There's been a screw-up in the production planning department," he reports. "Instead of producing 5 cc vials for us this morning they switched to making 10 cc ones. The wrong damn size."

"Jeesus effing Christ, Joe, we can't use 10 cc vials—they won't fit into the applicators we loaded into the system this morning. And we don't have larger applicators on hand. What monkey brain is running things over there today?"

"Dunno, Travis, but listen, I'm pretty sure I saw some extra boxes of the bigger applicators on a pallet at the Oakville warehouse yesterday when I picked up stock for today's shifts."

Travis thinks fast. "Save our asses. We could ship out the larger ones, call it a mistake. I don't think the hospitals would care; they'd get more for their money and the bosses upstairs might bitch a little, but they'll be okay with it in the end. Best they know after the deed is done. How long would it take you to go to Oakville and back, seeing as how it's worth two weeks' pay?"

"An hour, hour and a quarter max, staying out of traffic and using the back roads. You pay the speeding tickets?"

"Yeah, I have a little pull in accounting. Cindy up there still has a sweet spot for me. Here's what we do. Take the van and, to be on the safe side, get me two thousand large applicators." He throws Joe the keys. "Try to be back by three. That'll give us two hours to produce fifteen hundred units. Now step on it."

"Less the setup time," Joe reminds him.

"Joe, move it! We'll clear the 5 cc applicators out of the system while you're gone and I'll figure out something with the pasteurizing while you're away."

"What about the half hour it will take to load the new units into the system after I get back?"

The assembly lines at Plasmalab had been set to produce five finished kits per minute per line this week, but the equipment could turn out three times that much were it not for the pasteurizing section where the standby unit is under repair. If there were a way Travis could circumvent the pasteurizing problem and bribe a skeleton staff to stay on he could still make his quota and leave the plant by six.

"OK, OK, so we'll speed up the line a little."

"With both pasteurizing units working we could do it, Travis. But with the standby unit on the fritz . . . ?"

"For Christ's sake, get the bloody hell out of here and leave the pasteurizing problem for me to solve."

Travis waits until the last 5 cc vial is used up then gets his staff to clear out the applicators remaining in the system.

By three pm they are ready for Joe, but he is an infuriating half hour late.

Joe forestalls the outburst he knows is coming. "Friday afternoon, man, what can you expect?" he shouts. "Traffic is brutal. So lay off of me and let's do what we can to save the situation."

It takes Travis until four to get production rolling again. Tracy sees him struggling and sneaks up to him on her way to the restroom. "Don't sweat it, babe, we'll meet an hour later than planned—at eight," she whispers. " I think we're both worth waiting a little more for, don'cha think?"

Travis turns with his trademark smile on full jets. "Thanks, hon', I'm primed. I'll make it up to you, you'll see!"

Watching Tracy's rear end and very attractive legs disappearing up the metal staircase, Travis reviews what he knows about pasteurizing, which, in truth, isn't much. The process is what kills the microorganisms that "spoil" beer, wine, milk, fruit juice and other kinds of liquids intended for human consumption. To kill them you have to heat the liquid in which they reside to fifty-five degrees Celsius for several minutes. The cavities in each of Plasmalab's two pasteurizing tunnels, one of which is always kept on standby in case the other fails, measure two meters by one meter and can accommodate only 250 kits at a time. Since the pasteurizing process requires 30 minutes, including preheating, pasteurizing, cooling and unloading, the installation limits the plant's capacity to 500 kits per hour.

"Face it, man," Travis mutters to himself under his breath. "You need three hours to produce the fifteen hundred units we need to meet quota, and you can't squeeze it. Our goose is cooked." He laughs out loud, getting a sudden brainstorm. "I'll be buggered if it isn't cooking that this whole damned mess is all about."

He takes a deep breath and waves at Joe to join him in his foreman's cubicle.

"Increase the two assembly lines' speeds gradually so that by six, —he glances at the clock—"we have fifteen hundred units ready for pasteurizing."

"That's about eight units per minute per line, boss. We're pushing it, no?"

"But still, Joe, you're well within the maximum capabilities of the system."

"True, *and so?*"

"If we start pasteurizing the first batch of kits an hour from now—"

"Around five. But—"

"I hear you." Travis gives Joe a wide grin. "We'll cut down on the cooking time so we can do three batches an hour—not two."

"How do you think we can do that?"

"We increase the temperature."

"How high?"

"We'll go as high as ninety degrees Celsius. Have you ever heard of flash pasteurization?"

"Vaguely." Joe is mystified.

"It's the same as regular pasteurization except at higher temperatures—as high as what we're going to use: just below one hundred degrees Celsius—but only for a very short time."

"How short?" Joe asks.

"Thirty seconds. We can do this, man. And the beauty of it is that no one but us will ever need to know."

Joe leaves to reset the assembly line speed controls. Travis grabs an instruction manual and heads for the rheostat regulating the heat within the tunnel's cavity and the timer that opens and closes it.

The staff's work is complete by seven and everyone leaves on the run, heading for vacation city; everyone, that is, except for Joe and five stalwarts who help extract the last batch of kits, which they box, shrink wrap and stack on pallets ready to forklift into the shipper's eighteen-wheel van parked at the loading dock.

While Joe and his assistants shut down the assembly line, Travis takes a lightning-fast shower, changes into street clothes, then completes the day's production report at his terminal, switches off the lights and locks up. But in his haste to fall into Tracy's open arms, he fails to return the temperature controls to their original settings. *Time enough for that when we start up again in two weeks,* he thinks as he turns the ignition key of his Yamaha R1 motorcycle.

    The work problem already behind him, concentrating on how Tracy will look with nothing on and how fast he can accomplish that, he takes off in the direction of the Meadowvale Inn on Mississagua Road and fails to see the semi, now full of his flash-cooked glue, come roaring around the corner of the plant building, the trucker thinking to himself that the weekend was starting much too damn late.

    Travis never feels a thing after the initial millisecond of shock. The impact of the collision throws him for forty-five feet, and despite his three hundred dollar crash helmet, his neck breaks on landing. Death is instantaneous.

CHAPTER ONE

Deputy Director of NATO Intelligence Robert Lonsdale—formerly Bernard Lands—knew his Christmas Holidays were going to be special: As of December 1, he would be on six months' leave of absence with full pay.

He planned to spend most of the month, at least until Christmas, with the family of his friend Nicola Bianchi near Venice then cross the Atlantic to visit his Israeli-American buddy, Reuven Gal, for a couple of weeks in Florida.

Lonsdale had become involved in the intelligence community when the CIA recruited him out of college. He had served first as an idealistic, somewhat naïve, but versatile field agent, then as a hardened, cynical, embittered senior operative, having somehow survived years of double-dealing, treachery and assassination attempts and the death of his wife Andrea. "Survived" was, perhaps, an inaccurate characterization. Although he was alive and in good physical condition for his age, the state of his mental health left a great deal to be desired: The years of stress, insecurity and loneliness imposed on him by his responsibilities had weakened his psyche.

Before the death of his wife, for which he still blamed himself, he had been gregarious and action driven. A hard-living raconteur with a busy social life that served to conceal his real activities, he had developed a profile some may have thought too high for a man in his profession. But all that changed after he lost Andrea. He rapidly became a social recluse and introspective—and even better at his job, which was to coordinate counterterrorist activity worldwide from a secret location in Bethesda, near Washington, less than a couple of dozen miles from the White House.

Then, in the mid-nineties, with Slobodan Milosevic stirring up trouble in Belgrade, the West became nervous about what was happening in the Balkans. NATO was asked to intervene and the United States, NATO's principal member, insisted on direct access to the Alliance's intelligence harvest. Washington wanted an American to be NATO's Director of Intelligence. But to remove the present incumbent, General Joachim Richter, would have insulted the Germans needlessly and this the U.S. did not wish to do because the benefits, it was agreed by consensus, were unlikely to outweigh the drawbacks.

The next best solution was to get an American appointed as Richter's second-in-command. This meant finding a multilingual, seasoned senior intelligence manager with field experience, superior language skills and familiarity with Europe's ways.

The computers at Langley and at the National Security Agency did their dance and came up with Lonsdale: multilingual, born in Hungary, naturalized Canadian, granted U.S. citizenship when he was placed in the CIA's employee protection program, he was a savvy field operative and an excellent program administrator with remarkable successes to his credit.

Lonsdale was senior enough to hold down the job, but not senior enough to make General Richter feel threatened. In the late stages of his career with the Agency and not in line for further internal promotion, Lonsdale's career was at a dead end. He jumped at the opportunity, moved to Brussels, but kept his apartment in Washington and focused his energies on monitoring the roiling and murky waters of the Balkans.

Richter and Lonsdale found they could work well together and did so for three years. Intelligence from Belgrade turned out to be a mine of information on the fault lines of the region that would soon widen into tragedy. Then Lonsdale became eligible for a six-month leave of absence. He decided to take it: The job was beginning to wear him down. He briefed his assistant in depth on important files, set up an email address where he could be reached if it were absolutely necessary, sublet his Brussels apartment on Avenue Franklin-Roosevelt and was in the process of locking his files before leaving for Italy when there was a knock on his office door.

"General Ricther would like you to stop by his office." His secretary gave him a warm smile. "I guess he wants to wish you '*bon voyage.*'"

Lonsdale was pleased. The General and he had gotten along well from the very start. It was nice to think that the crusty old Kraut wanted him to know that he would be missed. He pocketed his keys and crossed the reception area. The door to his boss's office was open.

Richter held out his hand. "Come in, Robert, come in. Let me wish you a good stay, wherever you are going, and a safe return." He handed Lonsdale a glass of schnapps and picked up his own drink with the faintest tentative smile on his lips. "*Prosit.*" They emptied their glasses in unison, shook hands again and Lonsdale left.

The flight from Brussels to Venice the next day had been uneventful and, remarkably, arrived on time. Even so, Lonsdale caught himself checking for surveillance as he got off the aircraft.

Old habits die hard...

Before collecting his luggage at Marco Polo International Airport, a spanking new edifice, all chrome and glass, Lonsdale stepped into the men's room to freshen up; he wanted to make a good impression on his hosts. While washing his hands he cast an appraising glance at his image in the mirror. Under the circumstances he was not too displeased.

He saw an athletic-looking man with rugged features and short sandy hair graying at the temples. The speckled, hazel eyes, though showing fatigue as the result of having taken a very early flight in Brussels after a long, brutal last day at the office, had the piercing look of intelligence. He smiled at his image: His regimen of jogging five miles three times a week was paying off. He looked fit and slim and younger than his years, except for his eyes, though the fine lines around them, betraying pain and suffering and a deep-seated weariness that no amount of sleep could cure, barely showed.

Lonsdale had met Nicola Bianchi in Budapest some years back while jogging. Guests at the Forum Hotel, they both got up at the crack of dawn to run before the air became fouled from the exhausts of the city's automobiles, most without catalytic converters. By coincidence, they kept running along the same route along *Akademia* Street to Parliament Square.

After two days of listening to the footfalls of the silent runner behind him, Lonsdale, forever suspicious of "coincidence," made discrete enquiries about his "jogging partner" and found that the man was a restaurateur-hotelier from Venice, in Hungary on a five-day equipment-buying trip. That evening, Lonsdale left word at the Reception Desk, suggesting they meet at six in the lobby, run together rather than one behind the other, and then share a light breakfast. The run was invigorating as always and over coffee, when the Italian let slip that, this being his first trip to Budapest, he was looking for a guide to show him the sights in his spare time, Lonsdale—who knew the city well and spoke Hungarian fluently—volunteered his services.

It was the beginning of a beautiful friendship.

Over the years the two kept in regular contact and Lonsdale, a bachelor with no particular romantic commitments and living alone, was happy to accompany Bianchi and his large family on holidays to the seaside where an extra adult, willing to help supervise and amuse the six children, was always welcome.

Lonsdale delighted in these times; oases of normalcy in a life that was anything but.

The family lived in Conegliano, a small town about thirty kilometers northeast of Venice. Four hundred years back, Nicola's ancestors had acquired a farmhouse able to accommodate a large family. In the late 18th Century, with the arrival of Napoleon's armies, the building was enlarged and converted into a way station for voyagers on their way to Venice.

Nicola's great-great-grandfather, an outstanding cook, sired three talented assistants. As their reputation spread over the decades, and their own descendants' culinary skills increased from generation to generation, the restaurant side of the way station business developed to the point where *l'Osteria d'Oro* had, by the 1930's, become *the* restaurant of the region.

After World War II, Nicola's grandfather, perhaps the most famous of the Bianchi chefs, a man with an infectious smile and bursting vitality, sold off most of the land he owned, renovated the building and founded a hotel school whose students were provided practical experience through working at *l'Osteria d'Oro*—by now a modern and comfortable hotel behind an ancient façade with a famous restaurant and a popular bar.

The hamlet that had once been Conegliano had by then grown into a prosperous town of fifty thousand with an international reputation for the fine food of its eateries and the excellent *Prosecco* wine produced in the surrounding hills.

When Lonsdale stepped out of the terminal into the blinding December sunshine he at first had difficulty spotting his host. But Nicola, looking healthy and relaxed, was there all right and so were three of his six children, lined up against their father's impressive-looking Mercedes SUV. They helped to get Lonsdale's luggage squared away in no time and piled into the vehicle giggling and tugging at each other and their guest.

The cordiality continued through a pleasant lunch after which the kids swarmed Lonsdale who spent the afternoon playing with them and the presents he had brought each of them. The evening featured a more adult activity: a wine tasting at *Alice,* a *Relais Nelle Vigne* or country inn in nearby Vittorio Veneto.

Busy tasting *Prosecco* and *Grappa* and shaking hands with friends, the very popular Nicola left Lonsdale in the care of Germano DalMolin, chef at *l'Osteria*. It was a brisk, but beautifully clear night. DalMolin led Lonsdale out onto the terrace, to the huge pedestalled brazier in which the embers of the fire their host had lit earlier in the evening to ward off the night's chill were still smoldering. The sound of laughter and excited conversation carried from the inn, contrasting starkly with the almost ominous quiet of the huge vineyards that surrounded the building on all sides.

"How do you like Alice*'s Prosecco,* Mr. Lonsdale?"

Lonsdale raised his glass and took a sip.

"Quite exceptional, I must say." He was on his third round by now and thoroughly enjoying the feminine elements of the gathered multitude. The women looked truly stunning.

"I have just spent a wonderful six months in America you know," the chef confided, "and I mean all of America."

"Whereabouts?" Lonsdale, whose eyes were focused on a statuesque blonde, inquired absentmindedly.

"Mexico, the United States of America and Canada."

"And what, may I ask, were you doing over there for six months?"

"Sampling the cooking and looking for new ideas."

"How long have you and Nicola known each other?" Reluctantly, Lonsdale's eyes refocused on the pleasantly rotund Chef.

"Forever." DalMolin emptied his glass. "We went to classes together from elementary school onward. When we graduated from *gimnasio* Nicola went to Lausanne to learn how to cook and run a hotel and I went to medical school."

"You what?" Lonsdale looked at DalMolin in amazement, not sure whether the Italian was pulling his leg.

But DalMolin was in earnest. "That's right, I went to medical school in Milano, at the university there. I was only twenty years old."

"And what happened?"

"I was a very good student."

"You must have been brilliant to have gotten into medical school at twenty."

DalMolin shrugged. "I guess I was." He sighed and reached for another glass of *Prosecco* at a nearby table. "Anyway, it would have been better for me to have waited a little."

"Why?"

"I was too young, too ambitious and too immature and, for me, you understand, the pressure was too much. I always wanted to be first in my class and—*come se dice*—how do you say—I drove myself too hard." DalMolin looked at Lonsdale as if assessing whether the American could be trusted with a confidence.

Lonsdale, who knew the look, waited and said nothing.

After a minute, DalMolin went on. "I was in my final year at *La Scuola della Medicina,* you understand, and Nicola was in London, working at the St. James Hotel, learning English, that's when I burned out."

"What happened?"

"*No lo so—*I don't really know." DalMolin's voice was low. "All of a sudden I lost interest in everything. I stopped studying, didn't attend classes and did not show for my exams—*niente.*"

"What did you do?"

"Went for long walks in the spring rain, talked to myself, cried a lot and got so depressed that, in the end, I let everything slide—*tutto, tutto.* I stopped going out even for food. I didn't eat for days and was contemplating, how you say, *suicidio.*"

"Sounds like a complete nervous breakdown..."

DalMolin nodded. "*Si.* My mother came to see me because my landlady called her. She took me home and put me to bed. I turned my back to her and lay there for two weeks staring at the wall."

"What about your father?"

"*Morto*—dead."

"Any brothers or sisters?"

DalMolin shook his head. "My mother, she was getting by on a modest widow's pension, she didn't know what to do for me. One day she spoke with Nicola's mother about me and she must have told Nicola, because a week later Nicola came to visit. He spent three days in my stinky room and on the fourth day, instead of going back to London, he took me to a *psichiatra* in Treviso who agreed to see me."

DalMolin stopped. Lonsdale was going to prod him to go on, but Nicola appeared out of nowhere and the spell was broken.

"Come on you fellows," he shouted, slapping DalMolin on the back, "don't look so glum. It's St. Nick's Day tomorrow and we have work to do. Time to go home."

CHAPTER TWO

It is the Austro-Italian custom on December 6, St. Nicholas' Feast Day, to have a person dressed as the Bishop St. Nicholas parade through the streets with a bag of candies and small toys over his shoulder, accompanied by a little "devil's assistant," called a Krampus, wielding a tied bundle of birch with which to thrash children who'd misbehaved during the year.

After the procession had passed *l'Osteria d'Oro* the Bianchi children trooped back into the hotel to decorate the main dining room for the festive private lunch planned to celebrate Nicola's name day.

Attending the meal, in addition to the Bianchis and Lonsdale, were DalMolin's mother, and several of Nicola's friends—all locals, except for Pietro Biscontin, a handsome, bearded Trevisano, and his American girlfriend, Joelle Delatour, an attractive New York literary agent in her mid-forties. Biscontin and Delatour were staying at the *Osteria* on their way to the Milan leather show.

There was a third "outsider," Gerry Sidarenko, an American from Atlanta, a regular at the hotel, whose company manufactured transponder keys in Vittorio Veneto.

Lonsdale was seated between Sidarenko and Delatour.

"What's with these non-Italian sounding names?" she asked Biscontin across the table. "Biscontin, DalMolin." She waved the menu at her boyfriend. "See, here it is—the chef's name is DalMolin and the man we met at the gallery across the street this morning was DalCol..." Delatour looked at Lonsdale. "Should these names not end in I's or O's?"

Lonsdale could not resist teasing her. "Like Sidarenko, you mean?"

"But I'm of Ukrainian descent," the man protested, smiling.

"Ah, well, there goes your Italian theory." Lonsdale laughed, but Delatour was not one to give up. "Come on, be serious. Pietro, what's with these names?"

Biscontin finished his soup and wiped his mouth. "These are typical names from the Province of Treviso, which is where we happen to be. DalMolin used to be Della Molina—'from the mill,' DalCol comes from Della Collina or 'from the hill', while Biscontin is derived from Viscontino, 'little Viscount'."

"Just a local affectation then?"

Lonsdale was about to say something about the etymology of names, but the main course arrived to much oohing and aahing and he became distracted. On finding a veal chop on her plate Delatour turned to her boyfriend, somewhat embarrassed. "Pietro, I thought you had told our hosts that I am a vegetarian."

"I did, *cara mia*. The veal chop on my plate is a real veal chop, but rest assured, the veal chop on your plate is not a real veal chop at all."

"What is it, then?"

"It's a veggie chop," said a voice behind her. DalMolin, all smiles, and dressed in his full Chef's regalia explained. "I did not want the *Signorina* to forego the delicious flavor of my specialty, so I created a unique copy in vegetables."

Loud "bravos" rang out, the guests tucked in and the imbibing began in earnest.

After lunch Lonsdale, who had drunk little, volunteered to drive the exhausted DalMolin and his mother home.

Mrs. DalMolin sat in the back of Nicola's Audi—one of his several cars—with her son sitting in front, next to Lonsdale, giving directions as they drove.

"Finish your story," Lonsdale said after a while.

"What story?"

"The one you started telling me last night—about not being able to afford to continue seeing a psychiatrist."

"Oh, that." DalMolin dismissed the subject with a wave of his hand. "The psychiatrist, he told me he took on one patient a year free as *pro bono* work and said that if I were willing to work hard he would choose me as his 'patient of the year.'"

"Did you accept?"

"*Certo.*" The Chef smiled, remembering. "It took us six years to put the insides of my head together to the point where I could function stress-free and hold down a job, as long as it did not involve too much responsibility. Nicola gave me a job washing dishes at the *Osteria.*"

Lonsdale kept on listening as the car sped through Vittorio Veneto.

"And six years later I became the Executive Chef of *l'Osteria d'Oro.*"

"Well done, Germano."

As he was getting out of the car, DalMolin turned to Lonsdale. "Nicola didn't tell me for years that his psychiatrist friend had no *pro bono* patients."

"Why then did he make an exception with you?"

"He didn't. My friend Nicola Bianchi—a *real* friend—swore my doctor to secrecy and financed my entire rehabilitation out of his own pocket, then gave me a job to start me on the road to self-fulfillment."

* * * * *

Germano DalMolin reported back to work on Monday still feeling hung-over, though he had done no serious drinking on Sunday. When, on Tuesday, he fell down the stairs on his way to the wine cellar for the second time, Nicola took him to see a doctor. Noticing DalMolin's general disorientation, the baffled physician ordered a battery of neurological tests and sent the patient home.

By Friday, DalMolin was running a high fever and bleeding from the nose. On Sunday he began having difficulty focusing and started to vomit uncontrollably at the Treviso General Hospital, where his frantic mother had arranged to have him taken by ambulance.

He died on Monday night.

The Bianchis and the staff of the *l'Osteria d'Oro* went into deep mourning. Lonsdale shared their grief.

On the following Thursday, while DalMolin's autopsy was being performed, Pietro Biscontin telephoned Nicola for the name of a good doctor in Milan. Joelle Delatour was running a high fever and bleeding from the nose. Biscontin had gotten her admitted to the local Santa Cabrini Hospital, but the doctors there were charlatans in his opinion—they seemed to be able to do nothing to alleviate the woman's condition, which was deteriorating by the hour.

On Saturday, the day he was supposed to return home for Christmas, Gerry Sidarenko lost his balance in the shower. He managed to get dressed and to pack, but when, briefcase in hand, he tried to walk to the taxi that was to take him to the airport, he fell again and had to be helped to get up. As he was trying to catch his breath, he began to vomit and his nose started to bleed.

The police rushed him to the hospital.

On Sunday, December 21, Joelle Delatour died.

The morning of December 24, *l'Osteria d'Oro* and its famous centuries-old restaurant were ordered closed by the Provincial Health Authorities. The autopsies performed on DalMolin and Delatour had revealed the cause of their demise as being a new and virulent variant of Creutzfeldt-Jakob disease: Their brains were riddled with multiple microscopic aggregates encircled by holes, making the brain resemble a sponge—the hallmark of bovine spongiform encephalopathy(BSE), or mad cow disease.

The authorities feared this new variant of CJD to be far more virulent than its predecessors and ordered a thorough inspection of the *Osteria*'s food inventory and installations to determine the extent of the contamination.

At this stage of their work they assumed—in error, as it would turn out later—that what the three victims had in common was having eaten the same meal. Consequently, they began to investigate the origins of the meat the late Germano DalMolin had served his guests on December 6 since Biscontin was not there to tell them that Joelle Delatour, a vegetarian, had eaten none of the meat. Two months would go by before their discovery of the true commonality among those who had fallen ill: DalMolin, Delatour and Sidarenko had all undergone minor surgery in October in different hospitals, in different parts of the world.

For the Bianchis the traditional meal on Christmas Eve turned out to be a somber affair. Nicola's wife, Anamaria, an unusually upbeat and energetic woman at all times, tried her best to cheer the family up, but to no avail. The downcast faces along the long dining room table contrasted strangely with the cheerfulness of the room decorated with Christmas baubles. Lonsdale felt frustrated, helpless, and angry. He wished with all his heart that he could think of a way to alleviate the situation somehow, but things were so obviously tragic, it was a hopeless task.

Still, they did attend Midnight Mass, and afterwards Lonsdale and Bianchi stayed up until dawn, sipping *Grappa* in the stillness of the once-so-busy kitchen and reviewing the Italian's options, one of which was to close the business for good and sell the real estate.

Lonsdale counseled waiting. "Let things settle down. Go skiing with your wife and kids in Cortina and give your head a couple of weeks' rest. Exercise. Don't drink too much and force yourself not to think about your business. You'll see—when you come back after Epiphany you'll feel more positive about everything. Besides, the situation may change. There's always the possibility that the authorities will exonerate you."

"Where will you be?"

"A phone call away."

"No—seriously: Where do you go from here?"

"The day after what they call Boxing Day in the U.S. I'm off to Palm Beach to visit a friend."

"One of your 'special' friends from the old days?"

A shadow crossed Lonsdale's face. It still hurt to remember that episode in his life.

"As a matter of fact, yes. His name is Reuven."

"Reuven? What kind of a name is that?"

"Israeli."

"And he is a good friend—yes?"

"The best."

"Then go in peace to see him. And tell him he has a very good friend in you."

"How would you know that?"

"Because, Roberto, you are a very good friend to me."

Lonsdale was touched. "You need anything Nico, you call me

rightaway. If I can help, I will. If I can't, I'll be able to send you to someone who can."

They embraced and went into the living room to watch the children open their Christmas presents.

On December 28, the day after Lonsdale left Italy, Gerry Sidarenko died.

CHAPTER THREE

Fred Keller was thirty when he first became involved in the blood-derivatives business. Born in the mid-fifties in the small town of Forch just outside Zurich, he had a miserable childhood. Pedantic and picky, he had hated the sloppiness of his house, the resigned, ineffective subservience of his mother, the insensitivity of his father to his son's emotional needs, the rigid small-mindedness of the townspeople, the ostracism of his classmates because he was skinny, awkward, unattractive—and different. Although he was ashamed to admit it, he had been relieved when his father died the year before Fred's admission to the ETH: Zurich's equivalent of Boston's MIT.

At the university his isolation continued. Girls shunned him because he was pimply and awkward and because he spoke with a slight stammer. His bookishness and academic pedantry didn't help either. Even the whores on the Niederdorfer Strasse, whom he frequented in hopes that regular sex would quiet his raging hormones and clear up his acne, mocked him.

Nothing seemed to help. His skin improved only after he graduated with an engineering degree and started living with Katya.

He had been trolling for prostitutes on Mullerstrasse when he spotted her in a bar. She had looked up when he passed, smiled, and had waved for him to join her. Taken aback by her open friendliness, he had done so. After buying her drinks, he had invited her to dinner during which she confessed that she was a Russian citizen without proper papers working in Switzerland illegally. They had then gone back to her room where she had given him unprecedented pleasure by performing unprotected oral sex on him.

Next had come a brutal surprise: When she took her clothes off he saw "she" was a transsexual. To his surprise, he didn't seem to mind, on the contrary, it was a revelation!

In the sixth month of his living with Katya his newfound happy little world came crashing down around him: One Sunday evening the Zurich Morality Police arrested her, charged her with soliciting without a permit as an illegal immigrant and deported her to Russia.

Fred never heard from her again.

Devastated, but sure of his sexual orientation at last, Fred decided to emigrate, more to get away from the narrow-minded and nosey burghers of his native Switzerland than because of a burning desire to settle elsewhere.

Canada was actively looking for qualified Europeans, so Keller moved to Montreal where he obtained a Master's degree in biochemistry and a second Master's Degree in virology and microbiology at McGill University. While working on his PhD thesis for his second Master's degree he was offered the position of Associate Scientific Officer at Continental Plasma. He accepted the job without hesitation because he knew the position would give him the prestige he was looking for and the money he needed to complete his post-graduate studies.

At Continental Plasma Fred Keller met Mike Martin.

Born Jean-Michel Martin (pronounced "Marten") in Quebec City, "Mike" Martin was the youngest and only male of five siblings. As a result, his mother and four sisters had spoiled him rotten, turning him in the process into a selfish, intolerant male chauvinist. Like Fred, he had attended McGill University, where he obtained an MBA with First Class Honors and was arrogantly expecting to take over his father's business one day. This, however, was not to be; the day Mike graduated his father, who recognized his son for being what he was, announced he was selling his tire distribution company.

Mike's disappointment was profound. In a pique, he moved to Toronto and became Assistant to the Marketing Manager of Continental Plasma a few days after Fred Keller's arrival there.

Mike was a quick study. He realized within days that his knowledge of biochemistry and biology was totally inadequate. In a bold move to turn this shortcoming to advantage he asked for help from his boss, the Marketing Manager, who introduced him to Fred Keller.

Sensing a mutual advantage in pooling their abilities, the two young men disciplined themselves to work together so that, by the time Fred left Continental five years later, they had become close, though they were quite different in character: Mike wanted more than anything to be his own boss, while the bookish Fred craved academic recognition as an admired expert in his chosen field.

The elder Martin died the month Mike turned twenty-six.

Never having forgiven his father for selling the family business out from under him, Mike listened in silence, unmoved, to the eulogy delivered by his oldest sister. When his turn came to cast a handful of dirt into the open grave he did so with glee, swearing to best the old man at everything: being a father, being a husband, and—above all—being a successful entrepreneur.

It took Mike ten years of hard work to identify his business niche— the blood derivatives industry. He sought out Fred who, by then, had impressive academic credentials and years of research in molecular biology and virology under his belt as Chief Scientific Officer of Warner-Lambert Canada.

Fred bought into Mike's dream. The two pooled their resources and founded Plasmalab using Mike's inherited money and Fred's professional contacts. Through these, Plasmalab obtained a license to distribute products derived from whole blood.

During the first five years of its existence the company had to struggle hard to survive. In the end, however, Fred's brilliance and Mike's tenacity paid off. Fred had been able to create a revolutionary surgical glue, Plasmacol, derived from bovine blood, which had not only remarkable healing qualities, but was also inexpensive to manufacture.

By then Mike had become an even more selfish, cynical man who felt life had dealt him an unjust number of disappointments. To the litany of imagined wrongs, including his father's unfairness toward him, he now added his perception that Fred Keller had treated him shoddily when they renegotiated their relative positions in their company at the time Plasmalab had to be taken public. Although Mike and Fred had started off as equals Fred had insisted that he be allowed to keep the patents for Plasmacol in his own name in exchange for granting exclusive manufacturing and distribution rights to Plasmalab worldwide.

Mike had argued that such an arrangement was neither within the spirit nor the letter of their shareholders' agreement, but Fred had dug in his heels and would not budge. He knew that unless Mike agreed, the company could not go public and, as a consequence, would go under—no one was willing to invest in a Plasmalab held in private hands.

Mike had been forced to capitulate, but did so with great reluctance and unresolved grudge.

The Initial Public Offering (IPO) was very successful and yielded over fifty million dollars to the company, enough for Plasmalab to build a plant in Toronto and to finance the rigorous two-year testing program required by the FDA and Health Canada before Fred Keller's magic glue could be marketed to the general public.

The success of the IPO increased Mike's resentment of the way his crafty Swiss partner had out-maneuvered him. He swore to get even, and, in the end, to oust Fred from the partnership. As a first step, he established a secret offshore bank account in Bermuda through which he began to trade Plasmalab shares.

Plasmacol became very popular—surgical professionals liked the easy-to-use glue that saved time during operations and was inexpensive. Plasmalab did well. Sales climbed to two hundred million dollars by the seventh year of its existence and after-tax profits that year reached twenty-four million dollars, a dollar per share. The stock was trading at sixty times earnings or sixty dollars per share. Mike and Fred each owned six million of them in Canada, but Mike also owned four hundred thousand Plasmalab shares in his secret account.

CHAPTER FOUR

Reuven Gal, deeply tanned and full of energy, was waiting for Lonsdale as he emerged from Concourse B at Palm Beach International Airport.

Reuven was a Sabra—an Israeli-born Jew—with an attitude seeded in the Holocaust. His mother, a concentration camp survivor, had emigrated from Transylvania to Israel where she married his father, a member of the Haganah, the underground fighting the British before independence. When the son came of age, he had followed in his father's footsteps by enlisting in the Mossad—the Israeli secret service—where he served with distinction for twenty-five years, after which he retired as a security consultant.

He greeted Lonsdale with an affectionate "You got old!"

"And you're still ugly," countered Lonsdale. Then they laughed, embraced and took the escalator down.

Lonsdale reached for his luggage on the carousel, but Gal shoved him aside. "Let go," he commanded. "This work is for strong men. I'll take you home and get you settled. Perhaps we'll even have a swim if you feel up to it. My housekeeper has prepared snacks for us—unless, of course, you'd prefer something more substantial."

"That'll be just fine." In fact, Lonsdale was longing to sit in the sun for a while after the flight and do absolutely nothing.

Gal, a few years younger than Lonsdale, was driving a Jaguar, as always his signature choice. This one was a kick-ass bottle green SXR. "For dinner we're booked at *Café l'Europe* on South County Road. The girls will come by to pick us up around seven. We'll have drinks and eat around nine."

"Whoa, big guy," Lonsdale raised his hand. "What's all this about girls?"

"My girlfriend Gina and her sister Adys." Gal tried to look innocent, but was making a poor job of it.

Lonsdale pretended to be put out. "Reuven, you're incorrigible. How often must I tell you to stop trying to fix me up? When I'm ready I'll organize my own dates, thank you."

"Come on, old boy," his host protested. "I'm just asking you to do me a small favor, that's all."

"What favor?"

"Gina's twin sister is here from New York for the Christmas holidays and if I want to see Gina I'm obliged to drag Adys along. You'll be my guest for dinner if you'll help me out."

"No way," protested Lonsdale. "The deal is as always: You feed me and lodge me, but when we go out, I pay!"

Gal gave in. "Very well then. Now let me tell you about Adys."

Lonsdale pretended to listen, but his mind was still on Nicola and his misfortunes.

"...and I'd really appreciate your help old friend because I'm serious about this woman," Gal was saying. Lonsdale put the thoughts about Bianchi out of his mind and focused on the moment.

"I don't believe it."

"What is it you do not believe?"

"A leopard does not change his spots."

"Really?"

"Really. You fall in and out of love all the time."

Lonsdale, whose friendship with Gal dated back two decades, knew that the Israeli's psychological make-up was complex. In spite of his apparent bonhomie and swagger he was an insecure product of the post-Nazi era during which Israel had to fight two wars of survival in the Middle East and Jews around the world had to put up with continued harassment and violent acts of discrimination. Such a background and the indirect trauma of his mother's suffering in the camps had produced a hard, focused egocentric unable to form intimate lasting relationships.

Lonsdale knew the syndrome well. He had been thirty-eight by the time he had become mature enough to settle down and get married. Three years later his wife, whom he had loved deeply, had gotten killed. Since the time of her death he had only had one meaningful relationship, and that had lasted for less than two years.

The Israeli shook his head in exasperation as he crossed the bridge to Palm Beach and pulled into the driveway of the large, well-protected house he owned on Ibis Crescent alongside the Inter Coastal Waterway. He did not like it when someone, especially Lonsdale, saw through his protective shield.

Lonsdale dumped his bag in one of the guest bedrooms and walked out to the pool patio situated between the house and the waterway. Gal handed him a Pacifico beer and poured himself one too. He raised his glass. "Nice to see you alive and well and healthy. Now help yourself to some grub." Gal couldn't help sounding somewhat English; he had learned the language in a school run by Brits.

"Cheers." Lonsdale saluted with his beer.

Once the dishes were out of the way, they settled into comfortable armchairs facing the canal and neither spoke until Gal broke the silence. "After dinner we might drive over to a *salsateca* in West Palm. I presume you do dance?"

"Used to, Reuven, used to. In fact, I was quite good at it. Learned to dance Latino-style in Cuba from a wonderful *Santiaguera*." Lonsdale smiled, remembering. "But that was some time ago."

"I'm not worried about you." The Israeli took off his shirt and Lonsdale saw Gal must have been pumping iron. His musculature was well defined and his stomach flat. "It's like riding a bike—once you've learned how, you never forget."

"Are you telling me these two ladies like dancing?"

Gal sighed, at peace with the world. "I don't know about Adys, but Gina is a marvelous dancer."

They stayed by the pool well past four, catching up. Gal, whose security business was booming as more and more of the wealthy people making Palm Beach their home began to fear for their physical well being, had more on his plate than he could manage alone. "Why the hell don't you take early retirement from NATO, secure your pension and join me here?"

"Jesus, Reuven, when will you start teaching yourself to be less pushy? I haven't even unpacked and you already have me fixed up with a woman and working with you. What's there left for the rest of my stay—marriage and twins?"

His host smirked. "Don't you think it's about time you ceased being a civil servant and joined the exalted ranks of the entrepreneurial elite? I'm not asking you to work *for* me, I'm asking you to work *with* me—to be my partner. And by partner, I mean a full partner."

"Fifty-fifty?"

"Yes—fifty-fifty."

Lonsdale shook his head. "That's unfair to you. During the last ten years you've built a solid business here. What could I contribute—besides money, of which I don't have that much—to qualify for equal partnership?"

"Your contacts, your rank, your name, your reputation."

Bewildered, Lonsdale looked at the Israeli in astonishment. "You're really serious."

"That I am."

"You've taken the wind out of my sails Reuven. I don't know what to say."

"Say yes, then. With you in Washington and me down here, we could develop the corporate side of the business that is nonexistent at present. We'd make a fortune."

To hide the turmoil within him Lonsdale got up and walked around the pool, pretending to inspect the potted plants along the way. Then he sat down again next to Gal. Accepting the Israeli's proposition would mean moving back to Washington and giving up his present lifestyle, that of a senior, well-respected bureaucrat in a comfortable position with a secure and ever increasing pension.

Once on the "outside" he'd soon be forgotten by his contacts on the "inside," unless he spent a great deal of energy and money to continue cultivating them. He would also have to start working hard again for a living—selling his own and his partner's services in a very competitive environment. Although he'd have his substantial pension to keep the wolf from the door, he'd have to watch his expenses to start with—no more perks, no official car and driver, no duty-free liquor, no first class travel around the world.

But he'd be his own boss in charge of his own destiny. This was worth something. He could settle down and wouldn't have to worry about the treachery, danger and double-dealing that had characterized the last three decades of his life... Or was he just kidding himself ... again?

"Let me think about all of this." He looked at his watch. "I'm not saying 'yes,' but I'm not saying 'no' either. Let me shower and get ready for my date." He winked and went into the house.

The Martinez sisters arrived a few minutes after seven.

Standing on the seawall overlooking the canal and enjoying the spectacle of the setting sun's dying glitter in the windows of the houses on the other side of the Waterway, Lonsdale was daydreaming about what life would be like after having accepted Gal's generous offer, and didn't hear them come in.

"Ola, Caballero," a husky, melodious voice called out behind him. Startled, he spun around, almost losing his balance.

A smiling woman with a drink in each hand stood before him. "I did not mean to frighten you," she went on in Spanish. "Reuven asked me to pour you a drink and bring it out to you." She handed him a glass.

Flustered, Lonsdale took it from her. The woman raised hers. "*Salud*—to health." Her voice had a soothing quality.

"I'll drink to that," Lonsdale replied in Spanish. The drink was Absolut and San Pellegrino on ice, prepared just the way he liked it.

"I hope I got the proportions right. Reuven said it should be about one third-two thirds."

"Perfect." Lonsdale cleared his throat awkwardly and gave her an appraising look.

She was about five foot four inches tall, had long, reddish-blonde hair, and appeared to be in her forties though Lonsdale suspected she was older. Dressed with style in a body-hugging, light-green split skirt, a wide, black leather belt around her slender waist and a white silk blouse that showed off her full figure to great advantage, she met his gaze without blinking.

"Why are you staring at me?"

"Because you are very beautiful, A, and B, because before making a pass at you I should find out whether you are Gina or Adys and if Reuven will kill me or cheer me on if I fall hopelessly in love with you."

Her laugh was spontaneous and very pleasing. "I'm Adys. And Reuven was right about you being charming. By the way, your Spanish is almost accent-less. How did that happen?"

"*Gracias, Señorita.*" He bowed and stepped up to her to kiss her on the cheek.

Blushing, she pulled away. "Reuven should also have told me that you are a dangerous flirt."

"So I am Adys, so I am." As he joined in the banter Lonsdale realized that the woman had somehow managed to turn the clock back twenty years to the time when he was, indeed, a great and quite heartless flirt and *bon vivant*.

Adys took his hand. "Come, let's join the others." Her touch was cool and reassuring. Hand in hand they walked around the pool to meet Gina halfway.

"So this is the great Robert Lonsdale." She held out her arms to be embraced and Lonsdale kissed her on both cheeks, French style. "For the past couple of weeks Reuven has been talking about nothing else except your impending visit. I'm glad you're here so I can find out how much of what he has told me is true."

"About me?"

"Not only about you." Gina looked so much like her sister that Lonsdale had the impression he was looking at Adys' mirror image.

"Thank God you have a ribbon in your hair," he managed to stammer. "Otherwise I wouldn't be able to tell the two of you apart."

Reuven appeared with a bucket of ice in his hand. Gina turned to him. "Robert has worked out how we accommodate our friends so people can tell us apart." Her English had a distinctive Latino accent.

"Don't you believe a word of what Gina says." Gal turned to Lonsdale. "She is a cruel woman."

"That I don't believe."

"The other day she arrived wearing no ribbon in her hair and it took me half an hour to realize that I was talking to her and not to Adys."

It was shaping up to be an evening of fun, good food, fine wine and easy conversation.

The *Café l'Europe* seemed dropped into Palm Beach in one piece directly from Rome or, perhaps, Monaco. The food was expensive, but delicious, the service European and impeccable.

Gina was a bank manager in West Palm Beach, Adys the managing director of the *Repertorio Español*, a well-known Spanish-language theatre in New York City. The sisters, born in Santiago de Cuba, had lived sheltered middle-class lives until Fidel Castro came to power. By the time the family could move to Atlanta, after a two-year wait for permission to leave Cuba, the Martinezes had been stripped of everything they had once owned.

"Those were tough times," Gina recalled between bites of dessert, a delicious chocolate and praline cake. "But that's enough about us. How about your friend here?" She looked at Lonsdale.

"Me?" Lonsdale gave her a studied look. She seemed to bask in the warmth of his smile. "I'm a sort of Heinz 57 varieties kind of guy, born in Central Europe, Budapest, in fact—a mixture of Austrian, Hungarian, Swiss and Italian. I went to school all over Europe, emigrated to Canada and worked here in the U.S. and in South America."

"Have you ever been married?" Adys asked.

Lonsdale became disconcerted. Gal saw it and intervened. "Robert's wife was killed in an unfortunate accident."

"That's when Reuven and I met." Lonsdale pulled himself together. "What about you?" He wanted to change subjects. "Have you ever been married?"

"Yes, I have." Her beautiful green eyes were looking into his, searching. "And I have two grown children. They live in Spain—in Valencia."

"And your husband?"

"I'm a widow."

"I'm sorry. I know something about that." Lonsdale asked for the bill, then added, "Let's go dancing before our collective baggage wears us down."

They drove over to *Nessun Dorma*, the West Palm Beach *salsateca* featuring Meme Solis, the well-known Cuban singer, and his orchestra. Lonsdale accompanied Adys to the dance floor with some trepidation, but the moment he took her in his arms he knew things between them would be just fine.

Adys was not a good dancer—she was a great one. This inspired Lonsdale to let go and reveal the deep sensuality of which he was capable, amazed at the change within him. Contact with Adys' body seemed to want to make him celebrate. He wanted to forget Italy and death and celebrate being alive, and well, and happy.

He hadn't felt that way for years.

Because Gal was planning a barbecue to introduce his houseguest to his Palm Beach friends, Lonsdale was dispatched to the Presidente supermarket for Argentine churrasco steaks the next morning and he took Adys with him. Gina stayed behind to help their host tidy up.

There were only four invitees: Ralph and Fortune, an elegant Moroccan Sephardic couple now residing in Palm Beach, specialists in renovating and reselling houses built by Addison Mizner, the pre-eminent Florida architect; Karl Hauser, a handsome, urbane senior Delta Airlines pilot from Austria and Gal's occasional assistant on special assignments; and Dr. Fred Keller, Hauser's partner.

"Fred's a brilliant virologist," Gal had told Lonsdale before their guests' arrival, "and his company's products are great commercial successes. His company is a target for industrial espionage and needs the type of services we can offer."

"We?"

Gal grinned. "I know, I know, I'm pushing again, old chap. It's just that, with your credentials, selling Fred could be quite easy..."

Lonsdale grinned back. "Leave it be pal, for just a bit. Give me time to think. I'll let you know by the end of my stay here. But tell me about Karl."

"He is a somewhat uptight pilot, but pleasant. He's also a bit of a whiz at lamplighting—you know, shadowing people. He's helped me out on occasion in the past with, I dare say, more than a modicum of success. He and Fred are a couple, by the way."

Reuven got the barbecue going around six and Gina began serving Sangrias spiked with brandy. The ambiance soon became very laid-back and mellow.

After some light hors-d'oeuvres Reuven started to cook the steaks. Then the housekeeper put a huge plate of piping hot Cuban-style French fries on the table and everybody tucked in.

"Amazing, these steaks," Gal was saying, as he brought more meat to the table. "Robert has just visited Italy where nobody dares eat beef anymore."

"You mean because of the foot and mouth disease?" Having helped herself to a large portion of fried potatoes, which she loved, Fortune cut into her meat with gusto.

"No, no," said her husband. "That's not a people problem. It's that other thing, that mad cow disease thing, that humans catch."

"That is correct." Keller sounded like a teacher addressing his class. "It is, in fact, a variant of the mad cow disease that is highly dangerous for us."

"You mean Creutzfeldt-Jakob disease, don't you?"

Keller, who was reaching for the wine, almost dropped the bottle. "How do you know about CJD Mr. Lonsdale?" His voice had an edge to it. "Are you a virologist?"

"No. I work for NATO, but I've had recent contact with people who contracted the disease."

"Where?"

"In Italy."

"But that is impossible, quite impossible. There have been no reported confirmed cases of CJD in Italy." Keller sounded so insistent that Lonsdale's professional interest was aroused.

"Why are you so sure?"

"It's Fred's business to know," Gal interjected. "His company is in the business of manufacturing a surgical glue made of bovine blood. Am I not right, Fred?"

Keller, mouth taut, nodded agreement, then excused himself and went to the washroom. By the time he returned Lonsdale was listening to Ralph telling a risqué story.

"Can I have a word with you?" asked Keller after the laughter died down. He seemed troubled.

"Of course." Surprised, Lonsdale followed the scientist to the sea wall.

"You said that you were in recent contact with suspected victims of Creutzfeldt-Jakob disease in Italy. Am I correct?"

"Almost. What I had meant to say was that I had been in contact with three people who contracted a new variant of CJD, two of whom then died."

Keller paled under his suntan. "Where was this?" His voice sounded strained.

"Near Venice."

"And how do you know these people died of CJD?"

"Because their autopsies showed that their brains were riddled with signs of CJD." Lonsdale noticed that Keller's hands had begun to tremble and that, all of a sudden, he had developed a nervous blink.

"What is it you do at NATO, Mr. Lonsdale, if you don't mind my asking?"

Lonsdale had not intended to upset Gal's guest and could not understand why his words had triggered such an intense reaction in the man. "I am NATO's Deputy Director of Intelligence, presently on temporary leave of absence."

"How did you find out that the authorities were dealing with a new variant of CJD?"

"In my line of business we keep asking questions when things don't sound right. The victims died within a few days of falling ill. The normal incubation period for CJD is one year or more—but you know that. Under the circumstances I wanted to be sure that the authorities had gotten their diagnoses right, so I kept after them until they told me that they thought they were dealing with a new variant of the disease."

His answer seemed to upset Keller even more. "Would you mind giving me some details?" He sat down on the wrought-siron chair next to them. "Please forgive me," he added, "but, as a virologist, I am very interested in CJD in all its manifestations."

Lonsdale obliged and related what had happened in Italy, keeping his narrative succinct and leaving out the names of the people and the places involved. When he had finished Fred forced a smile and held out his hand. "Sorry for taking up so much of your time."

"Don't mention it. We can talk some more the day after tomorrow. I understand we're invited to your house on New Year's Eve."

"Quite right, quite right," Keller confirmed as they walked back to the other dinner guests. "We'll see each other at my place on Wednesday night and speak again."

He buttonholed Gal inside the house. "I must thank you for a very entertaining evening, a delightful meal and for providing, as always, most interesting company. I'm afraid Karl and I have to take our leave—he has an early departure tomorrow."

"Oh? Will he be back by New Year's Eve?"

"He's returning a favor to someone who had helped him out at Christmas. He is working the flight to Boston and back on the thirty-first." Keller sounded angry.

Gal was pleased to hear that. "I'll probably need his services again early in the New Year, by the way." Never too sensitive about when not to push, the Israeli felt he had earned the right to do a bit of self-promoting. "Should you and I not discuss how my firm could be of assistance to yours?"

"Yes, we should... and soon... but now we must be off."

The Moroccan couple also took their leave. While the housekeeper was cleaning up, Gina put on a CD featuring The Buena Vista Social Club's Omara Portuondo and Adys asked Lonsdale to dance.

It felt so natural. He held her body close, Cuban-style, and let the Latin beat overwhelm them.

The bolero ended much too soon and she went to get them something to drink. As he watched her walk away he realized that, somehow, it hurt him to see her go.

CHAPTER FIVE

As far as his circle of friends in Toronto was concerned, Fred Keller was a confirmed bachelor. Some suspected he was gay, but so what? Good old Fred could always be counted on to make up a missing fourth at bridge, or to act as escort for an unattached female—educated, sophisticated and well-mannered, he was a safe and enjoyable date.

Few of his acquaintances in Toronto knew about Karl Hauser, with whom he kept company in Palm Beach and elsewhere whenever he could.

Keller lived in an exclusive condo on Toronto's Harborfront. He also had a sumptuous Palm Beach penthouse at Bradley Place in a luxurious five-storey building with only two apartments to each floor. He and his fellow condo owners, all Canadian Snowbirds who used their Florida apartments in the winter season only, took turns hosting a New Year's Eve party for those in residence and their friends. This arrangement—a party once every ten years—was, to be sure, not pushing the social obligations envelope too much.

Unfortunately, Keller, whose turn it was this year to play host, wasn't much good at arranging social gatherings so he hoped Karl would take charge. Knowing Fred's predilection for unreasonableness Karl organized everything down to the last detail so that all Fred had to do was uncork the champagne. In spite of this, Fred, on edge, made it clear to Karl that he felt he'd been let down somehow and the two had a bit of a row.

Of course, Karl had no way of knowing what Fred was really worried about: He had become so preoccupied with what Lonsdale had told him that he had contacted the World Health Organization for an update on the incidence of "new variant" Creutzfeldt-Jakobs Disease (nv CJD) worldwide.

The devastating answer from the WHO—confirming *three* cases of new variant CJD in Italy and reporting five, possibly six, additional cases across the U.S., one in Canada and eight in the U.K.—had reached Keller late the night before his party.

The epidemic he had predicted three months earlier was beginning to take shape.

In late August Fred had hosted a high-powered Japanese delegation, interested in acquiring Plasmalab.

He had taken his visitors on a tour of the company's facilities, starting with the Quality Control Lab where he explained the biochemistry of surgical sealants, outlining in detail Plasmalab's patented process for producing Pharmacol, the miracle glue and accelerator of wound healing.

"What about the problem with bovine blood?" one of the visitors had asked. "We understand that Pharmacol is manufactured from animal blood."

Keller had answered without missing a beat. "You are, of course, expressing indirect concern about the danger of manufacturing a product that may propagate Creutzfeldt-Jakob Disease, which is linked to BSE, otherwise known as 'mad cow' disease." He looked around the room then continued, weighing his words with care. "Let me assure you gentlemen that I have studied this potential hazard carefully and designed a process which eliminates it to a degree of certainty of 99.9999%. Next, I built a pilot-plant to test the process and analyzed the product manufactured in that plant."

Since there had been no further questions, they continued the tour, reaching the pasteurizing unit a few minutes before lunchtime.

"Production capacity is limited by our ability to pasteurize no more than five hundred surgical sealant kits an hour," Keller had said in closing, "because we can only use one pasteurizer, though we have two."

"How come?" came a voice from the crowd.

"The second is on perpetual standby so as to guarantee continuity of production in case of a breakdown. As you have seen, we have backups for everything—we even have two assembly lines." He had ushered his guests toward the cafeteria where a gourmet meal was being catered for the distinguished visitors.

That is when, passing the controls of the pasteurizer, Keller froze as he noticed that the temperature rheostat was set at FLASH, *contrary to his strict instructions that pasteurization was NEVER to be higher than fifty-five degrees Celcius and NEVER for less than a duration of ten minutes.*

He had ordered an intensive investigation of the matter on the spot.

Three days later he had called Mike Martin, insisting they meet over lunch that same day. Mike, fed up with his partner in general, had initially declined, but finally gave in because Keller had been so adamant.

"Where's the fire, Fred?" he had asked the virologist as soon as they were seated. "What's so important that you made me drop everything to accommodate you—as always."

"Consider yourself lucky I haven't burdened you sooner with what I've found out recently." Keller had tried hard to remain in control of his emotions. "But then even I wasn't sure about what was going on until this morning." His voice broke—the stress was too much. "You remember the foreman who died, the fellow who was such a crackerjack?"

"And always chasing women," Mike had said without thinking.

"His name was Travis McNiff. You thought he could do no wrong."

"Right. He seemed to know his business and the staff adored him." Mike had gone on the defensive. "No one could get people to work harder and to get product out the door on time better than Travis. Besides, he was likeable. It was tragic the way he died in that stupid accident this summer."

"It seems, the afternoon of the accident McNiff's people were running behind schedule and in danger of losing their special bonus. To accelerate production he reset the pasteurizing rate to produce three batches of Plasmacol an hour instead of two by doubling the pasteurizing temperature to cut ten minutes off each half-hour cycle."

Mike had grasped the impact of what Fred was saying right away. "Instead of slow pasteurizing, he ran a bunch of product through a flash pasteurizing process?"

Fred had nodded primly. "That is correct."

"You say this happened at the end of the second week of July. We're in mid-September. The affected batches must still be in inventory; either in our refrigerated warehouses or, worst case, in the fridges of our client hospitals. We must identify and recall them." He had glanced at his partner. "That is, if you feel the change of procedure had an impact on the production process that would render the product unsafe."

"I wish it were as simple as that." Keller, fiddling with his cutlery, had been sweating profusely. "When I discovered what had happened, which, by the way, was during the visit of Dr. Seko and his Japanese delegation, I had the original pasteurizing parameters reinstated."

The blood had drained out of Mike's face. He felt as if someone had punched him in the stomach. "You're telling me we used an unapproved procedure for a month?"

"For five weeks, maybe six even."

"Oh Jesus God! How could such a thing have happened?"

"McNiff never turned the pasteurizing rheostats back to their original settings before leaving on vacation. I guess, he intended to do so after coming back, but he never did. He couldn't; he was dead."

"And his successor, Joe something or other?"

"Bucalo never thought about the matter."

"Don't tell me that when they started up after the shutdown they didn't recheck the equipment settings."

"They didn't have to. The first batches that came off the assembly line after the shutdown were run through the other pasteurizing unit, repaired the first day we were back in production. The settings on that unit were within the proper parameters."

"So what went wrong—"

Keller had cut Mike off. "The pasteurizing unit broke down again a couple of days later, so they went back to using the one McNiff had tampered with."

"And you're going to tell me they went on using it right up to the time you discovered that the settings were wrong?"

"Until August 31, to be precise."

"And that five, maybe six, weeks' production may have to be scrapped?"

"At a cost in excess of twelve million dollars."

"Half the profit projected for this year!" Mike's gut had begun to constrict again. "Do you realize what this will do to the stock price, not to mention the merger talks with the Japanese that are scheduled to start next week? Unless, of course, your tests... I presume you did some sample testing of the affected batches?"

Keller had nodded, forcing himself to swallow the spoonful of soup in his mouth. "Of course I have! During the past week I have done nothing but that. First, I designed a spot reagent test and looked for discoloration in the samples. It took me a day to find the right way to do it."

"And then?"

"My assistant and I uncapped a hundred vials at a time and, using a pipette, added a drop of reagent to each test sample. We then placed the trays containing the samples into a clean room and revisited them later."

"That's a lot of work."

"What else could I do?" Keller had shrugged. "I had to keep the problem under wraps."

"What did you tell your lab assistant?"

"That I was working on a new vaccine."

"How many vials did you test?"

"Believe it or not, we got so good at it that we could prepare almost two hundred vials for testing in an hour."

"That's pretty good—about twenty seconds per vial."

"Anyway, we averaged twenty-five hundred tests a day during seven days."

"That's over seventeen thousand vials."

"Close to one week's production."

"And?"

Keller had been showing signs of severe stress, squeezing his eyes shut then opening them wide again and again. "Here's the bottom line," he had whispered. "Out of the seventeen thousand five hundred kits tested we found ten were contaminated."

"With what?"

"We don't know, but it looks like a virulent mutation of the CJD virus."

"Oh, God Almighty," Mike had blurted. "And how large is the affected batch?"

"To be safe, let's say six weeks' production: one week in July, and five in August."

"That much?"

"We date our product by the week of its manufacture. We can, therefore, identify the kits made during the last week in July, and in each of the four full weeks in August. But product manufactured during the last three days of August is labeled as having been produced during the first week of September—which of course it was."

"So we're looking at a twelve million dollar reduction in our forecasted earnings for this year. The stock will halve in value; it may, in fact, go lower, perhaps to one third." *And make me poorer by a quarter of a billion dollars in the process,* Mike had added to himself.

Keller had looked at him in amazement. "Have you taken leave of your senses? When I start recalling product I will have to advise the FDA and Health Canada and give them the reason. They'll insist we 'temporarily' shut down, decontaminate our equipment and retest. We're talking about having to suspend production of Plasmacol for at least six months. By the time we get back into the market, our competitors will have stolen all our clients. Let's face it: Plasmalab, as we know it now, is *kaput*—finished."

"Come on, we have other products beside Plasmacol."

"Yes, but they account for only a third of our turnover. We'd never weather the storm with them, never..." Keller had shaken his head.

"What would happen if we did nothing?"

"We would run the risk of killing between fifty and a hundred people, or more."

"Why more?"

Keller's squinting had been getting worse. "Because, I don't yet know what kind of a mutant virus we've accidentally created. As you know, CJD is a horrendous, fatal, brain deteriorating disease—Alzheimer's on fast forward—which is quite rare. A new variant, nv CJD, which made its appearance in January 1994, has been related to what people popularly call 'mad cow disease.' Its incubation period is much, much shorter than that of ordinary CJD. About a hundred nv CJD cases have been reported to date. The disease is transmitted from cattle to humans through food, and between humans via contaminated surgical equipment, or as a result of cornea transplants."

Beads of perspiration had appeared on Mike's forehead and his hatred of Fred increased by an exponential leap. The effort of not betraying his emotions had made his stomach feel like a block of concrete.

"My fear," Keller had continued, "is that this new mutant we've created may turn out to be transmittable between humans the way the Ebola virus is, through the blood or other body fluids, and like the flu, by air by people breathing on each other."

"When will you know?"

"About the transmissibility you mean?"

"Yes."

"By Christmas."

Mike had pulled himself together. "Let me get this straight. Either we pull our product off the market, hoping we can do so in time to stop human contamination. Even so," Martin gave Keller a withering look, "we have no guarantees. Some of the contaminated stuff might still get through and cause a death or two, maybe even a small epidemic, if your mutant strain turns out to be what you fear it is." He stopped to catch his breath. "Or, we do nothing, in which event our product might cause up to a hundred deaths over a period of—"

"Two, perhaps three months..."

"Which is about the time you say you need to determine whether or not the new strain is transmittable between humans."

"But we can't wait that long! The danger of a worldwide epidemic is too great!"

"Listen, if what you say is true, we've unfortunately passed that danger point some time ago. As we speak, our contaminated product is being used in operating rooms everywhere. We were falling behind in deliveries before our shutdown—remember? The material we manufactured in July and shipped in August has already been forwarded to, and is presumably being used, in hospitals across the U.S. and Canada."

"And the rest of the world, Mike, don't forget the rest of the world. We were so short of inventory in Europe that we had to effect direct shipments via FedEx to hospitals in the U.K., France and Italy."

"There you are." Martin had seen clearly that he had to slow Keller down. He needed time to figure a way out of the threatening disaster. "We are no longer in a position to prevent the product from being used. Why create a panic?"

Ever since Keller had sold him short by retaining the Plasmacol patents in his own name, Mike had been searching for a way to rid himself of the virologist. First he had thought of buying him out, but that would have been too complicated and very expensive. Then he had tried to sell Plasmalab to its competitors, but to no avail: They felt the company's product line was not diversified enough.

A disappointed Mike had chosen to grit his teeth and bide his time.

Now this! He would never be able to recoup. He and Fred would lose all their money, their reputations ruined forever. The customers' and shareholders' suits would see to that.

There was no way Mike was going to let that happen. He had to gain time to mount a rear-guard action.

"Let's wait for three months and monitor the world for sudden, inexplicable occurrences of Creutzfeldt-Jakob Disease. Perhaps you might even consider trying to develop a vaccine against this new strain of CJD, more so since you have samples of it and are ahead of the curve, so to speak."

The last argument had appealed to Keller the scientist, as well as to Keller the pseudo-moralist. Doing something positive to correct an inadvertent mistake, thereby saving lives, was obviously the right thing to do.

Sensing Keller's hesitation Mike had cast about for a workable idea, a plan—anything with which to make Fred see the situation his way.

Then it came to him in a flash. MONEY—of course, the Swiss panacea!

He had taken a deep breath and started to improvise. "It has just occurred to me that, if we played this thing right, instead of losing everything we own, we could not only walk away tall, but also with quite a bit of money; money nobody could take away from us."

Keller had been all ears. "How?"

"We each have six million Plasmalab shares which, at least in my case, I own in the form of twelve share certificates for five hundred thousand shares each."

"Me, too."

"Well then, give your mother one of them with the understanding that she is to give it back to you in three months' time. Have her remit the certificate to her banker as security, not for sale, instructing him sell five hundred thousand shares of Plasmalab 'short' over the next three months at an average price of eighty dollars."

"Will they go that high?" Keller had sounded doubtful.

"Fred, we had a terrific year! Even if we were to write off six million dollars of inventory, we would still show a profit of a dollar and a quarter a share for our last fiscal year. Because of our stellar performance, the street will apply a higher multiplier—say seventy times profit—and the stock will peak at eighty-five."

Fred had licked his lips. "All right. Suppose I do that. Then what?"

"Your mother will have forty million dollars in her bank account from the sale of five hundred thousand Plasmalab shares at eighty dollars."

"And?"

"After the world discovers our little 'difficulty' and we close down operations, the stock's value will plunge—probably to a quarter of what it is today. This cannot happen before Christmas because you'll need about three months to sell that many shares without making the price of the shares go down."

"All right. Assume everything goes the way you see it. What happens next?"

"You tell your mother to buy half a million Plasmalab shares on the stock market for twenty dollars each, which will only cost her ten of the forty million in her bank account."

Fred's eyes had flashed with greed. "So she will end up with a thirty million dollar profit. And you're sure nobody—not the shareholders, not the creditors, not the government, nor Plasmalab's clients, nor the relatives of the people who were killed by our glue—will be able to take it away from her?"

"That is right Fred, as long as she gives back the original certificate for half a million shares."

"What will I do with it?"

"After Christmas all our assets—yours and mine—will be seized by the people who'll come after us for damages." Mike had sighed. "You'll have to give the certificate to your bankruptcy Trustee. But the thirty million will still be there."

"And you?"

"What about me?"

"Will you be doing the same thing?" The moment Fred had asked the question Mike knew he won.

"I would," he had replied, "except that I don't have a mother living in Switzerland!"

Raging against what he felt was an unjust fate that threatened to destroy his professional reputation, Keller had driven out to his lab in Mississauga to set to work on a vaccine to eradicate what he had created.

His lab assistant was on maternity leave so he had to start from scratch.

He ordered the material and equipment he would need for his work from a laboratory supply house with which Plasmalab had never done business. He hired an assistant, Jason Moscovitch, a post-graduate student working on his bio-chem thesis in virology at the University of Toronto, and told him only that they had three months in which to find a vaccine to counteract a virus that Keller had stumbled upon by chance during his research.

* * * * *

The New Year's Eve guests began to arrive and Fred forced himself to be outgoing and hospitable, though he felt quite lost without Hauser whose flight had been re-routed to Miami because of weather. He was aching to talk to Mike whom he had tried to contact after hearing from the WHO, but Plasmalab's CEO had not been at home—out celebrating, no doubt.

He did his best to hide the disappointment he felt because of Karl's tardiness, but made a poor job of it to the point where both Gal and Lonsdale noticed their host's ire: The virologist seemed distracted and was discourteous to the staff. When Hauser finally arrived shortly before eleven Keller kept snapping at him with childish petulance. To his credit, Hauser tried hard to ignore his partner's barbs, but to no avail. It soon became apparent to all that the two were having an argument.

As the evening wore on Fred began to drink hard and, succumbing to liquor and stress, went to bed before midnight.

Hauser soldiered on alone, staying to oversee the caterer's efforts at cleaning up. At four am, with Fred's condo more or less tidy and his host fast asleep, Karl let himself out without making a sound.

CHAPTER SIX

Lonsdale woke up late the morning after Keller's party, feeling restless and frustrated. Less than a month into his leave, a time for forgetting about making choices, circumstances were forcing him—on New Year's day, no less—to deal with two matters that would surely affect the rest of his life: what to do about Reuven and Adys.

Lonsdale agreed with Reuven: The sum of the two of them working together would equal more than the sum of their individual efforts. Therefore, logic dictated that they combine forces. But his relationship with Adys was not a matter for logic.

He seemed to have fallen in love.

They had spent only five days together, but under ideal conditions: relaxed, on holiday, eating, drinking, dancing, fishing and partying, though almost always with people around.

Even so, their brief time together had been enough for him to become smitten with her maturity and the compassion she exuded when she was with him, even in a crowd. He also found Adys so physically attractive, her touch so calming yet alluring, her entire being so sexy and desirable that he became hopelessly obsessed with the want to bed her.

He realized with a shock that she had managed, apparently with no effort on her part, to enslave him with her animal magnetism to the point where he could not think objectively.

And that's what worried and frustrated him. He feared he would once more surrender to a relationship that would expose his heart to the pain of the kind of loss that had affected him so profoundly in the past.

He was afraid to fall in love again, but was it not already too late? What to do?

Lonsdale had sensed that, although the four of them had become very good friends very quickly, Gina and her relationship with Reuven inhibited Adys. That she desired Lonsdale became obvious every time they danced. But she couldn't let go in front of her sister, and nor could Gina. Both women insisted on returning to Gina's apartment every night to the considerable frustration of not only Lonsdale, but his host as well.

Such behavior, Lonsdale knew from past experience, was due to the inbred shyness of well-brought-up middle class Latinas who did not wish to appear "easy" though their hot blood was driving them insane.

He picked up the telephone and called the Breakers.

Then he phoned Adys.

"*Feliz Año Nuevo,* whoever you are," said a sleepy, but melodious voice.

"To you too, but am I speaking to Adys or Gina?" It was impossible to tell the twins' voices apart.

"It's Adys, Roberto. How come you're calling so early?"

"Because I can't live without hearing your voice first thing on New Year's Day."

Silence. Then: "Are you kidding or are you serious?"

"Deadly serious. You're going back to New York tomorrow and I must speak with you alone before you go."

"I'd like that. Where and when?"

"Have tea with me at the Breakers at four this afternoon."

"How do I dress?"

"Informal chic. Do you want me to pick you up?"

"No. Gina will drop me off on her way to Reuven's."

"That's perfect. Meet you in the lobby at four."

Punctually at four, Adys walked into the hotel's huge lobby. Without a word Lonsdale took her hand and led her to the bank of elevators.

When they entered the room he had rented on the sixth floor the music was playing softly. Lonsdale poured champagne for them and raised his glass. "Happy New Year, my darling."

Her eyes brimmed with tears and her lips began to tremble. "I don't think I can live without you, Roberto…"

"Nor I without you…"

He opened his arms to her and she came to him eagerly.

El Cigala was singing *Veinte Años* and his almost raucous flamenco-trained voice gave incredible poignancy to the words. They danced and Adys held him close. He felt safe. She kissed him repeatedly on the lips, first gently then with insistence, until he could bear the tension no longer.

He led her into the bedroom and watched her take off her clothes while he undressed.

Then he knelt down before her reclining figure on the bed and tasted thin honey and milk.

She pulled him close with her strong thighs around his neck and reached orgasm almost at once. He straightened up, rock hard, and she guided him into herself. His thrusts became urgent, demanding. He pulled out, but before she could take him into her mouth he came all over her beautiful breasts.

She laved his sex with her lips until he became erect once more. Then she made him penetrate her again and they began to keep time to a slow but ever-increasing rhythm of love that mercifully culminated with simultaneous release.

They dozed, then awoke together, their limbs entwined.

Languorously, she began to stroke his face with her slender, long fingers.

She looked into his eyes. "Tell me how your wife died." Her gaze was steadfast.

Remembering, he began to weep.

Two decades earlier almost to the day, Lonsdale had been in hospital under guard, recovering from a bullet wound in his shoulder, the result of a failed assassination attempt against his life by a Palestinian terrorist.

It had started to snow early on that fateful day in Montreal and, by evening, a full-blown storm was raging outside the windows of the Royal Victoria Hospital. Lonsdale—his name had been Bernard Lands in those days—had eaten dinner in the company of his wife, Andrea, and they had turned in early; he in his hospital bed, she in the room adjacent.

It had been the oh-so-familiar recurring nightmare about the wolf, coming at him with fangs bared, that had saved Lonsdale's life.

He had been restless, tossing and turning until he dozed off around two and had slept fitfully for about an hour and a half, awakening in a cold sweat, trembling. His spare pillow and bedcovers were on the floor, the bed sheets all rumpled. He looked at his watch: three thirty-eight in the morning and, from what he could see, a blinding snowstorm still blowing outside.

He got up awkwardly, favoring his wounded shoulder, picked up the pillow and bedclothes with his good arm and threw them on the bed. He walked over to the window and looked out; the storm was so bad that all he could see was a white glow: the diffusion of the parking lot lights off the sheet of snow in front of his window.

He trotted over to the bathroom to relieve himself then, with a wet towel, wiped his face and neck.

It was at that moment that he heard it first; a noise as if someone had thrown a snowball against the mosquito-screen covering the window.

"Must be the wind," he muttered as he dried himself with a fresh towel.

But then he heard the noise again and looked over to the window. An immense shadow was sliding into view from above. His instinct and training alerted him right away to what was happening, but he was powerless to act. His pistol and walkie-talkie were on the night table beside the bed.

He screamed for help.

The window exploded into a thousand splinters of glass. Bullets and the smell of cordite filled the room. He took refuge between the toilet bowl and the bathtub, and watched, frozen in place, as the assassin's weapon raked his bed with long bursts of gunfire. The Good Lord must have been looking after him because he did not as much as get nicked by either the flying glass or the ricocheting bullets. The firing stopped as abruptly as it had started and he knew very well what would come next:

the familiar thud and rolling noise. He screamed "Grenade" at the top of his voice and dived into the bathtub.

And that's where they found him; temporarily deaf, stunned and with a nose bleed from the concussion. His head and injured shoulder were aflame with pain, but otherwise he was all right.

Pandemonium dominated the fifth floor of the hospital. The guard in the adjacent sitting room, hearing his charge's screams, sounded the alarm on his walkie-talkie, but had time for nothing more. He was under strict order to protect the patient first and to worry about capturing any would-be-assassin later. In the event of an attack the guards were to follow a well-rehearsed drill: Alert all security personnel on duty, relay the alarm to Central Command via the patrol car's radio, then converge on the patient's room as quickly as possible. The guard in the sitting room was to protect Lands with his body if necessary, the guard by the Nursing Station was to take up position in his room's doorway to keep everyone out, the car was to race to the hospital's front entrance, one of its occupants was to jam all elevators with a special key, the other was to back up the car, and, at night, train its headlights on the front door.

In theory, it was impossible for anyone unwanted to get near the patient; however, reality is different.

The attack was over in less than a minute—not much time, yet time enough for many terrible things.

Andrea, awakened by the gunfire, had rushed to her husband's room, and was killed instantly by the grenade.

The guard from the Nurses' Station had come running to take up his position in the doorway and had been upright when the grenade exploded. Although he would live, the grenade fragments had done terrible damage to his left arm and neck.

The bedroom was a shambles, as was the sitting room. Andrea was dead, the patient semi-conscious, deep in shock, the second guard unconscious. Luckily, the first guard, young, fit and quick-witted, made three crucial decisions: He raced to the window to make sure the attack was over, ascertained that his charge was safe, and ordered the medical staff to minister to the badly wounded man. Andrea was beyond help.

Barely able to speak and trembling uncontrollably Lonsdale told the guard to keep everybody out of his room; to seal it off until the Royal

Canadian Mounted Police liaison team and the senior operations officer from Central Command arrived. The guard was to tell everyone except the senior man that both the patient and his wife were dead. The senior man was then to arrange for transportation for Lonsdale and his wife, both in body bags. These were to be loaded into an RCMP morgue wagon and driven to RCMP Montreal Headquarters where the coroner was to take charge of the "bodies."

The RCMP coroner on duty was to issue two death certificates: one in the name of Bernard Lands, the other in the name of Andrea Lands-Nesbitt. The "bodies" were to be transported to St. Hubert Military Air Base, a short distance from Montreal, for immediate transfer to Washington.

It took two hours to organize the trip and another to get the "bodies" to St. Hubert, an hour that Lonsdale spent in the back of the morgue wagon, silently saying goodbye to Andrea and begging for her forgiveness, over and over again.

The convoy arrived at the Air Base around seven, in the darkness of a winter morning. The storm had broken and the Agency's jet had no trouble landing.

During the flight to Washington, Lands would speak to no one, not to his friend and boss, Jim Morton, who had flown to Montreal to share his grief, not to the guards, not to the pilots. He sat with his wife's stiffening body strapped into the seat next to his and would not let them take her from him until the Agency's doctor came on board at Dulles Airport to give him a shot of Demerol to ease his pain and put him to sleep. By that time Lands had sunk into a seemingly bottomless pit of depression from which he would only emerge months later...time, which he would spend at Bethesda Naval Hospital, first to heal himself physically, then, ever so slowly, to begin focusing on the state of his mental health.

In the end, the man to emerge from this intense physical and emotional ordeal was a physically very fit, aloof, calculating, ruthless and implacable foe of terrorism—in other words, the ideal type of person to direct the Agency's counterterrorist activities.

Realistic and opportunistic as always, the Agency knew very well how to take advantage of the situation. Lonsdale was enrolled into the

CIA's employee protection program and reassigned, deep under cover, where he would be most useful—in the Agency's brand new, super secret counterterrorism and counternarcotics division.

It took the plastic surgeons at the hospital about four hours to alter his facial features sufficiently to make people think twice before calling him Bernard Lands. The CIA's experts then fabricated an in-depth "legend," a new persona: Robert Lonsdale, an obscure analyst with the U.S. Environmental Agency... a seemingly colorless man, devoid of emotion, incapable of love or mercy—even toward himself.

"...and you have lived alone, ever since." Adys' voice was barely a whisper.

"Sort of, but there was, of course, my work and, after a decade, there was also Micheline."

"Micheline?"

"An old, old pre-Andrea flame that I rekindled when I ran into her accidentally during one of my missions. For a while we were an item. Things were going quite well considering my crazy state of mind caused by the job-related stress I was under. She even moved in with me." Lonsdale suddenly stopped talking.

Adys looked at Lonsdale and saw the spasm of pain cross his face.

"What happened?"

"A year into our relationship we discovered that Micheline had leukemia. Less than six months later..."

Without a word, Adys wrapped herself around Lonsdale and held him as tight as she could.

Next day, in the car, on the way to the airport, she asked Lonsdale to help her find a job in Washington.

CHAPTER SEVEN

On New Year's Day, Fred Keller came to at the crack of dawn with a splitting headache and a very upset stomach. When he found his bearings he realized he was sprawled on top of his bed in his tuxedo. He had no recollection of how he got there.

He pulled the covers off the bed, stripped the pillows, took off his clothes and bundled the lot into the laundry chute. Then, with trembling hands, he made himself some toast and a weak cup of tea and crawled back into bed.

He awoke to the shrill bell of the telephone ringing next to his head. Groping for his glasses, he knocked the instrument off the night table. "Coming, coming," he croaked and picked up the receiver. "Hello, this is Fred Keller." His alarm clock showed eight am.

"Jesus Fred, you sound awful." It was Mike Martin. "Are you all right?"

"Why shouldn't I be?"

"I phoned you yesterday evening around eight to wish you a Happy New Year and again at ten, but there was no answer. Where were you?"

"I was here." Fred's head began to throb again. In the deep recesses of his brain he remembered hearing the telephone ring, but had thought it had been a dream. "I called you on New Year's Eve, Mike, but your answering machine was on."

"What time?"

"Around nine."

"Oh." Mike did not feel like telling Keller that, at that very moment, he had been engaged in the mother of all battles with his wife, Donna, a fight that had been long in coming. During the summer she had warned him that unless he began to spend more time with her and the children she would leave him. To humor her, Mike had promised to attend family counseling starting in September, but when he failed to make good on his undertaking Donna had told him that she would seek a separation early in the New Year.

"Why did you call?" Mike asked.

Keller felt his eyes beginning to blink. "I found out on New Year's Eve that there have been repercussions about the Italian thing we discussed."

Mike understood right away. "How many?"

"Three—one native, the other two Americans."

"Then we're not the initiators."

"What makes you think so?"

"Because it doesn't make sense that two different nationalities so far from each other should have the same incubation period."

Keller did not agree. "What has geographic separation got to do with this? Wait till I find out about what real communality there is before jumping to conclusions."

"Where did you get your info?"

Keller was getting angry. "From the World Health Organization, if you must really know."

"Not the Italians?"

"No, not them."

"Then the information you have isn't worth shit!"

"Is that so? Next you're going to tell me you've become an expert in virology overnight." Keller's temples were pounding.

Mike sensed he was pushing too hard. "Okay, okay," he said, backing off. "It's just that your bad news comes on top of some other bad news. My wife and kids have left."

"What do you mean?"

"Donna and the kids went home to Toronto."

"When are they coming back?"

"That's just it—they're not. She's left me for good."

"Oh. Well, look, I feel for you, but perhaps it's for the best in the long run. You've known for some time that you were headed for divorce." Keller's reaction was automatic and entirely superficial. At that moment he couldn't have cared less about his partner's marital problems.

"I guess so, but it's a shock nevertheless."

Keller decided to take the bull by the horns. "Mike, under the circumstances I must insist that I go to Italy to investigate."

"Are you out of your mind? You are to go nowhere near the place."

"And why the hell not?"

"Because by doing so you'd be drawing attention to us, and that is the last thing we want!"

"I must know what is going on. I cannot just stand by doing nothing until it is too late."

Martin forced himself to sound calm and reasonable. "Fred, you're a scientist. Apply logic and common sense to the situation. Your being there would change nothing, even if it turned out that we were involved. You haven't yet developed an antidote, so what could you do...how could you help? Instead of going to Italy you should return to your lab in Toronto and continue your work there."

"I need more information on the pathology before I can do that," insisted the Swiss, "and for that I need specimens."

They argued the point for a while. In the end, the virologist agreed to defer his trip until the following Wednesday, since, in any event, European government offices would not reopen until Epiphany—January 6.

"I'll be staying in Sarasota until Tuesday night. I have to sort my stuff out down here because of this thing with Donna." Mike felt it was time to hold out an olive branch. "I have to drive over to Palm Beach on Sunday anyway. We could revisit the subject at an early dinner and proceed from there."

"You can revisit as much as you want Mike." Keller was still put out. "But my mind is made up. On Monday at noon I fly to Toronto, and on Wednesday night to Italy to see the authorities there."

"I respect your decision Fred, but have dinner with me anyway."

Keller sighed. "I'm attending a concert at the Kravis Center on Sunday afternoon which will end at six. At night I have a dinner engagement at eight thirty. If you can be punctual, come by at seven fifteen sharp. We can have a drink and a half hour or so together." He hung up.

Mike felt as if someone had kicked him in the head. He knew Keller. Once the Swiss got to Toronto it would be impossible to stop him from going to Venice; he was bound to cave in under the pressure of uncertainty.

Everything in Mike's life was heading downhill. His family was breaking up, his business was in danger of imploding, his personal fortune in the process of evaporating. He stood to lose everything he had worked for all those long, hard years. To boot, instead of helping, his business associate, King Shit - insecure, unimaginative, cowardly and incapable of flexible thinking—was threatening to spill the beans sooner than necessary.

But then Mike had known that Keller was a stubborn, dangerous royal pain in the ass. He had had lots of proof of it in the past.

Mike owned a condo in Sarasota on Florida's West Coast. He and his family spent every Christmas there. The unit had been built by a development company run by the Antonucci brothers. Carmelo Antonucci, the Sicilian patriarch of the family, had immigrated to Montreal in the mid-fifties and had set up a cheese manufacturing business that had done very well. Success prompted him to diversify into real estate, so he set up a development company in Florida for his three sons to run.

The Antonuccis believed in delivering dependable quality to their customers who, in turn, rewarded them by recommending Antonucci condos and homes to their friends. In fact, Mike had bought his Sarasota apartment on the recommendation of his stockbroker—a satisfied Antonucci customer—and Mike had, in turn, talked Fred into buying a condo in one of the luxury buildings the Antonuccis had put up in Palm Beach.

Mike should have known that Fred Keller would not be an easy customer. Finicky in the extreme, he was forever badgering Paolo, the brother running the development company's East Coast operations. Paulo, exasperated, had asked for Mike's help through his brother Tony who had been the one to sell Mike *his* unit.

To smooth ruffled feathers, Mike volunteered to act as a buffer between Keller and the Antonuccis. This satisfied Fred who then gave Mike a key to his apartment so that Mike should have access to the place. The Antonuccis were pleased because they had rid themselves of a headache, and so was Mike because he had averted an embarrassing situation. Moreover, he gained a new friend in Tony Antonucci who lived in Mike's complex in Sarasota.

Alone in his apartment, Mike spent New Year's Day raging against a fate that had smitten him with such great cumulative misfortunes and cursing Keller whom he blamed more than he blamed McNiff for the contamination accident at Plasmalab. He felt that Keller, as the company's Chief Scientific Officer, should have foreseen the eventuality and have provided safeguards.

As the day progressed Mike gradually convinced himself that Keller was the direct cause of most of his miseries. His animosity toward his partner kept increasing until, by mid-afternoon, it turned into hatred and he began to think about killing Fred. Of course, the intent to murder Keller was not motivated solely by emotion. Mike had realized very soon after he'd been told about the problem that, with Keller dead, no one could prove he had known about the accident before it became public knowledge—which meant he might be able to get off scot-free.

He began to perceive the possibility of carving out a new life for himself far from the suffocating attachments that now weighed him down. No family ties, no business partner, no lawsuits, no pressure...and plenty of money, even in exile.

Which he had managed to accumulate, thanks to his foresight!

Prompted by a natural distrust of everyone, at the time Plasmalab was arranging to go public Mike had made discrete arrangements with some of his stockbroker friends to shield at least some of his assets from an eventual divorce-inspired grab by his wife, Donna. He was also seeking a way to retaliate against Fred for having treated him unfairly during the IPO.

In return for exaggerated allotments of Plasmalab shares in the IPO at issue price, his friends agreed to pay him an offshore "service fee" equal to half the profit they would make by taking up their allotments and selling them the same day.

Since the IPO, with a two-dollar issue price, had been heavily oversubscribed as a result of the biotech hype, the shares had closed at six dollars and ten cents at the end of their first day of trading. Within a week, Mike's offshore bank account in Bermuda, which he owned through an Isle of Man bearer share company resident in the Channel Islands, showed a credit balance of close to six million dollars.

Four years had gone by since then, during which this sum had grown to ten million, thanks to the astute management by Mike's offshore investment counselors who had no inkling of their client's true identity.

As soon as Fred had told him about the accident, and knowing that, barring public knowledge, Plasmalab's stock would soon be worth over eighty dollars, Mike instructed his bankers in Bermuda to start buying Plasmalab shares in small, but constant, quantities. This they did, with the result that, by the end of October, Mike had accumulated close to a million shares in Bermuda at an average price of sixty-seven dollars that he then resold during the next sixty days, making a twelve million dollar profit.

The transaction more than doubled the value of his offshore portfolio.

Not content, Mike went one step further. In mid-December he instructed his offshore bankers to start selling Plasmalab shares short at the rate of twenty-five thousand a day. He aimed to sell three hundred thousand shares (which he did not have offshore) by mid-January then cover his short position when the stock's price plummeted the moment the contamination problem became known to the public.

He calculated that he could make about twenty million dollars on the deal, thereby bringing the value of his portfolio to over forty million dollars—plenty of money to live on, even as a fugitive.

Mike snapped out of his reverie when the phone rang. It was Tony, the youngest of the Antonucci brothers.

He had invited the Martins to their New Year's Eve bash in Sarasota, but only the children had attended because, after their fight, neither Mike nor his wife felt like celebrating. Mike owed Tony an apology, but the Montrealer had forestalled him.

"I saw Donna and the kids leave this morning. You know how

kids are," Antonucci added. "They talk to each other. I'm sorry you're having a rough time and I can well understand why you and Donna didn't show at the party."

Mike started to hem and haw, but Tony cut him off. "Why don't you come with us to Paradise Island on Sunday? The trip will take your mind off your marital problems. My brothers and I are flying over to Nassau in the company plane for an overnight gambling junket—we've booked a suite at the Paradise Island Casino Hotel. There are four beds; you can have one of them, though I don't think any of us will be doing much sleeping. On Monday we'll fly back to Sarasota because we have a meeting to attend late in the afternoon."

Mike hesitated. "Give me some time to think it over." He was very tempted.

"There's no rush. As long as you meet us at the West Palm Airport private jet terminal by eight thirty Sunday night you're cool. Take-off time is nine pm"

"When are you guys driving over there?"

"Tonight. But Lino can't get to West Palm from Montreal before Sunday night."

"Isn't he flying commercial?"

"No, no. He's coming in the company plane."

Mike hung up in a daze. Tony had just given him an idea about how to fabricate an alibi that might enable him to kill Fred and get away with it.

He took a slip of paper from the secret compartment in his wallet and, after consulting it, composed a message in code for his bankers in Bermuda, instructing them to sell whatever was left of his Plasmalab holdings immediately, to complete any outstanding part of the "short sale" transaction involving three hundred thousand Plasmalab shares, then to cover it by buying when the price of the shares dropped to a quarter of its present value.

He wrote the message out on a sheet of blank paper and signed it One, Eighty-one, Two, Five, Sixty-two. Next, he made three phone calls: the first to Tony to confirm he would be joining him and his brothers on Sunday for their overnight junket; the second to Henry Sokolowski, a locksmith in the village of Jackson Point near his Ontario country cottage

67

on Lake Simcoe whose services Mike had used before; and the third to Air Canada to book an evening flight from Sarasota to Toronto and back.

On his way to the airport he stopped at a copy shop and, paying cash, sent his message by fax to a number he had been given when he opened his account in Bermuda.

CHAPTER EIGHT

It took Mike six hours to get to his cottage, thirty miles north of Toronto; ample time to reflect on the consequences of his proposed course of action. Although he realized that the risk he was about to take was great, his hatred of Fred had grown so strong that it overrode all reason. He felt no qualms about taking his partner's life. On the contrary, he could hardly wait to exact the ultimate revenge on the man who had double-crossed him in the past and whose self-righteousness was now jeopardizing everything Mike had struggled to attain.

To get away with what he was planning to do, Mike needed a perfect alibi and a foolproof fallback position. He soon concluded that the ideal backup plan would require that he disappear after faking his own death, which meant he would have to create a new identity and eschew all contact with present friends and family.

Could he manage the psychological stress? Mike felt he could. He had no close friends and his family meant little to him; his relationship with his wife was at an end and, as for his daughter (a carbon copy of his wife)... he could do without her. Which left his son of whom he was fond, but if it came to a choice between his son and prison Mike knew he wouldn't hesitate for a second to opt for freedom.

The trip itself had been uneventful—a half-hour drive to the airport, a four-hour flight to Toronto, where he bought himself a jogging suit and a pair of running shoes, then another hour by rented car to the lake. He was at his cottage by eleven thirty on Friday night.

He made himself coffee and, while eating the pizza he had picked up on the way, reviewed his plan once more in the minutest of detail. Satisfied, he prepared a short checklist that he placed in his wallet, then went to bed.

After a frugal breakfast, Mike opened the wall safe in the basement, pocketed the "emergency wad" of twenty thousand U.S. dollars he kept there and extracted copies of the real estate tax bills relating to the cottage. He also took out a small, stoppered test-tube containing about an ounce of liquid Curare "sufficient to kill the entire rodent population of Southern Ontario," to quote Fred Keller. He poured the liquid into a vial he had brought with him, sealed it and carefully inserted it into a pencil holder in his briefcase. Then he rinsed out the test-tube, walked into the woods, smashed it under his heel and buried the shards.

How ironic, he thought, that he should be using the poison provided by the poisoner to kill the poisoner. He remembered the event well. One summer, during a rampant field-mouse invasion of the cottage, he had asked for Fred's advice and then received some custom-processed Curare from the company lab to help destroy the rodents.

Always methodical, Mike had kept what had been left over from the deadly, odorless, colorless liquid for subsequent use, locking it away in the safe, out of harm's way.

The locksmith arrived at nine sharp.

"I don't want to create problems for you, Henry," Mike said to the man after the locksmith had changed the exterior locks, "but if Mrs. Martin contacts you to change the cylinders again, please tell her that I told you not to do so. As you can see from the tax bills, I am the registered owner of this property and you should, therefore, tell Mrs. Martin that before you can act you must have my authorization or that of a judge." Mike scribbled a few lines on a sheet of paper, signed it and handed it to the locksmith with the tax bill copies. "If you run into problems please show Mrs. Martin these documents and contact my secretary."

"Don't sweat it Mr. Martin." Sokolowski understood at once. "I know what to do; I've had plenty cases like this in the region." Mike paid him for his work, then locked up and left. He felt well satisfied. The locksmith would tell everyone who cared to listen that Mr. Martin had come back from vacation early to lock his wife out of their country house in anticipation of a bitterly contested divorce.

Mike was back in his Longboat Key condo by six pm on Saturday night.

Next morning he called his house in Toronto, and when his son, Kevin, answered, asked for Donna. The boy came back crestfallen. "Mummy says she's busy. Can she call you back?"

"Sure. I'm going to the store to pick up some groceries, but I should be back by noon. Ask her to call between twelve and two."

"I will, dad." A silence, then "I miss you."

"So do I, buddy." Kevin, only nine, was the more vulnerable of his two children. Karen, his daughter, thirteen, was already turning into a harpie. "Don't worry, we'll work things out, your Mom and I," he reassured the boy although he knew the chances of seeing his children again were remote.

"I love you daddy," the boy whispered and hung up. Mike shook his head then took a deep breath. There was no turning back now.

He drove to the local Publix supermarket in Donna's BMW and bought a dozen small bottles of Naya Water, a whole barbecued chicken with fries and an apple crisp. He left the car in the parking lot and walked home. In his running shoes, sweat shirt and shorts he looked like any other Sunday morning shopper.

Back at his apartment he drilled a small hole in the cap of one of the bottles, inserted a pharmacist's funnel into the opening and poured the poison into the water. Then, using his wife's mini soldering iron, plugged the hole with plastic from another bottle top, and pocketed the empty vial. As a final precaution, he stuck a red marker on the bottle containing the poison. Having donned surgical gloves, he then wiped the bottle clean of fingerprints and placed it into his waterproof, corrosion-resistant aluminum briefcase.

At noon he went for a dip in the pool and did some laps, then heated up the chicken and fries.

He was eating lunch when the phone rang. It was Donna.

"What did you say to Kevin to make him cry?" she asked by way of greeting.

"Nothing," Mike made himself sound casual. "I asked for you, he said you were busy. Then he told me he missed me."

"A likely story," Donna continued, determined to seek confrontation. "I would appreciate your acting like a gentleman and not involving the kids in our fight."

"I couldn't agree with you more, but I assure you—"

"Anyway, I went to the bank yesterday."

Mike knew what was coming. "On Saturday?" he asked.

"Yes, the branch was open because of the holidays."

"And?"

"There were eighteen thousand dollars in our joint account. I took the money." She waited for him to remonstrate.

"That's OK," he said instead, his voice neutral. "I was going to give you money anyway. You'll need some ready cash for living expenses and for a lawyer." He paused. "I presume you have one"

She did not know how to react to his cooperative attitude. "Yes, I do."

"Good."

"What did you call about anyway?"

"I want to keep things as civil as possible between us and I don't want you to think I'm doing anything behind your back. I wanted you to know that I visited the cottage yesterday and had the locks changed."

"You did what!?"

"Today, I'm putting your car in storage. The cottage, its contents and the car are joint property. Once we've sorted out our problems we'll settle who gets what."

"If that's the way you want to play it, so be it," she said with biting sarcasm. "First thing tomorrow morning I'm selling my Plasmalab shares." He had given her ten thousand shares as a present when the company had gone public, worth two dollars each then; today they were worth eighty-five.

"Why the hell would you want to do that?"

"Because I don't want to have anything to do with you or your company anymore," she shouted and banged down the receiver.

Mike smiled and congratulated himself. He had achieved his purpose. Although appearing to be the epitome of rectitude by pretending to be telling her everything he was up to, he had managed to goad his wife into selling her Plasmalab holdings worth close to a million dollars. There was, consequently, no way she could accuse him later of having done anything underhanded—at least not as far as his visit to the cottage was concerned.

With over eight hundred thousand dollars from the sale of her Plasmalab shares, plus the house in Toronto's fashionable Forest Hill worth more than three million, and the cottage at Lake Simcoe another million, Mike figured Donna would end up with close to five million dollars—enough to bring up the kids even without Mike around. His conscience was clear, his children's future assured.

After lunch he called the garage and confirmed with Phil, the attendant, that he would pick him up a few minutes before three so that Phil could service his Audi. Then he fetched his roll-on and packed, limiting himself to clothes and toiletries a person would need for a two-day stay in a place like Nassau.

It was one thirty pm—time to get a move on.

He deleted the greeting from his answering machine and, after practicing for ten minutes, substituted the text he had memorized the night before. "Phil the Pill, is that you? (pause). Do me a favor, will you? [pause]. Put the car in the garage and leave the keys with the Super. Tell him I'll pick them up from him in due course. Got to run, I'm late [disconnect]."

At two Mike reviewed his checklist to make sure he hadn't overlooked anything. Fifteen minutes later, satisfied, he exited the apartment carrying a garment bag, his briefcase with his computer in it and dragging his roll-on behind him. He didn't bother double-locking the front door. In the garage he made sure no one saw him place his things in the trunk of his car.

At two thirty Mike drove to the shopping center parking lot and transferred his gear into the trunk of his wife's BMW.

At a quarter-to-three he was at the gas station to pick up Phil, who drove him back to his apartment.

"What time do you figure you'll have my car ready?"

"Give me an hour."

"Perfect. I'm not going anywhere in a hurry. Suppose you call me between four and four fifteen from the gas station and I'll tell you where to leave the car and the keys. Can do?"

"No problem, Mr. Martin." Phil was eager to cooperate. He liked Mike; the man paid well and was easy to deal with.

Mike gave Phil thirty dollars and watched him drive off. He then let himself out the back way and walked over to the shopping center.

He was behind the wheel of the BMW by three fifteen, on his way to Palm Beach.

Somewhere along Alligator Alley he opened the window and pitched the vial that had contained the Curare. He stopped the car a couple of miles down the road and changed into the jogging suit he'd bought in Canada.

Mike made good time from Sarasota to Palm Beach; he was in the Publix parking lot less than two blocks from Fred's condo by five forty.

He took his time getting out of the car: he was still shaking with rage.

He had tried once more to think things through with objectivity, but had failed: His hatred of Fred kept growing with every minute he had spent on the road until it had turned into such venomous loathing that it seemed to permeate every cell, not only of his brain, but of his whole body.

"Calm down," he exhorted himself. "Focus on the task at hand, like you did when you were preparing the IPO and nobody would underwrite it. You were out of funds—finished, unless you could get money from the public. You almost had a heart attack from working too long and too hard without sleep. But you pulled through." He took a deep breath and continued. "You pulled through because you had to. Well...you have to again—because unless you do, you're finished."

He leaned forward and forced his head down toward his chest to ease the muscles in his neck. Then, rocking back and forth, he began to chant the mantra he had used the last time. "I'm strong, I'm smart, and I will pull through...I'm strong, I'm smart, and I will pull through..."

Within a minute he became calm and his usual efficient self.

"Go to work," he whispered and exited the vehicle.

In his jogging suit, wearing sneakers and a wide-brimmed straw hat, and with a beach bag strung over his shoulder, looking like any other beach tourist, Mike walked to the back of the Bradley Place apartment building and let himself into the cabana area with the key Fred had given him.

He made sure he kept his head down to avoid having his face photographed by the security camera above the entrance of the door leading from the pool into the building proper.

On his way up in the elevator he donned surgical gloves.

Inside the apartment, he wasted no time.

He checked the alarm. There was no need to disable it; Fred seldom, if ever, set it during the day. In any event, it would not have mattered had it been on: Fred had given him the code. Sixteen paces got him into the bedroom. As always, a pristine bottle of Naya water graced Fred's night table. He dumped it into his beach bag and, after removing his red marker, put the bottle containing the poison in its place. Another sixteen steps took him into the kitchen where he found five more Naya water bottles in the fridge, which he also dumped into his bag.

He let himself out without making a sound.

Total time spent in the apartment: less than three minutes.

Mike left the building at one minute to six the way he had entered it, via the swimming pool area.

From the Publix parking lot he drove to the Breakers where, in the men's room off the lobby of the famous old hotel, he exchanged his sneakers and jogging suit for Guccis, an unlined natural linen jacket, an exquisite Yves St. Laurent shirt and elegant slacks. He stuffed his jogging clothes and hat into the garment bag and headed for Fred's apartment a few minutes before seven.

He pressed the Super's buzzer at seven ten sharp. "I'm here to see Dr. Keller and I've forgotten my keys. I'm not sure he's in though—doesn't seem to be answering."

Ramon Sanchez, the Super, knew Mike well. He called Keller on the telephone. When Keller answered Ramon buzzed him through.

After exchanging a few words of small talk Mike got down to business.

"I spoke to Donna this morning. She's back in Toronto with the kids and, although I'm trying to keep things friendly, I'm not doing a good job of it; she's plenty fed up with me."

"How will this affect the company?" Fred was focused on one thing only—himself.

"She said she's selling her Plasmalab holdings first thing Monday."

"Will that hurt the stock price?"

"The sale of ten thousand shares? Not right away. But when, as an insider, she reports the transaction at the end of the month, it might."

"That will be the least of our worries by then." Fred was glum.

"Meaning?"

"By the end of January, we will have either infected a hundred people with nv CJD who, in turn, will infect thousands more, or, if the virus is not transmittable from human to human, the death toll will remain at the hundred level."

"Why the end of January?"

"Because by then, the entire affected inventory will have been used up by our client hospitals."

"Will you have a vaccine ready by February first?"

Keller shook his head. "Maybe in preliminary form, but not in sufficient quantities to stop an epidemic."

"So what's the sense in going to Europe, for God's sake? Your presence in Italy would only add to the confusion. Why precipitate a crisis before it is necessary to do so?"

Fred was adamant. "We cannot avoid the loss of at least a hundred people because of our carelessness—but tens of thousands more might die unless I get to Italy without delay. I need to obtain samples of the diseased brains and rush them back to Toronto to use in cultures for developing an antivirus in sufficient quantities to control any impending epidemic."

"Are you sure the Italian cases were caused by our glue?"

"No, I'm not, and I cannot make sure unless I go to Italy and investigate the medical histories of the three victims."

"Suppose you tell me what you've found out so far."

It took Keller less than five minutes to relate his conversation with Lonsdale and to brief Mike on what he had found out from the WHO.

"Whichever way I analyze this thing we're too late." Mike shuddered. "The victims may have already infected dozens of others, but we won't know this for another couple of weeks. It seems this new variant's incubation period is about a month."

"Correct."

They continued the discussion, but their arguments soon became repetitive.

At seven forty-five on the dot, Fred rose. "I cannot be late for this dinner. I'm the guest of honor."

"Very well, Fred. Have a safe trip home. I'll see you in Toronto on Tuesday after lunch."

"Oh? Aren't you coming home tomorrow?"

Mike shook his head. "I have some things I have to take care of in Sarasota tomorrow."

"Because of Donna?"

Mike nodded. "I'm booked to fly back to Toronto from Tampa on Tuesday morning."

"Very well then," Fred said as he saw Mike to the door. "See you on Tuesday."

There was nothing more Mike could do, there was no way out. Fred had to die. As for the new vaccine... Moscovitch, Fred's understudy, could deal with that.

On his way out Mike, stopped by the Super's flat on the ground floor. "I've just come from Mr. Keller's place, Ramon, and I forgot to ask him something. Would you mind ringing him for me?"

"Not at all Mr. Martin. Come in, come in."

When Keller answered Mike took the phone from the Super. "Mike here Fred. In the heat of our discussions I forgot to ask your permission to park Donna's car in your second parking spot for a while."

"For how long?" Keller sounded annoyed, he was running late.

"Just a few days."

"Oh, all right, but not longer than a week." Typical. Keller was being difficult for no reason.

"Thanks Fred," said Mike. "A week is plenty. Now would you mind confirming this to Ramon so we're not at cross purposes?" He handed the receiver to the Super.

Mike looked at his watch: eight o'clock—it was getting late.

"Do me a favor Ramon and call me a cab. If I don't hurry I'll miss my plane." He gave the man twenty dollars. "While you're on the phone I'll unload my gear, and you'll perhaps be good enough to park the car to save me time."

Traffic was light along Okeechobee Boulevard and he got to the airport at a quarter to nine, just in time to hook up with the Antonuccis.

Mike and the Antonuccis made it to the hotel on Nassau's Paradise Island a few minutes before eleven after a twenty-minute alcohol-laced flight with Mike leading the drinking with three very large double gin-and-tonics.

They dumped their luggage in their suite, had a fast sandwich in the cafeteria then headed for the gaming tables reserved for high rollers—mostly baccarat aficionados.

Mike could do no wrong. He won big at blackjack, had fantastic success at roulette and even greater luck at craps. By one am he was up fifteen thousand dollars.

He wandered away from the high rollers, cashed in his chips and began playing the slots, waiting for his buddies to tire of gaming. He drifted over to the one-armed bandits programmed to accept only ten-dollar tokens and sat down next to a very attractive thirty-somethingish woman.

For a while they played side by side, at times winning, at times losing. Then, Mike suggested they switch machines.

On her first pull the woman hit the jackpot of ten thousand dollars!

Wildly excited by her good fortune, she kept hugging and kissing Mike. "If you hadn't made us switch machines," she screamed above the ruckus, "it would have been you the winner."

Mike helped her collect her winnings. It surprised him that he wasn't at all upset. He had, he felt, been lucky enough for one night.

"I'll buy you the best champagne supper you've ever had," she said. "Do you know a good restaurant around here?"

Mike laughed. "Before you do, why don't you tell me your name?"

"Marilyn," she held out her hand. "I'm a widow—from Atlanta. This is my first trip ever to Nassau."

"Alone?" enquired Mike, hoping for a "yes." He found the woman vivacious and full of energy.

"I'm here with my girlfriend—she's around here somewhere. And you?"

He told her about the Antonuccis as they walked back to the high-rollers' section. Tony was still at the baccarat table.

"Takeoff time is one pm tomorrow. Meet us in the lobby no later than noon," he said to Mike then looked at Marilyn and smiled. "Take care of my buddy. He needs some TLC."

Mike decided to take matters in hand. In the lobby, he grabbed Marilyn by the waist and kissed her on the lips. She responded eagerly.

"Where to?" he asked.

"Let's get a couple of bottles of champagne, and some snacks and take the stuff back to where I'm staying. We can party there."

"Where's that?"

"At Club Med." When she saw the look of alarm on his face she burst out laughing. "Don't worry about my friend Doris. She's not coming back to sleep in our room. She found herself a beau yesterday."

Within fifteen minutes, in high spirits and armed with backup supplies of champagne and sandwiches, they were on their way to the club.

In the back seat of the cab the action instantly spun out of control from hot to hotter to hottest on a flash-fire course. By the time they raced the stairs to Marilyn's room they couldn't get their clothes off fast enough. Shirt and pants, bra and G-string flew through the air and landed in a heap on the floor.

Again and again they tore at each other like two seasoned vultures attacking the carrion of their pent-up sexual frustrations in a run of raw, savage attacks, rutting like crazed predators soaked in musky sweat— yielding nothing, taking brutally, they surfaced only to ease swollen lips and burning throats with countless glasses of ice-cold champagne. Reckless lust drove their bodies long past endurance until dawn broke, when they collapsed into bruised, exhausted stupor.

* * * * *

A few minutes after five o'clock on Monday morning the shrill, insistent ringing of the telephone woke Gianni Gianotti, the night watchman at the Gelateria Viotti, located in the heart of Montreal's Little Italy. Cursing the crazy bastard foolish enough to call at this ungodly hour, Gianotti fumbled his way to the phone.

"*Pronto,*" he croaked.

"Is this the *Gelateria Viotti*?" a voice inquired in Italian.

"*Si, si*, this is the Viotti Ice Cream Parlor."

"Is Umberto there?"

"Of course not, *stupido*. It's five thirty in the morning. He's sleeping."

"Wake him up and tell him to get in touch with Cesare Uno right away." The line went dead.

The night watchman was in a quandary. On the one hand, not to transmit the message to Umberto Viotti, head of Montreal's prime Mob Family, might cost him his life. On the other, waking Don Umberto for nothing because some *matto* (joker) called might also have dire consequences—such as the temporary loss of the use of his two legs.

He debated the matter for five minutes then decided that discretion being the better part of valor, he'd better wake his boss, asleep in his house across the street.

To Gianotti's surprise, Viotti was not upset. He asked the night watchman to drive him to the nearest subway station and to wait for him there.

By the time Umberto Viotti called Cesare Uno in Nassau from a payphone it was six am

Very few people knew that Cesare Uno's real name was Salvatore Setto and that he was Umberto Viotti's uncle. Gifted with an incredible memory for numbers that made him the terror of card counters and other types of gambling cheats, he also had a talent for never forgetting a face once he'd met its owner. Although he had not seen the Antonucci boys for decades he'd recognized Lino and his brothers the moment they entered the Paradise Island Casino's high-rollers' area, Salvatore Setto's domain.

He was the Casino's Senior Pit Boss.

As a matter of course, he dispatched one of his favorite waitresses to find out all she could about the Antonuccis' plans for the next twenty-four hours, then called his nephew in Montreal. Their conversation was brief and innocuous to the uninitiated.

"Buongiorno Cesare. You called?"

"*Si*. I have three small cheeses here—your favorite brand."

"Did you say three?"

"Yes. And they are being shipped out of here early this afternoon."

"How early?"

"One o'clock."

"I see. Well, I want you to make sure all three parcels reach their destinations?"

"Their final destinations?"

"*Si, si*—their final destinations."

"It's a bit tight, but I think I can manage it." Cesare Uno hung up.

Viotti returned to the car and made a mental note to reward his uncle hugely should the attempt to kill the Antonucci boys succeed. "What a coup," he muttered. "For centuries—in Sicily and in Canada—the Antonuccis have been at war with the Viottis. No more. With Lino, Paulo and Antonio gone there will be no male Antonuccis left since their offspring are all women!"

Mike woke up with a start and leapt out of bed when he saw the time. "Where's the telephone?" he yelled; it was twelve noon.

"There are no phones in the rooms at Club Med," Marilyn groaned at the noise.

"Jesus Marilyn, I'm late as hell. Tell me quick—where's the nearest place I can make a call?" Mike already had his shirt and shorts on and was climbing into his pants.

"At reception."

"We're scheduled to fly back to the States at 1 pm and I was supposed to meet my buddies at noon at the hotel. I've got to run," he shouted, kissed Marilyn on the cheek and took off in search of a phone like a scared jackrabbit.

When he saw the lineup at the front desk he changed tactics and asked the *gentil organisateur* (gracious organizer) on duty to call him a cab. He told the driver to make for the airport as fast as he could.

But traffic at lunchtime is always heavy across the bridge connecting Paradise Island with downtown Nassau. By the time they managed to fight their way across, it was a quarter to one.

The taxi got to the airport at ten past the hour, but it took the driver another five precious minutes to locate the building housing the private aircraft departure lounge.

By then it was too late—the Antonuccis' plane was already on the runway.

Mike called the Paradise Island Casino Hotel from the airport's VIP Lounge and inquired about messages. As he expected, Tony had left word, which the clerk read out over the phone. "Twelve twenty and you're not here. We can't wait any longer. Presume you'll meet us at the airport, so took your luggage with us. If all fails, see you in Sarasota. T."

Mike did not know whether to laugh or cry. His reason for accompanying the Antonuccis to Nassau had been to establish clearly that he had been away from Palm Beach during the night Fred Keller died. Upon his return to Sarasota by private plane he intended to take the next flight to New York and disappear.

Now, however, because of his lust for a woman he'd known for all of ten hours, he'd lost his luggage, his precious computer without which he could not access his database and his briefcase with all his papers in it.

He went rigid with fear!

Was there anything in the briefcase that could incriminate him?

He forced himself to recall every item in that damned box of his.

After ten minutes of agony, he heaved a great sigh of relief. There was nothing in there that could hurt him.

Next, he took inventory of what was in his pockets and the little leather satchel he used to carry his identification papers: his passport, wallet, driver's license and credit cards, thirty-six thousand U.S. dollars in one hundred dollar bills, and a business card Marilyn had thrust at him just before he had dashed out of her room.

And, of course, his famous checklist... He glanced at it and noted with concern that the previous night he had forgotten to erase the message he had left on his answering machine for Phil, the garage attendant.

Damn Marilyn.

Using his credit card he telephoned his condo and keyed in the code to wipe out greetings and messages.

He went into the washroom to relieve himself and tidy up a little. When he got back to the lounge he found the girl at the reception desk crying.

"What's the matter?"

"We lost one of our pilots," she sobbed. "He was killed ten minutes ago! There was an explosion. I knew him so well. He was such a nice guy."

"In a crash?"

"Yes," the girl answered. "The plane blew up, no one knows why."

Mike felt as if, inside, an icy hand were reaching for his heart.

Somehow he dragged himself into the main lobby where he approached the Bahamasair Information Desk. "What's this about a plane crash?" he demanded to know. "What happened?"

"It was not one of our aircraft, sir," the harassed clerk answered, her lips trembling. "I was told it was a private plane belonging to the Antonucci Group, a Canadian company."

"How many dead?"

"We don't know yet, sir."

"What happened?"

"It seems the aircraft just blew up in the sky a few minutes after takeoff."

Mike went to the bar and ordered a double gin and tonic, then asked the bartender to turn the sound up on his TV set. Sure enough, at two pm there was a news flash.

> "At one thirty-seven pm a private aircraft owned by the Antonucci Group of Montreal, Canada, crashed into the sea shortly after takeoff from

Nassau International Airport. Eyewitnesses report an explosion on board prior to the aircraft plunging into the Caribbean. Rescue operations are underway. It is not known whether there are any survivors."

The six o'clock edition of the *Nassau Times* had the full story, listing the names of the dead: the pilot, the copilot, the three Antonucci brothers and a Canadian businessman, Michael Martin. Four of the six bodies were recovered. The copilot and Mr. Martin were listed as "missing."

CHAPTER NINE

"You know, I could get used to this lifestyle." Lonsdale sighed with contentment as he scrutinized the remains of his breakfast on the dining room table; the weather, though sunny, had turned cooler and they had decided to eat inside. "I like the idea of having to worry about nothing more important than how to keep myself busy for the rest of the day."

Gal laughed. "You're full of it. By the end of your stay you'll be antsy, you'll see. I know you." He bit into an apple. "Let's see—you've been here for a week."

"With another week to go."

"Not bored yet?"

"Far from it. As I implied a moment ago, sloth seems to sit well with me."

"Then I dare say it's a bit early to start badgering you again about joining forces."

Lonsdale finished his coffee and got up. "It isn't actually. I've given the matter serious consideration during the last forty-eight hours."

"And?" Gal tried to sound casual, but Lonsdale felt the tension behind the single syllable.

"I think I'd like to give it a try."

Gal was speechless. He was expecting to be turned down. "My dear fellow," he blurted, and stepped around the table to embrace Lonsdale and shake his hand. "When can you start?"

Lonsdale held up his hand. "Don't misunderstand me. I said 'I'd give it a try!' What I have in mind is to start working with you on January 7—"

"That's the day after tomorrow."

Lonsdale nodded, " and go on working with you for four months."

"That brings us to the beginning of May."

"If things work, I'll give NATO notice in mid-May."

"How much notice do you have to give?"

"Three months minimum—maybe four."

"So you'll be my official, full-time, partner by September 1 at the latest." Gal's mind was in overdrive. "That's quite a long time from now. It'll be a bit of a stretch to have to cope for nine months without you. Still..."

"As you've said: nine months."

"Long enough to have a baby."

They spent the next couple of hours discussing the nuts and bolts of their cooperation, and then went shopping for groceries.

They were helping the housekeeper to put the food away when the telephone rang.

It was Hauser.

"I need to see Reuven urgently. Are you fellows busy?"

They weren't.

Karl arrived within minutes, pallid and looking very worried. He asked for a double vodka right off the bat.

Lonsdale excused himself to give Hauser and Gal privacy, but Reuven wouldn't hear of it. "Are we partners or are we not?" he asked and told Hauser about Lonsdale's probationary employment with RG Security Services.

Hauser didn't object, which surprised Lonsdale.

"I'm in serious trouble," the Austrian led off. "Fred Keller died of poisoning this morning and I seem to be the most likely suspect for having done it."

"What?!" Lonsdale and Gal were stunned.

"You heard me. Fred was supposed to return to Toronto this afternoon and I said I would drive him to the airport. I figured this would give me an opportunity to say goodbye since he was planning to be away for a month." Hauser took a sip of his ice-cold Absolut. "I got to Fred's apartment early—around eight—and we fooled around a bit."

Hauser had the grace *not* to blush.

"Then I had a shower and he started packing. When I got back to the bedroom Fred was just opening the bottle of water he always kept at his bedside in case he got thirsty during the night. He held it out to me and I took it, but then the phone rang. I handed it back to him and I picked up the receiver; the phone is on the night table on the bathroom-side of the bed. Fred took a swig of the water, went into convulsion and died within minutes." Hauser's face was ashen. "It was awful. During those last few minutes he was in absolute agony and there was nothing I could do to help him. I even tried to give him more water from the bottle, but I couldn't."

"Why not?" Lonsdale was watching Hauser intently.

"Because I couldn't get his mouth open."

"And who was it that called?"

"The housekeeper. She heard the whole thing. Fred had dropped the receiver."

"What was she calling about?"

"I don't know. I never got to ask her. For all I know she wanted to say goodbye to *Señor* Keller before he went away"

"Where is she from?"

"Guatemala."

"How long has she been employed by Keller?" Lonsdale kept his questions coming in rapid succession.

"I don't know. She's been with Fred forever—even before I met him."

"When was that?"

"About four years ago."

"What were you and Fred arguing about on New Year's Eve?"

Lonsdale's question took Hauser by surprise, but it didn't faze him. "He was pissed at me for having come late to the party. I couldn't help it, you know. My flight got rerouted to Miami."

"What did you do next?"

"After getting to Miami?"

Lonsdale shook his head. "No. After Fred died."

"I called 911."

"Why didn't you get the maid to do so while you were trying to help Fred?"

"I did. I kept screaming 'call 911,' and then I called them myself."

Lonsdale looked at Gal.

"What happened then?" the Israeli asked.

"The police and the ambulance got there at the same time. They took poor Fred's body to the morgue after photographing him and securing the crime scene—you know."

"And then?"

"They started asking me questions."

"Where?"

"In the apartment."

"Where in the apartment?"

"In the living room."

"What did you tell them?"

"What I've just told you." Karl was getting upset. "Why all these questions? I've come here for help, not questions."

"Never mind that," Gal cut in, his voice cold. "Did the police ask you to go to the station with them?"

"No, but the detective in charge gave me his card and said he'd be in touch and not to leave the area without calling him." Gal glanced at it. Detective Sergeant Henry (Hal) Dorff, it read. Gal knew him.

"What area?"

"Palm Beach, I guess."

"But you live in West Palm, don't you?"

"Yes. On my salary I can't afford to live here."

"So why did you poison your lover?" asked Lonsdale out of the blue. "Were you afraid he'd cut you out of his will?"

Hauser lost it. "Are you mad?" he shouted. "How dare you accuse me of such a thing. I loved Fred. I didn't want to hurt him."

"Just frighten him—right?"

"No, goddam it." Hauser was livid. "I did not kill Fred, I don't know who did, and I don't know what happened."

"So how did you know he was poisoned?"

"Because the police told me he had been."

"When?"

"When what?"

"When did the police tell you?" Lonsdale made the question sound unimportant—an old trick.

"After the coroner came and told *them*." Hauser was calming down.

"And how did the coroner know before running tests?"

"Because poor old Fred was doubled up in the fetal position and they had to carry him out like that, doubled up. His muscles were rigid, rigid; they could not straighten him out," Hauser whispered.

Lonsdale felt for the pilot. "I'm sorry Karl. I just wanted to make sure you had the right answers." He looked at Gal who nodded.

"I suppose we had better get you a lawyer before the police talk to you again," said the Israeli. "But lawyers cost money. Do you have any?"

Hauser was embarrassed. "I have some money saved, but I can't afford a big-name defense lawyer."

"Let me call a friend of mine then, and see what we can do. By the way, did the police ask you to surrender your passport?"

"They did at first, but I told them what I did for a living and that I needed my passport for work, so they gave up on that."

"Good man." Gal was pleased. "Now let me call my lawyer friend while Robert gets you another drink." He went into his bedroom to make the call.

"What will you have?" asked Lonsdale.

"A very tall, very cold glass of water."

"No more alcohol?"

"No, thank you."

After gulping down his drink, Hauser turned to Lonsdale. "You know, it's strange. One of the questions Detective Dorff asked me was where Fred kept his bottled water supply."

"I suppose you told him."

Lonsdale winced in anticipation of the answer.

"Yes, I did."

"So where *did* Fred keep the bottles?" Under his breath Lonsdale was cursing Hauser. The man should never have admitted familiarity with the workings of Fred's household.

"On the shelves of the fridge door. He always bought Naya water in six-packs. You know, in small bottles."

"What's Naya water?"

"Canadian bottled water."

Lonsdale couldn't follow. "So what's strange about this?"

"There wasn't a single bottle of Naya water in the apartment—not on the fridge door, not in the fridge itself, not in the pantry, nowhere!"

"Except, of course, on Fred's night-table."

Hauser looked lost for a moment then caught on. "Yes, of course. You mean the bottle from which he drank before he died."

"That's right." Lonsdale thought he understood what Hauser was driving at. "You think the murderer found out that Fred was down to his last bottle and put the poison in it?"

The Austrian surprised him. "No, I don't think so. Fred always kept lots of Naya around because he never drank tap water." Hauser smiled in remembrance. "He was a fusspot to the extreme: only bottled water for him and only from an unopened bottle."

"Oh?" Lonsdale's antennae began to twitch. "What do you mean by that?"

"Fred was worried that I, or the maid, or whoever was visiting would drink from a bottle in the fridge without using a glass and then put back the half-empty bottle. So he always insisted on drinking from a bottle he opened himself."

"But, this time he didn't."

Hauser shook his head. "That's what's so strange. When I picked up the telephone I was watching Fred. He was struggling to uncap the bottle and he was having a hard time turning the cap."

"But, in the end, he succeeded."

"He sure did," said Hauser sadly. "He sure did."

Gal's lawyer, Melvin Rosenstein, agreed to see Hauser at four in the afternoon, and the Austrian left to reorganize his schedule to accommodate, promising Gal to call as soon as he had finished with Rosenstein.

"What kind of a lawyer is Rosenstein?" asked Lonsdale.

"The expensive kind. And very good."

"No doubt, since he is doing business with you. What I wanted to know was his specialty."

"Criminal Law. He's well known in South Florida." Gal's head was bobbing up and down. "I know Detective Sergeant Hal Dorff—his nickname is Hanging Hal. He goes for the jugular and gets a conviction in seven cases out of ten." All of a sudden Gal became very serious. "He's quite ruthless and bigoted, you know. Does not relate to gays, Jews and Blacks."

"Do you think Hauser did it?"

"Too early to tell, but I don't think so." Gal was thinking out loud. "Maybe it was just an accident."

Lonsdale shook his head. "I doubt it. From what Hauser told me while you were on the telephone with Rosenstein, Fred's death was no accident. It was premeditated murder, planned with precision and executed with daring." Lonsdale then told Gal about Fred Keller's insistence on drinking water only from bottles he uncapped himself.

CHAPTER TEN

Two weeks after Dr. Frederick Keller's death, the Palm Beach County Sheriff's Office arrested Karl Hauser and charged him with homicide.

The authorities felt they had a strong *prima facie* case against the Austrian: Keller had died of drinking poison from a bottle with only Keller's and Hauser's fingerprints on it; the bottle had been tampered with; Hauser knew about Keller's habit of drinking only from bottles he unsealed himself; Hauser had a key to Keller's apartment; Hauser had been present when Keller died; and—last but not least—Hauser had a serious motive or so Detective Dorff thought: jealousy. His not-so-discrete inquiries within the area's gay community had indicated, erroneously, that Keller had frequent dalliances outside the "couple" relationship with Hauser.

"Keller was discrete, but very promiscuous," Dorff told Gal after bail of two hundred and fifty thousand dollars had been posted by the pilot, "and Hauser found out. They had a big fight on New Year's Eve. I have a witness who heard Keller tell Hauser he was fed up and thinking about terminating their relationship. The rest is history."

"Who is this sterling witness of yours?" Gal asked.

"The man who catered Keller's New Year's Eve party."

"Is he gay?"

"As a matter of fact, he is."

Gal protested. "A man of Hauser's intelligence and composure would not commit an amateurish, improvised, spur-of-the-moment murder driven by as flimsy a motive as the one you've just outlined."

"I admit that it seems out of character," Dorff retorted. "But combine it with a very strong financial motive and the conclusion is inescapable."

"Such as?"

"Keller owned two-thirds and Hauser one-third of a six-million dollar apartment building in West Palm, which they had financed by Keller putting up a million, Hauser half-a-million and Southeast Bank four and a half million, secured by a first mortgage. Their partnership agreement contains interesting insurance and shotgun clauses."

"You mean each could force the other out of the partnership at any time?"

"As long as the one who started the process had the money to follow through..."

"And if he didn't?"

"The other would have to knuckle under and sell for a song."

"What if one of them died?"

"The survivor would get enough money from the partnership life insurance to buy the deceased partner out, and also to pay off the mortgage."

"So Hauser stands to profit by about five and a half million dollars from Keller's death?"

"Right on."

Gal left the detective to meet Rosenstein at the holding cells where the lawyer was completing the paperwork for getting the Austrian released on bail.

"I called Robert Lonsdale, my partner, in Washington this afternoon after I heard our client had been charged," he told Rosenstein, "and asked him to come back here as soon as possible." The three were in Gal's Jaguar, on their way to the lawyer's office.

"What for?" Rosenstein was puzzled.

"Because he has an excellent analytical brain and even better contacts," Gal continued. "This case involves a capital offense, punishable by death. From what I've just heard, Sergeant Dorff, our worthy opponent, has already mobilized the gay community to testify against your client and we've just started."

"You're not serious." Hauser and Rosenstein were aghast.

"Trust me, I am." Gal was not happy. "Rather than having to repeat myself, why don't we do this: I'll get Lonsdale back here by tomorrow afternoon and we'll have a full-scale pow-wow with him present."

"Where and at what time?"

"What about at my house on Ibis Crescent at five pm? I'll have my housekeeper prepare a cold meal so we can strategize while we eat."

Rosenstein was the first to address the four-man meeting. "The evidence against Karl is circumstantial, since no one saw him put the poison into the bottle nor did anyone see him hand the bottle to Keller. However, the *prima facie* case is good: Karl had the opportunity, which he never denied—and was present when Fred Keller died. As to motive: It is based on hearsay evidence as well as on hard financial facts."

"What do we do?" Hauser wanted to know.

"Find another suspect with a stronger motive," was Lonsdale's gut reaction. "In other words, find the real murderer."

"Do we have any other suspects?" This from Gal.

The silence that followed was deafening.

* * * * *

Dog tired from a tough day at the office in Washington, the subsequent flight to West Palm and the conference about Hauser that finished after nine, Lonsdale called Adys to say, "Goodnight, I love you," and went to bed early. But it took him a long time to fall asleep without Adys breathing serenely beside him, her warm body coaxing the tension away. And when he finally did doze off he slipped into one of his two recurring nightmares. This time it was not about the wolf, but about his brother, Anthony, whom Lonsdale had idolized.

A restless, curious kid, three years older than Lonsdale, Anthony had a mind of his own. During the siege of Budapest in 1944 he had disregarded his mother's orders on Boxing Day against venturing into the street.

Lonsdale had gone looking for him after Anthony had failed to return for lunch, and had found him not ten yards from the entrance of their apartment building, sitting on the curb, facing the street, his back against the base of a lamp that shielded him from view. To Lonsdale, he had appeared to be asleep. The sliver of metal from an exploding mortar shell that had killed him was so small that the entry wound could not be seen for the hair covering it.

Lonsdale had given Anthony a playful shove to wake him up.

Anthony had keeled over and Lonsdale had kept on shoving. "Come on Anthony, soup's on and Mom is waiting. Stop fooling around Anthony. Anthony!" He kept tugging at his brother's corpse, as he continued to shout louder and louder, "Anthony, come on Anthony."

Lonsdale awoke with a start, his scream still echoing in his brain.

He looked around, quite lost. Then he got it. He was in Gal's guest bedroom in Palm Beach, working on exonerating Hauser from Fred Keller's murder.

The scene of Keller sitting in the metal armchairs on the seawall, talking about CJD, came floating up from his subconscious. He remembered being surprised at the virologist's agitation. The man had been very tense and sweaty. Lonsdale's soothing words had not assuaged... what? It came to Lonsdale all of a sudden that Keller had been terrified.

What had he been so afraid of that night?

Lonsdale got out of bed, pulled a sweater over his pajamas, paddled out to the seawall in his loafers and sat down in the same chair he'd sat on the night he had first met the virologist.

That's what the emphasis had been on: virology—the new variant of CJD. Keller had given Lonsdale the distinct impression that an epidemic involving a new strain of mad cow disease was imminent.

Things were beginning to make sense. What if Keller had some connection with the expected epidemic and the deaths in Venice? Had there been others? Did someone kill Keller because he knew too much?

Lonsdale kept playing "what if" until he began to feel cold. At half-past-three he went back to bed, but couldn't sleep.

At six thirty he woke up Gal.

"Reuven, I've got to talk to you," he said to his astonished host. "It's about Fred."

Gal staggered out of bed and headed for the kitchen. While he made coffee Lonsdale told him about his musings during the night.

"Have you come to a conclusion?"

"Karl Hauser did not murder Fred Keller." Lonsdale's reply was firm. "His motive is not strong enough and he is far too intelligent and levelheaded to have committed a crime of passion in a way that would inculpate him right off the bat."

"If not he, then who *did* murder Keller?"

"Someone with a strong financial interest in keeping Keller from revealing something he knew about nv CJD; a business partner or competitor, for example."

"Competitor?" Gal sounded surprised.

"Sure—someone who is perhaps working on a better surgical glue or vaccine or antidote against CJD, hoping to market the stuff before Keller did."

"I see your point." The Israeli began fiddling with his sunglasses. "Fred had a partner in his business, a man with the same number of shares Fred had - a dynamo of a man called Mike Martin. Fred often talked to me about him. Unfortunately, he can hardly be considered a likely suspect."

"Why's that?"

"Because Martin died in a plane crash in the Bahamas the same day Fred died."

"Come again?"

"Martin had gone to Nassau with friends to gamble at the Paradise Island Casino. On their way back their plane blew up and everyone on board was killed."

"How did you find out about this?"

"Detective Sergeant Dorff told me."

"Quite a coincidence, wouldn't you say?" Lonsdale challenged.

"You mean that they should both die on the same day?"

"Yeah. And you know what?"

"What?"

"I don't believe in coincidences."

CHAPTER ELEVEN

During their Wednesday afternoon strategy session at Rosenstein's office Gal announced that, henceforth, Lonsdale would be in charge of the case.

"To start with," Lonsdale led off, "let's agree on fees." He glanced at his notes. "Karl's comfortable, but not rich, so we need to be careful about how we spend his money."

"You're not kidding," Hauser jumped in, concerned. "I can lay my hands on about a hundred thousand dollars, at most."

Lonsdale was matter-of-fact. "We'll need half of that for preliminary investigation work, travel and incidental expenses."

"Figure at least another sixty for the trial," Rosenstein chimed in, "if we're lucky."

"Which leaves me ten thousand short and no reserves if things become complicated," Hauser observed. "Unless you fellows can wrap this thing up in ninety days my life's savings will be soaked up by defending myself."

Lonsdale wanted no misunderstandings. "Let me make this clear, Karl. Our job is to find a way to prove you're innocent. There's no way we can tell today in what direction our investigation will take us tomorrow."

"Where and when do we start?"

"Right now, by you making an "In Trust" check to Melvin for fifty thousand dollars."

"And then?"

"I'll start at the scene of the crime by interviewing Ramon Sanchez the building Super. Do you know him?"

"I sure do. He's a good fellow and we get along well. Do you want me to come with you?"

"Yes." Lonsdale looked at the lawyer. "Is that OK?"

"I'm glad you asked." Rosenstein turned to Gal. "You have to get Robert a temporary permit to act as your consultant and you have to inform the police about him. Make sure Robert explains to everyone that he is acting on Karl's behalf, and also make sure Robert does not carry concealed firearms or commit acts of violence."

The meeting broke up and Hauser drove Lonsdale to Bradley Place.

Lonsdale felt kinship for Hauser, whom he perceived as yet another displaced Central European with no family in North America, working in a chauvinistic environment in which his being gay isolated him even further from the mainstream.

Lonsdale was aware of how petty and gossipy the gay community was in Southern Florida; as were, for that matter, the Cubans, the Colombians, the Mexicans, the Italians, and the Jews....

"How is all of this affecting your position with Delta?"

"It's a sticky situation. Technically I'm innocent as is everybody in this country until proven guilty. But the publicity has hurt my career. Nobody wants to be flying with a pilot who is a murder suspect. I'm getting lots of peer pressure, but my union is protecting me and so far so good."

Lonsdale mentally complimented Hauser on putting up such a brave front, but couldn't help wondering what the poor bastard did when he got off duty after a grueling flight. Probably went home to his bachelor's flat and stared at the walls.

"What about your friends? Are they supportive?"

"Robert, my only close friend was Fred, and he's gone. As for our acquaintances..." he caught himself, "as for *my* acquaintances...well...what can I say?"

"Being ostracized, are you?"

"You can say that again. You and Reuven seem to be the only friends I've left. And, of course, Rosenstein."

Lonsdale felt very bad for him.

When they got to the building at Bradley Place, Sanchez was just finishing dinner. It was obvious the Super liked the pilot and invited Hauser and Lonsdale in for coffee.

"Ramon, are you from Cuba?" Lonsdale asked in Spanish.

"Yes, from Pinar del Rio—you have heard of the place?"

"Yes, I have. Used to go there regularly during my visits to Cuba in the sixties."

"You an American?"

Lonsdale smiled, but did not answer the question. "A namesake of yours in Pinar del Rio used to make the best *lechones* I've ever tasted. He grew tobacco and raised cattle on a *finca* near Ovas."

Sanchez was thunderstruck. "Are you talking about Enrique Sanchez, the owner of *La Finca Adorada?*"

"That's the one. He had a wonderful Canadian wife."

"Alma Granda, from Montreal. She was my aunt."

From then on Ramon Sanchez could not do enough for them.

He told them in detail about Mike Martin's visit to Fred the night before Fred died, and took them to see the BMW still parked beside Fred's car.

"Who came to visit Dr. Keller that Sunday beside Mike Martin?"

"Nobody I know of. But then both Dr. Keller and I were in and out of the building all day. Being the end of the holiday season every apartment was bursting with regulars and visitors—you know, the children and grandchildren of the owners and their friends."

"How do you cope with this from the point of view of security?"

"Good question. A very good question, as a matter of fact."

Sanchez then told Lonsdale that owners were required to provide the Super with the names of those who had been given keys to the apartments and to the front door. "The front door key also opens the garden gate beside the tennis courts on the street side of the pool area, and the door leading from the pool to the garage."

"In other words, to go to the pool or to the tennis court you go down to the garage and out into the garden. To go back to the apartment, you retrace your steps. Have I got it right?"

"You do, *Señor* Lonsdale. You can also get into the pool area from the street."

"Provided you have a key to the front door."

"As a matter of fact," the Super loved the phrase, "many people do enter from the street after their walk along the beach. That's why we have a security camera above the door leading from the pool to the garage. It's trained on the pool area and the entrance from the street."

"Does the camera record what's going on?"

"Yes. As a matter of fact, all cameras in the building do that."

"Are there cameras in the corridors?"

"No, there are only two altogether: the one at the pool and the other in the main lobby."

Sanchez then explained that the police had viewed the tapes from the two cameras and identified almost every person who had entered and exited the building between noon and midnight on the Sunday before Fred Keller died.

"That must have been one hell-of-a-job."

"Not really," retorted Sanchez. "As a matter of fact, the owners helped a lot by identifying their own gangs as it were. We counted fifty-seven different individuals"

"That averages out to about six per apartment," Lonsdale observed. "Did you identify all fifty-seven?"

"No, *Señor*. As a matter of fact we couldn't identify six of them."

Lonsdale's instincts were telling him he was on to something. "Could I see the tapes?"

"Sorry, the police have them."

"If I could get them copied, would you view them with me?"

"You bet. For a box of *Romeo y Julietas*, I would."

Lonsdale shot him a grin. "Cuban cigars? You've got a deal. I'll get them from Canada."

* * * * *

Next day Lonsdale got Rosenstein to apply for official permission to view the tapes, then borrowed Gal's Jag and drove to Sarasota to interview the Super of the complex where the late Mike Martin and Tony Antonucci lived.

The Super, Ricardo Flores, also Cuban, knew Ramon Sanchez and was cooperative, but could shed little light on what interested Lonsdale. He did, however, confirm that Martin had spent most of the Sunday before the murder in Sarasota.

"Would you know what time he would have left for Palm Beach?"

"No sir, but Phil Grover might."

"Who's he?"

"The attendant at the gas station not far from here who washes some of our tenants' cars."

Lonsdale left in search of him.

"I spoke with Mr. Martin around four on Sunday afternoon, so he must have left after that," Phil told Lonsdale during their chat. "I remember he asked me to call him between four and four fifteen because he needed to tell me where to leave his car after I finished washing it."

"Then you spoke with him on the phone, not in person?"

"Yes sir. I called Mr. Martin at his apartment and he told me to park the car in the garage and leave the keys with the Super."

"Are you sure it was with Mr. Martin that you spoke?"

"Absolutely. He's the only one who calls me Phil the Pill."

Lonsdale drove back to Palm Beach, digesting what—if anything—Phil's story meant, and timing the trip. It took him two hours and forty minutes at an average speed of seventy-five miles per hour.

The following Monday, Lonsdale flew to Nassau to see Chief Inspector Edward Triggs of the Royal Bahamian Police Force.

The Chief Inspector was anxious to assist: The Bahamas, being an important drug trans-shipment point, needed all the good will they could generate within the international law enforcement community. Lonsdale, as NATO's Deputy Director of Intelligence, though not strictly speaking a part of that community, was close enough to it to merit special cooperation.

Triggs, a Scotland Yard-trained detective, met Lonsdale at the airport and drove him straight to the Central Police Station where he handed him a thick file. "Read this," he said and poured Lonsdale some coffee. "I'll be back in half an hour." He lit his pipe and smiled. "Forgive me, but I'm so busy I'm having difficulty coping."

"We have established with some certainty," Triggs said when he returned, "that the Antonucci crash was mob related, the result of a vendetta between the Antonucci and Viotti families, both from Montreal. The Viottis saw an opportunity to wipe out all the living Antonucci males and took advantage of it." He pointed to the file in Lonsdale's hand. "As you can see, they arranged for the Antonuccis' aircraft to be blown up."

"How did you manage to put this information together?"

"We have informants in the casino. They reported the extraordinary interest one of the pit bosses manifested in the Antonuccis' activities. The rest is conjecture."

Lonsdale was skeptical. "Pretty flimsy information on which to base firm conclusions."

"Agreed." Triggs took a puff of his pipe. "But we also intercepted a couple of telephone conversations between Nassau and Montreal that reinforced our beliefs." Triggs pointed his pipe at Lonsdale for emphasis. "The Bahamas are besieged by high profile international gamblers, pimps, whores and drug dealers. The only way we can cope is by ignoring certain regulations."

"Such as?"

"The requirements for permission from a judge for wiretapping."

"Probable cause," Lonsdale murmured.

Triggs smiled. "I knew you'd understand." He got up. "Come, I'll show you the personal effects we managed to retrieve from the tail section of the aircraft that was still afloat when the rescue vessels reached the crash site."

As they walked up the street from the Central Police Station to Police Headquarters, Triggs kept up a steady stream of complaints and apologies. "We're understaffed and our office facilities are, to say the least, inadequate. Please forgive me for shunting you around like this. However," Triggs brightened, "thanks to the Americans our aerial drug interdiction facility is one of the best in the world."

"I suppose that's why your rescue craft got to the downed plane so soon."

"Not quite." Triggs led the way into the building housing the

Police and Fire Brigade Directorates. "The main reason we arrived so quickly was that the crash occurred within minutes of takeoff, with the aircraft going down very near the airport."

"Who got there first?"

"The traffic helicopter."

"Which then directed the surface craft to the crash scene, I suppose."

"Absolutely right." Triggs relit his pipe. "Now let me have a word with the sergeant here, and get you sorted out." He waved at a man in uniform who seemed to be in charge of the immense evidence room chock full of a bewildering variety of objects.

They were led to a table in a corner. The sergeant consulted a thick loose-leaf book and went off to fetch the victims' personal effects, of which there were only four: a roll-on suitcase belonging to Lino Antonucci (it had a tag with his name on it), a garment bag that Tony Antonucci's wife had identified the previous week as containing her late husband's clothes, a Compaq laptop computer in a metal briefcase with Mike Martin's name on it, and a second garment bag that Triggs thought may have belonged to one of the pilots.

"Thus far no one has identified the owner of the articles in the bag."

Lonsdale was puzzled. "That's strange. Haven't the relatives of the victims picked through what you have here?"

"The Antonucci relatives did, when they came to identify the brothers' bodies and to make arrangements for their return to Canada. Mr. Martin's widow telephoned, but did not visit. Of course, she had no body to identify."

"What about the pilot's and the copilot's relatives?"

Triggs shook his head. "They had no reason to show. The copilot's body was not recovered; the pilot's was identified by a local ground crew member who knew him."

Lonsdale picked up the garment bag and looked at Triggs. "May I open it?"

"Help yourself - we've already seen the contents."

Lonsdale unzipped the bag and took out its contents: a pair of Nike sneakers, a jogging suit, and a wide-brimmed straw hat bent out of shape as a result of a soaking.

"I asked Mrs. Martin about these items over the telephone," Triggs said, "and she said they might very well have belonged to her late husband, but she needed to see them before making a positive identification."

"What about the computer in the case?"

"That Mrs. Martin did identify as being her husband's."

"Where do you go from here?" Lonsdale asked while repacking the items.

The Chief Inspector gave a resigned sigh. "We'll go through the motions of an investigation, but it's a foregone conclusion that, even if we did manage to identify the perpetrators, we'd never be able to bring them to justice."

"How come?"

"This is a mob-inspired contract killing, Mr. Lonsdale. Those directly involved have long since left the Bahamas and are, as we speak, no doubt engaged in similar activities in South America, or Europe—or China, for all I know. The jurisdictional problems involved in attempting to apprehend them, extradite them, try them and condemn them are monumental." The detective glanced at his watch. "It's half past twelve. What say to a pint at the local and a quick sandwich?"

"I'm game," Lonsdale replied, "as long as it's my treat."

Triggs took Lonsdale to the Cracked Crab, an eatery that vaguely resembled an English pub.

"This case must be pretty small beer compared to the files you usually handle. How are things in the Balkans?" inquired the policeman.

Lonsdale tried to sound noncommittal. "Unstable as ever. The Albanians won't leave well enough alone and the Serbs keep cheering them on."

Triggs wanted to pursue the subject in depth, but Lonsdale was tired and fended him off with generalities. They had a bit of a tug-of-war when it came to paying the bill, but Lonsdale won that with ease.

"What happens to the items you showed me this morning?" Lonsdale asked on their way out.

"They remain in our custody until the Magistrate approves their release to the heirs of the deceased."

"How long will that take?"

"Oh, at least another three months, I should say."

"The wheels of justice," murmured Lonsdale, and took his leave. He had a feeling he would be seeing Triggs sooner than the Chief Inspector suspected. The temptation to look inside Mike Martin's computer was overwhelming: Lonsdale had not failed to notice that Martin's metal briefcase was watertight and that its contents seemed to be undamaged.

CHAPTER TWELVE

"I don't think we should eliminate Mike Martin from our list of murder suspects," Lonsdale told his colleagues at their Wednesday afternoon strategy meeting back in Palm Beach. "Sanchez, the Bradley Place Super, saw Keller on Sunday midmorning. We can, therefore, assume that, unless Keller drank no bottled water during Saturday night, the murderer must have placed the bottle on the night table on Sunday some time between, say, eleven am and Keller's return from a concert he attended at West Palm Beach at six pm"

"How do you know that?"

"It was in the papers—in the social column. After the concert Keller went to a dinner in his honor, which started at eight thirty."

Gal chimed in. "So he had less than an hour to shower, get dressed and meet with his partner Martin."

Lonsdale nodded. "Martin arrived a few minutes before seven. He had forgotten the key Keller had given him to the apartment and asked Sanchez to call upstairs because Keller would not open the door."

"How come?"

"Most likely in the toilet. Who knows?"

"Where was Martin between eleven am and seven pm?" Rosenstein was keeping track of the timeline.

"The Super at the Sarasota condo complex saw him at noon in the pool area, chatting with Mrs. Antonucci. At three he drove his car to a nearby gas station to be serviced. He told the attendant to call him when he was finished, which the attendant did a few minutes after four. Martin then told him to leave the car in the garage and give the keys to the Super."

"How long does it take to drive from Sarasota to Palm Beach?"

"Two hours and forty minutes at seventy-five miles per hour," Lonsdale replied. "I timed the trip twice—once coming, once going. Driving faster than ten miles above the speed limit," he added as an afterthought, "is an invitation for the cops to pick you up, especially along Alligator Alley."

"It would seem that all of Mike Martin's time on Sunday is accounted for and he couldn't have been the poisoner."

"Unless?"

"Unless he put the bottle in place on Saturday and not on Sunday," Gal completed the thought for Lonsdale.

Hauser was disappointed. "Do we know how Plasmalab's CEO spent his day Saturday?"

Lonsdale shook his head. "That's my next assignment. No one in Sarasota saw him much that day, but Tony Antonucci did speak with him by telephone around noon. I'm flying to Canada tomorrow for a chat with Mrs. Martin first, and then with the people at Plasmalab to try to flesh out his movements that day." He turned to Rosenstein. "How's the request to view the videotapes coming?"

"It's taking forever, but I'm hopeful we'll have copies by the time you get back from Canada. By the way, how do you propose to get Mrs. Martin and the people at Plasmalab to talk to you?"

Lonsdale shrugged but said nothing. He did not feel like sharing his little secret that through his very special contacts in Brussels and Washington he had managed to obtain a list of the telephone calls made from and to Mike Martin's telephone in Sarasota during the week prior to the man's demise.

Three of these he found of particular interest: one to Air Canada, one to a locksmith just north of Toronto and one *from* Nassau on the day Martin died.

* * * * *

The Canadian Passport Office, a special operating agency of the Department of External Affairs and International Trade, is located in the city of Hull, Quebec, just across the Ottawa River from the Canadian House of Parliament.

The Director of the Passport Office is, by tradition, a senior Foreign Service Officer, but it is the Deputy Director, secunded from the Canadian Security Intelligence Service (CSIS), who runs the show. It is his job to ensure that Canadian passports are no longer as easy to obtain by international crooks, drug dealers and terrorists as they once were. That Ernesto "Che" Guevara had traveled on a Canadian passport in the late sixties and that, in 1998, four Mossad agents had been caught in Lebanon with Canadian passports in their possession still rankled. Not to mention millennium bomber Ahmed Ressam who, but for a sharp U.S. border guard, was headed to blow up Los Angeles International Airport using a valid Canadian passport issued to Beni Noris—a wholly invented person.

The day after the meeting in Palm Beach Lonsdale flew to Montreal then drove to Hull to visit the Passport Office's Deputy Director, Ben Svoboda, an old friend from CIA days when Svoboda was the CSIS liaison man in Washington.

They met at *La Grenouille*, an elegant Paris-style bistro outside the central core, little frequented by civil servants because it was out of the way and pricey.

Svoboda was manifestly pleased to see Lonsdale. "You could have bowled me over with a feather when you called to say you were coming. How long has it been since we last had a meal together?"

"Twelve years, Ben, if it's a day."

"Who paid?" Svoboda asked.

Lonsdale smiled. Svoboda, a notorious penny pincher, was running true to form. "All right, all right Ben. This meal's on me."

Svoboda surprised him. "OK, Robert, but let me pay for the wine."

Over coffee, Lonsdale got down to business.

He told Svoboda about Keller's murder and Hauser's suspected involvement in it, then gave a brief account of the virologist's relationship with Mike Martin and described the way in which, and the reason why, Martin and the Antonuccis died.

"It was a vendetta killing Ben, and Martin was an unintended victim—a man in the wrong place at the wrong time. However," Lonsdale stopped long enough to savor a mouthful of the excellent Napoleon brandy that Svoboda, in an uncharacteristic gesture of largesse, had ordered to finish off their meal in style, "as the saying goes, 'a funny thing happened to me on my way to the Forum.'"

Svoboda leaned back, smiled and waited for the penny to drop; he enjoyed the way Lonsdale told his stories.

"Langley provided me with a list of the telephone calls to and from the late Mike Martin's apartment in Sarasota. Unbelievable as this may sound, I found one that had originated from Nassau about five or six minutes after the Antonuccis' aircraft had taken off."

Svoboda snapped forward, all ears. "You don't say!"

"Nassau air traffic control clocked the takeoff at 13:23 hours. Cable and Wireless, the Bahamas telephone company, claims the call to the Martin residence emanated from a public telephone situated in the main hall of the Nassau International Airport at 13:29 hours."

"Who do you think made the call?"

Lonsdale shrugged. "Damned if I know." He took another sip of his brandy. "But the call was dialed without operator assistance and charged to Martin's credit card."

"But by that time Martin was in the Antonucci aircraft, in the process of being blown to pieces over the Atlantic."

"So it would appear."

"Could be Martin lost his wallet, or had it stolen, and the person who found or stole it made a test call to his house to see if the card still worked, or the person who found the wallet called Martin's house to advise that the wallet had been found."

Lonsdale nodded. "Possible, though somewhat contrived. And how would they know the PIN? In any event, I haven't yet been able to check out this hypothesis. I have no access to the late Mr. Martin's telephone answering machine in Sarasota."

"Oh?" Svoboda, surprised, carried on theorizing regardless. "What about this: Martin had given his credit card number and PIN to someone in Nassau with instructions to call his house to leave some sort of a message like 'I'll be coming home late tonight'—that sort of a thing."

"To what end? Anyway, as I said, I haven't yet been able to access Martin's answering machine or speak to his wife."

"Wife? Surely, you mean his widow."

"No Ben, I don't." Lonsdale was emphatic. "I'm convinced Martin made that call himself."

Svoboda laughed. "That's my third scenario, too. But it makes no sense."

"Why not?"

"Because either Martin was already dead, or he wanted people to think he was dead. He did not come forward after the crash—did he?—to announce that he had missed the flight. Why would he then do a stupid thing like using his credit card? Even a moron knows nowadays that credit card transactions are easy to trace."

"Agreed. My problem is I need help in getting the information that would allow me to discard two of the three possibilities we just outlined."

"What kind of help?" Svoboda became wary.

"I need someone with some sort of official standing, like you, to help me interview Mrs. Martin who will probably scream for her lawyer as soon as I go near her."

Svoboda was nonplussed. "Come off it Robert. I couldn't possibly intervene in an official capacity."

"Why the hell not? You'd only be doing your job!"

"How so?"

"I am giving you information to the effect that a man, who is supposed to be dead, may be using a valid Canadian passport fraudulently. Is it not your duty to prevent such a thing from happening?"

Svoboda had to think that through and it took him some time. "I suppose you have a point," he allowed in the end, feeling very tempted to get back into action again. "What do you have in mind?"

"Ask for an interview with Mrs. Martin and take me along."

"To Toronto?"

Lonsdale smiled. "Don't worry, OK? I'll pay for the plane tickets and the hotel. Won't cost the Canadian taxpayer a plugged nickel."

Lonsdale then suggested they make the most of the opportunity and arranged to arrive in Toronto on the Thursday afternoon before the interview, in time for a decent evening meal and a concert by the Toronto Symphony at Massey Hall.

The day after the concert, weather in Toronto was, frankly, miserable. It was blowing snow off the lake and bitterly cold when their taxi pulled up in front of the Martins' spacious residence on Forest Hill Road. They were received in the drawing room where a fire had been lit for the visitors' benefit. As foreseen by Lonsdale, Donna Martin had insisted that her lawyer, Jeff McHenry, be present.

They were forced to spend the first ten minutes of their visit reassuring McHenry that Mrs. Martin was *not* the subject of an official inquiry by the Passport Office.

"We're here to seek Mrs. Martin's assistance in establishing whether or not her late husband had been in possession of his passport at the time of his death. Nothing more," was the way Svoboda put it. His rank, as it appeared on the business card he handed the lawyer, and Lonsdale's taciturn presence, playing the subaltern, seemed to do the trick. McHenry allowed the interview to proceed.

The meeting lasted close to an hour during which, as a result of a few short, skillful questions, interposed by Lonsdale at opportune moments, Mrs. Martin told her visitors just about everything Lonsdale had come to find out.

Their chat ended on a polite note. "I cannot tell you how glad I am to know," Mrs. Martin said as the meeting broke up, "that at least one branch of the government is mindful of its taxpayers' needs, and attempts to protect them."

Svoboda squared his shoulders. "Mrs. Martin, the Passport Office is run by professionals in an entrepreneurial environment. We use the latest techniques available. We fund our operations by charging for the service we provide. Public opinion forces us to give value for money."

On their way out Lonsdale turned to his hostess. "Are you a director of Plasmalab, ma'am?"

"Yes. Why do you ask?"

"Must be pretty difficult to direct that company these days."

Donna Martin looked uncomfortable. "What makes you think so?"

"Losing its CEO is always hard on a company, but losing its Chief Scientific Officer at the same time, that must be pure hell."

"You are quite right," the woman replied. "You cannot imagine how difficult things are just now." She was going to say more, but a warning look from McHenry stopped her.

On their way to their hotel, Svoboda could not stop congratulating himself. "I thought the interview went very well, didn't you?"

"Yes I did, but I don't think Mrs. Martin told us everything she knows."

"About Mike Martin, you mean?"

"No—about Plasmalab. I'm sure you noticed how worried she became when I began to probe her about the company."

Svoboda shook his head in disbelief. "Of course she's concerned. Geez you're obtuse. She must own a bundle of Plasmalab stock that has taken a shellacking in the market during this past month. The price is down by fifty percent."

"She will inherit six million shares when this mess gets cleared up," Lonsdale told Svoboda. "Even with the stock as low as twenty bucks a share, she'll still be a very wealthy woman."

"So why do you think she's holding out on us?"

Lonsdale shrugged. "I have no idea, but my gut says there's more trouble ahead for Plasmalab."

It was at that moment that Lonsdale's inner voice—the voice that he always obeyed—chimed in. "Stay in Toronto and wait," it commanded.

And Lonsdale did.

After lunch he sent Svoboda back to Ottawa and resolved to talk Mrs. Martin into showing him around Plasmalab on the Monday.

Lonsdale called the Martin house at eight in the morning, but was told Mrs. Martin had already left. He asked the maid to have her call him at his hotel, then phoned Plasmalab, but was informed she was not expected until after lunch. He left her a message there too then went downstairs for breakfast.

The lobby was full of people on their way to a power breakfast in the hotel's main ballroom, courtesy of Yorktown Securities. On impulse, Lonsdale joined their ranks and soon found himself seated next to a personable man in his mid-thirties. His business card said he was Josh Meltzer, the Manager of Yorktown's Bloor Street branch. "And you?" he challenged Lonsdale. "What's your connection with us?"

"I'm a potential client," Lonsdale answered, improvising as an idea emerged from his subconscious. "I need information." Before Lonsdale could go on, a speaker extolling the advantages of using Yorktown's services interrupted their chat. This gave Lonsdale time to refine the story he intended to lay on Meltzer to inveigle the broker into helping him.

"I'm very interested in bio-surgicals," he told the man after the speeches were over, and handed him his NATO business card. He noted Meltzer's reaction of awe with satisfaction. "I've heard that there is a great deal of activity in Canada in this sector of the market."

Meltzer, sensing a potential new client, spent the next thirty minutes chatting up Lonsdale, who used the time to work his way around to the subject of Plasmalab.

Meltzer's knowledge about the company was superficial. "Tell you what…When I get back to the office I'll talk to the analyst who follows the stock and have him send you more information."

"Good. I'm staying in room 1471. Tell him to fax me the stuff here by noon and I'll call him back after I've read it."

Meltzer was very much on the ball and, by lunchtime, Lonsdale had a six-page summary on Plasmalab, prepared by Paul Savard, one of Yorktown's analysts.

He called Mrs. Martin again after lunch, but couldn't get through so he decided to call Savard.

The analyst explained that Plasmalab was in the process of rebuilding its management team to overcome the loss of the company's CEO, Martin, and its Chief Scientific Officer, Keller.

"Rumor has it," Savard went on, "that there will be an announcement about Keller's replacement today. The betting is on Jason Moscovitch, the Acting Chief Scientific Officer."

"Is he any good?"

"Supposedly a genius in virology, shy on experience but a crackerjack researcher, which is what the company needs just now."

"How come?"

"Plasmalab's most successful product is its magic surgical glue, Plasmacol. But one product is not enough. The street expects Moscovitch to come up with something new that's just as exciting as Plasmacol. Otherwise, the stock won't regain its lost luster."

"Where's it at now?"

"Forty dollars—up from its low of eighteen the day after Keller and Martin died, but way off its high of eighty-five last fall."

Lonsdale was having breakfast in his room the next day, still waiting for a callback from Donna Martin and re-reading the material Savard had sent him, when his phone rang. It was the analyst.

"I thought you'd like to know," he said, "trading has been halted in Plasmalab and an announcement is expected before noon."

"Regarding the appointment of new executive officers, I suppose...."

"I don't think so." Savard sounded worried. "That's not the sort of thing to cause the authorities to suspend trading, not before the start of a trading day anyway. Something else, something important, is up."

"Keep me posted, would you? And thanks." Lonsdale hung up and tuned his TV to the local financial news channel.

He didn't have to wait long.

At about eleven twenty the NEWS FLASH logo filled the screen, with the legend MAD COW DISEASE *MADE IN CANADA* underneath it. "We interrupt our regular programming," said the voiceover, "to bring you this special announcement. Health Canada has ordered the closing of Toronto-based Plasmalab's operating facilities pursuant to a request by the World Health Organization. WHO investigators have traced the cause of a frightening spate of recent cases of Creutzfeldt-Jakob disease worldwide to the use of Plasmalab's surgical glue. Trading in Plasmalab shares on the Toronto Stock Exchange has been halted until further notice."

Everything suddenly snapped into focus. Keller had to have known that his product was contaminated. Martin must have killed Keller to stop him from revealing this knowledge too soon. DalMolin, Delatour and Sidarenko must have undergone surgery during which Plasmacol was used. That would explain how three people—one of them a vegetarian—living in different regions of the world contracted Creutzfeldt-Jakob disease more or less at the same time. Nothing else made sense.

The revelation also cleared up yet another point that had been bothering Lonsdale: CJD's usual incubation period was months, not weeks. Yet DalMolin and his fellow victims had died within ten days of having eaten at *l'Osteria d'Oro*.

It was quite obvious that Nicola Bianchi's restaurant had not, in any way, been responsible for its luncheon guests' deaths.

CHAPTER THIRTEEN

The day of his supposed demise Mike Martin managed to get on board an Air Transat late night charter flight from Nassau to Montreal with a one-way ticket purchased for cash. He passed through Customs and Immigration on arrival using his driver's license, and gave his name as Jean (his full name was Jean-Michel) Martin on the Customs Declaration form. The sleepy officer on duty never noticed the slight discrepancy between the two documents and hardly gave Martin a second look.

He took the airport bus downtown and checked into an anonymous B&B in Montreal's Gay Village for one night.

The next morning, since he had purchased only the bare essentials in Nassau, he rounded out his wardrobe to fit his new persona: jeans, flannel shirts, heavy shoes, a sweater, a lined windbreaker with a hood, a pair of workman's boots and a backpack to stow everything. In the afternoon he went searching for more permanent lodgings and settled into a rooming house on St. Denis Street, near Viger Square where he stayed while his beard grew out.

He'd known all along that the most difficult part of disappearing would be the establishment of a new identity. Therefore, planning ahead with diligence, Mike had confirmed, by calling his family in Quebec City at Christmastime, that his uncle Jean-Yves, nicknamed Joe, who suffered from cerebral palsy, was still alive and living in a nursing home in St. Georges de Beauce, close to the U.S. border.

On the pretext of having business in the provincial capital, he had visited his uncle and other relatives in the area. While visiting the nursing home Mike had lifted from his uncle's medical chart the information he needed for completing a Passport Application Form: date and place of birth, social insurance number, and so forth.

At the end of January, with his bushy, gray-streaked black beard neatly trimmed, and sporting a pair of ten-dollar optically neutral eyeglasses with heavy frames, Mike had his passport picture taken. The likeness showed a robust man in his mid-forties, which pleased Mike very much since he was only thirty-nine, but his Uncle Joe, his father's youngest brother, was forty-nine.

All Mike now needed to obtain a *genuine* Canadian passport bearing his photograph, but issued in the name of his uncle, Jean-Yves Martin, was a certified copy of his uncle's baptismal certificate. *But for that I have to go to Port-Alfred—Uncle Joe's birthplace*, Mike decided, and packed his bag.

CHAPTER FOURTEEN

In spite of pursuing Mrs. Martin with determination, Lonsdale was unable to secure an appointment with her before having to return to Palm Beach.

He did, however, obtain more information about the situation at Plasmalab from Savard, who provided valuable details about the contamination incident, and said it was estimated that at least a hundred people were infected worldwide.

"Of course, the product has been taken off the market. Existing stocks of Plasmacol are being destroyed worldwide. The manufacturing facility has been closed until further notice."

"Then the company is out of business. Right?"

"Not quite. Remember Moscovitch, the virologist Keller had hired before his death?" Lonsdale nodded and the analyst continued. "Well, he's working on some sort of an antidote for nv CJD. This vaccine will be in great demand—believe me—when the expected epidemic develops."

"What epidemic?"

"Keller, it seems, had found out about the accident in early September and hired Moscovitch to help develop an antidote because Keller did, in fact, anticipate that the contamination would spread like wildfire. No one knows what the incubation period or virulence of this new strain is, not even Moscovitch, who has had access to samples of the strain since September."

"Why is that?"

"Keller fed a bunch of baloney to Moscovitch when he hired him in September about stumbling on a new strain of CJD by accident. He then provided Moscovitch with samples, which must have come from the contaminated inventory—"

"So all of Plasmalab's senior managers must have known about the contamination," interrupted Lonsdale. "Certainly the CEO must have."

The analyst disagreed. "Maybe. But Keller played everything very close to the vest. For example, Moscovitch's research equipment was bought from a company with which Plasmalab had never done business, and was paid for by Keller out of his own pocket."

"You really believe that?"

"That the CEO did not know?" Savard took a moment to think before replying. "We'll never know, will we? He's dead. It's possible that other senior managers didn't know either. Research companies such as Plasmalab compartmentalize their activities because they're always afraid of industrial espionage."

"Where's the stock?"

"At twenty-eight"

"That's high. How come?"

"More than a million and a half Plasmalab shares were shorted during the last three months, of which most were covered only after the bad news hit the street. That stopped the price from sliding much below twenty."

"Isn't that unusual for a company the size of Plasmalab?"

"You mean a million and a half share short position?"

Lonsdale shrugged. "I suppose so." He didn't quite know what he meant.

"It represents less than ten percent of the total shares issued." The analyst sounded pensive. "I can see nothing highly suspect about the size of the shorts, but I do find it remarkable that people should have had the nerve to wait for so long before covering in a steadily rising market."

Lonsdale was out of his depth and said so. Savard was glad to explain. "When you sell short, you sell shares you don't have, so you have to buy them later to be able to deliver them. Suppose you 'shorted' at eighty dollars and the stock went to eighty-five."

"I would have lost five dollars a share."

"You've got it. The Plasmalab share price has been on the rise since September. Those who shorted the stock must have been pretty nervous by New Year's, yet most of them covered their positions only after the bad news hit in early February."

"Which means they probably knew the bad news was coming," Lonsdale cut in.

This stopped Savard cold. "I never thought about it that way. Be that as it may, short covering alone would not have brought the stock back from its eighteen dollar low to its present level of twenty-eight."

"What did then?"

Savard suddenly sounded impatient. "Think about it, man. Suppose that the incubation period is four months and that people can infect other people as soon as they, themselves, become infected. Under such circumstances there must already be a whole bunch of people running around out there, sick and not knowing it, busily cross-infecting one another. Within a couple of months we might have hundreds of thousands of new cases of CJD and the only hope of stopping worldwide contamination would lie with Moscovitch's ability to come up with a serum really quick..."

"Which, if Moscovitch were successful, would send Plasmalab's share price through the roof."

Savard's laugh sounded cynical. "True, provided there would still be people left alive to buy the stock!"

* * * * *

"He's quite right you know," Lonsdale told his colleagues at Gal's house in Palm Beach, and bit into a chicken sandwich. Ever since getting involved with CJD he had stopped eating red meat. "We don't know squat about this disease, which started when cows in England acquired it after eating enriched foods. It seems the renderers ground up dead cattle bones and mixed this protein-rich powder into the fodder they sold to the farmers to feed their cattle. The disease is transmitted by prions, an organism we do not yet know how to kill."

"Do you really think there may be a worldwide epidemic in the offing, comparable to AIDS?" Rosenstein asked, obviously uncomfortable with the thought.

"I don't know." Lonsdale shrugged. "In fact, I don't think anybody knows." He sat up and looked at his notepad. "Let's stop worrying about things we can't do anything about. There's enough on our plate as is." He ticked off a few items on his list. "I think I've just about told you everything I found out. The two open items I seem to have at my end are..." he counted them off on his fingers, "the viewing of the video tapes from the cameras at Bradley Place; and that unexplained telephone call from Nassau to Sarasota, placed a few minutes after Martin was supposed to have died."

"You seem to be pretty sure Martin is still alive." Hauser, whose trial for murder was scheduled for mid-September, was looking for any port in the storm.

"It's a definite possibility as far as I'm concerned. Although, when I told Mrs. Martin about the phone call she said she had no recollection of any such thing on the answering machine. Then, when I asked her to let me listen to the tape so I could judge for myself, she told me she had erased all messages. So you see, my gut says Martin's alive, but I have no proof."

Gal swore under his breath. "Then, damn it, we're at a dead end. So where do we go from here, Robert?"

"We view the tapes from Bradley Place."

Lonsdale turned to Rosenstein. "When?"

"We'll receive a certified copy tomorrow morning."

"At last." Lonsdale grabbed the phone. "Let me call Sanchez and see if he's available to lend us a hand. By the way, how do we feel about the trial?"

Rosenstein sounded non committal. "All evidence against Karl is circumstantial. However, he did have a strong motive. I'd say our chances are sixty-forty in favor of acquittal."

Lonsdale was surprised. "That isn't too good."

"Our chances would be enhanced if we could present a plausible theory involving Mike Martin. It would confuse the jurors and plant the seed of reasonable doubt in their minds."

Hauser was taut-faced. "You mean: give them an alternative suspect, don't you?"

Rosenstein stood up. "To conclude that there is reasonable doubt and, thus, grounds for an acquittal, jurors need to be presented with an alternative explanation of the crime. If there's only one suspect to the exclusion of all others, juries tend to return guilty verdicts." He headed for the door.

"Hang on, hang on," Lonsdale called after him, holding the receiver away from his mouth. "Can we get together Saturday afternoon at two to view the tapes? Sanchez is available then."

"How long will it take?"

Lonsdale made a face. "I'm afraid it will take at least a couple of hours."

"Too long," cried Gal and Rosenstein in unison. "How come?"

"There are two tapes and the time span we have to review is six hours—from, say, noon till six on Sunday afternoon. Even with Sanchez prompting us, two hours may not be long enough."

"Must we all be present? I promised my kids that I'd play baseball with them." Rosenstein sounded especially disappointed.

Lonsdale took pity on him. "Well, a father's promise should be inviolate. Let's do the thing from five to seven. Two hours should be enough for a first run through and you can keep your word."

"Will there be more than one?"

"If I don't find something we can use, there sure will be!" Lonsdale told Sanchez about the arrangements and hung up. "Sanchez will be here at five on Saturday."

Gal turned to Hauser. "I'm putting you in charge of drinks during the afternoon and dinner at night; you Delta guys ought to be good at hospitality. I'll ask Sanchez to bring his wife. She'll spend the time with Gina. Unfortunately, Adys isn't in town."

"Can I bring my wife too?" Rosenstein asked sheepishly.

"Of course you can you silly bugger. Melissa needs no invitation to come to this house."

* * * * *

"Why don't we start with a quick run through?" Sanchez suggested. They were seated in front of Gal's giant TV screen amply supplied with espressos and key lime cookies. "I can remember the interesting parts—you know, the parts where we could not identify some of the people. There were only six, as a matter of fact. Five on the tape showing the pool area and the entrance from the street, and one on the tape showing the main lobby."

Gal turned on his machines and handed the remote to the Cuban. "It's your show."

"Hold on for a bit." Lonsdale went to his room and reappeared a few moments later with a plastic DUTY FREE bag from which he took two boxes of *Romeo y Julietas*. One he handed with a wink to Sanchez who grinned and nodded his head in thanks. The other he opened and set on the table. "Help yourselves gentlemen," he said, and sat back to watch the tape.

"The police are not being very cooperative," Rosenstein said, nursing his cigar to life with loving care. "They have stills of all persons appearing on the tapes, those they've identified and those they haven't, but they won't give us their analysis until we do our own homework."

Hauser was indignant. "Do they have the right to do this?"

"Well, the law says that both sides have to cooperate in a situation such as this." The lawyer turned to Sanchez. "Fire away and tell us what to watch for."

It took ten minutes on fast forward to get to the first "unidentified" person, a young man carrying a skateboard.

"Pass," said Lonsdale, and the others agreed.

Forty minutes later they got to two very well endowed women, one a blonde, the other a brunette.

"They're a matched pair, as a matter of fact," said Sanchez smacking his lips. "Although nobody would identify them, I know they're high-class call girls who regularly service the old guy in apartment twenty-one. But you know how it is," the Cuban shrugged, "hear no evil, see no evil, speak no evil. I need my job."

There was an embarrassed silence while the tape rolled on, then, with the clock on the tape player showing a few minutes before six, Lonsdale suddenly called out, "Stop. Go back."

Sanchez obliged and then pressed the button for regular play. They watched as a man in a jogging suit, wearing sneakers and sporting a wide-brimmed straw hat, came in through the street side entrance of the pool area with an empty beach bag over his shoulder.

"Bingo," said Lonsdale and Sanchez almost in unison to Lonsdale's great surprise.

"What do you mean by bingo, Ramon?"

"I know why I said bingo, but why did you say bingo?"

Lonsdale was adamant. "You first."

"This guy with the hat and the jogging suit," the Cuban explained between puffs on his cigar, "is the one the cops picked as the number one target for their investigation"

"How do you know this?"

"*Señor* Rosenstein, I worked with the police for days on these tapes. They must have asked me and the other people about this guy a hundred times, but nobody seemed to know who he was or why he came to visit."

"Does the tape show him leaving the compound?" asked Lonsdale, noting the time of the man's arrival as being five forty-seven pm

"Sure it does," answered Sanchez, "just watch."

Twelve minutes later—at five fifty-nine—the man reappeared.

"Stop the tape," commanded Lonsdale. "See his bag? It looked empty going in, but it looks full now."

"What do you think he went to get?" Gal was baffled.

"Or steal," added Hauser.

"The Naya water in Keller's apartment that you said you couldn't find anywhere. Do you remember?" Lonsdale said.

Stunned, Hauser nodded, his eyes glazed.

"Run the sequence again, please, Ramon," Lonsdale requested.

After they had reviewed the scene a half-dozen times Lonsdale allowed Sanchez to continue with the show.

By seven forty they were through with tape one.

Gal got up and stretched. "Do we do tape two now?"

Sanchez got up too. "I need to go to the bathroom."

Lonsdale shook his head. "I wouldn't bother with tape two. I'm pretty sure I know who the guy in the jogging suit is."

"You do? Who?" Three sets of incredulous eyes bore into his.

"Mike Martin," replied Lonsdale and told them about the contents of the garment bag in the Evidence Room at Nassau Police Headquarters.

Whenever Lonsdale spoke in support of his theory that it had been Martin who killed Keller, Rosenstein systematically demolished his arguments. There was no way, the lawyer said, that Martin could have gotten to Palm Beach from Sarasota by the time the jogger first appeared in the tape, which was at five forty-seven pm—not with Phil, the garage attendant, testifying that he had spoken to the man at four: Lonsdale knew damn well the trip took at least two and a half hours.

The police claimed, Rosenstein continued with determination, that the reason why the jogger had not been identified was that his face could not be seen on the tape and the tenants did not recall what their friends, drifting in and out of the building, were wearing that particular Sunday afternoon.

As for the hat and jogging suit, they were of a common variety. The black-and-white tape showed that several other "identified" visitors were wearing similar outfits that day, though not in the same combination.

"The theory of the jogger arriving with an empty beach bag and then leaving with a bagful of Naya water bottles is pure conjecture for which you cannot produce factual support," the lawyer concluded. "And your request that the Palm Beach County's Sheriff's Office ask Interpol to watch for someone using the late Mike Martin's passport will not be acted on."

"How do you know?" Lonsdale sounded frustrated.

"Because Dorff told me so!"

"What am I supposed to do then?"

Rosenstein softened his stance. "Don't misunderstand me; the stuff you've dug up is useful. I will lay it before the jury, be assured of that, but there is a possibility the judge won't allow it in."

"Why not?"

"Irrelevant evidence. Pure conjecture. I can just hear the Assistant District Attorney screaming 'objection' after 'objection.'"

"Am I right to suppose then," a subdued and disappointed Lonsdale asked, "that unless I can produce Mike Martin in the flesh for the trial there is not much chance of an acquittal?"

"That just about sums it up."

"I guess I had better get hold of the late Mike Martin's briefcase then and rummage around in it to see what I can come up with."

"That won't be as easy as you think."

"Why not?"

"To make whatever you unearth in the Bahamas admissible evidence in a Florida Court you must obtain such evidence in accordance with strict rules. First, I'd have to engage the services of an attorney in the Bahamas to file a Request for Permission to Examine Evidence. This request will have to be supported by a similar request, made here in Florida. Shall I go on?"

Lonsdale had heard enough. "Forget it Melvin," he said. "Forget the straight and narrow. Let me try it my way."

* * * * *

Triggs was glad to see Lonsdale again—all the more so since he arrived bearing gifts: a bottle of rare, seventy-five-year-old cognac for the Chief Inspector and a case of Boddington beer for the sergeant in charge of the Evidence Room.

Over dinner, Lonsdale brought the policeman up-to-date on the Martin file, and expressed the hope that a way could be found in the interest of justice to allow the examination by experts of the contents of Martin's briefcase which, Lonsdale felt, would yield proof positive that his theory was valid.

Triggs was sympathetic, but non committal. He reiterated that the Crown did not have the resources to pursue an investigation into a crime that involved non-Bahamians and their assets and the perpetrators of which, even if identified, would not be within the reach of the rather short arm of the Royal Bahamian Police Force.

Lonsdale had foreseen all these objections.

He poured Triggs a generous helping of cognac. "Suppose you could assure your superiors that such an examination would involve no costs and the expenditure of only minimal time by you and your staff."

"What do you have in mind?"

"If permission were granted by a magistrate as a result of an application by the police to have the contents of Martin's briefcase analyzed by recognized forensic experts willing to donate their time in the interests of justice, I think I could persuade a computer expert and a forensic scientist to spend a long weekend in Nassau and do the work without charge."

"Under police supervision?"

"Yes."

Triggs pursed his lips. "It's a thought. But who would defray their traveling expenses?"

"I was hoping the Royal Bahamian Police Force's Benevolent Fund might find a way around that problem."

"How do you mean?"

"I hear the annual Nassau Policemen's Ball, the proceeds of which go to the Fund as a matter of tradition, is scheduled to take place in three weeks. Suppose a generous donor would buy fifty tickets. Do you think you could find a couple of willing policemen whose families would feed and lodge my two experts for four days?"

"What about their airfare?"

"They'd fly on points. No cost involved."

"Are you aware that the tickets for the Ball are a hundred dollars each, Robert?"

Lonsdale smiled—he had his man where he wanted him! "Indeed I am."

Triggs almost grinned as he knocked back the remains of his drink. "I'll see what can be done." Neither of them alluded to the fact that, to encourage the sale of tickets to the Ball, the Benevolent Fund sold ten-ticket booklets to policemen at a twenty percent discount.

Lonsdale's five-day trip to Nassau in late February turned into a series of maddening frustrations, not the least of which was the tension that soon developed between the two experts he'd brought with him.

No wonder. His computer specialist, Mark Randolph, a brilliant, gregarious, disorganized protégé of Gal's, all of twenty-two, had little respect for Lonsdale's generation, while the forensic scientist, Joe McGregor—an old connection from CIA days—was a dour, methodical Scotsman in his fifties whose services Lonsdale had retained because of his analytical mind, his vast experience, and his ready access to the crime lab at Langley.

Lonsdale's principal concern was to get them all to work together without upsetting their host, Chief Inspector Triggs, who was required, by court order, to be in constant attendance while Mike Martin's briefcase and its contents were being examined.

Randolph got past Martin's computer security code within hours, and, by the end of the second day, produced a hard copy of the machine's entire contents that would take Lonsdale some time to review. Ready to goof off since his work was done, Randolph left in search of ice cream while McGregor focused on the notepad Martin had left behind, which was the only item in the briefcase other than the computer.

The sum total of the two experts' findings was minimal: one—Martin's log-on password was ARBEZ (Lonsdale immediately spotted the ZEBRA palindrome), and two—the pad had been used to prepare a checklist of which only a small fragment could be deciphered.

"Martin was careful," McGregor reported. "He tore off the sheet beneath the sheet on which he wrote so as not to leave a trace. He must have been in a hurry though because, when he tore off the second sheet, he ripped the paper and left the top part behind—a strip of paper about an inch and a half wide on the left side tapering off to almost nothing on the right."

"Could you reconstruct anything?" asked a very disappointed Lonsdale.

"Yep," was McGregor's laconic answer. "But, as you can see, it's mostly gibberish." McGregor handed out copies of the enhancements of his findings.

"Try me." Lonsdale was willing to listen to anything.

"See? There's a 2 right on top." The Scotsman pointed out.

"Meaning, it's page two."

The Scotsman nodded. "Most likely. Beneath it we have 'LEAVE FOR PB NO LATER THAN 3'. I must assume PB means Palm Beach." McGregor went on. "The next line is 'dispo ial A.A.' followed by 'Change' on a line by itself. The last line I can make out reads 'take bag, and bot to B.P.' with a possible final line that starts with HA."

"I presume you've done all the tests you could think of?"

McGregor looked pained. "The lab did infrared and ultraviolet enhancements and some dust testing. There's not much more I can do."

Randolph, who, having returned with several containers of ice

128

cream, was in the process of spilling Coke all over Trigg's office floor, piped up out of nowhere. "From what Mr. Lonsdale has told me about the case I'd guess that the second line stands for 'dispose of vial along Alligator Alley'."

McGregor and Triggs were too stunned to say anything.

Lonsdale was flabbergasted, but capable of speech. "How the hell did you come up with this idea?"

"Free association, I guess." Randolph opened another bottle of Coke. "I also looked at some of the stuff that came out of the computer."

"And?" They were all ears now—the kid was making sense.

"I couldn't find anything interesting, except a strange-looking table that looks as if Martin may have been charting the price performance of Plasmalab's stock."

"What's strange about that?"

"Nothing, except that, every now and then, he'd insert a notation like (20-) and (10+) and (105 y)." Randolph handed out copies of the chart.

Lonsdale nodded. "I saw the chart, but I haven't yet had time to figure out what the entries mean. Have you?"

"No sir, but, since they look strange, we should all spend time thinking about them. That's why I wanted to draw your attention to them."

After Lonsdale had thanked everyone for their cooperation, Triggs drove them to the airport for their respective flights back to the U.S.

Contrary to expectations, Rosenstein was happy with the results of the foray to Nassau.

"There's enough material here to distract the jury," he told them at their regular Wednesday work session in early March. "I think our chances in favor of acquittal have just increased to seventy percent."

"A modest improvement," remarked a caustic Hauser who was becoming more and more withdrawn as the date of his trial approached.

"What's your next move?" Gal enquired of Lonsdale.

"A visit to my stock analyst in Toronto would be in order, I believe."

*****

The first face-to-face meeting between Lonsdale and Savard took place over lunch at Hy's Steakhouse in downtown Toronto. It turned out to be an unqualified success since Lonsdale, having ascertained Savard's habits in advance, opened the proceedings by ordering two double Martinis. Savard, a heavy drinker, felt immediate kinship with Lonsdale and let his guard down.

"Plasmalab—what a mess," he said as he cut into his juicy sirloin and looked with an appreciative eye at the expensive Bordeaux being uncorked. "A tangle of lawsuits from which only the lawyers will profit."

"As usual, but who's suing whom?"

"The Directors as a group are being sued by the shareholders in a Class Action for criminal negligence; Keller's and Martin's estates are each being sued and have had their assets seized. In addition, all parties, however connected to Plasmalab, are being sued by the eighty-two victims whose deaths have been attributed by the WHO so far to the use, during surgery, of Plasmacol."

"Any sign of an epidemic?"

"Not yet, but eighty-two is a pretty significant number, no?" Savard emptied his glass. Lonsdale poured him more wine.

"What about Moscovitch?"

"He's no longer at Plasmalab."

"Oh. Where's he now?"

"In Europe somewhere."

"Can you find out where? And while you're at it, can you give me the name of the lawyer who is coordinating the victims' lawsuits against the company and the other defendants you've mentioned?"

"That part's easy," the analyst was sipping the brandy Lonsdale had ordered to go with the espresso the waiter had just brought him. "His name is David Jackson and he's a Senior Partner at Osler, Hoskins."

Lonsdale called Jackson's secretary and asked if the lawyer could receive him late that afternoon.

After the obligatory preliminary skirmish to establish pecking order, which resulted in a draw, the two men got down to business.

"Thus far I have seized about three hundred million dollars worth of assets," Jackson told Lonsdale, "the bulk of which is represented by the Plasmalab shares owned by the Keller and Martin estates."

"Aren't they contesting?"

"Of course they are, but Keller's side is bound to lose."

"What about Martin's?"

"They claim Martin knew nothing about the accident and that, therefore, he had no personal liability."

"Except as a Director."

Jackson acknowledged the remark with an affirmative nod. They continued exchanging bits and pieces of information, until, around seven, Lonsdale stood up.

"Let me summarize. You feel your side can lay its hands on about three hundred million dollars on behalf of the victims, provided you can prove that Martin had prior knowledge of the accident on which he then failed to act in a timely manner, and provided also that the value of the seized shares does not slip below twenty dollars a share."

"That would be about right, including the payout from the insurance company to cover Directors' liability," agreed the lawyer.

"But if you fail to prove that Martin had prior knowledge you're looking at a great deal less, by about a hundred million dollars, right?"

"About."

"How much would you be willing to pay my client, Hauser, if his defense team's assistance would enable you to prove that Martin had full knowledge?"

"Fifteen percent of the value of the Martin estate."

Lonsdale let out a sharp laugh. "I was thinking about fifty percent."

Jackson looked into Lonsdale's eyes and shuddered. He had rarely seen such unrelenting, impersonal ruthlessness.

They bargained for a while, agreeing in the end on one third. "Draw up the papers," Lonsdale said, "and I'll come by at ten tomorrow to sign them. Set aside an hour for our meeting—I have lots to tell you."

As it turned out, Lonsdale stayed for two hours, and left a David Jackson drooling in anticipation of the size of the bill he would be sending his clients for having recovered an additional million dollars for each of them.

* * * * *

"He's probably being paid a monthly retainer plus a result-oriented bonus," observed Rosenstein. "An extra hundred million will get his firm five million dollars."

Gal looked at Hauser. "We shouldn't complain. I estimate we'll get about the same when we get Martin."

"But we haven't laid our hands on Mr. Martin yet." Lonsdale's observation was to the point.

"Is the stuff you found in Nassau not enough?" To Hauser it seemed every time he got his hopes up Lonsdale would dash them with unreasonable disregard.

But Rosenstein was nodding his head. "Lonsdale's right—to establish without doubt that Martin had knowledge and did not act on it, we need either a credible witness to that effect or, even better, an admission from Martin himself."

"Fat chance," Hauser muttered in disgust. For a moment he had thought the potential windfall Lonsdale had engineered would obviate the need for him to pay for his defense team's services.

"My next move is to find Jason Moscovitch," Lonsdale announced.

"Any idea where he is?"

"Savard told me he is now the Chief Scientific Officer of a Hungarian veterinarian pharmaceutical company called Phylaxos."

CHAPTER FIFTEEN

Two things had troubled Jason Moscovitch from the very start about his work at Plasmalab: Dr. Keller's reluctance to provide a formal letter outlining Moscovitch's terms of employment with Plasmalab; and his insistence on paying everything from his own pocket against invoices for services Moscovitch submitted to him personally every month.

"Let's keep the paperwork to a minimum," the virologist had said. "Besides, doing things my way is more advantageous for you from an income tax point of view."

Moscovitch acquiesced in the end. He hated paying taxes.

By mid-December, Moscovitch began to suspect that Dr. Keller was "moonlighting," working on a discovery on his own that he did not intend to turn over to Plasmalab, something he was bound by law to do as an officer of the company using the company's facilities. What other reason could there be, Moscovitch asked himself, for his boss's insistence that they use the lab only in the evening, after all other employees had left?

Though Moscovitch was just starting his career, he wasn't naïve, and had no intention of jeopardizing his reputation by becoming involved in a questionable operation. After much soul-searching he took the bull by the horns and wrote to Mike Martin requesting that Plasmalab's CEO confirm his awareness of the project on which Dr. Keller insisted Moscovitch work in the utmost secrecy.

To make sure the letter would reach the CEO without being read by anyone other than the addressee, Moscovitch obtained Martin's Florida address in Sarasota and sent it by FedEx a few days before the Christmas holidays.

Moscovitch reported back to work on the Monday after Keller and Martin died and, having gotten five by putting two and two together, deduced that the deaths of his boss and Plasmalab's CEO were part of a sinister Mafia plot to take over the company.

This frightened him, but he soldiered on at Plasmalab for four weeks at the request of the Directors, who needed time to find a suitable replacement for Keller. Then the CJD virus accident came to light. This time, Moscovitch arrived at the correct conclusion: Only three people could have known about this unfortunate event the previous September: Keller, Mike Martin and himself. There was also Joe Bucalo, shift foreman at Plasmalab, but Joe was a follower of orders, not bright enough to have interpreted the consequences of his actions. As for Monique Martelle, Keller's regular lab assistant and Moscovitch's predecessor, she had been out of the loop on maternity leave.

To Moscovitch the implications were clear because, though he was innocent, neither Martin nor Keller was around to exonerate him from blame. Consequently, he had to distance himself from the situation as fast as possible. He thanked his lucky star for having used FedEx to send his letter because this enabled him to prove that it had been written and sent to Martin before the man's demise, packed up his notes and samples and, having declined the offer to become Chief Scientific Officer of the company, left Canada.

Moscovitch was not without an ulterior motive; while working on his own during Dr. Keller's frequent absences, he had found a way of at least directing, if not destroying, the prions that transmitted mad cow disease. The discovery of this new technique would have an enormous impact on the veterinarian pharmaceutical industry worldwide—and Moscovitch intended to profit from it. He began to search for a place where he could set up shop and be assured of competent professional help without having to invest too much money.

His research indicated that, of all places, Hungary had been producing effective blood-based vaccines for prophylaxis in cattle for almost a century. For Moscovitch, the country held additional attractions: it was far from Canada; it was not a member of the European Union and, thus, not subject to reciprocal Western copyright infringement agreements; its economic climate, now embracing entrepreneurial principles, rewarded North American-trained scientists with generous participation packages in exchange for know-how; Budapest was a civilized city in which a dollar stretched far; and, above all, U.S. Food and Drug Administration regulations did not apply.

What better place than Hungary, then, to start a modest manufacturing operation for the production of a new, untested vaccine with considerable potential for eradicating mad cow disease?

CHAPTER SIXTEEN

Mike genuflected in front of the altar and headed to the sacristy to assist Father Lachance with dressing for mass. Hired in early February as church handyman-caretaker and part-time sacristan as a result of a series of fortuitous coincidences, Mike was still having difficulty finding his way around the building.

He had taken the train from Montreal to Quebec City and then a bus to Port-Alfred, a small town near the confluence of the St. Lawrence and Saguenay Rivers where ships, laden with bauxite from Jamaica and Demerara, unloaded their cargo destined for Alcan's aluminum smelters in the Saguenay Valley.

The bus had dropped him off across the street from l'Hôtel Central into a Saturday night blizzard of sleet and snow. Seeking shelter, he'd hurried toward the building and almost been bowled over by a young priest slithering downhill on his bicycle, quite out of control. Mike jumped away at the last moment, watching as the priest hit the curb and went flying over the handlebars.

He ran over to help.

The stunned clergyman had difficulty getting up. "I think I'm all right," he stammered, "except for my ankle." He looked around, dazed. "Please see if you can find the sacraments. I must have dropped them on my way down."

"Father, I should get you inside first." He helped the priest through the front door and handed him off to a sobbing woman there.

"How is he, Madame Habib?" the priest asked.

"Still alive, Father, but fading fast."

The priest turned to Mike. "Quick, my son, go up the street and see if you can find my little black bag. It should be lying in the street close to where I fell. Hurry!"

Mike put his belongings down and hustled himself ostentatiously outside.

He was back in minutes with the bag.

"Thank you, my son, thank you for your kindness. Now, can you help me up the stairs?"

That had been four weeks earlier, during which Madame Habib's father, having received the last rites of the Holy Roman Church, died in peace, absolved of his sins thanks to Mike's intervention after which Madame Habib—the owner of L'Hôtel Central and an attractive, energetic and passionate widow—had hired Mike as the hotel's *homme-à-tout-faire* at a modest salary plus board and lodgings and, two weeks after his employment, occasional and very discrete access to her bedchamber on the building's top floor.

The grateful and overworked young priest, Father Lachance, also volunteered to contribute to Mike's sustenance in exchange for clerical and general assistance during weekends, an offer Mike eagerly accepted because his sole reason for coming to Port-Alfred had been to gain access to the parish records. Canadian passports for native-born French Quebecers were easy to obtain since a baptismal certificate, issued by a parish priest, was deemed sufficient proof of citizenship. All Mike needed in his quest for a valid passport in the name of his uncle Jean-Yves Martin, was a copy of that parish certificate.

To be on the safe side, Mike waited until mid-March before approaching Father Lachance's superior, Father Pratte, who was also the parish priest in charge of documents.

"Have we received a donation from *Monsieur* Martin for this request?"

"*Oui, mon Père.*"

Mike handed Father Pratte a postal money order. "*Monsieur* Martin was very generous. With his request for a copy of his baptismal certificate he sent along a donation of fifty dollars. I took the liberty of composing a short note of thanks for your signature."

Mike laid the baptismal certificate form and the note on Father Pratte's table.

"Splendid work," the priest said with a prim smile as he signed the papers. "Since *Monsieur* Martin has been so generous we could, perhaps, reciprocate by having the certificate notarized, and sent out as soon as possible."

"I shall attend to the matter immediately," Mike replied and set off in search of the nearest notary.

At the end of March, Mike, pleading urgent family business in Montreal, said goodbye to the widow Habib and left Port-Alfred with two important documents in his pocket—the certified true copy of his Uncle Joe's baptismal certificate, and the "thank-you" note signed by Father Pratte.

Back in Montreal he rented a modest, one-bedroom furnished apartment on St. Hubert Street near the Notre Dame Hospital and paid cash for three months' rent in advance. By early April he was dating a registered nurse, Nicole Lafleur, who, after a month's whirlwind, passionate affair, readily signed the Passport Application Form of Jean-Yves (Joe) Martin as guarantor, attesting to the veracity and accuracy of the information contained therein, because Mike had told her he needed the passport to be able to take her to Bermuda for a few days' vacation.

She also certified that the photographs accompanying the application were a true recent likeness of the said Jean-Yves (Joe) Martin, a man she had known for more than two years.

The application was sent off by certified mail, and seven days later the passport was duly issued in Ottawa and mailed back to Mike—now Jean-Yves—Martin, at his St. Hubert Street address.

True to his word, Mike took Nicole to Bermuda for ten days at the end of May. They stayed at the Sonesta Princess Hotel and laughed a lot, drank a lot, danced a lot and made love a lot. They even played a little golf—a sport neither knew much about and that both came to dislike by the end of their stay.

Mike had given Nicole five hundred dollars to go shopping, so they drove into Hamilton on the fourth day of their vacation (a Tuesday) and split up in front of the post office for a couple of hours so as 'not to interfere with each other's craziness' as she put it.

As soon as Nicole was out of sight, Mike ducked into The Pickled Onion restaurant on Front Street to use the washrooms and to have a word with one of the waiters. Then he located a telephone cabin in the post office and called his Bermuda banker.

"Please put me through to the person in charge of account number 1, 81, 2, 5, 62." Within minutes he was speaking with Llewellyn Edwards, Senior Account Manager at Butterfield Bank.

"I'm the owner of the account you're looking at," Mike said. "I would like to get some information about it please."

"I'm sorry sir," Edwards was polite but firm. "We do not give out information about our accounts over the telephone."

"That's, I suppose, because you don't know who's at the other end of the line."

"Quite right."

"Let me provide you with identification." Mike made himself sound persuasive. "Take a pencil and a piece of paper. Write down the alphabet vertically. Number the letters, from 1 to 26. Got that?"

"Yes, I do."

"We're talking about account number 1, 81, 2, 5, 62."

"Correct."

"Very well then," said Mike. "What does 1 stand for?"

"The letter A."

"Correct—and 81?"

"Nothing, there are only 26 letters in the alphabet."

"The inverse of 81 is 18."

"Ah, that's R."

"Exactly. And what is 2?"

"B."

"And 5?"

"I've got the rest," Edwards cut in, "but what does Arbez mean?"

"ZEBRA spelled backwards."

"I'm still not convinced."

Mike thought furiously.

"Would it help if I told you about the last few equity transactions that you were instructed to carry out?"

"Yes, it would certainly help."

Mike rattled off six of them.

"You've got me convinced. What can I do for you?"

"Answer some questions."

"Go ahead."

"How much is the portfolio worth?"

"Forty-two million six hundred and eighty thousand Canadian dollars, give or take a few thousand."

"Invested in what?"

"Provincial and municipal bonds and certificates of deposit, yielding, on average, five percent per annum."

"No equities?"

"No. As per instructions, we completed all equity transactions in early January."

"All short sales were covered?"

"As per instructions." Edwards sounded smug.

"Thanks," said Mike, well satisfied. Five percent per annum on forty-three million dollars gave him an annual income of over two million dollars. "Here's what you do," he continued. "Get hold of twenty one-thousand dollar bills, put them in an envelope and seal it. Then lay your hands on two hundred one-hundred dollar bills and divide them into four envelopes, which you are also to seal."

"We're talking Canadian dollars I presume?"

"We are."

"What do I do next?"

"Put the envelopes in your pocket and walk them over to The Pickled Onion on Friday at noon. There are, in addition to the stand-up urinals, two sit-down stalls in the men's washroom. One of them will be out of order between twelve and twelve fifteen on Friday. At twelve ten sharp, go inside, sit down, and wait." Mike paused. "Do you have any problems with this so far?"

"It's somewhat unorthodox, but no..."

"Some time after you've sat down, someone will enter the stall next to yours and say 'Stripes, are you there?' Instead of answering, you'll slide the five envelopes under the partition between that stall and yours. In return, you will receive an envelope containing a receipt for forty thousand dollars, together with further instructions *and* ten one-hundred dollar bills to cover your *personal* expenses."

"That is quite unnecessary," Edwards protested. "I'm paid to look after our clients."

"As you wish," Mike replied. "The money will be in the envelope in any event. If you feel you have to turn it over to your employer that's your business."

"Understood. Anything else?"

"Yes. Give me the names of two senior members of the staff whom I can contact should you not be present when I call next."

"Andrea Boswell and Ken Shanahan."

"Are they both officers of the bank?"

"They are."

"Good," said Mike. "We're almost done. Two more points: Make sure you have the five envelopes ready by ten am on Friday at the latest and stick around until noon, in case I call to change the venue at the last moment for security reasons. Can do?"

"No problem. What's the second point?"

"If no one shows by twelve thirty, take the envelopes back to the office and redeposit the money. In that event, I'll contact you next week." Mike hung up.

* * * * *

Nicole had been so excited about the wonderful duty-free bargains, especially the cashmere, that Mike had no difficulty persuading her to repeat "the shopping thing" again on Friday morning, more so since he gave her another five hundred dollars "to go crazy with."

He arranged to meet her at The Pickled Onion for lunch and insisted that she be punctual. "Be there no later than noon," he said. "Otherwise the place gets busy and we'll never get a table."

"So let's make reservations."

"With half the islanders receiving their payroll cheques on Thursday night and blowing a good part of it on food and booze every Friday? Besides, they don't take reservations at The Pickled Onion."

"OK, OK," she gave in, laughing.

He kissed her. "I'll try to get there a little early and hold a table for us."

Of course, he made sure to be there by eleven thirty. He had work to do.

In a brief printed note he instructed Edwards to convert his entire portfolio into U.S. Treasury Bills, and wrapped the note around ten one-hundred dollar bills. He slipped the little package, together with a receipt for forty thousand dollars, into a blank envelope he had picked up at the post office. Then, using paper he had borrowed from the barmaid, he fashioned a crude OUT OF ORDER sign and affixed it to one of the washroom stall doors. He returned to his table, ordered a drink and sat back to wait for Nicole.

She slid in beside him a few minutes past noon, nervous and out of breath. "Boy, am I glad you're here," he grinned, hiding his annoyance at her tardiness. "I didn't dare leave our table even for a minute. Look! The place is jammed." He gestured toward the entrance where a line had formed. "I'm bursting. Got to go to the can!"

He made it to the washroom at twelve minutes past the hour, but "his" stall was occupied and he had to wait a minute before he could get in. "Stripes, are you there?" he called out.

The five envelopes came sliding across. He reciprocated with the package in his hand and heard Edwards pick it up and tear it open.

A few moments later Edwards got up, flushed, and left the cubicle.

Mike waited five minutes before doing likewise.

That afternoon, while Nicole was snoozing in the sun poolside, Mike rolled the contents of each envelope lengthwise into tight cylinders and wound elastic bands around each, then slipped the five rolls into two hikers' aluminum water bottles, which he placed into the safe provided for guests' valuables.

Back in Montreal Mike renewed his apartment lease until the end of August and continued to share it with Nicole, but the bloom was beginning to wear off their relationship. After they had attended one too many Montreal summer festivals together (the one that broke the camel's back was the Festival of Asian films with English *and* French subtitles) they realized that they were not really on the same wavelength.

When the lease ran out Mike and Nicole parted company by mutual consent.

CHAPTER SEVENTEEN

Jury selection for Karl Hauser's trial on the charge of first degree premeditated murder began during the first week of September. The trial, which lasted two full weeks, ended with a major shock: the Austrian's acquittal.

Rosenstein had anticipated that introducing evidence about Mike Martin, whom he intended to portray as a plausible alternative murder suspect, would not be easy. As expected, he was forced to circumnavigate a barrage of objections from the prosecution. He managed to accomplish this by calling Ramon Sanchez as his first witness.

The Cuban testified to Martin having visited Keller the day before the virologist's death, which led to speculation about who else might have had access to Keller's apartment. This allowed Rosenstein to introduce the security tapes as evidence. After viewing them the judge had no choice but to allow argument relating to the identity of the "jogger," which got Chief Inspector Triggs on the stand.

Rosenstein led the policeman through testimony about the items recovered at the scene of the plane crash, including the tracksuit and sliver of paper containing fragments of an incriminatory checklist.

The prosecution attempted to discredit the theory of Mike Martin's involvement by producing Moscovitch as a material witness, whom the Florida District Attorney had arranged to have flown in from Budapest. The scientist, referring to the letter he had sent Martin, testified to his conviction that Plasmalab's CEO had known nothing about the accident and that, therefore, he had no motive for killing Keller. On the contrary, Moscovitch went on to say, Martin had every reason to want Keller alive—the virologist's presence and reputation had been essential factors in assuring that Plasmalab was respected in scientific circles and that its stock's price remained high.

On cross-examination, Moscovitch confessed that the motivation behind his leaving Plasmalab had been his concern about organized crime's involvement in the deaths of the company's two most senior executives.

Monique Martelle, Plasmalab's regular lab technician, corroborated what Moscovitch had said about her boss's mania for secrecy. She recounted how she had been told only the absolute minimum necessary for her to conduct a statistical survey on almost twenty thousand samples of Plasmacol. She claimed to have been unaware of the "accident" and, therefore, to have had no reason for questioning Dr. Keller's motives.

Joe Bucalo, McNiff's successor, testified that, as far as he knew, only Dr. Keller and Bucalo himself were aware of a "problem," which Dr. Keller seemed to consider "minimal." In fact, Bucalo said under oath, the problem could not have been "serious" since no disciplinary action had been taken against him.

The prosecution then put Mrs. Donna Martin on the stand. She had viewed the security tape twice, and testified that her husband had not owned the type of hat nor the kind of tracksuit the "jogger" had worn.

"How did you come to such a conclusion?" a frustrated Melvin Rosenstein asked her.

"He was a 'cap' kind of a man and did not like hats with wide brims. 'They blow away too easily in a wind,' he used to say."

"Did he own any wide-brimmed hats?"

"No."

"What about the tracksuit? How can you tell it was not your husband's?"

"My late husband hated stripes of any kind. He wore dark blue or gray or white tracksuits, sometimes with the name of a club or team on them, but never stripes."

Rosenstein then questioned her about the telephone call from Nassau made minutes after Mike Martin was supposed to have died. He drew a blank there, too. Mrs. Martin said that when she checked her answering machine on her return to Florida after her husband's death there had been no trace of any such call.

Rosenstein made a great show of how discouraged the defense was and asked for a recess.

The following day, in his address to the jury, he pointed out the obvious: that all evidence against Hauser was circumstantial; that Hauser, a seasoned senior pilot, was not given to impulsive action and was not the kind of person to commit as clumsy a crime as the one of which he stood accused; that he would benefit from a substantial pension upon retirement and was far from being in need of money.

"Other than a compelling financial motive—which he obviously did not have—what other motive could the accused have had to kill his companion?" Rosenstein asked the jury. "Jealousy? Hardly: As we saw from testimony during the trial, neither man played the field; rumors of the victim's affairs were, as you heard, nothing but unsubstantiated gossip. As for opportunity—the defense admits Mr. Hauser did have the opportunity. BUT, so did at least TWO others!" He paused for effect. "Yes, TWO others: Mr. Michael Martin, who, as you heard Mr. Sanchez testify, visited the victim the night before he died and the unidentified "jogger." For all I know, to borrow a phrase from Mr. Moscovitch's testimony, the jogger was an organized crime hit man. The prosecution has taken so much time and trouble over the identity of this person that even I am now convinced that he was NOT Mike Martin."

The last sentence did the trick: the seeds of reasonable doubt were sown and the jury given a plausible logical alternative.

After the acquittal Lonsdale bought Moscovitch a drink at the bar of the Breakers Hotel.

"How goes the battle in Budapest?"

Moscovitch laughed. "Quite well, thank you." He shook his head. "Your team sure suckered the opposition."

Lonsdale pretended to be puzzled. "What do you mean?"

"Come on, don't play innocent with me," the virologist protested.

"The trial is over." He drained his glass. "First you call me in Budapest, and ask me to testify on Hauser's behalf. I refuse, but the prosecution gets wind of your plans and puts pressure on me through the Canadian authorities to testify on behalf of the prosecution. Mrs. Martin and I are brought here at the expense of the State of Florida—in first-class style—and the prosecution redoubles its efforts to disprove your theory that the "jogger" was Mike Martin. Which, of course, was exactly what you and that wily Rosenstein wanted in the first place."

"What on earth for?"

"So that you can tell the jury that, in addition to Hauser, there were at least TWO other people—Martin and the "jogger"—who had the opportunity to do Keller in."

Lonsdale silently raised his glass to Moscovitch, impressed by the young man's read of the defense's strategy, then they chatted for a half hour, during which the scientist allowed how well pleased he was with his progress in Hungary. "I should be ready to file three patent applications for new vaccines by the spring," he bragged. "Then I'll need to raise a couple of million bucks to build a little plant, and with that money I'll be off to the races."

"What are your chances of getting the money?"

"Fair to middling," came the reply. "Strange, but the modest fame I gained during the trial helped. All kinds of people have offered to find me capital—from as far away as Japan and as near as Yugoslavia. The Italians are also interested. They want no mad cow disease in their country."

"Don't I know it." Lonsdale's stomach twitched. He couldn't help recalling Nicola Bianchi and *his* predicament. He left, after promising Moscovitch to keep in touch.

The celebratory dinner took place at Gal's home on the Saturday following Hauser's acquittal. Adys and Gina were invited, of course, as were the Rosensteins, Sanchez, and Hauser with some of his friends.

Everyone was in high spirits, except Lonsdale, who slipped away from the crowd to sit by himself near the seawall. Adys noticed and joined him there.

"What's troubling you *querido*?" The touch of her hand on his forearm was as light as a feather. "Your team has won; your man was acquitted. You have done a wonderful job for him, and you should feel proud."

"He's out there, you know," Lonsdale muttered, "and he'll never be brought to justice"

"Who?"

"Mike Martin, of course." He looked at his girlfriend and, seeing her concern, tried to make light of the situation, but failed. "Even if I were to catch him—which now seems only a remote possibility—he'd never be found guilty. There's no tangible evidence against him"

"But if you proved that he was still alive. Wouldn't that be enough?"

Lonsdale laughed. "Running away is not a capital crime. Thousands of people flee their wives, their debts, their responsibilities." He shook his head. "What crime could they convict him of? Using a phony driver's license, or a phony passport maybe?"

CHAPTER EIGHTEEN

A methodical man, Mike Martin prepared his departure from Canada with care, knowing full well that even the tiniest oversight might lead to his downfall.

Although he was in possession of a valid passport, he had no credit cards, no driver's license and no bank account. Only cash, but lots of that.

As a first step toward "normalizing" his situation he enrolled in a driving school and, having passed his tests, applied for a license that he duly obtained in the name of Jean-Yves Martin. Next, he deposited ten thousand dollars with the Bank of Nova Scotia and, having pledged his deposit as security, obtained a Visa Gold credit card with a fifteen thousand dollar credit limit, since his uncle's credit history showed no blemishes.

His greatest concern was his uncle's health. As long as the old boy was alive there was no problem; however, if he were to die, Mike's new persona would evaporate—his documents would become invalid. Therefore, he made sure to check on uncle Joe's welfare by calling the nursing home once a month, each time from a different pay phone. Deep down, however, Mike knew that, sooner or later, he would have to start afresh in a country that had no extradition agreements with the U.S. or

Canada and preferably where English or French was spoken,

In July, he purchased a Notebook computer and subscribed to an Internet service enabling him to get updated on what was happening at Plasmalab and with Karl Hauser, the murder suspect. His gut told him he should attend the trial, but he was concerned about it being scheduled for September. He would have preferred to have been given longer lead-time to prepare his disguise.

The consensus on the Internet was that Keller had been the "bad guy" who had covered up the "accident," thereby causing the death of eighty-two surgical patients whose surgeons had used contaminated Plasmacol while operating. Nobody was sure whether Mike had known about the mishap, but the point was moot—Martin was dead and gone.

"And even if they did find me," he mumbled one sleepless night while thinking about the many "what ifs" in his life, "who could testify about my knowing? Only Fred..."

Although the thought reassured him, he was far from satisfied. To get on with his life he needed to know where the investigation stood. And the easiest way of finding out without arousing suspicion was to attend the trial and listen to the proceedings. True, there was a risk, but it could be minimized with careful preparation.

At the end of his lease, Mike put his few belongings in storage and flew to Atlanta where he checked into a nondescript motel, bleached his hair and beard white and purchased a second-hand Volvo for cash. Then he drove to Fort Lauderdale where he settled into a two-bedroom furnished apartment.

During the trial, Mike would arrive at the West Palm Beach Court House every morning a few minutes after nine and sit as far away from the witness stand as possible. The well-attended event was held in a room that got increasingly stuffy as the day wore on, but Mike never left his seat; he needed at all cost to avoid chance encounters with participants.

When his wife was sworn in he noted with surprise that, contrary to what he'd expected, he wasn't much affected by her presence. What did move him, though, was the flood of memories of his time with his children. He missed his son a great deal and the realization that he might never see him again brought tears to his eyes.

Amazed by the thoroughness of Hauser's defense team he went into mild shock when Rosenstein started to cross-examine his wife, Donna, about that cursed telephone call to Sarasota from Nassau. Of course, there had been no choice: it had been imperative that Mike erase the message to Phil the Pill.

The attempts by the defense, disallowed by the judge, to interpret what the scribbling on his rule lined pad meant, also gave him a bad turn, in particular when one of Hauser's investigators—Robert Lonsdale—managed to slip into his testimony that he interpreted a line on the scrap of paper as reading "disposal of vial along Alligator Alley." That had been far too close for comfort!

He was surprised when the prosecution made the point, based on Donna's testimony, that he had never owned a wide-brimmed hat or a striped jogging suit. This was untrue, and he could not figure out why Donna was dissembling. When Rosenstein asked whether anything had been removed from the cottage, she said "no," thereby making herself a possible accessory to murder; she had not only known about the poison and his twenty-thousand dollar emergency stash, but also the combination of the safe. That's when the reason for her lying dawned on him. She wanted him innocent of all wrongdoing—of murder, of suppressing information about the accident, of fleeing—because she didn't want the children to have to live with the stigma of a father who was a poisoner, and because she had no desire to share his estate with those who were suing Plasmalab and its officers and directors.

At the start of the trial it had seemed to Mike that the person he needed to fear most was Rosenstein, whose probing questions kept coming closer and closer to uncovering the truth. He changed his mind, however, when he saw with what deference the lawyer consulted Lonsdale whenever a delicate situation developed that threatened the defense's case.

By the end of the trial Mike had become convinced that Lonsdale had seen through his alibi and figured out how Mike had killed Keller and why.

This was valuable information. To know your enemy without your enemy knowing that you knew gave you overwhelming advantage over him.

Another piece of important information he developed by listening to the witnesses related to Moscovitch, who told the Court in detail about his plans in Hungary. To Mike it was obvious that Moscovitch was using the lead time given him by his "nonengagement" at Plasmalab to best advantage, racing to patent a vaccine against mad cow disease before anybody else did.

On the Saturday before the murder Mike had been so preoccupied that he hardly glanced at the FedExed letter from Moscovitch that Flores, the Sarasota condo Super, had given him. He tore off the sender's address and phone number, intending to reply later, then threw away the letter.

The sliver of paper was still in his possession. Mike made a mental note to call Moscovitch as soon as expedient.

* * * * *

After the acquittal, Mike bought himself a set of golf clubs, dyed his hair and beard back to their original color and went on a cruise to Bermuda, satisfied that officialdom considered him dead. He contacted Edwards and, using the same procedure as before, took fifty thousand dollars home with him in his aluminum water bottles.

Back in Fort Lauderdale, he called Moscovitch's home in Toronto from a payphone and spoke with the man's mother who, after Mike had told her he represented a Japanese company interested in funding her son's Hungarian venture, was glad to provide Jason's phone number and e-mail address in Budapest.

In mid-October Mike took a cruise through the Panama Canal and, calling himself James Grey, stopped to visit the Panama International Trust Company, a discreet and flexible private bank, which he retained, after depositing twenty-five thousand dollars in cash, to form Kyoto Veterinarian Pharmaceuticals (Panama) Inc., a bearer share company.

The e-mail Mike sent Moscovitch from Panama was a masterpiece of fabrication. He introduced himself as a consultant to KVP, and said he had read about Moscovitch's plans for manufacturing inexpensive vaccines in Hungary. "*The Miami Herald* reported your testimony at the Keller murder trial in some detail. The article caught my eye because of

the veterinarian connection rather than the criminal aspects of the case."
"Mr. Grey" went on to explain that Kyoto was always on the lookout for new talent and suggested that, should Moscovitch's Hungarian venture require financing, KVP might be interested in helping out.

In closing, Mike encouraged Moscovitch to verify "Mr. Grey's" bona fides with Dr. Eduardo Samos, President of Panama International Trust, a forty-year-old financial institution. (To ensure that Dr. Samos said the right things, Mike paid the good doctor a ten-thousand dollar "consulting" fee.)

He then returned to Fort Lauderdale, taking his Kyoto bearer shares with him.

During the following two months Mike, posing as an avid golfer in love with Bermuda's links, made five weekend trips to the island, during which he accumulated over three hundred thousand dollars in cash, which he stashed under the floorboards of his Fort Lauderdale apartment.

A week before Christmas, he chartered a modest, crewed motor yacht for cruising the Caribbean to learn boat handling and navigation and to slip into Panama again without having to go through Customs and Immigration through popular—and therefore well-watched—airports.

With Hauser's trial behind him and confirmation that he was considered dead, Mike felt relieved and grateful to the fates. Of course, he realized that his troubles would never be over as long as he paraded around as his own uncle, because, sooner or later, Uncle Joe would die. And although he was worth close to forty-three million dollars, access to his money was cumbersome.

Even had he been able to get to his money easily he would still not have been able to use much of it; nothing attracted attention faster than conspicuous spending. So he established four ironclad rules by which to live: be modest in your habits; always have at least half a million dollars in cash, gold or diamonds within reach; avoid crossing borders as much as possible; show your passport only when absolutely necessary.

Having devoured all the books he could lay his hands on about notorious fugitives such as Robert Vesco, Baby Doc Duvalier, Fulgencio Batista and Idi Amin Dada, he concluded that if you were rich enough you could escape being punished for breaking the law in spite of your whereabouts becoming known. Trouble was, being worth forty odd million dollars did not necessarily qualify one for being considered "rich," still less so if all one's money was in a place where the authorities could get to it. To be safe, he calculated he required at least a hundred million *more,* spread around the world in an intelligent manner.

During his four-week boat trip from Florida to Panama, Mike worked out the ideal arrangement: a number of unconnected and untraceable bank accounts operated by bearer-share companies in Switzerland, Brazil, Costa Rica, Hong Kong and Hungary (the latter was fast emerging as *the* stable financial center in Central Europe), administered by professionals who couldn't identify the companies' beneficial owner. In other words, the arrangements he had put in place in Bermuda were what he needed to replicate everywhere else.

Mike knew that his Bermuda bank account was not totally "unconnected." A clever and patient investigator could uncover the short sales he had orchestrated through that island by analyzing Plasmalab share trading patterns. Thus, his money in Bermuda was tainted and would have to be given up in case of discovery—something to be yielded to the enemy when withdrawing to an alternate, secure redoubt.

Consequently, the challenge facing Mike was how to overcome the problem of using some of the money in Bermuda to make more money—lots of it—without leaving a trail, and then to create, with this new, untainted money, five twenty-million dollar pools of unconnected, untraceable, yet accessible capital, each situated in a different jurisdiction.

It seemed to Mike that he could keep himself busy and his mind stimulated for years by devoting his time and energies to meeting this challenge.

* * * * * *

Ghal'al Behna, Consul General of Belize in Panama, who needed to supplement his meager salary with whatever scheme he could develop from time to time because he was constantly overspending on whores and drink, wiped his sweaty face with a not-too-clean white handkerchief. He squeezed out of his Toyota Echo that he had managed to park in a very tight spot between a Mercedes 450SL and a BMW 735 in the parking garage of the Sheraton Four Points Hotel, the erstwhile Radisson Royal, on 53rd Street in Panama City.

It was steaming outside, but, of course, it is almost always hot in Panama, and humid too during the rainy season—to the point where, if you did not have air conditioning with dehumidification in your house, you could expect mildew to form by the following morning on the shoes you were wearing the previous night.

In Behna's modest two-bedroom apartment on *Avenida* B near the *Mercado de Mariscos* the only air conditioning was in the master bedroom because electricity was very expensive. Luckily, there was a bit of a breeze off the ocean at night so life was bearable in the rest of his home, but just barely.

And, of course, his wife, the fat bitch, never ceased to complain about it.

Ghal'al Behna's father, Anwar, a member of the Muslim Brotherhood, had to flee Nasser's Egypt in the early fifties because of his extreme religious views. After a two-year stint as a seaman, he had settled in Belize where he married a Colombian woman he had met on the beach, and fathered three children of which Ghal'al was the oldest.

Ghal'al was a bright boy, deserving of an education. Since the family had no money, Anwar turned for help to the Brotherhood which, recognizing an opportunity, provided the child with the wherewithal to finish his schooling and enter the civil service.

Ghal'al had slugged away at menial tasks until the Brotherhood intervened once more and arranged for him to be named Vice-Consul in Panama.

By age thirty, again sponsored by the Brotherhood, Behna had risen to the rank of Consul General and had added part-time ship chandelling, smuggling and passport selling to his repertoire of activities.

Of course, continued support of the Brotherhood was not free. Behna and his family were expected to make an annual contribution to Hamas—the militant group which had taken over the Brotherhood in 1987—and to provide whatever occasional "services" that organization required from time to time. This included looking for new ways of killing non-Muslims.

Behna, a Muslim in name only who did not follow the rules about praying and not drinking alcohol and who was married to an unconverted infidel, kept his political opinions to himself and tried to blend in as much as possible. However, he recognized the indirect debt to Hamas and tried to repay it by regularly providing bits of gossip and information he felt could prove useful to the Cause.

He certainly didn't consider himself to be a true follower, just a fellow traveler.

Gasping in the suffocating heat of the garage Behna headed for the elevators and, grateful for their coolness, pressed the button for the floor housing the two public watering holes in the hotel.

He preferred the Trade Point Bar to the Sports Room because his chances of picking up useful gossip from his diplomatic colleagues there were better. Besides, the bartender was a sort of friend who always kept the most recent copy of *The Miami Herald* for Behna.

He ordered his usual light beer, took a long thirsty gulp and looked around the room. It was early and the only other patron at the bar was the Australian Third Secretary, working on a huge mug of ale and reading Ghal'al's *Herald*. Spotting Behna, and seeing his downcast look, he smiled.

"Now don't be getting your water all hot, Al, just because I'm reading your paper," he boomed with good humor. "I'll shout you a beer which you can drink while I finish reading this article."

True to his word the Aussie handed the paper to Behna as the Belizean was finishing his drink.

"Was the article interesting enough to warrant your generous offer of a beer?" Behna had trained himself in Spanish and English to be good at repartee. That's how he got most of his information.

The Third Secretary nodded.

"It was fascinating: all about a murder trial in Palm Beach involving Creutzfeld Jakob Disease."

"What's that?"

"A sort of mad cow disease for humans. Very lethal."

"Tell me more."

The voluble Australian did and they each had another beer. Behna was glad to pay: he had just discovered a new weapon of mass destruction.

After carefully re-reading the article about Dr. Keller and Plasmalab, Behna concluded that, although the product did not quite fall within the parameters set by Hamas for WMDs, the opportunity to manufacture a virulent strain of BSE, or mad cow disease, with which to infect and kill humans, was worth pursuing. As a consequence, he passed the article on to Selim, his contact in the organization, with a brief outline of how the BSE opportunity could be exploited. He emphasized that the "heir" to the Plasmalab technology was Dr. Jason Moscovitch, a Jew now working in Hungary for a pharmaceutical company called Phylaxos.

Selim turned to the Internet for information about BSE and when he realized that the Consul's idea was workable, he sent Behna's annotated file to his superiors for comment. To his great surprise, he was ordered to Budapest to discuss the file in depth with a "brother," Esad Delic, an Iranian-trained Bosnian Muslim virologist.

CHAPTER NINETEEN

That Mike Martin had escaped retribution was a persistent nagging frustration for Lonsdale. He returned to Conegliano on December 6, and brought Adys with him. This turned out to be an excellent idea. Her vivacious personality helped ease the pain felt by those who recalled that, in addition to Nicola's name day, the date was the anniversary of how something quite unforeseeable could destroy a family's happiness and the reputation of a proud man.

The authorities had tried to right the wrong done to *l'Osteria D'Oro*, and the Italian media had cooperated by giving the Keller murder trial high profile coverage. As a result, Nicola's restaurant had become even better known than before, but, somehow, the food did not taste as good as it once did: DalMolin, the creative genius, whose flavorful, well-balanced and delicate dishes had been so popular, was gone.

"I think next year I'm going to retire to the farm my grandfather left me and grow zucchini," said a depressed Nicola, sipping his fourth after-dinner *grappa*.

Lonsdale tried to lighten the gloom threatening to engulf their little gathering. "You wouldn't last a week. You're a man of action—no way would you have the patience just to sit and watch things grow."

They were in the Bianchis' living room, seated in front of the blazing fire the valet had lit before dinner; the winter was turning out to be colder than usual.

The apartment was quiet: The children were in bed. "Listen to you," Nicola stared at Lonsdale. "From what Adys tells me you haven't been your positive self since the trial either."

"It's just that I'm overworked." Lonsdale was on the defensive. He had, as promised, resigned from NATO and joined Gal's firm full-time in October. No sooner had they hung out their shingle in Washington than he'd been inundated with so many requests for assistance that they were having difficulty coping. "To make matters worse, combining our households had taken a greater effort than I anticipated."

Using his share of the generous fee Hauser had paid Gal's firm for orchestrating the pilot's acquittal, Lonsdale had bought the apartment below his own in Washington. He'd then arranged for the construction of an inside connecting staircase because he wanted lots of living space. To his great surprise he had, in spite of having lived a bachelor's life for decades, fallen so in love with Adys that he was willing to give up his independence.

At first Adys was leery; she, too, had been single for years and was unwilling to put up with the constraints of living with someone else, but after Lonsdale had walked her through the ample living space they were to occupy, she accepted the idea and found a part-time job for herself in Washington.

"From what I hear it's not the combining of households, but the other kind of combining that's been tiring you out," Annamaria chimed in and grinned at Adys who blushed a crimson red.

That broke the somber mood. "You must come and stay with us." Adys quickly changed the subject. "The apartment looks beautiful. We have two floors and a roof garden. Three bedrooms, on the lower level, have *en suite* bathrooms. The living space is upstairs."

"Is there a kitchen somewhere?" Nicola was needling.

"An immense one, don't worry." Adys would have none of his nonsense. "And very well equipped. Come and cook for us—we'll provide the ingredients."

"We might just do that." Annamaria seemed to like the prospect.

After the women went to bed Nicola stretched out on the rug in front of the fire and looked up at Lonsdale relaxing in a deep leather armchair beside the stone hearth. "So what's your next move, hotshot?"

"With Mike Martin, you mean?"

Bianchi nodded. "Who else?"

"Our lawyer says I should forget about trying to bring him in. He says there just isn't enough concrete evidence on which to convict the bastard."

Bianchi sat up and finished his drink. Then, speaking softly, he made a remark that Lonsdale would long remember. "There is more than one way to make sure a man is held responsible for his wrongdoings. Bringing him before a judge and jury is just one."

CHAPTER TWENTY

By the time Mike got to Panama the second time—in mid-January—he was a changed man. The four-week sail had made him fit, tanned and focused. His goals were clear—make money, change persona once more, stash the money and get on with life.

Making money would be no problem. Fred Keller had told him enough about Moscovitch for Mike to realize that the young man would come up with a revolutionary vaccine against mad cow disease well ahead of his competitors. Therefore, by buying into Moscovitch's Hungarian venture Mike was bound to make the money he felt he needed to be safe. Stashing the money would be no problem either, provided he could establish a new persona without connections to his old life. But there was no rush: Uncle Joe was still alive and Mike felt he had time before having to do something about a new identity.

However, the obstacles he would have to surmount to avoid attracting the authorities' attention were formidable because he was proposing to play—simultaneously—a deadly game of Hide and Seek and Monopoly, but with real money.

He needed to establish a security screen around himself that had to be impenetrable.

This required fierce discipline.

To safeguard the secret of his identity he would have to communicate with the professionals, whose services he would require in the future, only through the Internet, sending and receiving messages by signing in as a guest from a different Cyber Café each time—a convoluted, time-consuming process, but necessary under the circumstances.

To keep his whereabouts unknown he couldn't risk traceable credit card charges; he would have to pay cash everywhere to avoid hassles. This meant he'd have to wear a bulky money belt to ensure he had enough of the "ready" on him at all times.

To be able to escape at a moment's notice, he would have to acquire a hoard of gold coins or diamonds worth at least half a million dollars, hidden nearby for fast access in case he had to flee.

This meant he'd need a car on constant standby—not a practical thing to do. The only realistic alternative Mike could come up with was *to live on a boat*.

From Panama Mike, as James Grey, e-mailed Moscovitch, expressing his regrets about not having heard from him and to remind him that Kyoto Veterinarian was still there to help. This time the virologist bit. He was fast running out of capital.

Moscovitch had arrived in Budapest with thirty-six vials containing samples of his work on the vaccine against mad cow disease, six hundred pages of lab notes, thirty thousand dollars (his life's savings), and a letter of introduction to Abel Drusza, a Deputy Managing Director of the State Property Agency (SPA), Hungary's Privatization Authority.

Born in the southern Hungarian city of Szeged to a Bosnian father and a Hungarian mother (who converted to Islam to please her husband), Abel Drusza was brought up a Muslim in the relative comfort of Sarajevo until 1989, when civil war broke out in the Balkans. Sixteen years old, he was present at the abduction of his father by the Serbs to a concentration camp from which he never returned, and was made to witness the rape and execution of his mother for being a turncoat—a Christian Hungarian woman who had allowed herself to be sullied by marrying a Muslim.

The loss of his parents under such desperate circumstances had almost been more than Drusza could bear.

Raging against NATO for its hands-off attitude while these atrocities were being committed, he became fanaticized and turned into a secret supporter of Jihad to wage holy war against the West and Christianity. Somehow, he managed to end up in a refugee camp run by the Knights of Malta who arranged for him to immigrate to West Germany, where he graduated from Dresden University with a degree in biology and another in business administration. Fluent in English, German, Hungarian and Bosnian, he returned to Hungary where, hiding his Muslim affiliations, he got a job at the State Property Agency. His timing was lucky—it took him less than five years to become Deputy Managing Director of the Medico-Pharmaceutical Division.

To Drusza, Moscovitch was a godsend: a means to justify the SPA plowing more money into Phylaxos Ltd., once the pride of Hungary's veterinarian pharmaceutical industry, but now teetering on the verge of bankruptcy. Drusza could not allow Phylaxos to go under—the company's international reputation demanded that the government keep it afloat somehow.

As a first step, Drusza appointed Moscovitch Phylaxos' Chief Scientific Officer. Within a month Moscovitch reported that the company was beyond salvage, so Drusza sold Moscovitch, for a hundred thousand dollars, Phylaxos' almost new laboratory equipment and the right to use the name "Phylaxos Veterinary Pharmaceuticals."

But Moscovitch didn't have that kind of money—he was short seventy thousand dollars.

Sensing an opportunity to further his cause, Drusza called a fellow Bosnian Muslim, Esad Delic, his roommate at Dresden University who, after graduating with a Ph.D. in virology had gone to Pakistan and then Iraq to learn how to manufacture biological weapons for Saddam Hussein.

Delic was quick to realize the potential of nv Creutzfeldt-Jakob disease as a biological weapon of mass destruction. He persuaded the Iraqis to "lend" him the seventy-odd thousand dollars to buy part of Phylaxos.

For thirty thousand dollars, plus the work he had done to date, Moscovitch was given eighty percent of the new company. Delic got twenty percent for his money though he had tried to hold out for a fifty-fifty partnership, but Moscovitch was not about to give half of the technology away. However, Moscovitch did hire Delic, which was all that the Bosnian had really wanted.

Next, again with Drusza's help, Moscovitch sold ten percentage points of his Phylaxos holdings to Investments Hungary for six monthly payments of ten thousand dollars, sufficient to cover the fledgling company's overhead for half a year.

For five months Moscovitch and Delic worked twelve hour days, seven days a week, to perfect a technique to direct prions, the propagators of Creutzfeldt-Jakob disease. This enabled them to produce a number of CJD variants, including one that was contagious and, therefore, very dangerous. Unless checked by a vaccine, it would spread through humankind like wildfire.

However, the method of fabricating the vaccine kept eluding Moscovitch. This frustrated Delic's plan. He couldn't risk getting rid of Moscovitch by killing him or buying him out before the Canadian scientist produced the antidote that Baghdad needed to protect the lives of the True Believers while the infidels continued to die of nv CJD like flies in autumn.

The company was just about out of money when "Mr. Grey's" providential e-mail arrived, enabling Moscovitch once more to divide and conquer. Instead of being forced to accept Delic's persistent offers of additional funding (which would have meant having to surrender control of Phylaxos to the Bosnian) he could negotiate a standoff with the Japanese.

After a rapid-fire exchange of messages in the second half of January, Mike advised that he would submit Moscovitch's latest business plan to Kyoto's "board" with a recommendation that Kyoto invest enough money into Phylaxos to become a fifty percent shareholder of Kyoto.

"How much should I say you want for fifty percent?" "Grey" e-mailed.

"Two million U.S.," replied Moscovitch, who figured he needed working capital for at least two years at a burn rate of forty thousand dollars per month.

"One million is tops—and no bargaining." "Grey" sounded stern.

"I'll accept a million and a half and not a penny less," countered Moscovitch.

They finally agreed on a million and a quarter, with a one hundred thousand dollar nonrefundable deposit, whereupon "Grey" advised Moscovitch that Kyoto's Hungarian attorneys, Baker McKenzie, would be contacting him within the week to commence drafting legal documents.

From the stash he had brought with him on board the boat, Mike gave Dr. Samos a hundred thousand dollars in cash, which the banker, for an "origination" fee of ten thousand dollars, forwarded to Baker Mackenzie in Budapest.

It took Mike, communicating only through the Internet, all of February to get the relevant documents ready for signature. Closing took place on March 1, and the papers were deposited with Baker Mackenzie in trust. Mike now had thirty days to arrange for the payment of one million one hundred and fifty thousand dollars, failing which he'd lose his deposit.

Money was running through Mike's fingers like sand; his cash on hand was down to a hundred thousand dollars after paying Samos, the lawyers, the boat charter and the deposit.

It was time to visit Bermuda again.

He sailed up the coast to Puerto Limon in Costa Rica, paid off the charter, and took a car to San José from where he traveled to Bermuda via New York. He contacted Edwards and explained what he wanted done in Budapest (wire, with instructions, one million one hundred and fifty thousand dollars to Baker Mackenzie, the lawyers), then picked up fifty thousand dollars the usual way and flew to London. He spent two weeks in England buying clothes, going to the theatre, attending concerts, relaxing—and visiting coin dealers and yacht brokers.

He landed in Budapest on a British Airways flight from London a week before his deadline was due to expire.

CHAPTER TWENTY-ONE

Spring arrives early in Budapest. By the second half of March the sun is strong and the city sparkles again after the drabness of winter. The turning point is March 15, Hungary's National Day, celebrated in remembrance of the 1848 Revolution when, against all odds, the Hungarians, united by widespread revulsion against tyranny, defeated the occupying Austrian Army.

But their days of freedom were short-lived. Within the year, allied with the Russians, the Austrians were back to hand the Magyars a resounding defeat from which they never recovered.

Mike Martin felt at home in Budapest from the very start. Though their language was incomprehensible to him, he found the Hungarians helpful and willing to make the effort to communicate. This made him feel comfortable: He required all the help he could get because what he had to accomplish in the Hungarian capital was crucial to his meticulous plan and needed to be done with zero tolerance for error.

He checked into the Taverna Hotel, a modest establishment, but well located for his purpose on Váci Street in the city center.

From an Internet café he sent a terse message to Baker Mackenzie. "Please confirm by return e-mail the availability for delivery of five valid and fully paid bearer share certificates, each representing ten percent of the paid up capital of Phylaxos." The reply arrived within the hour. His lawyers confirmed that the certificates were ready.

Mike rented a second hotel room; this one at the Hotel Central—two blocks from Baker Mackenzie's offices near Heroes' Square. He dyed his hair and beard ash gray with Grecian Formula and put on a DHL messenger's uniform he had brought with him from London. Using the public telephone in the restaurant across the street from the lawyers' offices, he called Mr. Madarász, his contact at Baker Mackenzie.

"This is DHL in London," he said to the man in English. "Our messenger will be at your office some time this afternoon to pick up the Phylaxos package in exchange for some documents we were asked to deliver at the same time. Will that be convenient?"

"Can you make it between two and three?" Madarász asked.

"Between two and three it is," Mike agreed and hung up. Although he hated the idea that someone would know his whereabouts during a specific period of time, he reasoned that trying to avoid being pinned down would make matters worse. If he could have avoided meeting Madarász personally he would have, but he'd come to the conclusion long ago that the only way to insert a clean "cut out" between himself and the eventual ownership of the shares by a series of holding companies was to take physical possession of the shares and then transport them himself to their final destinations.

Mike opened the satchel hanging from his shoulder and reviewed its contents. As a precaution, he had prepared a couple of small parcels and five letters—all fictitious. The only genuine item in the lot was an envelope he'd picked up in the lobby of the Ritz Hotel on Piccadilly and which now contained a Barnes and Noble Bookstores loyalty card in the name of James Grey. (He had obtained a number of such cards at City Place in West Palm Beach for future use in several innocuous names: John White, Peter Brown, Benjamin Black, Basil Greene, Abe Braun, Marc Laviolette—Mike liked colors.)

He crossed Andrássy Boulevard, climbed the steps leading to the main entrance of the mansion housing Baker Mackenzie's offices and asked the receptionist for László Madarász.

Madarász took him to a small conference room, but did not ask him to sit. "Do you have something for me?" he enquired in Hungarian and held out his hand. Although Mike did not understand a word, the lawyer's gesture was self-evident, so he made a big show of sorting through his papers, then handed over the Ritz envelope inside a standard DHL pouch, complete with phony waybill, which Mike had painstakingly forged in London from genuine material "lifted" from DHL's offices there.

Madarász carefully compared the name and number on the Barnes and Nobel card with information in what, to Mike, looked like a printout of an e-mail message. Satisfied, the lawyer signed the attached receipt, handed Mike a thick DHL pouch and asked him to sign the waybill, which Mike did, printing "Schwartz" neatly beneath his signature. (There was a forged DHL identification tag for D. Schwartz in his pocket that he was prepared to flash, but the lawyer did not ask for it.)

With measured steps, Mike Martin, escaped murderer and fugitive from justice, strolled out of Baker Mackenzie's premises with five Phylaxos common share certificates, made out to bearer, each representing ten percent of the ownership of the company, leaving the lawyers and Moscovitch with no means of finding out the identity of the ultimate owner of these certificates.

Moscovitch had told Mike that Phylaxos was about a year from marketing its vaccine, at which time the value of the company's shares would rise spectacularly: After going public, Phylaxos' capitalization would pass the quarter billion dollar mark with ease. If all went well, within two years the bearer shares in the satchel hanging from Mike's shoulder could be converted into shares, tradable without restriction, on any one of the world's major stock exchanges and would fetch upward of a hundred million dollars.

Back at the Central Hotel Mike washed the Grecian Formula out of his hair and beard, changed into a pair of gray designer slacks and a blue blazer and bundled his DHL uniform and toilet articles into a big plastic bag. He took a circuitous route to the Heroes' Square subway station; when he emerged from the hotel, instead of walking along Andrassy Boulevard he turned left on Bajza street, deposited his bag in a dumpster on the corner of Benczur street, strolled all the way down to the artificial skating rink located on the Városligeti pond then doubled back to his left and took the stairs down to the train.

He got off at the first stop—the Municipal Zoo—and wandered

about for half an hour, then left the animals to their daily distractions and walked by the world-famous Gundel Restaurant on his way back to Heroes' Square again. Once sure that no one was following him, he rode the subway to Deák Square and walked to the Taverna Hotel where he packed his bags, took a cab to the airport, and caught the seven ten BA flight to London's Heathrow Airport.

He sailed through Customs and Immigration easily.

The following morning he addressed the delicate problem of implementing Phase Two of his Master Plan, the principal feature of which was the acquisition, without leaving a trail, of a not too flashy-looking, second-hand yacht between eighty and a hundred feet long.

During his two weeks in London prior to visiting Budapest, Mike had stumbled on a ninety-foot 1993 Benetti-designed, Azimut-built motor yacht, the Polyd, whose owner wanted a quick sale, if possible to someone in a tax haven.

Before leaving for Hungary, Mike had retained a marine surveyor, Edward McInnis, who, in return for a fixed survey fee plus a bonus for completing his work quickly, undertook to have his report ready by the first week of April.

As soon as he got back to London Mike made two phone calls: the first to check up on McInnis; the second to his uncle Jean-Yves, whose well-being he had last verified five weeks earlier.

He got the shock of his life! Jean-Yves Martin had died in his sleep of an unexpected heart attack three weeks earlier, which meant that the passport Mike was using had become invalid.

After the initial panic, Mike rationalized his position. Since he had passed through U.K. immigration control without difficulty the previous day he concluded that the news of his uncle's death had not reached the authorities as yet; so he was safe as long as he stayed in Britain, or visited a country where passport verification was manual rather than computerized. What Mike feared was the optical reader used at most large airports which, he presumed, read not only the security dots on the passports, but their serial number as well. He tried to remember at which airports such readers were not in use. Instantly, Panama came to mind.

Relieved, he spent the next two days at the surveyor's office in consultation with McInnis. He concluded that Polyd was the vessel he needed: she boasted stabilizers, a water maker, heating and air conditioning; her twin engines could develop enough power to give her twenty-plus knots' cruising speed; and the electronics and communications equipment on board were state of the art. Two very large and two smaller staterooms could accommodate eight passengers with ease and there was sleeping room for a crew of five. The upper sundeck that shaded the afterdeck and covered the saloon and dining areas had been reinforced to allow for a light helicopter to land. But what finally sold Mike on Polyd was a wall safe located in her master stateroom, accessible only from under the vanity opposite the stateroom's king-size bed.

Mike figured he could, indeed, have use for such a facility in his future!

"As I told you when last we met, I work for a Panamanian shipping company. I believe my employer may be willing to accommodate the owner's fiscal requirements." They were in McInnis' office, developing a strategy with which to approach the estate's attorneys. "I understand," Mike went on, "that there are serious tax considerations to contend with."

The Scotsman nodded. "Well, obviously, the estate would like to transact the sale outside the U.K.."

"And time is of the essence."

"Quite so. The creditors are pressing."

This was the kind of deal Mike liked. "Who are the agents?"

"Camper and Nicholsons. My contact is one of the Assistant Sales Managers at the London office."

"Where's the vessel lying now?"

"In Guernsey."

"Please arrange for me to see her this week. After I've made my inspection I'll let you know how we stand." Mike smiled with all the sincerity he could muster. "I must tell you, though, that I have a timing problem."

"What does that mean?"

"I might have to go away on business for a week or two. You might have to close the transaction for me. Would you?"

"For the right fee—yes." There was no nonsense about McInnis; he was all business.

After his return by ferry from Guernsey a few days later, Mike visited the surveyor for the third time. He came straight to the point. "I liked what I saw. I have been in contact with my superiors and, on the strength of your report—a copy of which I faxed them—they authorized me to retain your services for a fee of ten thousand pounds sterling. They will pay no more than two million seven hundred thousand dollars for the vessel." Mike looked at the surveyor. "Is such an arrangement acceptable?"

"Provided I get a nonrefundable advance of five thousand up front—yes."

"Done deal," replied Mike, "but you pay your own expenses."

"Agreed." They shook hands.

* * * * *

Mike spent the following week revisiting the coin dealers he had contacted prior to going to Hungary, chose seven establishments with which to deal, and instructed Edwards in Bermuda by e-mail to wire one hundred thousand dollars to each of the seven. He then returned to selected dealers and gave them individual lists of gold coins he wished to purchase, restricting himself to half-, one- and two-ounce coins, figuring that with gold at three hundred dollars an ounce, for seven hundred thousand dollars he would have to purchase about two thousand four hundred gold coins, weighing approximately seventy kilos in total.

At the end of the week he contacted McInnis.

"I'm back from Panama. How're you getting on with your negotiations?"

"I've got agreement on a price of two million seven hundred thousand dollars provided we can close within the month."

"Is that feasible?"

"Yes, as long as we start right away. Have your people wire a hundred thousand dollar nonrefundable deposit today to Messrs. Adams, Drury & Paget-Brown, the owner's attorneys, in Guernsey. Once they've received the money they will arrange for Polyd to be sailed to London where I will inspect her once more and arrange for whatever final adjustments are required to bring her in compliance with Triple A ABS Certification."

"At the owner's expense, I presume," Mike interjected.

"Correct. This will take three weeks, at the end of which your company will have to wire another two million six hundred thousand dollars to the attorneys who will then transfer ownership of the vessel to whomever your people designate, and release her in the care of their nominee."

Mike sent an e-mail to Dr. Samos requesting him to incorporate a Panamanian bearer-share company in the name of Panama Vessels Inc. and to send the issued share certificates by FedEx to the Ritz in London for pickup by Benjamin Black, the alias Mike was using in the U.K. Then he leased a garage-equipped flat for a month in one of the West End's myriad mews and parked his modest rented car there.

Every other morning, dressed like one more of the army of drab professionals working in the City, Mike sallied forth with a large briefcase that he dragged behind him on a foldable trolley, the kind commonly sold at airports for carting around hand luggage.

He called on each of the seven selected coin dealers in turn and picked up his coin "orders"—about three hundred and fifty coins per order, weighing close to ten kilos, paying for them, as pre-arranged, by handing each coin dealer the appropriate Barnes and Nobel loyalty card stipulated in the wire transfer. (The coin dealer would get his money by presenting the card at the bank on which the wire transfer Letter of Credit was drawn.)

Mike was very careful. He changed his routine daily and saw only one dealer per day. After each visit he would walk home part of the way, using a randomly selected route and making sure he was not being followed. Then he would take a cab, but never from the same rank twice.

At night he would transfer the coins from the briefcase into the trunk of the Opel.

After accumulating seventy kilos of gold he contacted McInnis for an update.

"Polyd is at the Camper and Nicholsons facility south of London, near Tilbury," reported the surveyor. "I plan to issue a Certificate of Completion of Work within the week. Have your people open a letter of credit for two million six hundred thousand dollars payable against delivery of a signed copy of my Completion Certificate together with the documents transferring ownership of the vessel to Panama Vessels Inc."

"I'll get cracking on that." Mike was over the moon. "But I'll ask for fifty thousand dollars more."

"Why?" The Scotsman sounded suspicious.

"My company wants Polyd delivered to Balboa, in Panama, and asks that the owners arrange for transport to that destination, at our cost, on board a freighter. After they've paid for the vessel and before shipment, they want a week's sea trials, which are to be conducted by you, with me present. For this we need a crew. Their wages will also have to come out of the fifty thou."

"Are you telling me in a backhanded way that you've arranged for a week's paid vacation on board Polyd for you and me?" The Scotsman was thrilled.

"It's not really a vacation." Mike was laughing. "You'll have to put up with me for a week and help me familiarize myself with the boat."

Mike retained a solicitor friend of the Scotsman to represent Panama Vessels in the transaction and Polyd's ownership was transferred to Mike's company on a Thursday in mid-May. He spent two days with McInnis verifying that all of Polyd's equipment was in working order. On the Friday night he volunteered to stay on board for the weekend to act as watchman; the sea trials crew was scheduled to check in first thing Monday morning.

Alone at last, he transferred the gold to Polyd's safe in six quick trips during the night.

McInnis arrived with the crew on Monday morning, very pleased with himself, as he had the previous owner's captain in tow. This smoothed Mike's indoctrination, and the one-week trip from Tilbury to Plymouth, where the boat was loaded on a freighter bound for Panama, was an easy and exhilarating pleasure.

Polyd and Mike left England for Central America on board the freighter on a beautiful, sunny morning during the first week of June.

CHAPTER TWENTY-TWO

Khalil Sedki could not believe his good fortune! Finally, he could show his Uncle Ramsi how wrong he had been about his nephew, how badly he had misjudged him, how he had failed to recognize his true mettle.

Feeble-minded he had called Khalil, and gutless, when—almost three decades ago—Uncle Ramsi had asked the boy to stow away with him and go to Canada to help avenge the murder of the great Abu Ladin's son Mustafa, who had also been a member of their family. Now, try as he might, Khalil no longer remembered how they were in fact related.

But he did remember what a great leader Abu Ladin had been, and how good to his people... the people of Ras as-Sudr, the place where Khalil was born, an Egyptian industrial town near the Ahmed Hamdi Tunnel that connects mainland Egypt with the Sinai.

Life had been hard at home and the hated Israelis had made it even harder, especially for the poor people. They could surely not have managed without the Brotherhood and leaders such as Abu Ladin—and Hamas.

Everybody owed gratitude to Abu Ladin and everybody was expected to help ease his grief when his son was murdered in Canada, at the airport in Montreal.

And his uncle, his mother's brother, had been the first to heed the call, because he, like Abu Ladin, was from Jordan and because, by then, he had become a radicalized and well-trained member of the Movement, in fact one of its great assassination experts. His full name was Ramsi Al'Hassan, but they called him the The Mechanic—he was that good at his job.

Maybe Khalil should have gone to help when Al'Hassan had asked him to, but he hadn't and that was that...the past could not be altered.

In the end, as conditions in Ras as-Sudr deteriorated and the Brotherhood refused to help him any longer because of his cowardice (so they said), Khalil did finally stow away on board a freighter loaded with raw cotton for the textile mills of England.

He tried to settle there, but the British would not let him. After living in England for fifteen years as an illegal the colonialists caught him and ordered him deported, so he ran away from them at the airport to which they had taken him.

It had been the smaller airport, Gatwick, not Heathrow, and there had been a private jet there on the tarmac. Khalil had run to it in the darkness through the rain to hide, and saw that the luggage bay had been left open. The aircraft was being loaded, but the heavy gusts of wind, whipping the rain into walls of painfully sharp droplets of horizontal spray, had forced the handlers to take temporary shelter under a nearby truck.

No one had seen Khalil catapult into the belly of the aircraft. With teeth chattering from the cold, he had made himself as small as he could and squeezed into the space between two luggage containers.

He would have frozen to death or died of oxygen starvation had the jet's luggage compartment not been equipped to carry pets.

Fate would have it that one of the Sultan of Brunei's wives loved pets and insisted on taking at least two poodles with her on every trip—and a cat. And of course, her pet monkey.

The Sultan, on whose aircraft Khalil had found himself, hated that beast with all his heart, much more than he loved its owner. She was, however, his favorite wife and he did not wish to offend her by discriminating against the monkey. So he ordained that all the animals, without exception, make the trip from London to Washington in the jet's luggage compartment.

Khalil emerged from the hold at National Airport with the whimpering monkey clinging to him for dear life and refusing to let go.

That's how Khalil became a member—a very junior member—of the exalted Sultan's entourage.

At least for a while.

When the Sultan left Washington he ordained that Khalil be cast adrift, and the Egyptian, who had, by then, picked up the rudiments of short-order cooking, joined the ranks of the millions of illegals in the U.S..

Slow-witted, but lucky, he got a job near the area known as the Shops at Georgetown Park, at a *loncheria* run by a Cuban couple who needed an extra pair of hands behind the counter willing to work for less than the minimum wage. Khalil didn't mind. He knew he would make up for the low wages by getting generous tips for superior service. And the tips were tax-free—he was yet again an illegal, a person that did not exist as far as the U.S. government was concerned.

It had been about halfway through his fourth year of slinging hash when a handsome *Cubana* began to frequent his place of work for late breakfast, always alone. Well-built, with generous hips and proud breasts, she had an air about her that Khalil found irresistible.

And her green eyes—just like his mother's—were driving him crazy.

He waited on her at every possible opportunity and listened intently to her conversations with his boss's wife whenever the two got together for a few words of idle chatter.

He discovered that she was new to the neighborhood, that she lived in an elegant condo on Canal Street, that she was from the town of Santiago in Cuba and that she had a twin sister in Miami.

As far as he could understand the two women were both unattached, but he wasn't sure.

And the thought that she might have a boyfriend was driving him crazy.

He lived in a modest apartment on K Street, the rent of which was partially paid by Uncle Ramsi who used the place as a crash pad whenever he passed through Washington.

Khalil, forty-five, wanted badly to get married. He had set a little money aside, enough, he figured, to make a down payment toward buying the *loncheria*. He and *La Cubana* would then work for twenty years, pay off the balance of sale, sell the place and retire to Santiago, Cuba.

He had it all figured out. But first, he had to conquer her, and for this he needed his uncle's help. But he was afraid that Uncle Ramsi might laugh at him and his ambitions so he kept them secret until he felt he knew enough about *La Cubana* to be able to make a case for marrying her.

Ramsi Al'Hassan's abilities as an imaginative assassin who would almost always kill his target had been recognized early in his career. His uncanny ability to get close to his victim without detection until the very last minute and his talent to be able, somehow, to walk away not only without being captured, but, more importantly, without being identified, was much envied. Of course, the Western anti-terrorist authorities, especially the Mossad, were aware of his existence, but they were unable to put a name or a face to this elusive terrorist.

Al'Hassan, who spoke Hebrew, Arabic, accentless American English (which he had learned in school and perfected by watching movies) and Spanish, could easily be mistaken for a suntanned Spaniard or Mexican because he strongly resembled his Andalusian mother.

During a career spanning over a quarter century he had only "failed" twice.

The first time didn't really count as a failure: In Montreal he had been unable to immediately verify that he had actually killed his target because a howling snowstorm had obscured his vision, and he had had to flee. Although the target's death had been confirmed by the authorities and his body flown back to the States to be buried at Arlington Cemetery, The Mechanic had never been quite sure that the grave he had visited there really did contain the body of CIA contract assassin Bernard Lands.

The second instance had been a confirmed failure: In Paris, during a carefully planned, easy drive-by shooting, he had missed his man, the local Mossad station chief, because the car from which he was shooting hit a pothole the very instant he squeezed the trigger of his specially built, long-barreled Walther P-38 automatic pistol.

Al'Hassan was methodical, thorough and careful—and seemingly without feeling. Killing for him was a necessary task that someone had to perform to make the world a better place for his Muslim brethren. He was proud of his nickname and sought to live up to it by executing his work flawlessly, in a zero-error-tolerance environment. It irked him no end to have failed twice, as far as he was concerned.

Like all hunted men he kept on the move constantly, going to ground to rest only in countries where he had not killed. His favorite safe haven was the United States, a country in which he refused to undertake any terrorist activity—the rest of the world was a big enough operational theater for him.

As he got older and gradually withdrew from physically participating in assassinations, restricting himself instead to planning them, he frequently stayed in his nephew Khalil's Washington apartment, at irregular intervals, and never for longer than five days.

When Al'Hassan (whose Mexican passport claimed he was Ramon Zapatero) heard Khalil's news, he didn't know whether to laugh or cry. What he did know for certain was that his nephew, who seemed to be totally besotted with this Cuban woman, had to be treated with kid gloves, otherwise he might lose whatever was left of his mind and blow his uncle's cover.

Unless he wanted to eliminate his nephew, Al'Hassan had no choice but to play along.

He made Khalil repeat his story and wrote down the address of the building in which the woman was supposed to be living.

"Promise me you'll stay away from her until I finish my investigation of your beloved," he admonished his nephew.

"Why?"

"Because, since you don't want to frighten the bird away by making the wrong move, you must find out more about it first."

"But I know everything about her already."

Hassan sighed. "All right, then. How old is she?"

"She must be around the same age as me."

"Then she is too old to have children."

Khalil hung his head. "I never thought about it that way." Then he brightened. "But we could adopt one."

"Suppose she doesn't want any?"

"I'll persuade her."

Hassan tried another tack. "Is she rich or poor?"

"I think she has some money. She always wears attractive clothes and lives in a nice apartment building."

Al'Hassan gave his nephew an encouraging smile. "Tell you what. Give me two or three weeks to find the answers to all these questions. Then, if you still want to marry the woman we'll find a way to conquer her heart."

Tears of gratitude flooded Khalil's eyes. Wordlessly, he embraced his uncle. "Thank you, thank you, Uncle Ramsi. I'll never forget this."

The Mechanic's eyes, too, were moist with emotion. He realized he had, at most, a month to persuade his favorite nephew—and an essential part of his cover in the U.S.—to change his mind about the Cuban woman or to make him disappear without a trace.

The next day the he set to work efficiently and systematically. His plan was simple: get answers to his questions underlining that not only were Khalil's ambitions completely unrealistic (which would infuriate the fool and create animosity with which Al'Hassan could not live), but that, even if he were to succeed in wooing the lady, the marriage was bound to cause more misery and suffering than happiness.

His inquiries soon established that the woman did, indeed, have a boyfriend with whom she cohabited and that the reason why Khalil always saw her breakfasting alone was that the man went to work early and she liked to breakfast late.

"Saturdays as well?" a visibly shaken Khalil had asked.

"I don't know nephew, but the man is often away. He has another office in Florida."

"And maybe another woman there?"

"I don't think so. They seem to be very much in love."

"Who owns the apartment?" Khalil was grasping at straws.

"If you really must know, nephew, the apartment is owned by a Grand Cayman Corporation... probably for tax sheltering purposes."

"What's tax sheltering?"

Al'Hassan saw that the time had come to let his nephew down, but as gently as possible. "Listen to an older man's advice, *habibi*. The woman is five years older than you. She will give you no children, she does not speak your language and does not know our customs, our culture. In a couple of years she will be fifty-five and fat, she will be too old to work alongside you in the *loncheria,* even if she wanted to. But she won't want to, because she has much more education than you and she would always be able to get a better paying job than you could offer her."

Khalil was bewildered. "How did you find out all of this, uncle?"

"I went to the registry office to look up who owned the apartment, I made friends with the superintendent of the building where she lives and he told me where she and her boyfriend worked. I followed her around for a few days to see what sort of a job she had. Trust me, she has an important job in a real, live Spanish-speaking theater. She's the manager."

"So you think I have no chance? That my dream, it is hopeless?"

"Quite hopeless."

The younger man began to weep quietly. "What am I to do with my life then? I don't want to be alone anymore."

"Find yourself another woman—one from your village, perhaps."

"How can I do that? I have no papers. I cannot travel."

Al'Hassan took a deep breath. A way out of this mess had just occurred to him. "Don't worry. The next time I come to visit, or the time after, I will bring a wife for you."

* * * * *

Of course, The Mechanic did not tell his nephew about the shocking information he had unearthed by accident while checking *La Cubana*'s background.

The afternoon after his chat with Khalil, Al'Hassan had visited the Canal Street condo building in which *La Cubana* lived. Pretending to be a florist's delivery man, he made friends with the chatty doorman who was adamant: The occupant of the double-decker penthouse apartment was *not* Mr. Bernstein, so there was no *Mrs*. Bernstein whose birthday was being celebrated that day.

"The place belongs to a Mr. Robert Lonsdale and he lives there with his Cuban fiancée."

"Has he lived there long?"

"As long as I've been here and that's over ten years."

"Is he in advertising? I was told Mr. Bernstein was in advertising."

"He sure isn't." The doorman, of Italian descent, loved the word "sure." It sounded almost as good as the Italian "certo." "He used to work for the government, and then NATO, but now he works for himself."

The Mechanic first thanked the doorman then his lucky stars and went his way. He had enough information to go on.

It took him ten minutes in an Internet café to find Lonsdales's official biography as published on the website of G&L Personal Security Advisers Inc. He was intrigued to learn that the man had been NATO's Deputy Director of Intelligence before joining the firm as a full partner a few months earlier.

Before that, he had been Assistant Deputy Director of the CIA's Counterterrorism and Counternarcotics Division.

This was heady stuff for a terrorist, so Al'Hassan plunged on, but hard as he tried for a full month, he could develop no significant information relating to Lonsdale that was more than twenty years old.

And this, after consulting Federal and State Motor Vehicle Driving Permit Registration databases, Credit Bureau records, Washington area Golf and Country Club Membership Lists, Immigration and Naturalization Service files (where The Mechanic had a limited "in"), national records of births, yearbooks of significant schools and colleges, major national and local newspaper archives in New York, Miami, Los Angeles, Chicago, London, Paris, Berlin, Brussels, Montreal, Toronto, Ottawa, and, of course Washington.

No birthplace, no birth date, no schooling, no driver's license, no nothing, except a brief notation from confidential INS records that read: Dual U.S.-Canadian Citizen.

That did it for The Mechanic. He was certain that Lonsdale had originally been Bernard Lands whom Al'Hassan had been sure of having killed, but whose ghost was now reaching out from the grave to make of The Mechanic an imperfect man—a liar.

Time was running out. His obsession with Lonsdale was beginning to drive him crazy. He couldn't eat, couldn't sleep, had nightmares, lost weight and found it impossible to focus on anything but Lonsdale. He refused assignments and neglected to look after his own personal security by spending too much time in Internet cafés, chasing Lands' posthumous shadow.

Al'Hassan finally concluded that, to retain his sanity, he had no choice but to confront Lonsdale, then kill him.

CHAPTER TWENTY-THREE

They started calling Syd Bojarsky "Digger" when he was four years old because he kept digging for everything everywhere: for his toys in the pile on the nursery floor (he had three male siblings), in the laundry room for parts of his hockey equipment, in the garden for buried treasure when he was ten, for information he needed for his studies at high school .... All the way, all the time, until he finally got the job of his dreams: a position with the CIA.

Even there, he kept digging, thank God.

Digger Bojarsky, a tenacious scrapper, was small, built like a fire hydrant, strong as an ox, fit as a fiddle and the son of a Polish congressman from Sandusky, Ohio—attributes he thought would help him get a job at the spy agency. But it was, in fact, his ability and tenacity as a digger that clinched him his appointment.

And his exceptional memory.

Bojarsky leaned back in his comfortably upholstered armchair, took a puff of his cigar, scratched the side of his butt and surveyed his little kingdom.

Although smoking in the joint was strictly *verboten* he and his little crew of nine—eight computer whizzes and a very attractive and efficient secretary-administrator with fifteen years' seniority and a heart of gold the size of a bus—enjoyed special dispensation from the rule because, for one, they operated in an area with no windows whatsoever, and, for another, they were all heavy smokers of many years' standing who didn't mind the smell.

Which was, actually, not bad at all because their office had an especially built, extremely efficient air conditioning and purification system that sucked out and replaced the air they were breathing every half-hour.

And kept the ambient temperature and humidity at a rock solid, comfortable level—not because of the humans in the place, but because of the array of computer terminals crammed into their shop.

Bojarsky was the head of the nameless department that looked after the safety and security of the participants in the CIA's Employee Protection Program. And, although the department was very small, Bojarsky held GS Ten rank and was paid accordingly: over seventy thousand dollars a year, plus various special supplementary benefits that the "Upper Echelons" kept inventing annually to keep him happy.

Which he was—very. At a gross annual income in excess of one hundred and twenty thousand beans a year, a third of it tax-free, at the age of forty-five.

But he was worth every penny of it.

He was responsible—twenty-four/seven—for almost five hundred lives. Plus dependents.

He and his staff were just about ready to wrap up their weekly review and head for the door when Glynn Owen, the carrot-head, and most junior member of the team, piped up.

"Does the name 'Lonsdale' mean anything to anybody?"

Bojarsky snapped forward in his chair, the hackles rising on the back of his neck.

"Why?" he said.

Suddenly, his mouth felt very dry.

Taken aback by his boss's ferocity of expression, Owen hesitated before answering.

"Come on, out with it!"

"It's probably nothing anyway." Owen shrugged. "It's just that I had never seen the name before and now I have five hits this week alone. I checked the name against our database and yes, he's a client all right, but the inquiries look innocent enough." Owen shrugged again. "I did a light in-depth on him and it said he has recently quit his job at NATO. Before that he worked for us—openly. So I don't understand."

Bojarsky nodded. "Thank you, Owen." He looked around the room. "Is there anything else?"

Silence.

"Then have a nice weekend." He dismissed them with a wave of his hand and they trooped out.

Except Owen.

He hesitated. "Shall I drop the matter, boss?"

His question was rewarded with a bitter little smile from Bojarsky. "No, Owen. You are to do no such thing. Cancel everything you have planned for this weekend and devote your energies to finding out all you possibly can about these hits. And when I say 'all,' I mean 'all'."

"In depth?"

"All the way up the tree to Adam and Eve."

"By when do you want my report, Digger?"

"By Monday morning at the latest. If you finish earlier, call me and I'll send a car for you. You know where to reach me."

Dumbfounded, Owen nodded and left the room.

A few minutes after eight on Monday morning, Owen, bleary-eyed from lack of sleep and nervous because he felt his report was not up to scratch, began to hover at the entrance to Bojarsky's office.

Sylvia, Digger's administrative assistant, watched him with mild amusement then took pity on him. "Relax. He's not in yet, but on his way and he is in a foul mood. He knows you're waiting for him."

"How so?"

"I told him."

Bojarsky arrived before young carrot-head could digest the meaning of her words.

"Come in and close the door," his boss told him even before he reached his large, cluttered desk.

Without a word Owen, clutching two copies of his report, settled into one of the two comfortably upholstered armchairs in the room and faced his boss.

"So?" The question sounded like a pistol shot.

The young man held out a copy of the report, but Bojarsky waved it aside. "Don't want to read stuff. I want to hear what you found out, what you think."

"I spent two days almost without sleep on the file, Digger, and I had some help from the boys on duty here during the weekend. Even so, I didn't have enough time to completely follow all the hits we know about back to their origins."

"Summarize."

"The original five hits that drew my attention to the file were: three from NATO, one from the FBI and one from the INS. Of the NATO hits one was an inquiry from the Argus Corporation, located in Seattle. They design high-speed communication systems and wish to engage the security firm of which Mr. Lonsdale is a partner."

"What did they want?"

"Detailed information about our client."

"Next."

"The other two NATO hits were from an Internet café in Washington. They were for general background information on our client and were probing."

"Meaning?"

"The sessions were lengthy."

"Next."

"The FBI hit was on us, reporting that at least seven Motor Vehicle License Bureaus, namely California, Texas, Florida, DC, New York and Illinois, had had recent inquiries regarding a Robert Lonsdale whose correct address was provided in every instance."

"Here in Washington?"

Owen was taken aback. His boss seemed to know more about the file than he did. "No, Digger. Actually, in Georgetown."

Bojarsky swore under his breath. "What did they want?"

"General information again. All the sessions were long."

"Where did they originate from?"

"Three from an Internet café in Atlanta, the day after the Washington Internet café inquiry. Two from Miami, also from an Internet café, two days after the Atlanta inquiry and two from Mexico City the day after that."

"I suppose also from an Internet café and also requesting general information."

Owen nodded.

"What about the INS hit?"

"I left it for the last because it is the strangest of all the hits. It was an *internal* hit, Digger, and requested all available information on our client."

Bojarsky was struck dumb.

"You sure it was internal?" he finally managed to ask. "You're absolutely sure?"

"I am, Digger, I checked twice. I even tried to trace back, but I was denied access at INS and when I went through our contact there he told me they could not trace the hit because the sender had used a double blind re-addresser system. All he could confirm was that the inquiry had come from a terminal somewhere in the INS's vast internal terminal network."

Bojarsky's head began to throb. To ease the tension he began to massage his temples. "And what did the INS give the inquirer... what information?"

"Since it was an internal inquiry with low security clearance the inquirer was given permission to download the section of the Lonsdale file in the public domain, being date of birth, but not place of birth, social security number, and last known address."

"That's not too bad... not too bad," he mused somewhat relieved, but still very concerned. He looked at Owen. "I don't suppose you had time to obtain the addresses of the various Internet Cafes involved."

"No, Digger, I did not. I haven't had time either to check the various Credit Bureau databases..."

"Or newspaper archives in major North American cities..."

Owen's eyes widened with incredulity. His boss was asking him to undertake a monumental task, one that would take weeks to complete. Bojarsky saw the expression of consternation on the young man's face. It was time to ease up a little.

"You did a good job, Glynn, a very good job, considering the time constraints under which you had to work. And it was smart of you to have picked up on the bad vibes generated by the five original hits." The young man, flattered by the compliments, looked away, blushing with pleasure. Bojarsky waited for direct eye contact with his protégé, then said softly: "Glynn, Lonsdale's well-being is important to us. I know I'm asking for the almost impossible, but do you think you could, within a week, develop the information you know we need?"

"I'll give it my best shot, Digger."

"That's all I'm asking you to do. Now tell me, how do you interpret the big picture here? What do you think is happening?"

"Simply put, someone is trying to penetrate our client's background so that he can fry his royal Canadian ass."

"Canadian? Did you say Canadian? I never said Lonsdale was Canadian." Bojarsky was outraged. "Whoever gave you that idea?"

"It's in the INS file, Digger. Look." Owen fumbled for the right page in his report then handed it to Bojarsky. "It says it right here: Dual U.S.-Canadian Citizen."

Digger Bojarsky was near tears. Lonsdale's file was one of the special specials, Triple A1, Top Secret. There was to be no hint anywhere in the paperwork about his ever having been a Canadian citizen.

Shaking his head in disbelief he kept muttering, "The stupid fucking bastards; the stupid, fucking, cock-sucking, sloppy, no good sons of bitches."

He meant the assholes whose job it was to keep the files up-to-date at the INS.

Bojarsky reached for the phone and dialed an internal number.

CHAPTER TWENTY-FOUR

Tragedy had dogged Lonsdale all his life. He'd seen battlefield carnage and had lost a beloved older brother when he was ten. Nor could he avoid meeting death often in the wet end of his profession. As a result, by the time he reached his mid-thirties, he developed a thick carapace to shield him from hurt caused by personal loss. Then he'd fallen hopelessly in love with Andrea and, after a whirlwind courtship, married her.

Two years later she was dead.

The pain of losing his wife so soon after finding love had pierced Lonsdale's protective shell and crippled him emotionally... afraid to feel.

For two decades after losing Andrea, he refused to develop any meaningful personal relationship that wasn't job-oriented, focusing instead on his work with determination, ruthlessness and impersonal efficiency, asking no quarter and giving none, thereby earning the byname "Snowman." Then Micheline had come along and she helped him to learn how to feel again.

But Micheline, too, had been taken from him and he had vowed never to open his heart to anyone again, ever.

He was surprised and totally unprepared for the speed with which his relationship with Adys developed to the point where all his carefully built barriers—mental and physical—collapsed. The gentle, loving and persistent presence of the Cuban woman reached deep into his psyche and the emotional paraplegic began to walk once more.

But as his ability to feel returned so did self-doubt. Was it maturity or fear of loneliness, he wondered, that drove him to dare to love a third time?

* * * * *

Lonsdale and Adys planned to inaugurate their new home—the double-decker apartment—by hosting a gathering for their friends during the long Memorial Day weekend at the end of May.

They invited about forty people, among them the Svobodas, down from Canada; Gal and Adys' sister Gina; and, of course, the Rosensteins, up from Palm Beach. The party was a great success, with guests staying late into Saturday night.

The next day Lonsdale did a brunch for those staying over, which meant that Svoboda was unable to have a quiet word with his host before Sunday evening.

"Are you still chasing that Martin guy—the one involved in the Plasmalab scandal?" They were enjoying mojitos on the terrace, trying to work up an appetite for an evening snack.

"In a way I guess I still am. Why?" Svoboda's question had thrown Lonsdale.

"I shouldn't be telling you this," the Canadian went on, "but two years ago the U.S., U.K. and Canadian governments started a confidential, joint test project aimed at tracking the movements of international fraudsters, money launderers and drug dealers."

"I'm aware of that."

Svoboda nodded. "I thought so. That's why I feel comfortable telling you about what came to my attention a couple of weeks ago." He now had Lonsdale's full attention. "The pilot project became operational as of the end of February, with digital passport readers at Toronto's Pearson Airport in Canada, London's Heathrow Airport in the U.K., and Kennedy and La Guardia Airports in New York linked via Internet with three central locations, one in each participating country, where a list of "problem" passport numbers is being kept on line and up-to-date at all times."

"You mean, if a Canadian presents his passport at La Guardia in New York, arriving from Switzerland, for example, the reader identifies the document as being a Canadian passport and sends the information to Ottawa in "real time" where the data are compared with a master list."

"Yes and no. We can't operate on "real time" yet because there are bound to be delays—technical, human, timezone inspired—and this would slow down passenger flow. Instead, the readers accumulate the day's information and sort it by participating country. The sorted information is then batched and sent for action by high speed satellite link to each respective country's central clearing point."

"What kind of action?"

"Cancellation notices to Interpol, information about the movements of known members of organized crime to various police forces, and so on."

"Very nice, but what has all this to do with Martin?"

Svoboda held up his hand and took a gulp of his drink. "Let me finish. At the same time, we also improved information flow within Canada by obliging the provinces to share birth, death and suchlike information with us, which means we are now automatically provided with the social insurance number of every Canadian who dies."

"And?" Lonsdale was getting impatient.

Svoboda took a deep breath. "In mid-March a fellow by the name of Jean-Yves Martin died of a heart attack in a Quebec nursing home. Although he had been suffering from cerebral palsy for years and was quite incapable of traveling, he had applied for and obtained a passport about a year ago."

Lonsdale willed himself to be very still; his heart was pounding.

"On April fourth—three weeks after Jean-Yves Martin died—someone passed through Heathrow Airport traveling on that passport. Although we have a number of such occurrences, the list is not long and I scan it on a regular basis to get a feel of what's going on in the field. The name Martin caught my eye, and I got one of my people to investigate."

Lonsdale held his breath.

After what seemed an eternity Svoboda continued. "Jean-Yves Martin had a brother whose son was or is none other than Michael Martin of Plasmalab fame!"

Lonsdale exhaled audibly. "I knew it," he whispered. "I knew it all along. The bastard is alive and well and bound to be very rich."

"What makes you say he's rich?"

"Instinct, Ben, instinct."

"What are you going to do next?"

"Ask you to help me track him down, which, I admit, will not be easy." Lonsdale knew that more than a hundred airlines used Heathrow and well over a hundred thousand passengers landed there daily. Finding out where the flight of the person using the late Jean-Yves Martin's passport originated was akin to looking for a needle in a haystack.

But Lonsdale was undaunted: He knew he could rely on his friend—and he was right.

Ben Svoboda, who, as deputy head of the Canadian Passport Office disapproved of people making use of dead citizens' documents, demanded on the spot that Interpol immediately provide him with the airline passenger manifests of inbound flights to Heathrow on April fourth.

Since Svoboda knew that bureaucracies are slow-moving, which meant that the information being sought might get purged from the relevant airlines' computers before Svoboda's request could be acted upon, he cut through the red tape by phoning a friend at the Canadian Security Intelligence Service who, through his contacts with the U.S. National Security Agency, obtained the information directly by tapping into the computers of twelve of the world's leading airlines.

His search yielded fifty-nine "hits," that is to say, passengers named John, or Joe, or J. or Y. Martin—but no J-Y Martin.

"And here they are," said Svoboda with a grin, waving three sheets of paper at Lonsdale who was having difficulty stopping himself from tearing them out of his guest's outstretched hand.

The list, in addition to providing flight number, date and time of arrival, and passenger's name, also identified the point where the flight originated and the stops it made en route to London.

Lonsdale stopped scanning the list when he got two-thirds the way down the second page.

"I've got him," he said in a voice so soft it was almost inaudible.

"Bullshit!"

"I'm not joking, Ben," Lonsdale insisted. "Here it is: J. Martin on the British Airways flight that left Budapest at seven ten pm, arriving at Heathrow at ten pm, caught by the reader at ten twenty two pm. Makes perfect sense."

"But what makes you so sure it's him?"

"He was coming back from Budapest is my guess, after seeing Moscovitch."

"Why would he have gone to see him?"

"At the Hauser trial Moscovitch told the immediate world he was off to Hungary to work on a revolutionary mad cow disease vaccine. Martin must have read about it and decided to investigate. I bet he is thinking of going into business with Moscovitch."

Svoboda wasn't buying. "That sure would be tempting providence…"

"Not at all. It's been six months since whatever evidence existed against Martin was discredited at the Hauser trial. Martin is legally dead. Mrs. Martin has been paid the insurance on her husband's life. Those suing Plasmalab and its directors are at the point of settling with the insurance companies. It's all over for the forces opposing Martin." Lonsdale stopped talking—his emotions were beginning to show and he felt naked. "If I were Martin I, too, would pick now as the time to do something daring before it was too late."

"Too late for what?"

"Don't you see?" Lonsdale felt exasperated in his loneliness of perception. "Martin lost everything when Plasmalab went down: his wife, his family, his business. He even had to kill his partner to escape ruin." Lonsdale drained his glass and got up. "One of the few people who got out ahead on the deal was Moscovitch, who seems to have been smart enough to capitalize on the lead time Keller had bestowed on him. He's smart and talented and he will succeed. Mike Martin wants to be part of that success!"

"How?" Svoboda narrowed his eyes, far from convinced.

"I have no idea, Ben. Maybe he'll buy into Moscovitch's company through an offshore company or a bank"

"What will he use for money?"

"Don't ask me why, but I have this feeling that money is not one of Mike's pressing problems."

"What is, then?"

"Me," Lonsdale said and left Svoboda to finish his drink alone.

CHAPTER TWENTY-FIVE

During most of his time with the Agency Lonsdale's boss had been Jim Morton, now the Director of the CIA's Counterterrorism Division. Morton was a dedicated man who had made the CIA his first and only love. The middle son of a successful Boston liquor manufacturer, he had attended the right Ivy League schools (Exeter and Colgate) and was at ease with wealth and privilege. But this had not made him vain nor hardened his heart: He felt he owed his country for his family's franchise on ease and devoted his life to repaying the debt. His rise through the ranks of the Agency had been remarkable for a man with almost no experience in the "wet" end of the business. Morton had earned his promotions through brainpower; he was a superb analyzer and motivator of people.

Morton and Lonsdale had joined the CIA roughly at the same time and the two had worked well together for decades. They had remained in close touch even after Lonsdale's departure for NATO.

Everyone on the "top floor" knew about their long-standing relationship.

It was, therefore, quite natural for Bojarsky to want to share with Morton his preoccupations with Lonsdale's personal safety, first, because Morton was a friend of Bojarsky's "client" and, second, because the Digger knew that Morton was fully conversant with Muslim fundamentalism and the extremists associated with it.

The Digger was happy to see that Morton was as appalled by the INS foul up as he was.

"My concern is that if the person making the inquiries is a member of the Muslim terror firmament he is likely to remember the Lands incident. He will, no doubt, put two and two together..."

Morton, who had an extraordinary amount of work on his plate just then, had asked Bojarsky to come to his office in Bethesda because he just could not afford the time to leave his place of work. In fact, he and his two senior aids had been sleeping in Bethesda for the last three days. There were just too many rumors of impending disaster floating about.

Luckily, the Italian espresso coffee machine that had been Lonsdale's parting gift to the group was still working and the bakery around the corner produced freshly baked doughnuts daily.

Bojarsky bit into his chocolate pastry and took a slurp of the excellent *latte* Morton had procured for him.

"What do you propose we do?" asked Morton and laid down his espresso cup with care. He was fastidious in his bearing and habits; some went so far as to find his behavior prissy.

"Someone has to warn him, but not on the phone."

"I know, Digger, but I can't get away from here just now."

"I understand." Bojarsky was hearing the same rumors Morton was and understood the dilemma in which the head of the CIA's anti-terrorist operations found himself. What came first: loyalty to one's friend or to one's flag? "And, of course you can't send one of your people..."

"He won't listen to them... Besides, I don't know where he is just now and I can't spare the manpower to start looking."

"Is the Cuban woman living with him?"

"Definitely. She's a sensible sort—tough and resourceful."

Bojarsky felt guilty. He had waited for Owen to update his report, which the kid had done by the previous Sunday noon, but Bojarsky had been unable to set up a meeting with Morton before first thing Tuesday morning. Too many emergencies.

It was high time someone tipped Lonsdale off about what was going on. The Digger made up his mind. "On the way to the office I'll stop by and speak to her, and him, of course, if he's there."

Morton looked relieved. "Let me call to say you'll be over in a short while." He picked up the phone and spoke with Adys briefly, then turned to Bojarsky. "We're in luck. Lonsdale is having a shower and she is just making brunch for them, but she'll wait for you if you hurry. I told her you'll be right along."

The Digger said nothing. He had just finished demolishing three doughnuts and didn't much feel like stuffing his face again.

As they were saying their goodbyes it occurred to Bojarsky that he was unarmed. This made him feel uncomfortable; he was, after all, on his way to the lion's den in a manner of speaking.

"Let me sign out an automatic, just in case Lonsdale has no weapons at home. I'll have it back to you by tomorrow."

"Good thinking, Digger," Morton agreed. "Let me organize it for you. Pick it up at reception on your way out." He lifted the telephone receiver and Bojarsky got up to leave.

He was at the door when Morton called after him. "Thanks, Digger, I owe you one."

CHAPTER TWENTY-SIX

When Al'Hassan returned to Washington during the long Memorial Day weekend he found Khalil in a state of great agitation. "I've seen *La Cubana*'s apartment and met her boyfriend," he reported breathlessly as soon as his uncle sat down to have a soft drink with him. "She's even more beautiful when she's made up and has been to the hairdresser, and when she wears formal dress."

Al'Hassan was gladdened and saddened. Gladdened because his nephew was now in a position to provide invaluable strategic information that would just about guarantee the success of the assassination plot he was in the process of hatching; and saddened because he could see that Khalil was still as smitten with *La Cubana* as he had been before.

After debriefing the younger man in detail, Al'Hassan put the finishing touches to his plan that now included the unfortunate, but necessary, elimination of Khalil as well.

A little after nine thirty on Tuesday morning The Mechanic called the telephone number Khalil had given him as being *La Cubana*'s from a public telephone booth at the corner of Canal Street and Wisconsin Avenue. When a male voice answered he hung up and walked over to the apartment building, carrying a huge bouquet of yellow roses.

The doorman recognized him. "Looking for Mrs. Bernstein again?" he asked, laughing.

"No, actually," The Mechanic replied, shaking his head. He fumbled with the envelope attached to the plastic cover of the bouquet. "I think I got it right this time. It's for a Ms. Adys Martinez in the double-decker Penthouse. I'm supposed to deliver it personally," he indicated the flowers with his head, "and sing Happy Birthday to her." He showed the doorman the tuning fork in his hand. "Don't tip off my hand," he whispered conspiratorially, "it's supposed to be a big surprise."

The doorman opened the inner door for him. "Up you go, then. Take the elevator on the left and press P1."

The Mechanic knew that the main entrance to Lonsdale's apartment was on the eleventh floor where all of the "public" rooms were situated: the large living and dining rooms, the den and the library, and, of course, the kitchen. The kitchen, as required by fire regulations, also had an exit to the back staircase through a small "breakfast corner" where the Lonsdales took their meals when they were at home alone. The maid, who did not live in, but who came on duty five days a week at one and left at seven pm (unless her presence was required longer on days when the Lonsdales entertained at home—which was often) had her own little "rest" room, also off the kitchen.

The four bedrooms, each with its own *en suite* bathroom, were upstairs, as was a generous amount of cupboard and dressing room space.

The two floors connected through an internal staircase at the back of the apartment, away from the street-side of the building. The upstairs, like the floor below, had two exits: one in the front, the other in the back.

After leaving the elevator The Mechanic stepped into the stairwell, drew on his gloves, extracted his silencer-equipped Walther PPK from among the roses and a miniature phosphorus flare from the pocket of his florist's delivery uniform blouse. He put on a very dark pair of sunglasses, palmed the flare in his left hand, cocked his pistol, picked up the bouquet, stuck it under his left armpit and, shielding the pistol from head-on view with the flowers, walked to the apartment's front door and rang the bell.

Adys was in the kitchen when she heard the bell. She glanced at the clock on the wall: a quarter to ten. She wondered idly how Morton's man could have gotten from Bethesda to Georgetown in less than forty minutes.

She looked through the peep hole in the front door. All she could see was an enormous bouquet of yellow roses. *How nice*, she thought and half-opened the front door.

The Mechanic tried to push into the entrance hall, but the flowers slowed him down so he dropped them. Adys, seeing the gun and the dark glasses, tried instinctively to slam the door shut and caught The Mechanic off balance. She almost succeeded, but at the last milisecond, Al'Hassan managed to lift his pistol and jam it between door and frame. The automatic went off and the bullet shattered the mirrored wall behind Adys. The noise of crashing glass brought Lonsdale bounding into the room, but the assassin managed to light the flare, which blinded both Lonsdale and Adys temporarily.

By the time they recovered their vision The Mechanic, having closed the door behind him, was in complete control. He motioned with his pistol for the Lonsdales to back into the living room and to sit down side by side on the large sofa there. He placed the flare in the crystal ashtray on the coffee table in front of them then took his place in the armchair facing them.

The telephone began to ring, but the assassin shook his head. His hostages were to stay put.

Al'Hassan's tone was conversational. "Greetings from the Far Side, Mr. Lonsdale. Or should I call you Bernard Lands?" It gave him immense satisfaction to see Lonsdale's eyes widen in surprise.

Lonsdale said nothing. Adys shut her eyes.

"It took me decades to track you down Lands," The Mechanic continued, "because I half-believed that I had, in fact, succeeded in killing you. I must admit that the smoke screen the authorities deployed to cover up your survival was effective: I kept an eye out for you only half-heartedly."

He leaned forward, picked up the smoking, sputtering flare and stuck it into the pot of the magnificent hibiscus plant that stood beside his armchair. "But the world is small and Allah is great. I thank him for giving me the opportunity to make up for my failure."

He raised his pistol and pointed it at Lonsdale's head who, seeing that all was lost, stared at him defiantly, daring him to pull the trigger.

The assassin nodded. "I admire you for your bravery. The Mechanic salutes you for willing to die like a man."

"And what, pray, is The Mechanic's name?"

A flicker of a proud smile touched the Arab's lips. "I am a Jordanian servant of Allah the Merciful. My name is Ramsi Al'Hassan."

"Did you ever want to be a doctor, Ramsi Al'Hassan?" Lonsdale asked.

"What are you talking about, Crusader? Concentrate, you are about to die."

"Killing is like curing, you know, Ramsi, it's really a hit-and-miss business."

CHAPTER TWENTY-SEVEN

As the doorman opened the inner door to allow Bojarski access to the elevator that would whisk him up to Penthouse 1, he remarked chattily: "I guess you're here for the birthday party."

Surprised, Bojarsky stopped. "What birthday party?"

"I thought they were going to have a birthday party with the flowers and all that..."

"What flowers?"

"Five minutes ago I sent the florist's man upstairs with a huge bouquet of yellow roses. He was going to sing Happy Birthday to Ms. Martinez."

"Did you call upstairs to announce him?"

"Now that you mention it sir, I didn't. He asked me not to. Said it was a surprise. Matter of fact, he should've come back down by now." The doorman shrugged. "Probably they've offered him a cup of coffee."

Bojarsky sprinted back to his vehicle, parked curbside to the left of the building's entrance. "Steve, leave the car where it is and follow me," he told his surprised driver-bodyguard. "Call the Major for immediate backup. Tell him to send his people up after us to Penthouse One on the double. Make the call a Code Double Red event."

While they waited for the elevator the Digger turned to the doorman and showed his CIA identification. "In a few minutes there will be a group of men here looking for me. Send them up to Mr. Lonsdale's apartment on the double."

The stunned doorman tried to say something, but it was too late—the elevator had swallowed Lonsdale's guest and his driver.

"I may be overreacting Steve, but I have very bad vibes about this situation." Bojarsky unholstered his automatic and cocked it. The driver did likewise. "Did you get through to the Major?"

"Yes, sir. Help's on the way."

"Good. There are three people in the penthouse: one woman, two men. The bad guy is dressed as a florist's deliveryman. He's come to kill the good guy."

"One of ours?" Steve was a quick study.

Bojarsky nodded and put his finger to his lips. They were at the front door of the apartment. The Digger pointed to a fresh-looking gash between the doorjamb and the heavy oak door.

With pistols drawn they took up positions on either side of the entrance.

Bojarsky rang the bell.

No answer, but by then the Digger could smell burning phosphorus.

He rang the bell again, shouting, "Police, open up." For good measure he began to bang on the door.

At a nod from Bojarsky the guard shot out the lock and the Digger kicked the door in.

Al'Hassan's natural reaction to hearing the doorbell ring was to look behind his back toward the entrance hall. This allowed Lonsdale to execute an awkward somersault over the sofa's backrest. Groaning with pain, he picked himself up and sprinted into the kitchen where he grabbed one of the barrel-loaded automatics he kept hidden in strategic places in the apartment.

The Mechanic squeezed off four fast shots after the fleeing figure then spun around to face his attackers approaching from the vestibule. Adys hurled the crystal ashtray at the Jordanian's back, which made him scream out in pain.

But he didn't flinch and when Bojarski appeared in the doorway of the living room he shot the Digger dead.

Lonsdale reappeared with pistol in hand and, standing behind the sofa near Adys, screamed at the Arab to put his weapon down.

Al'Hassan spun around with his pistol raised and his face twisted with rage. Lonsdale shot him through the forehead. Then, as the man twitched and died, Lonsdale muttered, "Just like being a doctor, *habibi*. But I didn't miss."

Adys fainted.

* * * *

After the Digger's funeral, which Lonsdale and Adys attended with heavy hearts, deeply appreciative of Bojarsky's self-sacrifice, it took Adys two weeks to calm down and start functioning normally again, more or less.

Lonsdale also had difficulty coming to grips with the situation, not because of any psychological impact the physical danger to which they had been exposed had on him, but because he saw how much Adys had been affected by it. He feared that she would be unable, or unwilling, to face the stress created by having to wonder what kind of nasty surprise might be lying in wait whenever she opened her front door, or went shopping, or was confronted by a stranger in however innocent a manner.

So he spent every moment of that fortnight with her, repeatedly reassuring her that what had happened had been an aberration, very unlikely to happen again. He made love to her tenderly, comforting her, distancing her from the horror, making her feel protected, wanted and needed. As for security, the Agency provided that through a round-the-clock guard service resident in the building.

Lonsdale also felt duty-bound to explain to Adys that he was morally obligated to his good friend Nicola Bianchi not to rest until Mike Martin was brought to justice.

At the end of the two weeks, Lonsdale, who loved cooking, decided to prepare a gourmet dinner to celebrate Adys' recovery from her ordeal: smoked salmon for hors d'œuvres, followed by a beef rib roast basted in Dijon mustard, fresh asparagus tips, *pommes soufflées*, a light green salad with vinegar and sugar dressing, and, as *pièce de resistance,* a sweet omelette au chocolat that Lonsdale had learned how to make from his mother many, many years earlier.

He selected the wines with care, choosing Cristal champagne for the fish, a robust Chianti Classico, Riserva Ducale for the meat, and Inniskilling Ice Wine to accompany the dessert. He laid out their best dishes, silver and crystal, and lit half a dozen candles in strategic places around the apartment while she took an afternoon nap.

He didn't forget the centerpiece, either. A couple of dozen freshly cut flowers in a magnificent Baccarat vase graced the dining room table.

While sipping the last drops of his Ice Wine as the maid cleared away the remaining dishes from the table, Lonsdale squared his shoulders and braced himself for one of the most important conversations of his life.

"Do you remember the words of the song *Nosotros*?" he asked.

"The Cuban bolero? Of course I do. They're beautiful and heart wrenching in the context in which they were written. Why?"

He reached across the table and took her hands in his. "*Querida,* we need to talk about that song and those words."

She paled. "Are you telling me you're dying?"

"No, *mi amor*, worse than that: I'm an adrenalin freak. To feel alive I have constantly to spit in the eyes of death."

"What do you mean, Roberto?"

"All of my adult life I have been a man who could not stay away from danger. The rush of adrenaline that standing on the edge of the blade gives me is my addiction. But there is no cure, I'm afraid, except the fatal one."

She looked at him, quite lost, her beautiful green eyes brimming with tears, questioning.

Lonsdale continued: "I cannot bear the thought of subjecting you again—as I know I inevitably will—to the kind of horror you've just lived through. Unfortunately, my entire past is one huge provocation, the things I've done, the enemies I've made... My life is a magnet to dangers that I cannot foresee."

She cut him off. "Are you referring to the words '...*tenemos que separarnos - no me preguntes mas...?"*

His heart was breaking. "Yes, I am, my darling. We must split up, we must separate. How can I bear the thought of continuing to drag you into danger, of hurting you, of making you worry about me when I am not with you, of making you wonder every time I leave the house if you'll ever see me again—."

"Roberto," she replied softly, "have you heard me complain?"

"No, but—."

She cut him off again. "There is no but. I adore you. I told you on our first night together that I can no longer imagine my life without you and I still can't bear the idea of being without you."

She laughed. "Don't overdramatize. I've long since realized that you are, in fact, some sort of an international super-policeman, with lots of people who want you dead. So what? Look what I endured in Cuba. Do you really think I am a hot-house orchid? Is that what sort of woman you want with you for the rest of your life?" She squeezed his hands. "So I'm married to a policeman, and policemen's wives are a hardy lot."

"But—."

"Enough! I'm staying. Now pour me another glass of champagne and make love to me!"

A couple of days later they parted, reluctantly—she to stay for a week with Gina and Reuven in Palm Beach, and he to restart the hunt for Martin. The horror that had not killed them had made them stronger, and deepened their connection immensely. They now were certain that each could rely absolutely on the other, even in the most extreme of circumstances, and that was a gift that, in life, was matchless.

CHAPTER TWENTY-EIGHT

Lonsdale's Hungarian was fluent—it was after all, his first language—so he had no difficulty getting around Budapest, a city he knew well. Before getting in touch with Moscovitch he visited the Companies' Registrar's Office to obtain details on Phylaxos Veterinarian Pharmaceutical Inc.

Next, he called Gal to pacify him. His partner was very much against Lonsdale chasing shadows all over the world and neglecting their company's clients in Washington.

"I know you're pissed at me, Reuven," Lonsdale said, figuring the best strategy with the Israeli was to attack right off the bat, "but you're dead wrong. Moscovitch's company, I've just discovered, is forty percent owned by a Swiss holding company that, I suspect, belongs to Moscovitch and a Bosnian virologist, who is his partner, and half by a Panamanian entity called Kyoto Veterinarian, which, I'm sure, belongs to Mike Martin. The Hungarian government owns the remaining ten percent."

Gal was not impressed. "So what? How does all this put money in our pockets?"

"Think of David Jackson, the Toronto lawyer," Lonsdale reminded him. "We get a third of whatever assets belonging to Martin we discover.

According to the public record, Kyoto paid a million dollars for fifty percent of Phylaxos Veterinarian. One third of just that is three hundred and thirty-three thousand U.S. dollars."

"In the meantime who's paying your expenses?"

"I am, out of my own pocket." Lonsdale felt put-upon.

"You're a putz, you know that?" Gal said and laughed. "Also, incorrigible."

"I love you, too," said Lonsdale and hung up. Then he took a cab to Robinson's, a restaurant near the zoo on the shore of the little lake in the middle of the City Park.

Moscovitch was waiting for him, pleased to see Lonsdale again. "I'm glad you're on time. Let's order," he said, "I'm starving. But please, no beef."

They fed the swans and drank red wine mixed with soda water while they waited for their chicken paprikás. It was a beautiful, sunny day.

"What brings you to this part of the world, anyway?"

"You and your company."

"How come?" Moscovitch became apprehensive.

"I'm not sure you know who your partner in your company is."

"Of course I do. Beside me and my working partner, Esad Delic, a Bosnian scientist, there is the Hungarian government—we jointly own half. A Japanese veterinarian pharmaceutical company owns the other half."

"Have you ever met the Japanese principals?"

"No, I haven't. The negotiations were conducted by our respective lawyers."

"And I suppose that, after your lawyers ascertained that Kyoto had the money you wanted for half of your company, they never bothered to check further."

Moscovitch flushed. "Come off it, Lonsdale. Baker Mackenzie, one of the most prestigious law firms in town, acted on behalf of Kyoto. Their participation in the deal speaks volumes for the respectability and bona fides of Kyoto. It never occurred to me to probe further."

"All the more so since they forked over a million dollars in record time."

Moscovitch was beginning to look uncomfortable. "You know that too, do you? What else have you found out?"

"Everything that is on the public record, plus a thing or two that isn't."

"Such as?"

"Let's make a deal, shall we?" Lonsdale picked up his wine glass. "You tell me about the details of the million dollar payment—which, by the way, I could work out without your help, but your assistance would save me a lot of time—and I will tell you who your real partner is."

Moscovitch thought for a few moments, then also raised his glass: There was no way he could lose. "It's a deal." They downed their drinks in unison.

The longer Lonsdale listened to Moscovitch the more convinced he became of three things: that Mike Martin was a cunning and dangerous man; that it was, indeed, he who was behind Kyoto Veterinarian; and, lastly, that Mike Martin, ex-CEO of Plasmalab and fugitive from justice, was a very wealthy man who stood to become even more so when Moscovitch took his vaccine to market.

After an excellent meal, the waiter served them strong espressos and Lonsdale felt it was time for him to sum up. "You think it is Kyoto that has possession of the bearer shares that represent half your company's ownership, but you have no proof. Have Baker Mackenzie ever checked with Kyoto about receiving the shares?"

"We would have heard from them had they not done so."

"Yes, you would have, unless, of course—."

"Of course, what?" Moscovitch's guard was up.

"You know what I think?" Lonsdale couldn't resist tormenting Moscovitch a little. It was payback time for the scientist's testimony at the Hauser trial.

"Keep your side of the bargain, Mr. Lonsdale, and get on with it."

Lonsdale gave him an angelic smile and lit his cigar. "I think the DHL delivery man who picked up the shares was none other than Mike Martin, the ex-boss of your ex-boss, Fred Keller." Lonsdale put down his cigar and showed Moscovitch a copy of the late Jean-Yves Martin's passport picture, which Svoboda had "forgotten" on a corner of the dining-room table in Lonsdale's Washington apartment. "I have reason to believe Mike Martin looks like this today."

The flabbergasted Moscovitch could do no more than freeze. "I wouldn't know. I wasn't there when the guy picked up the package."

"But your lawyer, Madarász, was." Lonsdale looked at his watch. "It's ten to three. We have just enough time to walk over to see him. I took the liberty of making an appointment in your name for three this afternoon."

Lonsdale signaled the waiter for the bill. "It'll be interesting to see his reaction to the photograph."

Although the meeting with Madarász did not result in positive confirmation that the DHL messenger and the man in the photograph Lonsdale had obtained from Svoboda were the same, the visit to the lawyer's office had been useful: The Hungarian, less constrained in the scientist's presence, was glad to explain the mechanics of the transaction and revealed that the contact at Butterfield Bank was called Llewellyn Edwards.

Lonsdale flew to Bermuda to interview Edwards, aware that the slightest miscue on his part could not only make Edwards clam up, but would also prompt the Bermuda authorities to deport him and bar him from re-entry. Therefore, before approaching him, he spent a week observing the banker from afar and interviewing his acquaintances.

A stocky Welshman in his mid-thirties, Edwards was an enthusiastic rugby player whose passion for the game far exceeded his love for his wife. This led to regular confrontations between the two—some of them quite public—when Edwards, having imbibed unbelievable quantities of beer after a game, would refuse to take his spouse home at a decent hour.

Chatting with Edwards' mates at the banker's favorite watering hole, the Bear & Bull, Lonsdale found out that the Welshman, like most middle-management expats, was short of money most of the time, drinking too much, spending too much, fighting with his wife too much, and working too little, which meant that, unless he mended his ways, he'd lose his job one day and go bankrupt. Edwards appeared to be aware of this, but seemed to lack the discipline and strength of character to dig out of the mess he was in. So Lonsdale set out to entrap him with an easy, but compromising, way of making money.

He asked Edwards to lunch at Bermuda's most fashionable restaurant, the Four Corners, an invitation the banker eagerly accepted: Friday lunches were, by tradition, very "liquid," and, therefore, expensive.

After two quick gin and bitter lemons before the smoked salmon hors d'oeuvre, Edwards became patronizing.

"I've seen you around here and there, but can't quite place you."

"Mr. Edwards, I have a very difficult and confidential job and, to be frank, I have no idea where to start." Lonsdale sighed. "I'm just not familiar enough with Bermuda."

"Sounds ominous." Edwards reacted with a superior smile. "Perhaps if you told me more, I could help. I've been here for years and know just about everybody who matters in Bermuda."

"I wouldn't want to involve you, Mr. Edwards. The matter is complicated and would take up a great deal of your time." Lonsdale drank some wine. "I was wondering whether you would know of someone whose services I could engage to assist in my inquiries."

The banker drained his glass and addressed the steak before him. "You sound like a copper. Don't tell me you are one?"

"Hardly. I'm what's best described as a financial investigator."

"And what does that mean?"

"I work for a life insurance company that had to pay out ten million dollars a short time ago when the chief executive of a Canadian public company supposedly died in a plane crash. Rumor has it that the man survived and is now living the life of a fugitive—in great luxury, I might add."

"And you think he's living here in Bermuda?" Edwards thought he had the whole scenario figured out.

Lonsdale shook his head. "No, Mr. Edwards. The man has just purchased an interest in a Panamanian veterinarian pharmaceutical company. We think he lives in Panama."

Edwards gulped down another glass of wine to cover up his shock at hearing the word "veterinarian." "Why are you searching for him here, then?"

"Because." Lonsdale paused for effect, while keeping a close eye on his guest. "I believe this man is using a Bermudan bank through which to manage his financial affairs."

Edwards poured more wine to hide his unease. "Do you have any idea which one?"

Lonsdale lied without hesitation. "Either the Bank of Bermuda or Swiss Bank."

Edwards relaxed. Lonsdale had not mentioned Butterfield's.

"Of all things to want to invest in..." Edwards was going to say more, but thought better of it; he wanted more information before committing himself.

The question, "How many mysterious fugitives dealing in Bermuda could there be with an interest in veterinarian pharmaceuticals?" kept ricocheting around his alcohol-befuddled brain until it dawned on him that his own mystery client might very well be the man Lonsdale was after.

Did his client use the cash he kept picking up in Bermuda to fund a company in Panama? Was he using this Panamanian entity through which to own the Hungarian veterinarian company, half of which he had just bought for a million dollars a few weeks earlier? Was his client living on board his yacht *for which Edwards had arranged payment upon delivery to Panama, for God's sake*?

He tried hard not to show the turmoil within him. "Very interesting," he temporized, "but I fail to see how I could be of help."

It was time to deploy the bait. "I work on a contingency basis," Lonsdale continued without missing a beat. "My employer, the insurance company, is motivated by profit. It does not make moral judgments. Provided it can recover its ten million dollars, it is willing to suspend the investigation."

"What about your fee?" Edwards was no fool.

"My fee sir, would be twenty-five percent of the moneys recovered for my client. On ten million dollars this would be two and a half million dollars."

"But the insurance company would continue to push for recovering your fees as well—wouldn't it?" Edwards was beginning to see how he could develop a win-win scenario: get twenty million from his client, pay twelve and a half to the insurers, keep the balance and ask Lonsdale to split his own fee with Edwards.

Eight million seven hundred and fifty thousand dollars, for having lunch with this simple-minded American—not bad for a Friday afternoon's work.

Provided, of course, his mystery client really was the man the American was after.

Lonsdale was fascinated by the way Edwards changed—like a chameleon—from arrogant Welshman to flushed drunk, through cold-sober and ruthless double-crosser, to cunning negotiator.

"Suppose I could find a way to help. How would you recompense the person I would introduce to you?" Edwards thought he was being subtle.

Lonsdale gave the banker his I-want-to-be-your-friend smile. "Under the circumstances I would split my fee fifty-fifty with you. Of course, you would have to pay your associate out of your share of the fee."

"You mean I would get a quarter of the fee and so would he."

"If you decided to go fifty-fifty on your portion with him—yes."

"Tell you what." Edwards was all business. "Give me until Tuesday to see what I can come up with. Let's have lunch again then."

"Next Tuesday?" Lonsdale continued to play the simpleton; he wanted to be sure the hook was well set now that Edwards had swallowed the bait.

"Yes, yes, next Tuesday, and let's make it here again. I'll try to find someone at the Bank of Bermuda or at Swiss Bank to help you." Edwards could hardly contain himself—he had just discovered a way out of his financial problems. "Thanks for an excellent lunch." He signaled the waiter. "Allow me to buy you a cognac."

"No, no," insisted Lonsdale. "The cognac comes with the lunch."

Edwards acquiesced. As always, he was glad of a free ride. "Tell me more about this fugitive fellow. It would help me in my research."

Lonsdale reached into his wallet. "I believe this to be a recent likeness of the man," he said, handing the Welshman a copy of the Martin passport photograph. "Have you ever seen him?"

Edwards, who had never laid eyes on Martin, shook his head.

Then an idea struck him. "May I keep this picture?" he asked.

"Whatever for?" Lonsdale pretended to be surprised.

"I might show it to some friends this weekend." That was a blatant lie. He had no intention of doing such a thing. His plan was to use the photo in a confrontation with ZEBRA (as Edwards called his client) when the man showed up again.

"By all means do so, but with discretion of course."

"Rest assured of that." Edwards held out his hand. "Thanks again for a splendid luncheon. By the way," he asked, trying hard to sound casual, "what did you say the name of that Panamanian pharmaceutical company was?"

Lonsdale had to fight hard not to laugh at the Welshman's clumsiness. "I didn't."

"Didn't what?"

"Didn't say what the company's name was. But I don't mind telling you now." Lonsdale was watching the banker like a hawk. "It's Kyoto Veterinarian Pharmaceuticals Incorporated." There was no reaction. It was obvious that the name meant nothing to him.

"No matter," Lonsdale muttered to himself on his way back to his hotel. "The bait's been swallowed—hook, line and sinker."

CHAPTER TWENTY-NINE

Instead of going on a pub crawl—his regular routine on Friday afternoons—Edwards hurried back to his office and asked his astonished secretary for the one-eight-one file, the name under which his mystery client's affairs were being handled.

He could find no reference to Kyoto Pharmaceuticals in it.

He reviewed what he already knew: His client had requested that one million one hundred and fifty thousand dollars be wired to Baker Mackenzie, a firm of attorneys in Budapest, funds to be disbursed against the delivery of bearer shares, representing a one-half ownership of a company called Phylaxos Veterinarian Pharmaceuticals. Thereafter, he had told the attorneys, they were to stand by for further instructions.

But this was a dead end: The "further instructions," he presumed, would come straight from ZEBRA—and neither Edwards nor his bank would have any further involvement in the matter.

Divide and conquer! The payer bank did not know on whose behalf the purchase of Phylaxos was being made, and Kyoto's manager, fronting for the purchaser, did not know where the money for the purchase had originated.

The more Edwards thought about the situation the more logical his way of seeing the transaction seemed. His client appeared to have cleverly arranged payment for the Phylaxos bearer shares by and delivery to a company (Kyoto) the bearer shares of which he himself owned. To this extent, though the payment for the Phylaxos shares could be traced to Bermuda, and the source of the instructions relating to the transaction to Kyoto, ownership of Kyoto could *not* be traced—and whoever had possession of the Kyoto bearer shares would also own half of Phylaxos.

If the purchaser of the shares was Kyoto, Edwards reasoned, delivery or custodial instructions would also emanate from Kyoto. If the attorneys were to keep temporary custody of the shares on behalf of their client the matter would end there. But sophisticated investors did not believe in leaving valuable bearer shares lying around—the risk of their being stolen was too high.

No—by now, Baker Mackenzie would have received instructions to deliver those shares to someone, somewhere.

Why not, then, go on a fishing expedition and write the Budapest attorneys to elicit a reply confirming to Edwards that his mystery client was the owner of Kyoto?

As he composed draft after draft of the e-mail he would send the Hungarian lawyer, Madarász, Edwards reflected on the irony of fate. ZEBRA's scheme had been perfect: had it not been for the pure chance of that American simpleton, Lonsdale, approaching *him* rather than someone at Bank of Bermuda or Swiss Bank, no one would have put two and two together. Only he, Edwards, had access to file one-eight-one.

The e-mail Edwards sent in the end was simplicity itself:

Re: Phylaxos Share Acquisition. Our file number D-2771. For estate planning purposes it would be helpful, though not essential, for our mutual client if he could obtain a receipt from Kyoto Veterinarian Pharmaceuticals for the captioned shares. Should you have such a receipt to hand, a faxed copy would oblige.

Edwards was proud of his handiwork: it was formal, in the stilted style of the British civil service, and uninformative—no one could fault him for having sent it; he could always claim with justification that his intent had been to complete the documentation in a "sensitive" client file, thereby protecting the interests of the bank for which he worked.

After a nerve-racking weekend, during which he drank far too much and was more abusive to his wife than usual, Edwards found Madarász's answer on his computer on Tuesday morning.

> *Your detailed and very specific instructions regarding the documentation required for the transfer of the Phylaxos shares made no mention of a receipt from Kyoto Veterinarian; thus, we have no such item on file. Should, however, our mutual client require that we attempt to obtain same, we shall endeavor to do so after receiving his instructions to that effect through the usual channels.*

To Edwards, Madarász's reply clearly implied that the Phylaxos shares were, indeed, destined for Kyoto; therefore, he reasoned, ZEBRA and the man in the photograph Lonsdale had given him were one and the same.

Anticipating the riches that would accrue to him should he succeed in extorting twenty million dollars from his client got Edwards so excited that on his way to his luncheon appointment with Lonsdale the following Tuesday he almost fell off his scooter when he tried to cut a corner too sharply.

After the customary two gin prelunch drinks, they tucked into their respective starters—*velouté de crabe*, this time—and began working on the wine.

Lonsdale's game plan was to wait and see: Having obtained Edwards' e-mail address from the Butterfield directory, he had asked his friends at the Agency to "read" the man's e-mails for the last five days; thus, he was aware of the exchange between the banker and the Budapest lawyer.

Edwards had also intended to play the waiting game, and nothing of significance was said before dessert arrived, by which time Edwards was anxious and in his cups.

"What have you been able to find out for me?" After ordering the traditional espressos and cognacs, Lonsdale at last broke the ice since Edwards was on the verge of becoming incoherent.

"You haven't bloody made my life easy—have you?" The drink was making Edwards belligerent.

"How so?"

"A couple of the chaps I've spoken to seemed somewhat interested in pursuing the subject, but when they asked me about additional details and I couldn't come up with them, they shied away."

"What banks?"

"What banks what?" The banker's voice was now garrulous.

"Which banks do they work for?"

"Who?"

"The fellows you talked to during the weekend." Lonsdale was having a hard time hiding his impatience. Edwards seemed to be past being able to concentrate.

But the Welshman surprised him; he managed to pull himself together. "Bank of Bermuda and Swiss Bank, of course. Didn't you say you suspected your mystery man was dealing with one of these two institutions?"

"Indeed I did, indeed I did," Lonsdale conceded at once. He wanted no adversarial situation to develop.

Edwards looked at him with bloodshot eyes full of liquor and cunning.

"Well, then. Don't be so dense. I need more information about your man before I can go further."

"And if I provide you with some, can you guarantee success?" Lonsdale was continuing to play the simpleton.

Edwards was haughty. "In this game, Mr. Lonsdale, there are no guarantees. But the likelihood of your stumbling on the right banking officer—the one in charge of the ZEB... (he was going to say ZEBRA, but caught himself in time) in charge of the mystery man's file—is high."

"You think so?"

"I'm pretty damn sure, provided the information you give me matches the information my chaps have on the fugitive."

Lonsdale leaned forward and beckoned Edwards to do the same. "Let me tell you what I've found out since we last spoke." His tone was conspiratorial. "But first, give me your word that you will not repeat what I tell you to anyone except those who *must* know."

"You have my word as a gentleman."

They shook hands.

"The man in the picture I gave you—rumored to be dead—is Mike Martin, the ex-CEO of Plasmalab, a Canadian pharmaceutical company which, because of an accident on its production line, sold surgical supplies contaminated with mad cow disease. Over a hundred people have died as a consequence."

"Was it this Martin chap's fault?"

"As far as could be determined he didn't even know about the accident..."

"Whose fault was it then?"

"A fellow by the name of Keller, Dr. Fred Keller, the company's Chief Scientific Officer."

"Where is he?"

"Dead: murdered by persons unknown."

"And you think this chap Martin was the one who did him in?"

"I do, but that's immaterial. What matters is that, though Martin was at one time suspected of having killed Keller, the evidence against him was found to be so weak as to not warrant his being charged."

"Was someone else accused of the murder?"

"Yes, but he was acquitted."

"So then what is Martin guilty of?" Edwards was disappointed. His scheme of blackmailing Martin seemed to be evaporating before his very eyes.

"That's just it—Martin does not stand accused of anything: He is dead as far as the law is concerned. And, as far as my client, the insurance company, is concerned he can stay dead as long as Transamerica Life recovers what it had to pay out as a result of Martin's supposed demise."

"Plus your fee," Edwards reminded Lonsdale.

"Plus *our* fee," Lonsdale put a slight emphasis on the word "our."

The Welshman grinned. "Quite right," he said, choking with greed, "plus our fee!"

"What all this boils down to," Lonsdale gave Edwards a hard look, "is that we must first find out who Martins' banker is in Bermuda. Then we must make this person tell us how much money Martin has. Can he afford to lay out twelve and a half million dollars to buy off the insurers?"

"Suppose he can, but wouldn't want to?"

"Then it would be my job to track him down and turn him in."

"How would that give Transamerica Life back the money it has laid out?"

"I guess I would then have to locate all of Martin's assets, seize them, sell them and then distribute the proceeds among Martin's creditors."

Edwards was sobering up. "But a dead man can't have creditors"

Lonsdale gave the banker his earnest, you-know-how-it-is smile. "Everybody who had ever had anything to do with Martin and his company would sue the SOB for whatever reason they could think of, and that would be a hell of a mess."

He shook his head. "The best solution for my client would be to find Martin and somehow convince him to buy off the problem."

"Assuming, of course, he could afford it." It was a smug reply.

"Well, that's where you come in, isn't it? Your assignment is to find out how much money Martin has and where it is being kept."

Edwards was beginning to change his mind now about Lonsdale; perhaps the man was not as big a fool as he made out. "And if I do?"

"Find out you mean?"

"Yes."

"We'd work out a settlement between the insurance company and Martin, get paid our fee, and everybody goes home happy."

CHAPTER THIRTY

Mike's only contact in Panama was Dr. Samos, his "banker," whom he did not wish to involve in matters relating to Polyd. So the first thing he did when he arrived in Balboa was to get in touch with "Al" Behna, the shipchandler whom Camper and Nicholsons had recommended to him in England.

Behna turned out to be a very useful "fixer." He made short shrift of securing the permits, certificates and registrations required to sail Polyd from port to port in the region. He also identified a number of potential crewmembers in short order from among which Mike picked a New Zealand couple, the Andersens. Stan was a qualified captain with first-class references, Cathy a fabulous cook who loved the sea.

Mike figured that, with the Andersens and two "occasionals," he could sail around the world and be assured of all the creature comforts he could wish for. He settled on Puntarenas, Costa Rica, as his base of operations: the country was safe and stable, encouraged visits by rich "resident" tourists, the climate on its west coast was pleasant, and there were excellent repair and service facilities for luxury yachts in and around that port city. What's more—not to be overlooked—there was Nicaragua to the north and Panama to the south, both with bureaucracies riddled with corruption, each within a day's sailing, convenient to bolt to in case of trouble.

Having discovered that Behna was also the Consul General of Belize in Panama, doing a booming business in passports for affluent tourists who wished to avoid being branded "rich gringos" in South America—where kidnappings of wealthy U.S. citizens was on the rise—Mike shaved off his beard and, for a fee of fifty thousand dollars plus the strength of his Canadian citizenship, bought a Belize passport, complete with valid multiple entry visas to the U.S. and the U.K.

The similarity between the Canadian's name and that of Plasmalab's deceased CEO had not escaped Behna, but he let the matter slide because Martins were a dime a dozen, and, besides, the given name was different. By the time Behna received notification from the Canadian Passport Office that the rightful owner of Mike's document had, in fact, died, it was too late to change horses: Mike had his new passport and Behna and his colleagues at the Ministry of the Interior in Belize City (without whose approval the consulate could not issue passports) had their fifty thousand dollars and no one was about to give anything back.

Instead, Behna—now sure that Martin was Plasmalab's ex-CEO—got in touch via e-mail with Selim, whom he had never met face-to-face, and suggested that two qualified agents be placed on board the Canadian's yacht to obtain more information on the fugitive.

Within days Selim produced a couple, Mani Seykely, an experienced steward with a Canadian passport, and Layla Floren, a Norwegian-trained certified marine diesel mechanic. Mike liked them and hired them for a ninety-day trial period.

Polyd's shakedown cruise along the Pacific Coast of Central America in mid-July went off without a hitch. The new crew soon melded into an efficient team, so that by the time the vessel reached Puntarenas (the town was only two hours by road from San José, the capital) Mike could host a modest cocktail party for key dignitaries and selected visitors.

The event took place at the Yacht Club marina where Polyd was to be berthed for ninety days, the maximum time allowed for visiting yachts to remain in the country without having to go through the hassle of obtaining residency documentation. The cocktail party was a great success and Mike found himself with lots of new "almost friends."

Mike's plan was to stay at the marina for three months, then sail down to Las Perlas Islands in Panama and visit the region for six weeks, after which he'd return to Puntarenas for another ninety days. Thereafter, having befriended the Costa Rican immigration authorities, he intended to repeat this routine *ad infinitum* by paying off the right people.

With side trips to the Galapagos Islands (a six-month endeavor, he figured) and sailing into the Caribbean through the Panama Canal to explore the San Blas Islands (yet another six-month project) Mike reasoned he could keep busy for a couple of years without getting bored and without needing to submit to invasive immigration control.

There was also his project of placing his Phylaxos holdings in strategic locations around the world through bearer-share holding companies in Liechtenstein, Monaco, Hong Kong, Costa Rica and the Channel Islands. This he intended to accomplish during a two-year around-the-world cruise on board Polyd some time during the next five years. All in all, Mike's universe seemed to be unfolding as it should.

To pay for the lifestyle he was envisioning for himself, about fifty thousand dollars a month was required, an easily manageable task, since the annual income on his forty-odd million dollars in Bermuda approximated three million dollars a year.

The problem was how to access it.

Having had great success with converting gold coins into untraceable cash, Mike decided to work out a scheme whereby he could pick up a hundred thousand dollars in gold coins every other month at coin dealers in Panama City, San José, Acapulco and Puerto Vallarta. First he needed to identify reliable and discrete coin dealers in the appropriate cities; then he had to convey his wishes to his Bermuda bankers in an unequivocal manner, which meant he'd have to meet Edwards soon since he did not want to touch his gold reserves, most of which were stored in Polyd's hidden safe.

In early August, satisfied that his crew was reliable and well qualified, Mike booked a flight on Delta Airlines from San José to Bermuda, via Atlanta. He had no difficulty with either U.S. Immigration or the Bermudian authorities—the Belizean passport seemed to be working just fine.

CHAPTER THIRTY-ONE

The dream is always the same. She and her cousin, Ibrahim, ten years her senior, are at home, waiting for her parents to return from the movies. Ibrahim, the best couscous cook in the world, is finishing up in the kitchen; she, all of six, is setting the table.

Her father, Ahmed, has the day off and Ibrahim, just in from Morocco, suggests that Layla's parents go first for a swim at the public swimming pool, then, if her mother Inge, seven months pregnant, is up to it, to the movies. Ibrahim will stay home and make couscous for all of them while babysitting Layla.

Ahmed, a Moroccan immigrant, and Layla's mother, Inge, Norwegian born, are hard workers who had bought a small apartment in the little town of Lillehammer with the pennies they managed to save through the years. Layla was born a year later.

Layla's father is an accomplished waiter, gregarious with people and attentive to their needs. The owner of the restaurant where he works relies on him. Ahmed is popular and the tips he makes are plentiful. The family lives in modest comfort. After eight years of hard work, the time has come for Inge to stay home, have another baby—hopefully a boy— and enjoy the fruits of her labors.

It is a warm July evening. Layla finishes setting the table and goes out on the tiny balcony to watch for her parents. She sees them get off the bus and start walking toward her. Ahmed waves and Inge, holding Ahmed's other hand, raises it to her lips.

Out of nowhere, a white Mazda materializes and stops between her parents and where Layla is standing on the balcony. Two men get out and begin shooting at her father. He falls down and her mother falls on top of him.

Screaming, Layla runs into the kitchen and makes Ibrahim call the police.

In her bunk on board Polyd, Layla Bouchiki-Floren awoke with a start, her childhood screams still echoing in her mind.

Her father was dead; her mother in an insane asylum in Norway; her brother, born a couple of months after the assassination, dead also—victim of a stupid touring bus accident in one of Kenya's exclusive game parks.

After her father's murder she, her mother and little brother moved in with Layla's grandmother to start a new life on the pension the government of Israel had provided to right the wrong the Mossad had caused: the murder of an innocent man whose only crime had been to look like Ali Hassan Salame, the primary architect of the 1972 Munich Olympics massacre of the Israeli wrestling team by the PLO.

The Israelis had also offered psychological counseling and had promised to help Layla find a job after graduation. But Layla would have nothing to do with them. No restitution would ever be enough to make her forgive them for destroying her family's happiness.

While at university, having stood helplessly by as her mother's sanity succumbed to her nightmares, Layla had joined the Islamic Students' Society in honor of her father's memory. Soon she began keeping company with radical fundamentalists who lived outside the law and who made sure her resentment of Israel turned into blazing hatred.

After graduating with a degree in mechanical engineering from Oslo University, Layla spent three years working for Volvo's marine engine division in neighboring Sweden, then emigrated to the U.S. to take a job in Cincinnati with Diebold, the safe and ATM manufacturer.

There, she found her life's vocation.

By age twenty-seven, Layla was able to open almost any medium security safe manufactured by Diebold without having to know its combination; the Diebold tumblers were no match for her acute hearing, augmented by the use of a stethoscope, and the unerring touch of her long, sensitive fingers.

Before resigning from Diebold she surreptitiously obtained the name of every yacht on which the company had ever installed a safe. The list included the model type and number, the dates of installation and most recent service, and the name of the last known owner of the vessel.

During the next three years Layla burglarized the safes of ten luxury yachts without once getting caught. Before moving against a target, she would research each respective owner's background in depth. She would then rob only those who would not want to get involved with the authorities for one reason or another. Besides, since Layla left no trace, the targeted owner could never be sure whether he had been a victim of a supersophisticated safecracker or a disgruntled wife, mistress or employee.

But on her eleventh attempt, Layla's luck ran out. She was caught red-handed by the steward working on board the vessel anchored next to the one she was burglarizing.

Mani, the steward, had returned a day early from his vacation on purpose and had gone on board his employer's yacht, berthed in Puerto Banus on Spain's Costa del Sol. A member of Hamas, he had been briefed about Layla's background and had been waiting for an opportunity to recruit her talents for his cause.

Layla, who had arranged for the watchman to be kept busy in the empty crews' quarters by a compliant Spanish prostitute, had assumed that she would not be disturbed during the half hour she needed to open the safe in the owner's stateroom. But as soon as the steward noticed the glow of Layla's flashlight he came over to investigate.

Seeing the woman crouched in front of the open safe, Mani lunged, giving Layla only a split second to react. She smashed him in the face with the flashlight she was holding, but he felled her anyway with a well-aimed punch to the solar plexus. After she came to, Mani made her put everything she had stolen back into the safe, lock it, and wash his blood off the carpet while he obliterated all other signs of their struggle. Then he gave her a glass of cognac and made her sit down next to him.

"I know who you are and what you do for a living. I also know about your father's murder, your mother's pain and your brother's death in Kenya."

Layla was shocked. "Who are you?"

"In the name of Allah the merciful, a Moroccan and a Muslim like you. But instead of serving my selfish ends I am a servant of Islam."

"If you know about me you must know that I am against killing."

"But you hate the Israelis for having killed your father."

"That is true."

"Then listen to me Layla Bouchiki-Floren. The time has come to devote your full time to the Cause and avenge the death of your father. Henceforth, you and I shall operate as a team, go wherever the organization sends us, and do whatever our leader tells us to do."

"What authority do you have to ask such a thing of me?"

"My name is Osmani Rassam, your assigned superior. My authority over you flows from my knowledge of your background and the details of your past burglaries."

"In other words, your threat lies in that I have no choice but to obey."

The cold look of indifference the steward gave her made her shudder.

"You have a choice," he said, cold as ice. "Either you do our bidding or I'll turn you in and you'll spend the next five years in prison. That is, if someone doesn't rape and kill you in there first."

Layla paused, then seeing she really did have no choice, submitted.

"What is our mission?"

"We will work on board a Canadian's luxury yacht in Central America and take a look inside the safe he has in his bedroom, which will enable us to blackmail him into helping our cause."

CHAPTER THIRTY-TWO

Since ZEBRA was an important client, the Bank of N.T. Butterfield was willing to accommodate his eccentricities, but only to the extent prudent under good internal control procedures. Edwards was in charge of the file, but his work was monitored and he knew that any deviation from the contact routine established with ZEBRA would come under close scrutiny. Under the circumstances, though, Edwards was not good at waiting for something to happen; he had no choice but to do just that.

Lonsdale, who could read the banker's e-mail thanks to his friends at Langley, was less impatient: He figured Martin would surface in mid-summer, by which time, he hoped, Edwards would be frustrated enough—or short enough of money—to attempt something foolish.

The Welshman was a busy portfolio manager and traffic on his computer was heavy, so much so that Lonsdale was afraid he'd miss Martin's contact attempt unless he tracked down the origin of every incoming message. This required hours of daily time, even after eliminating recurring correspondents.

When the e-mail signed 1, 81, 2, 5, 62 hit his computer in late July, Lonsdale sensed he was looking at what he'd been waiting for, but became certain of it only after establishing that the message originated from an Internet café in Panama.

He called Karl Hauser.

"Would you be interested in doing a small job for our firm in Bermuda?" he asked the pilot.

"That depends," came the laconic answer, "on what it concerns." Having become a very wealthy man as a result of Keller's demise, Hauser had become aloof and choosy, accepting only those assignments that interested him because he didn't need extra work, in fact any work at all. He stayed on with Delta because it amused him.

"This job is bound to appeal to you. Besides being in Bermuda, where the golfing is very good," Lonsdale replied, "it's our opportunity to get even with Fred Keller's murderer."

It was a proposition the Austrian could not turn down.

Lonsdale's next call was to his friend Svoboda, in Ottawa. He needed to have the Royal Bermuda Police Force notify him as soon as any Canadian citizen named J. or John or Joe or J-Y Martin landed on the island.

* * * * *

The day after he arrived in Bermuda in early August, Martin telephoned Edwards and arranged for a meeting the following day at noon in the washroom of The Pickled Onion.

"Bring eighty this time," Martin told the banker. "I'll have written instructions for you."

"And a receipt please," Edwards reminded him.

"Yes, of course," Martin snapped. For some reason, he felt uneasy, exposed.

"It's just that things are getting a bit tight around here."

"In what way?"

"Internal control is very tight because of Uncle Sam." Edwards was following the script he had written for himself. "Money laundering is the big no-no these days and since your dealings are always in cash or near cash—such as the coins—you're beginning to attract attention." The Welshman judged the time had come to start sowing the seeds of fear in his client's mind. "Every time you visit, you take between fifty and a hundred thousand dollars with you"

"That's for my living expenses."

"Fine, except we don't know who you are and where and how you live."

"The money you're managing for me has been with Butterfield for years, and the bank knows where it originated." Martin was no fool. He knew the rules. "Hell," he added, "most of it is the result of your own people's work."

"You mean the way we've invested your money?"

"Right. No 'new' money has been sent to the account for years; all you're doing is managing my investments and giving me money to live on."

Edwards increased the pressure. "How about the seven hundred-odd thousand for coins? What did you do with that?"

Martin made a mental note to start looking for ways to transfer at least part of his money out of Bermuda—his banker's attitude was beginning to annoy him. "That's neither here nor there." He kept his voice even; now was not the time to start bickering. "Even if I sold the coins and then used the money for criminal purposes, your end of the transaction could not be characterized as money laundering."

Edwards had to concede the point. "True, but believe me, we're skating close to the line. Soon they'll be asking you to reveal your identity."

Martin did not like this at all. "I'll be damned if I will."

Edwards backed off. "It's not me who's putting on the pressure—it's the U.S. authorities. I'm just cautioning you about what to expect in the near future."

"We'll discuss the matter after our next meeting." Martin hung up.

In his room at the Hamilton Princess, Lonsdale re-read the transcript of the telephone conversation with great interest.

He and Hauser had flown to Bermuda by private jet the moment a Chief Inspector Foy of the Royal Bermuda Police Force had advised Svoboda that a Canadian-born individual, carrying a Belize passport and calling himself Joe Martin, had indeed arrived in Bermuda.

As requested by Svoboda, Foy, who, it turned out, knew Chief Inspector Triggs well, had obtained a court order allowing him to tap

Edwards' phone. The tap had been in place by the time Martin had called.

"The meeting is scheduled for tomorrow at noon," Foy had told his visitors. "But you'll be on your own. I cannot spare any of my men for a stakeout. Besides, as far as the Bermudian authorities are concerned, this man is accused of no crime."

Lonsdale nodded. Rosenstein had warned that arresting Martin in Bermuda would not work. The Canadian would be released in minutes and would certainly disappear without a trace within hours. Somehow, Lonsdale had to find a way to make Martin confess.

"Don't worry Inspector," he had told Foy, "Karl and I are capable of handling things at The Pickled Onion. The objective is not to grab Martin, but to trail him to wherever he is holed up so we can keep tabs on him."

"What about Edwards?" Foy didn't like the arrogant expat.

"Thus far, all he's doing is his job. But give me time and I promise I will hand his head to you on a platter."

"How do you propose to manage that?"

"My guess is that, very soon, Edwards will start dipping into Martin's money without Martin's permission. But even if he doesn't, I'll suggest to Martin that he is." Lonsdale grinned at the policeman. "You know the technique. Throw some dirt on the wall and see how much of it sticks."

"Might one ask when you intend to start sullying our pristine Bermudian walls?"

"Perhaps as soon as tomorrow at noon," Lonsdale replied and saw himself out.

The terrace of The Pickled Onion, situated on the second floor of a three-storey building on Hamilton's Front Street, overlooks the docking quay of the luxury liners that call in Bermuda. The restaurant is popular with the locals, as well as with tourists. The latter need only cross the street from their floating hotels to enjoy the establishment's excellent food and British pub-like atmosphere. So the place is always crowded.

Lonsdale and Hauser, equipped with walkie-talkies clipped to their hips and made to resemble cell phones, earpieces in their ears and handheld microphones up their sleeves, arrived separately a few minutes after eleven to look over the premises and test the equipment. While Lonsdale inspected the toilets Hauser chatted up the barmaid, and talked her into allowing him to sit in the little alcove near the men's washroom, screened from it by a lattice wall.

"We need the place for spare dishes," the woman protested. "Besides, why would you want to sit opposite the men's stinking loo?"

"The guy I'm meeting has a very upset stomach and wants to be as close to a washroom as possible."

"One of those is it?" She'd heard the story a thousand times—mainly from old people suffering from incontinence. "It'll cost ya. I ain't walkin' an extra mile today for nothin'."

Hauser didn't catch on, so she explained impatiently. "I'll have to put the dishes and the cutlery that's on the table somewhere, won't I? The only other place I got is the kitchen, which is further."

The pilot produced a couple of twenty-dollar bills and the dishes were gone by the time Lonsdale came out of the men's room.

He was about to join Hauser when a sickening realization dawned on him: Martin knew what both Hauser and Lonsdale looked like!

He raced downstairs and contacted Hauser by walkie-talkie from the street.

"I've just realized Martin would recognize us. Get out of there as fast as you can."

"How come?"

"Ever since I was given the picture of Martin, a copy of which you have, I had the feeling I had met the man somewhere. Seeing you sitting at the table near the bar—which looks like the barrier that separated participants from spectators at your trial—helped me remember: Martin was in the courtroom every day. He sat in the last spectator row near the exit, but never left the room, not even during breaks." Lonsdale was cursing himself. "To think I walked by the son of a bitch at least four times a day during the trial."

"Unbelievable!"

"I know, but it's history." Lonsdale was trying to regroup. "Get out of there now."

Hauser refused. "His knowing me doesn't mean I have to leave. If Martin was at the trial he knows I'm a Delta pilot and I'm sure he also knows Delta flies regularly to Bermuda from Atlanta."

After a moment's reflection, Lonsdale gave in. "OK—stay. But what happens if he makes you?"

"Nothing. I wait until Edwards comes out of the toilet so that I can tip you off when he's on his way. The only change in plans is that *you* have to stay away from here—that's all."

"And I will have to trail Martin from afar to avoid being recognized."

"That too."

Lonsdale was about to say something more, but Hauser cut him off. "The discussion is immaterial anyway because I think Martin just came in. He's alone, wearing a Los Angeles Kings cap, a short-sleeve pink Polo sports shirt, black slacks, black Gucci loafers and has a very expensive-looking leather satchel slung over his shoulder."

"You sure it's him?"

"Pretty sure, though he has no beard and is wearing frameless glasses, not like the heavy ones in the picture."

"Why do you think it's him?"

"When he passed me on his way to the washroom he was in the process of pulling some sort of a cardboard sign out of his satchel. He half turned and caught a good look of me. I'm pretty sure he recognized me, so I stared him down showing no sign of knowing who he was."

"Where is he now?"

"In the washroom." The pilot's answer was to the point. "It's ten to twelve. Edwards should be here any minute now. By the way, where are you?"

"Across the road, near the gangplank of the Carnival Queen."

"Can you see the restaurant's entrance?"

"I can. Why?"

"Martin has just come out from the washroom. He is going toward the exit. I guess he wants to see if I follow him." Hauser waited for a few seconds, then asked, "Can you see him?"

"He's just coming out." Lonsdale watched the man whom Hauser had identified as Martin walk down Front Street toward the shopping center in the next block. From his vantage point he couldn't tell whether the pilot's identification was valid.

"What do we do now?"

"Wait for Edwards—but first check the washroom, just in case." Lonsdale put on a nondescript straw hat he had brought along. "I'll follow my man and if he doubles back to the restaurant we'll know it's him."

Lonsdale had taken only a few steps when Hauser came on the air again. "For sure our man is Martin. I've just checked the washroom. There is now an 'OUT OF ORDER' sign on one of the cubicles, and Edwards has just arrived. I'll take a peek again in a few seconds, but I'll bet my bottom dollar he's sitting in the stall with the sign on its door, waiting for Martin."

"What's Edwards wearing?"

"Bermuda shorts, short-sleeve white shirt and a college tie."

"And socks up to his knees, I bet."

"You got it. What about you?"

"I'm following Martin who seems to be window shopping across the street, but, in fact, he's checking for pursuit. I'll keep you posted."

CHAPTER THIRTY-THREE

It took Martin a few minutes to get over the shock of finding Hauser at The Pickled Onion, but then, recalling that the man was a Delta pilot, he concluded that Hauser was overnighting in Bermuda. Just to make sure, however, he decided to go for a walk to see if Hauser would follow.

At the shopping mall near the restaurant he dawdled over some watches in a jewellery shop, checking the mirrors around him for pursuit, but could spot none.

"Weird coincidence," he muttered as he climbed the hill toward town, then cut through a store, rushed down an alley and quick-marched to the entrance of The Pickled Onion. He shot past the stairwell, then spun around: As far as he could tell nobody was tailing him. He doubled back, ducked into the stairwell and sprinted up the stairs leading to the restaurant where he headed straight for the bar.

Hauser was still at his table, but, in Martin's absence, had ordered a juicy steak.

Martin went into the washroom and sat down in the cubicle next to Edwards. It was twenty-seven minutes past the hour.

"Stripes, are you there?" he signaled his identity.

"I was just about to leave," came the testy answer. "What kept you?" Edwards' acid indigestion, aggravated by the half hour wait for Martin, was killing him.

"Never mind that." The Canadian stopped talking; someone had come in to use the facilities. Without a word, he slid an envelope across to Edwards that contained detailed instructions pertaining to the gold coin operations and a receipt for eighty thousand dollars, wrapped around ten one-hundred dollar bills, Edwards' standard "honorarium" for meeting him.

Martin heard Edwards rip open the envelope as he fielded the little package the banker sent slithering into his cubicle. He was in the process of undoing it when he sensed Edwards was getting ready to leave.

"Any questions?" he asked, but it was too late. Edwards had left.

The package contained only five envelopes, not the eight Mike had expected. Four thick ones and a very slim one. He peeked inside the thick ones first and saw they held ten thousand U.S. dollars each.

The content of the fifth envelope was a shocker; a 5" X 7" photograph of his own face—the one in Jean-Yves Martin's passport, with an inscription on the back: MICHAEL MARTIN, then the current date and, under it, a local telephone number followed by "one pm." The last line said simply "40K."

Martin was too stunned to move.

Llewellyn Edwards, his fucking trusted banker, had just ripped him off for forty thousand dollars!

As if that wasn't bad enough, Edwards had somehow discovered his identity and, quite obviously, intended to blackmail him.

He pulled himself together and checked his watch—thirteen minutes to one. He had less than a quarter hour to marshal his thoughts, find a secluded public telephone and call the s.o.b.

But where?

The post office, of course.

He got there with no time to spare; it was a few minutes past the hour before he could complete the call.

"You're late." Edwards took the offensive; he wanted to keep his client off balance.

Mike could not control himself. "Never mind that, you desperate fuck," he hissed into the receiver. "Just tell me what exactly you think you're up to with the stunt you pulled on me at The Pickled Onion."

"It's no stunt Mike—if I may call you Mike—but then everybody does, don't they?" Edwards' sarcastic voice, cold as ice, made Martin almost choke with rage. "You're upset with me now, but by the time you've heard me out you'll be grateful that I had the initiative to pick up the reins, so to speak, and try to save your neck."

The Canadian was close to having an epileptic fit. "You save my neck?" he stammered, fighting hard to regain control. "Why, you little shit, by the time I've finished with you, you'll be glad I haven't had you locked away for life or worse."

"Really?" Edwards was beginning to enjoy himself. Martin was out of control and, therefore, malleable. "I suppose you mean you're going to deal with me as you did with Dr. Keller." He let the accusation hang in the air for a moment then pressed on. "You disappoint me, ZEBRA. I thought you were more sophisticated."

The mention of Keller convinced Mike. The banker was soloing. None of the Welshman's colleagues or superiors were in on the blackmail scheme; it would have been too dangerous given the magnitude of what Edwards was threatening to expose. Therefore, taking Edwards out of the equation would solve Mike's problems. "Where are you speaking from?" he asked, forcing himself to sound neutral and calm. He needed to hook Edwards somehow, then trap him and kill him.

"A public telephone, if you must know—and I presume you're doing the same; that is if you have not allowed your blind rage to affect your considerable intellect." Edwards continued to needle, hoping to maintain the upper hand, but to no effect—Mike was now in control of himself again and looking for a way to turn the hunter into the hunted.

He said nothing.

The silence dragged on until Edwards caved in. "Here is the pitch," he announced, making himself sound far more self-assured than he was. "Transamerica Life has paid your wife ten million dollars pursuant to your apparent demise. It wants its money back. I have friends at Transamerica through whom I can arrange to have your file closed, provided the company recovers every penny of what it has had to lay out on your behalf."

Mike understood instantly. "How much would it cost me to retain the services of you and your friends?"

"Another ten million."

"Twenty million. Let me think about it." Mike quickly hung up, thereby disconcerting Edwards and robbing him of the initiative.

* * * * *

It didn't take Lonsdale long to figure out that all was not well between Edwards and Martin.

He saw Martin burst onto Front Street, then, spotting the traffic policeman at the flagpole, trot over for a consultation, after which he sprinted off toward the center of town. Lonsdale followed at a discrete distance. At the post office, Martin grabbed the first free public phone and dialed a local call—Lonsdale saw that only one coin had gone into the slot.

"Edwards is in the Bermuda Rugby Club—a private establishment. Since I cannot get in I have no idea what he's up to," Hauser reported on the walkie-talkie.

"Talking with Martin, I'm certain." Lonsdale ventured. "Our boy looks very upset."

"Edwards too."

The phone call lasted less than five minutes. Martin returned to his hotel, the Southampton Princess, and Edwards to his office at the bank.

Martin's hotel was way out of town. This meant he had to take a taxi to reach it and Lonsdale had no problem shadowing him in another. Nor did he have to hang around the place for long; Martin was back in the lobby within minutes, checking out.

Lonsdale watched him take an airport cab then followed him to his destination without difficulty.

"I'm at the airport, watching Martin check in," reported Lonsdale at three thirty. "Perhaps you could find out through your contacts where he's headed, since he's flying Delta."

Hauser was back on the air within half an hour. "He's booked to Atlanta on the flight leaving at six thirty, from there, on to Panama City, Panama, arriving at eleven thirty tonight."

Lonsdale called Reuven Gal, explained his predicament and asked the Israeli to meet Martin's flight then follow him to his final destination. At first Gal objected, but relented when Lonsdale told him about his latest theory. "My people," Gal understood Lonsdale to mean his friends at Langley, "tell me Martin's trip originated in Panama. He's running back there to meet with his banking connections. Remember, he owns Kyoto Pharmaceuticals, which we know is a Panamanian-registered company. My guess is Martin owns other assets through his Panamanian bankers—perhaps a condo or house where he lives."

"You might well be right about other assets, but it won't be immovable property."

"Why not?"

"Because by its very nature immovable property is immovable. You can't take it with you. I know, I'm a Jew."

"What's that supposed to mean?"

"Why do you think there are far more Jewish violinists than pianists?"

"I give up."

"Because when you're on the run it's easier to schlep a fiddle around than a piano."

"Does that mean you'll go to Panama?" Lonsdale couldn't help laughing out loud.

"It guarantees it. I bet you the bastard lives on a boat."

Lonsdale stayed at the airport while Hauser collected their luggage and checked them out of their hotel.

A few minutes after five, Inspector Foy called. "Martin just left a message for Edwards telling him to pick up an envelope with his name on it at the Delta counter any time after six pm"

Lonsdale reacted with blinding speed. "Inspector, is there any way you could keep Edwards away from the airport until after the Delta flight takes off?"

"What time would that be?"

"An hour and a half from now."

"Possibly."

"Keep me posted."

Hauser arrived at five thirty. Lonsdale told him to get on the plane with Martin somehow—he did not want the Canadian to give them the slip in Atlanta by changing his onward booking there.

Next, Lonsdale trailed Martin to the first class passenger lounge and watched him compose a lengthy note, which he delivered to the Delta ticket office a couple of minutes before six, as the Atlanta flight was being called.

Lonsdale let Martin's plane take off, then, pretending to be Edwards, sauntered over to pick up the envelope, the contents of which he gingerly extracted.

Any attempt on your part, Martin wrote, *to use information about me, of whatever nature, that may have come into your possession in your capacity as my banker is Privileged Information as defined by the Bermuda Bank Secrecy Act of 1939. Its divulgation to persons not authorized to receive same (as stipulated by the said Act) is a criminal offence punishable by four years of hard labour and a fine of four thousand pounds Sterling. Additionally, your employer would also be liable for a fine in the amount of forty thousand pounds Sterling for failure to protect Privileged Information from public dissemination.*

Unless you immediately refund the money you took from me and desist from further harassment I shall procede in the following manner:

1. Contact Transamerica Life directly and deal with the matter you raised today without having recourse to your or your friends' services.

2. Cease to deal with your employer through you, using, instead, the services of Andrea Boswell or Kenneth Shanahan. (I have their e-mail addresses and direct telephone numbers.)

3. Inform Shanahan and Boswell about your action today.

4. Make arrangements to move my account.

What happens to me as a result of whatever action you choose to take will have little impact on my lifestyle since, as you know, I am quite capable of protecting my identity and privacy.

I am neither accused of or have been found guilty of any crime anywhere in the world and even if I were charged, my attorneys assure me that prosecution of me would fail.

You, sir, on the other hand, will become a pariah, a felon convicted of embezzlement and breach of the Provisions of the Bermuda Bank Secrecy Act, who will surely have little chance of securing employment in your chosen professional field on either side of the Atlantic.

I shall observe your activities closely over the next sixty days, at the end of which I shall inform you of what action I have decided to take with regard to this sordid matter.

Under the circumstances I strongly urge that you a) redeposit into my account the forty thousand dollars you have extorted from me; b) show proof that you have done so by e-mailing me my bank statement covering transactions for the last sixty days and authenticated either by Ms. Boswell or Mr. Shanahan. (Whoever will authenticate can expect a telephone call from me seeking verbal confirmation of authentication); c) stand by to meet me the next time I contact you so that we may achieve closure of this distressing episode in our relationship.

Lonsdale had a photocopy made of the note, kept the original and then placed the copy into a new envelope, addressed it to Edwards once more and left it for the banker to pick up.

Inspector Foy called a few minutes before seven as Lonsdale was boarding his Miami-bound flight. "Be advised that Mr. Edwards, who was detained for some time for a Breathalyzer test, is on his way to the airport."

CHAPTER THIRTY-FOUR

On his way back to Costa Rica Mike reviewed his situation for the umpteenth time.

Fact: The Canadian authorities knew he had been using his late uncle's passport.

Fact: Edwards had somehow found this out.

Fact: Edwards was acting alone.

Question 1: Why had the authorities not acted on their knowledge?

Question 2: How did Edwards acquire his passport photograph?

Question 3: Where was Mike at greatest risk?

He had the answer only to the last question: The Canadian passport was "blown"; his Belize passport, on the other hand, could be used, but only at points of entry without sophisticated links to the Canadian Passport Office.

If he stopped using his existing passports and eliminated Edwards, the little empire he had built with such care could go on functioning for long enough to give him time to sever unwanted links and change identity again.

In any event, he had to reconcile himself to losing everything Edwards knew about: Kyoto, Polyd and, of course, his account at Butterfield.

Polyd represented a four million dollar hit—no big deal.

Kyoto did not matter, since it had no assets—the Phylaxos bearer shares belonged to whoever had possession of them, even though it appeared that they were Kyoto's.

The main problem was the Butterfield bank account, not only because it contained the bulk of his present wealth, but also because it could be associated with the purchase of the Phylaxos shares.

Was there anyone else in the world besides Llewellyn Edwards who could prove that account number 1, 81, 2, 5, 62 at Butterfield Bank belonged to Mike Martin?

It seemed to Mike that not even the person who had leaked the information about him to Edwards could make the required proof in a court of law without Edwards' help. If he stayed away from his money, Edwards' extortion plan would be foiled. The passage of time would erode whatever tenuous links there existed between himself and the bank account until the matter became moot and the holders of the Phylaxos bearer shares could make themselves known with impunity, provided they were well-distanced from Mike Martin.

Mike kept fretting. He could not believe the solution to his ills was as simple as eliminating his banker. Edwards was venal, but not entirely stupid—he was bound to have something up his sleeve that would stop Mike from killing him.

Could he be in possession of *tangible* proof that Mike Martin was, in fact, the owner of the bank account?

Had he managed to trace the origins of the money that had flowed into the bank account at its inception?

Impossible—too complex, too diffuse, too long ago.

What, then—dammit—did Edwards have up his sleeve?

The answer came to him with a terrifying jolt somewhere over the Gulf of Mexico. Not only did it awake him from his alcohol-induced slumber, but it also made him sick to the point that he wanted to throw up.

His fingerprints. For God's sake, his bloody fingerprints. They were all over the documents he had given Edwards: the receipts, the instructions—even that last note he had left for the bastard at the Delta ticket counter.

Where were these documents now? Copies of the receipts must be in his file at the bank—but the originals?

Only Edwards would know.

Trembling with exhaustion from the effort to control his fear, Martin checked into the Hotel InterContinental in Panama City, took two Tylenols to help him sleep and went to bed.

He awoke with a splitting headache after five hours' tossing and turning. During breakfast he kept remonstrating with himself for having been so stupid as to forget to wear surgical gloves to avoid leaving fingerprints.

As for DNA—he had licked the envelope before sealing it shut at the Bermuda airport, but so what. Edwards was not going to use that piece of documentation to burn him; it was too incriminating for Edwards himself.

But the fingerprints!

And what about Hauser?

It had been bad enough to run into him at The Pickled Onion, an event he had explained away by the Austrian being a Delta pilot, but could Hauser's presence on board the aircraft to Atlanta also be accepted as sheer coincidence, or was Hauser tailing him?

And if so, why?

Mike could think of no rational explanation. Hauser, acquitted of Keller's murder, had profited from the scientist's death to the tune of at least six million dollars. He was financially independent and could retire any time he wanted.

Why would he then still be working for Delta instead of enjoying *la dolce vita*?

Maybe because he liked the action his pilot's life allowed him to savor. The bastard did look handsome in his uniform.

On his way to check in for the flight to Panama, Mike had spotted Hauser for the third time that day, kidding around with one of the male Delta passenger agents whom he seemed to know well. He'd still been at it when Martin's flight had been called, but, thank God, hadn't followed Mike on board.

Stay away, stay away, stay away. That was the way out of his troubles. He had forty thousand dollars in his pocket, six hundred thousand dollars worth of gold coins in the safe on board Polyd, and another hundred and fifty thousand hidden in the tubular arms of the modified fishing chair he'd had installed on the boat in Panama. Eight hundred thousand U.S. dollars would last him for a year, with a couple of hundred thousand left over for emergency repairs of the boat and other unforeseens.

After breakfast, Mike bought a few essential toiletries, then returned to his hotel where, at poolside, he spent most of the day listening to a group of colorful characters haggle with each other as they fixed the gray market price for gold, diamonds and other "commodities," business with which Mike wanted to have as little to do as possible. The hotel was well known for being a clearinghouse for borderline transactions.

After dinner he went to the movies. Halfway through the film he slid out through the side entrance and took a cab to Panama City's most elegant whorehouse—Challo's—his favorite. After a drink with the owner, an amazing Mexican meztiza, who had managed to put together a chain of deluxe *casas de sita* stretching from Mexico City to Medellin, he bedded a new "import" from Sweden then left at five am for the airport, using the back door.

He took the early morning rattler to the small town of David, sixty kilometres south of the Costa Rican border where, from the post office, he called Stan Andersen and told him to bring Polyd to Golfito, a marvellous little port on the Golfo Dulce, much frequented by yachtsmen on their way to the Galapagos. Next, he called a limousine service and arranged for a car to pick him up at the border.

By nightfall he was at Golfito's Banana Bay Marina where he rented a room for the night at the Jungle Club, to await Polyd's arrival at noon the next day.

Martin was certain no one had followed him to Golfito—and he was right: Gal had lost him at Challo's.

CHAPTER THIRTY-FIVE

Layla needed an excuse to spend time in the master stateroom while its owner was away. As soon as Mike left for Bermuda, she had Mani the steward "discover" a leak in the toilet that he duly reported to Captain Andersen who directed Layla to fix it. This gave her the opportunity to examine and open Martin's safe, photograph its contents, dirty the bathroom carpet a bit to make the "plumbing job" look more authentic, and report her findings to Selim via fax in Panama.

Born Mourad Haouari, in Sidi Bel Abbes, Algeria, the headquarters until 1962 of the French Foreign Legion, Selim was a veteran Muslim fundamentalist. In the early eighties, he had joined the GIA (Armed Islamic Group) at the age of sixteen. Two years later he had gone to Peshawar, Pakistan, and wound up in one of the Taliban training camps where he became adept at using firearms, making bombs, blocking roads, and other acts of sabotage. From there he progressed to killing people with cyanide and developed an interest in mass murder through the use of chemical weapons.

By the time the Soviets withdrew from Afghanistan, Selim—a dedicated fighter for whom only the Cause mattered—was a rising star among Islamic radicals. His renown became such that he had to leave the region: The Pakistani Intelligence Agency was threatening to put him behind bars. Claiming refugee status, Selim entered Canada and, because of his French-speaking background, chose to settle in Montreal. The city was only a half hour from the U.S. border by car and ideally suited as a base for action against the Big Satan. Once established, he began to organize a cell of Al Qaeda, the recent brainchild of Osama Bin Laden.

Selim was very good at dealing with people, and the Montreal cell soon boasted a membership in excess of fifty young Muslims, composed of Algerians, Moroccans, Tunisians and Egyptians, who supported their activities through credit card fraud, document forging and bad check artistry.

After the bombing of the U.S. embassies in Kenya and Tanzania in 1998, Selim had to flee again; his cell's widespread international ties, which included a link to Mohamed Khalfan, one of the Tanzanian bombers convicted for the attack, had come to the attention of the Canadian Security Intelligence Service.

By now a senior Al Qaeda operative, Selim chose Panama for his next base of activity. He set about replicating his Montreal successes by enlisting, as a first step, the Consul General of Belize in Panama, Ghal'al Behna. This, in turn, led to the identification of Mike Martin as a target of opportunity, which was of sufficient interest for the Leadership to order Selim to Budapest. Of course, Selim had no idea that through the Iraqis, the Leadership was already aware of Phylaxos and the nv CJD virus thanks to Esac Delic, Jason Moscovitch's Bosnian partner.

Selim checked into the Hotel Korona on Kecskeméti Street, Pestside, because he had been told that the place would be well suited for his purposes.

The Korona, by no means a five-star establishment, was downtown, near the "big" hotels, and always full of bargain-hunting tourists from the Balkans. Since Selim was traveling on a Turkish passport he figured he'd easily blend in.

Dressed casually in designer jeans, an elegant long-sleeved shirt, Gucci loafers and wearing Fendi sunglasses, he went for a short walk to scout around a bit then bought a map at the Pilvax Kiosk and sauntered over to Gerbeaud, the famous pastry shop on Vörösmarty Square. As instructed, he sat down near the main entrance at a table on the terrace, placed his expensive light-brown leather briefcase on the table, ordered a 'presso and a slice of Dobos cake and settled in to wait. He might have been just another well-off Israeli tourist as far as anyone could see.

At precisely eleven thirty-five a man in his late forties and similarly dressed sat down opposite him.

"My name is Delic," he said in English, "and I am an avid fan of Cuban music."

"Any particular artist?" Selim inquired.

"The late Elena Burque," Delic replied.

"Sounds like 'burka' to me."

Delic nodded. "Me too."

Contact was satisfactorily established.

"Are you aware of the fact that I am intimately acquainted with the subjet matter on hand?'

Selim was not surprised, but played along. "Start from the top."

Delic told him about his work at the SPA and about Moscovitch and proceded to give the Algerian a no-nonsense analysis of what Phylaxos could mean to Al Qaeda and Baghdad, under the right circumstances.

"The setup is ideal for launching a full-scale biological warfare attack on the infidels through propagating the disease via an infected surgical glue."

Delic stopped. The waitress had arrived to take his order.

Selim was skeptical. "I don't believe such an operation to be feasible," he remarked after the woman left.

Sure of his facts, Delic continued with determination. "As I explained," he said, "Phylaxos already knows how to produce a glue which is fatal to humans. All that remains to be done is to devise a delivery system."

"Your suggestions?"

"The best known manufacturer of these glues is Glaxter Corporation, whose products are used by hospitals all over the world. Why not produce a large batch of infected glue, packaged in thousands of vials identical to Glaxter's? These could then be sent out to our operatives worldwide for placement in as many hospitals as possible."

"Sounds too simple to be true."

"It's just so easy and uncomplicated. There is one catch though."

Selim sighed. "There always is."

"Moscovitch has, so far, been unable to manufacture an antidote, a vaccine against this new form of BSE, this new version of Creutzfeldt-Jakob's disease."

"Which means?"

"That we might, without wanting to, infect the whole world, including our Muslim brothers."

It took Selim some time to digest this. "And you're sure Phylaxos has the capability to manufacture a product that would be impossible to differentiate from Glaxter's?"

"With the help of the Iraqi government—quite sure. Phylaxos would produce a few hundred liters of infected glue and send it via rail to Iraq to be used for filling vials made to look like Glaxter's. Packaging and labeling are easy to copy."

"Did you thoroughly check with your Iraqi friends about cooperation?"

"I did: Authorization has come from the highest levels."

"What about the Hungarians and Moscovitch?"

"Once Moscovitch gives us the vaccine he he is expendable. Our Palestinian brothers won't miss one more dead Jew." Delic's eyes bore into Selim's.

"And the Hungarians?"

"With Moscovitch out of the way, I could change the production staff so that the Hungarians would never find out what was going on. We have a contact inside the SPA who would block any possible leak."

"Provided, of course, we owned the majority of the company, which would enable us to place our own people on its supervisory board." Selim had begun to see what Delic had in mind.

"Quite so."

"Which means we have to lay our hands on the shares owned by this Japanese pharmaceutical company, though nothing stops us from starting work on the project now. Am I right?"

Delic thought hard for several minutes before answering. "The most popular size of surgical glue kit consists of two 5 cc vials, one containing thrombin, the other fibrinogen. Two hundred and fifty liters each of thrombin and fibrinogen would suffice to manufacture five thousand surgical kits, amply sufficient to start an epidemic in at least ten countries."

Delic closed his eyes better to envisage what needed to be done. "The thrombin and fibrinogen will have to be ordered from the British Blood Fractionating Company, but we will only need laboratory quantities. I will be able to get quick delivery—perhaps even within fifteen days if I paid a premium."

"How much?"

"Up to twenty-five percent above market value."

"What I meant to ask was, how much would the thrombin and the fibrinogen cost in total?"

"At fifty dollars per kit, including the premium, it would come to approximately two hundred and fifty thousand dollars." Delic pointed at Selim for emphasis. "I should add that we'd have to pay in advance to ensure delivery. Phylaxos's credit isn't good."

"Money? As you know, thanks to our great leader, peace be upon him, this is not a problem."

"Good. Then let me continue. Assuming the material would be in my hands by the end of August I could process it during the first week in September and have it in Iraq by mid-month. By that time the vials and packaging materials, which I'll buy in Hungary, will have been manufactured and delivered to Baghdad. We'll probably have to 'tip' a friend in the United Nations Food for Oil program."

"Are these Magyars any good at this sort of thing?"

"Glassware and packaging? Oh yes, very, very good. Smart people. And adaptable."

"No, I meant 'tipping.'"

"The U.N. is a supermarket. You can buy anything with the right amount of cash."

"Excellent. Go on."

"I would then have the Iraqis do the filling and boxing."

"But is this not cumbersome?"

"Yes, but secure. No nosy Western journalists in Iraq. Besides, I have no filling line I can use in Hungary without arousing suspicion."

"So by the end of September, at the latest, you'd have five thousand units ready for insertion in Western hospitals."

"Yes. Say three thousand units to the U.S., and five hundred each to England, France, Germany and Italy."

"What casualties could be generated?"

"Multiply the number of kits by ten for primary re-infection and then multiply by ten again for the ripple effect."

"That's half a million souls."

"Spread throughout the West."

Selim made up his mind. "Go ahead and buy the raw materials; I'll wire the British their money on your behalf within forty-eight hours. Leave Kyoto and getting the Phylaxos shares to me. Just make sure you and Moscovitch develop a vaccine by September so that we don't *all* die."

CHAPTER THIRTY-SIX

Mike was very much looking forward to getting on board Polyd—sleep in his own bed close to his emergency stash, in control of his environment—and to lunching on Cathy Andersen's excellent cooking.

He watched as Polyd maneuvered to dock, noting with surprise that it was Cathy rather than Mani, the steward, who was assisting in the operation.

"Why is your wife doing the heavy lifting?" he asked Andersen as soon as he boarded.

"The day after you left our Norwegian mechanic and her boyfriend had to fly home—her brother got hurt in an automobile accident and is not expected to live. She wanted to see him before he passed on."

"Is this a problem for us?"

"Not in the immediate. I can manage for a few days with just you and Cathy as my helpers, provided you don't mind pitching in when we enter and leave port. In the long run, though, we'll need another pair of hands—if Mani and Layla don't come back."

"What's the likelihood of that?"

"They left a contact number where they can be reached in Norway—I'll call tomorrow."

Cathy came up to them. "Lunch is ready, gentlemen. I'm afraid it's not elaborate. With the other lot gone, I've been double shifting."

"What else is new?" enquired Mike as he dug into the cold lobster laid out for him on the afterdeck.

"Nothing exciting. We had a minor plumbing problem, but Layla fixed it before she left."

"What kind of plumbing problem?"

"The water pipe to your toilet began to leak and created a bit of a flood. But we turned off the main and mopped up the mess, and Layla welded the broken joint—it seems the vibration caused by the engines had cracked it."

"Could this occur again?" Mike only half listened to her response; he was ogling two statuesque Costa Rican women (referred to as Ticas by the locals) sashaying down to an elegant yacht docked at the end of the pier.

"Layla said no. She used a special kind of solder that has extra give."

Mike stretched. "Good. I think I'll go below and sort out my papers." He looked at his watch. "Let's meet in a couple of hours and develop an action plan for the next two weeks."

He went to his cabin to use the head and noted with distaste the slight discoloration of the carpet along the wall behind the toilet. *We'll either have to have the carpet cleaned*, he mused as he flushed, *or replace it*. He wanted Polyd spotless.

In the bedroom, he pressed the hidden switch that turned on the light under the vanity and released the panel covering the safe. He slid the panel aside. On his hands and knees, he dialed the combination and turned the handle.

It would not yield.

He dialed the combination again and tried the handle once more. No go.

He crawled over for a closer look, but nothing seemed out of order.

He checked the combination in his records and dialed it for the third time.

To no avail—the safe would not open.

Damn, damn, damn—he needed help from Diebold, the manufacturer.

Thank God he had had the foresight to hide some of his gold elsewhere. He'd check on it after nightfall; it was important he give his crew the impression that all was well. He went to the minibar in his bedroom, extracted a small bottle of rum, mixed it with Coke and drained his glass.

He powered up his computer and, after patching it into the telephone line, was greatly relieved to see on the Internet that Diebold technical service was now available in Panama City.

Next, a quick mental calculation revealed that the gold he had hidden in the fishing chair was ample to carry him for a couple of months—and more than enough for a comfortable trip to Panama to have the safe serviced. It would also give him time to replace the crew members they may have lost for good and, with his crew at full complement, for a trip to Grand Cayman to visit the Bank of N.T. Butterfield branch in George Town.

Mike planned to entice Edwards to meet him there, perhaps with a promise to give consideration to his twenty million dollar blackmail proposal. He'd get the banker to bring him a couple of hundred thousand dollars in cash, just in case. Then he'd find a way to rid himself of the greedy s.o.b. for good. Edwards was bound to jump at the opportunity: He'd certainly try to rip him off for another forty thousand dollars. Whichever way it went, the money was a small price to pay for the chance to squash the sucking weasel.

He went topside, all smiles and cordiality, had tea with the Andersens and laid out his plan to pass through the Panama Canal, visit the San Blas Islands and then sail across the Caribbean to the Cayman Islands.

"How long would such a trip take?" he asked Andersen who went off to fetch his charts, cautioning that, for such a passage, they would either have to have Mani and Layla back, or find replacements for them.

By early evening they concluded that, including a three-day stay in Balboa and a week in the San Blas Islands, they could expect to reach the Caymans in three weeks' time—by early September. That suited Mike just fine. The gold in the fishing chair was plenty to last the course. As long as there were no hurricanes in the area!

While the Andersens were cleaning up, he took a turn on deck and, having used the special tool he had been given to unscrew the fishing chair's arm ends, extracted the two plastic cylinders into which he had concealed some gold coins and the five Phylaxos share certificates.

He checked their contents in his cabin. Nothing was missing—he had capital to work with.

He volunteered to stand dead man's watch to give the Andersens a chance to rest up. While they slept, he put the gold coins and share certificates back into the arms of the fishing chair.

Next morning he sent an e-mail to the Diebold office in Panama requesting that a serviceman meet Polyd in Balboa, fired off a message to Edwards to keep him off balance, and e-mailed Behna with instructions to start looking for replacements for Mani and Layla.

At noon, with Stan Andersen at the helm and Mike acting as Mate, Polyd left Golfito for Panama.

CHAPTER THIRTY-SEVEN

Mike's request for replacements upset Behna to the point where he felt he had to take immediate action. From a public telephone in the lobby of the Sheraton Four Points Hotel he dialled an unlisted number.

"*Salaam Aleichum,*" said a voice at the other end.

"*Aleichum Salaam,*" replied Behna. "Is Selim in?"

"Who wants him?"

"Mustafa."

Selim was on the line within seconds. "Why are you calling the emergency number?"

"I have a major problem."

"What kind?"

"I have just received a troubling message about some mutual friends."

"Meet me at the car place in half an hour."

At eleven ten am on the dot, Behna drove his Toyota Echo into an automatic carwash much frequented by Canal Zone workers. He punched the appropriate combination into the keyboard at the entrance and, following the instructions of the attendant on duty, positioned his car onto the sled that would drag the vehicle through the washing process.

The carwash's door behind him rolled down and the attendant got into the seat beside him just as the cleaning fluid began to spray.

It was Selim. "What's the problem?"

The Consul had to strain to hear the Algerian because he was wearing a painter's respirator mask that covered most of his face. Selim avoided as much as possible being seen with local members of his network—even in his own garage.

"The couple you sent me for the Canadian seems to have left."

Selim nodded. "That is correct."

"And I have been asked by the owner to find replacements."

"Can you stall for a few days?"

"Well, the yacht is at sea. It will not arrive here for another couple of days."

"Very well." Selim nodded again. "By the way, did the Canadian indicate why the couple left?"

"The woman's brother had an accident and is near death. She has flown home to see him before he dies."

"Don't bother with finding replacements. She and her boyfriend will return by the end of the week. Your task now is to make sure the Canadian takes them back."

"Why would he not? He was well satisfied with their services."

"So much the better. Find a pretext for telling the captain that he should keep checking the contact number the woman gave him. I'm sure she'll leave him a message on the answering machine within a few days."

Selim turned toward Behna. "I had the woman change the combination of Martin's safe, so he'll have to have it serviced by the manufacturer. This will slow him down. Try to be present when the safe serviceman comes on board."

"What for?"

"So you can tell me about the Canadian's reaction when he finds that nothing is missing."

After Behna left, Selim changed into street clothes and drove to the Chalet Restaurant where he was joined by Layla and Mani.

"Polyd is due to arrive here within forty-eight hours," he told them. "We must act quickly."

"Has Martin called the police?" Layla was anxious to know.

"No—he only contacted the Diebold service people."

"Are you sure?"

"Behna told me Martin has asked him for replacements, but is still hoping that the two of you will go back to him."

"What do you want us to do next?"

Selim considered his answer for a while. As coordinator of Al Qaeda's activities in Central America, he had disciplined himself to give information on a need-to-know basis only since he was running three independent terrorist cells, each with its own agenda.

"Based upon information I've obtained from other sources and from your report on Martin," he nodded to Layla, "and the copies of the Kyoto share certificates in his safe, it is clear that Phylaxos is half-owned by Martin. To gain control of the company we must somehow lay our hands on the original Phylaxos bearer sha—"

"I have looked for the originals everywhere," Layla interrupted, "but a yacht is a complicated place. I was hoping Martin kept them in his safe…"

"…and now we know that he does not," Selim helped her complete the sentence. "In fact, we're not even sure they're on Polyd."

"Where else would he keep them? He has no home." This from Mani.

"But he has bankers and attorneys in Panama, Bermuda and Budapest," Selim shot back.

"Where then do we start looking?"

"We don't." Selim's laconic answer to Layla's question disconcerted his listeners. "We ask him and if he doesn't tell us we'll ask his bankers in Bermuda or Panama who are bound to know."

Mani snapped his fingers. "Just like that."

"No—not just like that." Selim smiled, something he seldom did. He addressed Layla. "You and Mani will return to Polyd in three days and act as if nothing had happened."

"Except that I'm supposed to have lost a beloved brother."

Selim's smile vanished. "Don't interrupt, woman," he admonished her. "During the next seventy-two hours we shall develop a plan together to hijack Polyd and kidnap Mr. Martin and his bank account."

"Where and when?"

He looked at Layla. His eyes showed no trace of feeling. "I do not know yet, but it will be up to you to tell us. In other words, find out, as soon as you get back on board, where Martin plans to meet one of his bankers next."

The only way Enrique, the Diebold technician, was able to open Mike's safe was to drill it, which took an hour. Martin asked him to wait outside while he verified the contents.

"You have either marked the combination down wrong, or someone else has opened your safe and changed the combination," the man reported.

"But there's nothing missing." Mike was perplexed.

"Which proves my point," the technician was packing up his tools. "You won't believe how many people do this."

"What?"

"Either mark down the combination wrong, or remember the wrong combination."

Mike was not convinced. "Can you give me a lift into the city?" He wanted a word with Enrique in private and for that he had to get away from Consul Behna who had paid him a surprise visit that morning and was still hanging around.

"Sure. I'll be cleaned up here in ten minutes."

On their way downtown Mike gave the technician a fifty-dollar tip then launched into a story he had carefully rehearsed.

"Whether or not you're right about me getting the combination wrong, I no longer feel comfortable. I feel I need protection and for this I need the tools to defend myself." He glanced at Enrique and saw the technician understood. "Could you direct me to a place that provides security services for people in my position?"

"We often get inquiries like this from people on their way to South America, but it's best to be careful when dealing in such matters. Allow me to make an appointment for you with Jorge Puga, the manager of Servicios Ejecutivos, to whom I've sent a number of Diebold customers. His office is just around the corner."

The establishment turned out to be a franchise of a British organization called Executive Services, specialized in ensuring the safety of VIPs and the protection of their assets.

Mike spent a couple of hours with Puga, explaining his dilemma and listening to the man's suggestions. Then he enrolled in a two-day training course to learn how to defend himself and to test some of the equipment Puga suggested he buy.

"Your best bet is to get a trapshooting kit and some auxiliary gear," Puga said to him as they sat sipping their drinks at the bar of the Inter-Continental Hotel, to which they had repaired after Martin's "graduation."

"By the way, let me compliment you," the Panamanian sounded sincere. "Not only are you very fit for your age, but you are also a quick learner."

"Thanks." Martin was pleased. "I try. Now, tell me what you have in mind."

"You don't want to buy anything that would draw attention to you. Weapons requiring registration and background checks are, consequently, out." Puga could read his client like a book.

"That doesn't leave much, does it?" Mike was disappointed.

The Panamanian held up his hand. "Wait. With a trapshooting set we can stretch the point."

"How?"

"I have the right to sell you sporting goods without registration. Trapshooting is a sport; therefore, in addition to the clay pigeons and the mechanism for launching them I can also sell you a couple of shotguns, a reasonable amount of ammo and some auxiliary equipment."

They finished their drinks and walked back to Puga's office where Martin wrote out an order for two twelve-gauge pump-action trapshooting Remington shotguns, sixty clay pigeons, launching equipment (which could be activated by remote control), ten boxes of ammunition, six small cans of Mace, six stun grenades "for fending off sharks in case someone should fall overboard," and six explosive devices. Three of these had pencil timers, the other three detonators that worked by remote control.

"The beauty of this combo is that, as you saw during the course you took, the portable remote can be used not only for launching the clay pigeons, but also for detonating the explosive devices."

"And how do I explain having explosive devices on board without a permit?"

Puga looked at him with wide-eyed innocence. "They're for blowing up obstructions such as small sunken boats which pose a danger to navigation and which you're bound to encounter as you circumnavigate the world."

"How am I going to hide all this stuff?"

"From your crew, you mean?"

"From them and others."

"You won't. We'll install it in plain view, but safely locked away."

Martin shook his head. "Please explain."

"The launching device will be mounted on the afterdeck starboard side, on top of a corrosion-resistant, water-tight, lockable anodized steel trunk in which you'll keep half the clay pigeons. The other half will go into an identical trunk portside, which will make for symmetry. The shotguns and the ammo, together with the grenades, you'll keep locked up in a steel cabinet I'll sell you which we'll bolt to the wall and the floor of one of your bathrooms." Puga seemed to have all the answers. "It has sturdy locks and hinges and is water and tamperproof."

"And the explosive devices?"

"They come disguised as Tueros cigars—each in its individual aluminum tube. Keep them with your other cigars in a box or humidor."

"What about the remote?"

"Keep it where you store your binocs, cameras and night-vision glasses. As you saw, it resembles a miniature camera."

"How long will it take you to assemble and install all this?" Mike was anxious to be on his way: He had already lost a couple of days to attend Puga's training course.

"If you can pay me tomorrow, Friday, I'll get my men to do the work over the weekend and have everything ready Monday night. But it'll cost you extra for overtime."

"Won't my crew get nervous?"

"Not if you tell them that nobody can stand the boredom of long sea voyages and that you bought the trapshooting equipment to break up the monotony of the daily routine by organizing shooting competitions among yourselves every now and then."

As promised, Puga's equipment was installed and functioning by late Monday afternoon. Meanwhile, Mike put the delay to good use by arranging for Polyd to be renamed "La Pintada."

"That way," he joked with the Andersens who felt ill at ease about the change, "we don't have to worry about the initials on the towels and cutlery. All we need do is paint over the names on the bow and stern."

After a fairwell drink on board, Puga bade Mike *Bon Voyage* and headed for the gangway. "Don't forget that the remote I sold you has a maximum range of only a couple of hundred meters."

"With fresh batteries." Mike was, indeed, a quick study.

"Correct. That's plenty of distance for blowing up small objects without danger, but it never hurts to take cover."

It was, in fact, for that very reason Mike had his yacht renamed. He was beginning to feel that, unless he started to take cover again by obliterating at least some of the trail he'd been unable to avoid leaving behind, he would be seriously tempting Providence.

CHAPTER THIRTY-EIGHT

Anxious to share the information he had just obtained in the Martin case, Lonsdale looked forward to seeing his colleagues in Palm Beach. Living in Washington, he missed the frequent personal interaction with Gal and Rosenstein.

They were to meet late on a Friday afternoon at Gal's house, which meant Lonsdale could bring Adys with him for the weekend. He very much needed having her at his side at every possible moment; love had, indeed, changed the loner.

"You're all sick and tired of listening to me discuss the Martin situation," he told his friends after everybody had been served coffee, "but I now know for sure that we can nab him, and profit a great deal from doing so."

Rosenstein was skeptical as always. "Suppose you grab him—what would that do for you except get you charged with kidnapping."

Lonsdale disagreed. "I have proof that Martin's alive, rich and crooked."

"You don't say."

"I kept the original of the letter that Martin left for Edwards at the Bermuda Airport and sent it to my friend Svoboda in Ottawa who had it dusted for fingerprints. The Canadian authorities have a set of prints that Martin provided when he applied for a firearms license ten years ago.

Two of the prints on the letter match those on file."

"That's the ticket." Gal was elated.

"As for being rich, I have a listing of Martin's holdings provided by his banker via e-mail, which we intercepted, showing he's worth forty-nine million dollars. We would get a third of that from the Toronto lawyers."

"Sixteen million dollars for us," Gal whistled.

"Right on." Lonsdale's lips curled in satisfaction. "But first we have to reel the bastard in."

During dinner, Lonsdale outlined his plan.

"Martin needs money from Edwards on a regular basis to cover his living expenses. I'm sure that, within a month, my friends will intercept an e-mail pinpointing the time and place of their next meeting. That's when we'll move on both of them. Edwards will be easy to crack and Martin will implode once we seize his money."

"When do you expect that fortuitous event to take place?"

"No idea, but it shouldn't be long now."

Lonsdale understood his prey. On the following Wednesday Martin's e-mail, offering Edwards and his wife a week's all expenses paid holiday in Grand Cayman, found its way into Lonsdale's computer Inbox and Lonsdale advised Gal to stand by for action on short notice.

During the remainder of the month Martin sent Edwards several e-mails that enabled Lonsdale to follow the Canadian's progress through the Panama Canal into the Caribbean and up the coastline from Colon to Belize. The Israeli's guess that Martin was living on a boat had been right on the money.

When Martin reached Belize City Lonsdale called Gal.

"Martin is poised to cross the Caribbean on his way to Grand Cayman. We have ten days to assemble and train a snatch team."

"No sweat," replied the Israeli. "We need four people in total: you, me and two buddies from the good old days. Do you have anyone in mind?"

"'Fraid not."

"Then leave it to me. Just get down here as soon as possible."

* * * * *

Selim was in a frenzy. Word had trickled down from "the top" that there would be a major development in the autumn following which Al Qaeda would launch a biological warfare campaign of international proportions. Suggestions were being solicited and it infuriated Selim to know that he had a first class biological weapon within his grasp that he was unable to exploit.

He needed at least another month before he could start infecting the infidels.

Selim could see it all in his mind's eyes: the West begging Al Qaeda for the counter-vaccine and the Leadership acquiescing—for a price. And what would the price be? The annihilation of the hated State of Israel, of course. And the withdrawal of the crusading armies from Arab lands. Selim could already taste victory in the name of Allah the Merciful.

But what if the Jew Moscovitch failed to come up with the antidote in time?

His Muslim brethren, too, would drop like flies.

What to do? What to do?

The answer was simple: Islam was at war and, in war, weapons—especially weapons of mass destruction—took precedence over everything else. As a leader of the Jihad it was his duty to perfect his potential weapon as quickly as possible. This he was doing by initiating action through Esad Delic who had assured him that the infected vials of glue would be ready for distribution by the end of September at the latest.

So to hell with the consequences—even if it meant the lives of thousands of his co-religionists. They would become martyrs and enter Paradise where six beautiful virgins would attend on each one of them.

Since the cells of Al Qaeda are autonomous, Selim needed permission from no one to proceed, provided he had the means to finance the operation himself. He had the money to pay the British blood suppliers in advance, and, with Martin in his power, he would have the money to carry out the rest of his plan.

It was now up to Selim to ensure that the plan succeeded by protecting Phylaxos's secret through taking over the company, freezing out all infidels, including the Hungarian government, and eliminating Moscovitch after the Canadian had produced the vaccine.

When Layla advised that Martin would reach Grand Cayman during the first week of September, Selim flew to Jamaica with his nephew Hosni (also a graduate of one of the Islamic fundamentalist training camps in Afghanistan) and rented a sportfisherman, The Shark, from Ahmad Jabal, who was a secret sympathizer. The two-stateroom vessel, though fifteen years old, was still capable of a top speed of twenty-five knots from its twin Caterpillar diesels. To prove it, Jabal piloted it from Kingston in Jamaica to George Town in Grand Cayman—a distance of one hundred and eighty-odd nautical miles—in ten hours, at an average cruising speed of eighteen knots.

Saturday morning, September 8

The Shark dropped anchor in Spots Bay early on Saturday morning and Selim settled down to await Polyd's arrival.

Midmorning, Selim's radiotelephone buzzed. It was Layla.

"How are you this beautiful sunny morning my dear uncle?" she chirped into the mouthpiece.

"Just fine, just fine. Where are you?"

"I'm looking at perhaps the world's most beautiful, sandy beach and I see that tonight I shall be treated to every creature comfort to which I could aspire."

"How's that?"

"If I'm not mistaken the hotel I'm looking at through my binoculars is a Hyatt. Tonight, I shall ask for a night off and eat at least eight pounds of roast beef."

"You mean you've had enough of fish?"

Layla chuckled. "You can say that again." She hung up.

This innocuous-sounding conversation conveyed a simple message: Polyd—now renamed La Pintada—was anchored on Grand Cayman's west coast off Seven Mile Beach, opposite the Hyatt Hotel. Layla was proposing to take the evening off and to meet Selim at The Steakhouse on West Bay Road at eight o'clock.

Selim turned to Hosni. "La Pintada has just arrived. The banker Edwards and his wife are staying at the Hyatt Hotel. They got in yesterday. It's time for you to get over there to watch Edwards. My guess is

Martin will be contacting him within the next twenty-four hours to arrange a meeting."

*****

Ken Brooks, owner-operator of the dive shop located beneath the Lobster Pot Restaurant near the southern tip of Seven Mile Beach, was filling compressed air cylinders out back when he heard the taxi arrive. He didn't even bother to look up; its occupants were bound to be the usual low budget early morning tourists hunting for a deal on half a day's rental of his scuba-diving boat.

When he caught sight of the four men heading toward him his jaw dropped. For a moment he thought he was hallucinating—two of his visitors were ex-SAS, former comrades-in-arms.

"Sergeant Cartwright," he called out, "is that really you, and is that ugly-looking fellow with you Corporal Stirling, or am I dreaming?"

"May very well be, Corporal Brooks," the older of the two, a man in his early forties, replied, then added with a chuckle, "unless you've been smoking those funny cigarettes again."

"And what would you be doing in the Cayman Islands, then?"

"Same as you—trying to scrape together a dishonest living."

Brooks burst out laughing. "You, Sergeant?" he made a face. "That would be nothing short of a miracle. And your friends are...?" After securing the cylinder he had been working on, Brooks beckoned his visitors to follow him through the back of his shop.

"Never mind. Come inside and tell me all about it."

On their way they passed a young Caymanian cleaning scuba gear under the tap jutting out of the wall.

"Dilbert here is my junior partner," Brooks said and gave the youth a playful punch. "Let's have a Coke and get acquainted. Then we'll go for a spin in my Durango and I'll show you around. I presume this is your first visit to these islands." He kept watching Cartwright while he handed around ice cold Cokes.

Although Lonsdale and Gal in fact knew the Caymans quite well, they nodded assent—it was obvious that Brooks did not wish to include Dilbert in their possible secrets.

After a few minutes of polite chatter they left Dilbert to mind the store and piled into Brooks' SUV, but not before Brooks produced a case of beer to slake the thirst they were bound to work up during their sightseeing tour.

He drove them to the public beach near Governor's House, parked his vehicle at the edge of the dune overlooking the sea and broke out the beer.

"Alright fellows," he said after swilling down half a bottle of Heineken without taking a breath, "let's have it—what's your game?"

"We're bounty-hunting on behalf of Reuven and Robert," replied Cartwright, nodding toward Gal and Lonsdale. "They've retained our services to help them in a rather delicate endeavor."

"And why have you come to see me? Come to think of it, how did you know I was in the Caymans?" All of a sudden Brooks became cautious.

"Come off it, Brooks." Stirling was not amused. "You're still on the list at *Soldier of Fortune* magazine, so don't play the innocent with us."

"Too true, mate." Brooks' Australian accent became more noticeable with every gulp of the beer he consumed.

"Robert here was Deputy Director of Intelligence of NATO before he joined G&L Consultants, a security company he owns jointly with Reuven, who's ex-Mossad by the way. As for why we came to see you," Stirling continued, "we want to lease your dive boats for a week—the one with the cabin in the middle and the other with the parasailing platform—and we want you and your junior partner along to maneuver them around while we're busy doing other things."

"Such as?"

"Boarding the odd yacht or two."

"What on earth for?"

"Before I tell you more I want to know whether the proposition interests you." Stirling nodded toward Lonsdale. "Robert will give you the details once you've said 'yes'. He's the team leader."

"Provided we do nothing too illegal, and the money is right, I'm in."

"Very well, then." Lonsdale took over. "The object is to snatch a fugitive from justice and turn him over to the Cayman Islands' police for subsequent extradition to Canada."

Brooks made a face. "Why don't the coppers just board the yacht and arrest the bugger?"

"For two reasons: First, the man's status here will become that of a fugitive only next week; second, he's a slippery bugger who is hard to corner. In fact, he may very well resist arrest by using physical force."

"Will you put all this in writing?" The Australian, though needing the money and aching to get back into action, wanted to be sure his back was covered.

Lonsdale did not hesitate for a second. "How about a letter from the Canadian Passport Office vouching for our bona fides."

"Then I'm in, but it'll cost you."

It was Gal's turn to laugh. The bargaining had begun—always an essential part of any successful operation.

Saturday afternoon, September 8

"Edwards is in room 303," reported Hosni to Selim by walkie-talkie in Arabic. "He has a suite on the third floor overlooking the sea. I'm in a rented car in the parking lot."

"Is he in?"

"He was having lunch with his wife in the garden restaurant the last time I saw him," Hosni looked at his watch, "Which was at one thirty, fifteen minutes ago."

Selim, who had told Jabal to move The Shark to an anchorage off Seven Mile Beach just south of the Ramada Inn, looked northward through his powerful binoculars. "I presume you've got the front entrance covered, but what happens if Edwards slips out the back?"

"He still has to come back to the West Bay Road to go anywhere."

"Does he have a car?"

"He rented one from CICO, the local Avis rep, this morning," Hosni sighed. Why did his uncle keep assuming that he was an amateur? "I'm parked a couple of rows away from it."

"Good work, but keep on your toes. This man Edwards is unpredictable."

Selim characterized himself as an unfettered planner—in other words, he believed in improvising as he went along, working his way toward his objective by trial and error, relying heavily on intuition.

Since he had no living relatives other than Hosni, he could allow himself to be totally selfish and his lifestyle to reflect his way of thinking. He lived in a rundown section of Balboa, a dangerous suburb of Panama City, in the basement of a house belonging to Hosni's uncle. Most of his meals he took at his place of work (the carwash and garage) where he pretended to be the manager. In fact, he owned the establishment through several faceless corporations and left the day-to-day running of the business to his assistant. This arrangement allowed him to come and go as he pleased and to devote most of his time to furthering the objectives of Islamic Jihad, something he pursued with passionate intensity.

Ruthless, immoral and incapable of decency, he had few illusions about life and was ready to die for his cause, preferably in action during which he intended to take as many of the enemy with him as possible.

With Hosni watching Edwards, and Layla and Mani keeping tabs on Martin, Selim felt he had reached Level One of his vague, amorphous plan; the meeting between the fugitive and his banker from Bermuda could not take place without one of Selim's people being present. This was as it should be—somehow Selim needed to end up with Martin's money to finance Level Two of the operation: the kidnapping of Martin, the hijacking of La Pintada and the transportation of the yacht to a safe haven, either under its own power or on board a freighter.

He was about to tell Jabal to move the vessel further north when he noticed that La Pintada had upped anchor and was heading straight toward him. Selim changed his mind. He decided to stay put and watch.

Mike Martin's yacht sailed by twenty minutes later and dropped anchor near The Wreck, a favorite site for scuba divers and snorkelers. La Pintada's Boston Whaler soon detached itself from the vessel and made for The Wharf Restaurant's jetty with Mani at the helm and Martin up front.

Selim had no difficulty identifying the Canadian from the photo Behna had provided.

The ship-to-ship radiotelephone squawked. It was Layla. "Our man's gone sightseeing—did you see him go?"

"Affirmative. Any idea where?"

"He said he's going to rent a car and circle the island to look for a good restaurant to take us for dinner."

"Us?"

"Yes, us—the crew."

"No roast beef tonight?"

"I'm afraid not. Instead, I'll see you at eight at The Steakhouse tomorrow night."

Selim pondered the information for a while and concluded that Martin would not meet Edwards until Monday at the earliest.

He called Hosni on the walkie-talkie. "Where's Edwards?"

"Playing tennis with his wife."

"Keep your eye out for Martin. He seems to have gone sightseeing and might turn up in your neck of the woods."

* * * * *

Since it was the off-season, Lonsdale had no difficulty finding a three-bedroom luxury condo for his group's operational headquarters.

The apartment, on the top floor of the Islands Club in the complex's southernmost building, boasted three balconies, one seaward and two smaller ones in the back, one of which had a clean line of sight to the Hyatt across the West Bay Road about a quarter of a mile away.

While Edwards and his wife were lunching, Gal gained access to the Welshman's room with the help of Brooks (who knew one of the chambermaids), and installed a powerful, voice-activated transmitter in the banker's telephone. A recording receiver, placed in a rented Honda Civic stationed in the hotel's parking lot, was then activated as backup to ensure that none of the banker's calls went unmonitored. To ensure reliable reception, a twenty-nine foot collapsible antenna, sufficiently high to clear all structures between the Hyatt and the Islands Club, was erected on the apartment's southern balcony. The main receiver, operating on "real time," was installed in the bedroom adjacent to the terrace.

While Gal, Sterling and Cartwright remained behind to fine-tune the equipment, Lonsdale drove over to the harbormaster's office.

"I'm looking for Mr. Coe," he said to the wizened old man who met him at the door.

"That would be me."

"Mr. Coe, my name is Lonsdale. I work for the Canadian Passport Office." Lonsdale produced a letter signed by Svoboda and showed it to the man. "We have reason to believe that a vessel, bearing a certain John, or Joe, Martin recently entered these waters. I was wondering if you could confirm this?"

The old man took his time to look Lonsdale over. "I'm the harbormaster, not the Immigration officer. And he finished his shift an hour ago." Coe spat neatly into the spittoon near the door. "He'll be back at seven tomorrow morning. Come back then." He turned away.

Lonsdale was not about to give up. "Years ago in Miami I ran into an Air Canada stewardess named Allyson Alberga who was from here. Her maiden name was Coe. Would she be related to you?"

The harbormaster spun around, surprised. "My niece. Haven't heard from her for years." Though the statement was brusque, the tone had softened. "Wonder whatever happened to her?"

"After she divorced her husband?"

"Silby?"

"That's right. Now I remember," Lonsdale nodded. "As far as I know she moved to Atlanta when they promoted her to Purser, got married to a Colombian and had two kids by him before getting divorced again. After that, I don't know—I lost track of her."

"She should never have left here," Coe said, sounding bitter, and headed for the door. "Come along, young fella, it's time I locked up."

But Lonsdale stood his ground. "I wonder, Mr. Coe, if I could ask you a small favor, something that would save me the trip back here tomorrow. Although I don't know the name of the vessel on board which Mr. Martin is traveling I do know it's a fair-sized luxury yacht with Panamanian registry."

"Only two such vessels entered Cayman's territorial waters during the last forty-eight hours," the harbormaster replied. He consulted a clipboard hanging from a nail in the wall.

"Let's see, the Xanadu—that's with an X—and La Pintada."

He opened the door and motioned Lonsdale out. "I've got to go now—wife's waiting."

Lonsdale thanked the old man and left. On the drive home along West Bay Road, he noticed a helicopter flying on a parallel course landward of him, trailing a cloud of spray behind it.

'They're spraying for mosquitoes again,' he mused, surprised. He had been under the impression that the resident UN Mosquito Research Unit had gotten the pesty things under control long ago.

Back at the apartment, he sent an email to his friends at Langley. By six am next morning, Sunday, he had his answer: La Pintada—formerly Polyd—owned by Panama Vessels Ltd., had a registered address identical to that of Kyoto Pharmaceuticals Ltd.

CHAPTER THIRTY-NINE

Sunday morning, September 9

Martin, up early, went for a dip in the sea off La Pintada's swimming platform then breakfasted in contented luxury.

At seven thirty Mani ferried him to the dock in George Town so he could mingle with the day-trippers from the cruise ships anchored a few hundred yards offshore.

Front Street was teeming with humanity. A number of taxi-minibuses were lined up for those who wished to "do" the island or go swimming on Seven Mile Beach, a pristine stretch of glittering, cool, white sand. There was a lot of friendly hustle to and fro while the tourists sorted themselves out. Those that opted for exploring the quaint little town on foot soon found out that the Copper Kettle and the Bakery were the closest places for a quick breakfast.

Of course, on days when there are cruise ships in the harbor every business establishment opens up early, from straw market through exclusive jewellery store to art galleries hawking "native" art (mainly sculptures made of black coral, imported, ironically, from Korea because the local supply was all fished out).

It seemed to Mike that no one wanted to miss an opportunity to make money.

No one, except the banks—of which there are over three hundred in Grand Cayman.

They open for business at the leasurely hour of eight thirty.

Martin called Edwards from a public telephone at eight thirty sharp.

"Be prepared to meet any time between one and three pm tomorrow, or Tuesday or Wednesday," he said to the sleepy banker without preamble, "and have my package ready for me."

"Where?"

"I'll call you when I'm ready, to advise the venue. We'll use the same procedure as before." He hung up and headed uptown.

On a whim, he decided to buy himself a watch. After window-shopping for a while, he took a chance on a boutique called Caymania Three where, having looked at a half dozen timepieces, he settled on an expensive-looking TAG Heuer waterproof diving chronometer.

"That's a handsome, rugged watch," remarked the very attractive sales clerk, giving him a dazzling smile.

"With a price to match, I presume." His repartee was almost automatic.

"Not really," the woman's throaty voice excited Mike.

"How much are you asking for it?"

"Six thousand U.S. dollars."

"That's a bit steep. Could you not do a little better? Perhaps you might have a word with the man in charge. Tell him I'm willing to pay five thousand."

The woman returned his gaze without blinking. She had beautiful emerald-green eyes. "I am the man in charge, and I can assure you I cannot afford to sell you this particular watch for what you're offering. Five thousand dollars is my cost price." Her gaze was steady.

"You have the most beautiful eyes I've ever seen." Mike heard himself stammer. "Are you married?" he asked, without knowing why.

"As a matter of fact, I've just gotten divorced." She looked away, her smile gone. "But I still cannot let you have this watch for less than fifty-five hundred dollars." A hardness had crept into her voice that Mike felt he needed to dispel.

"I did not mean to offend," he said with great sincerity. "It's just that I really do find your eyes very beautiful and you disconcerted me when you said you were the owner."

"Why? You don't think a woman is capable of owning and managing a store like this?" The hardness was gaining, not easing off. "Besides, if the owner isn't willing to show early on a Sunday morning, do you think the staff will?"

Mike reached into the satchel he was carrying. "Tell you what. I'll pay the price you ask for the watch, but only on condition that you have a drink with me this evening." He held up his hands. "We seem to have gotten off on the wrong foot; but I'm no male chauvinist. Please let me prove it to you."

She relented. "I can't tonight, but if you're still here tomorrow, I'll have that drink with you." Her answer was well rehearsed and designed to separate the wheat from the chaff: Many potential male customers had tried to bargain with her by making a pass. At first she had fallen for their patter, but no more.

His answer surprised her. "Done deal. We'll go for a drink on Monday—let's say around seven—and if we hit it off I'll buy you dinner at The Wharf."

Her eyes widened with pleasure. "My favorite restaurant."

The previous night Mike had taken his crew to dinner at that very place, an establishment he'd found to his liking for many reasons. Located in a little inlet, the eatery was accessible by boat since half of it was built on a wharf that jutted into the water. This arrangement provided a welcome breeze to those who chose to dine outdoors in September, the year's hottest and most humid month.

The dinner was a way for Mike to show his appreciation of Mani's and Layla's return "to the fold," as he'd called it during the short toast he proposed to their health. He expressed the hope that the crew would stay together for a long time to share his enjoyment of the exciting parts of the world he planned to visit during the coming year—Europe, Asia, the Islands of the South Pacific...

He stood to make his little speech, noticing in the process that their group was the only one dining on The Wharf's promontory, a hexagonal gazebo one side of which was attached to the rest of the structure. There and then an idea began to germinate in his mind.

Just before leaving the restaurant Mike peeked under the table. Its metal base was bolted to the floor and an interchangeable plastic top, held in place by clips, served as its top.

They must have different sized tops, he thought as he hurried along to catch up with his crew.

"Let's start with drinks tomorrow, as you suggest. Then we'll see..." The woman held out her hand. By the way, my name is Lesley."

"I'm Joe." He gave her fifty-five one-hundred dollar bills, which one of her clerks ran through the verity light to make sure none of them was counterfeit.

"Where and when shall I contact you tomorrow?"

"Call me here any time after ten." She gave him her card.

He picked up his parcel and was gone before she could say another word.

It took Mike an hour and a half to hike from George Town to the Holiday Inn—a distance of about five miles along the West Bay Road. Parched and covered with dust, he headed straight for the pool bar and ordered a very large gin and bitter lemon.

As usual on a Sunday morning, there was a sprinkling of locals perched on the stools—mainly excursion boat captains looking for business. The conversation was animated and Mike listened to the wisecracks and snappy comebacks with unabashed pleasure.

When the bartender brought him his second drink he asked the man if he knew who owned The Wharf.

"Fellow by the name of Clemens—he be an Austrian. Used to be the maitre d' at Grand Old House."

"You know him?"

"Sure do. I be working with him often at parties."

Mike finished his drink and went inside to use the men's room. He was pleased to see that its layout suited him well for the meeting he was planning with Edwards.

On his way out he called The Wharf and asked for Clemens.

"Willy, the bartender at the Holiday Inn, suggested the Wharf as an ideal place for a very special, romantic dinner."

"Villy is a good fellow." Clemens' accent could be cut with a knife. "Vat can I do for you?"

"I want to have an intimate champagne dinner with the best fresh seafood you have. Maybe you could set us up on that little gazebo-thing off your dock."

"Vat time and vat day?"

"Monday at eight."

"Let me check."

Clemens was back in a minute. "It's OK—vat's your name?"

"Keller, Joe Keller."

"OK Mr. Keller, I got it. Vere are you staying?"

"At the Holiday Inn." Martin was betting that the mention of Willy's name would stop Clemens from checking back.

Sure enough, Clemens caught on. "Stupid of me. Villy recommended us. Thank you and see you Monday night."

* * * * *

Lonsdale went for a brisk walk along the beach toward George Town and took his binoculars with him: He was hoping to spot La Pintada on the way. When he got past the Ramada Inn, he came across not one, but two luxury yachts: a sportfisherman, called The Shark, and anchored about fifty yards south of it, La Pintada.

Playing the gawking tourist, Lonsdale climbed the outside stairs of the hotel to the third floor and focused his glasses on The Shark, the vessel nearest him. Two men were lolling about on the afterdeck, one talking into a satellite phone, the other playing with his binoculars, sweeping the shoreline, then the horizon seaward. Every now and then he'd look toward La Pintada.

On board Martin's yacht, things were equally quiet. In the stern, a woman was cleaning away the breakfast dishes, assisted by an athletic-looking, suntanned man in his mid-thirties. Under the Bimini top someone wearing a captain's hat was fiddling with the craft's instrument panel, cleaning and polishing the brass fittings.

Martin seemed to be nowhere in sight.

After fifteen minutes Lonsdale had enough. He took the stairs down to the beach and headed for the Harbormaster's office.

The Immigration Officer greeted him with outstretched hands. "You must be Mr. Lonsdale. Chief Inspector Bostock called me about you. My name is Rex Rankin."

Lonsdale was pleased; his old boys' network seemed to be operating efficiently.

As soon as his contacts at Langley had identified La Pintada as being Martin's yacht, Lonsdale had telephoned Inspector Triggs in the Bahamas. After apologizing for rousing the irate man from his Sunday morning slumber, he had explained his urgent need for information.

"Martin is here, on board his yacht. We propose to persuade him to return to Canada to face the music."

"Do you have irrefutable proof of identity?"

"I do, indeed. His fingerprints off a letter he left at the Bermuda Airport for Edwards."

"I heard about that letter." Triggs was no slouch.

"The Passport Office found a match for them on his application for a firearm registration certificate filed years ago."

"How can I be of help?"

"Do you know anyone at Cayman Islands Immigration?"

"I do—Chief Inspector Bostock, the Director."

"Could you ask him to help me?"

"I need a plausible reason for asking."

"Tell him I work for the Canadian Passport Office and that we suspect Martin, a fugitive from justice, is using a forged Canadian passport."

"You have anything in writing?"

"Yes I do—a letter from Director Svoboda."

That had been enough for Triggs.

Rankin couldn't do enough for Lonsdale.

"There are four people on board La Pintada beside Joseph Martin, the Canadian owner travelling on a Belizean passport. The Andersens, a New Zealand couple—by the way, he is the captain; a Canadian from Quebec called Osmani Seykely, who is the steward; and Layla Floren, a Norwegian woman. She is the mechanic."

"A woman mechanic?" Lonsdale was surprised. "She must be very good."

Rankin shrugged. "I wouldn't know." He handed Lonsdale a copy of the passenger manifest. "It's yours—just don't show it around."

"Thanks—I won't. I promise." An idea struck him. "Would you by any chance also know who's on board The Shark, a sportsfisherman from Jamaica?"

"Of course." It took Rankin a few seconds to find the manifest.

"Here—look for yourself. First off there's another Canadian, also from Quebec. What is this, a convention? His name is Sam Major. Then there is a fellow by the name of Hosni Alemani on a Belizean passport, and, finally, the owner of the boat, a Jamaican by the name of Ahmad Jabal."

On his way back to the apartment, Lonsdale tried to digest what he had learned.

To encounter such a diversity of nationalities was not particularly surprising in the Caribbean. That there should also be a preponderance of funny-sounding names was not out of the ordinary either.

What bothered Lonsdale was Layla Floren. He was sure he had heard the name before.

Preoccupied, he fired off an urgent request for information to his contacts at Langley, asking for an in-depth report on Layla and her colleague, the steward Norris.

Then he sat back to wait and see, his curiosity in overdrive.

Sunday afternoon, September 9

By one in the afternoon Lonsdale was antsy, to say the least. He left Gal at the apartment and drove Stirling and Cartwright to Brooks' dive shop.

"I want a close look at The Shark," he announced to the surprised Englishman who, having just finished a hasty lunch, was preparing to take a group of tourists parasailing on one of his boats.

"Come with us and I'll fly you past the boat if you wish."

"Could you fix it so that I can take a couple of pictures?"

"I can probably rig the halyards so you needn't hold on to them while flying." Brooks scratched his head, "but it'll be a bit tricky."

They rode out to The Wreck alongside the dive-boat with the tourists on board.

"I'll go up third," Lonsdale told Brooks who was fiddling with the spare parachute. Stirling was at the wheel. "We'll give a couple more tourists a turn, then it's you." He pointed to Cartwright. "I want you to fall out of your harness somehow and splash down as near The Shark as possible. Climb on board and we'll come and rescue you. That'll give us a chance to look around the place."

It took them very little time to get organized and by three Lonsdale had his pictures of The Shark and its occupants taken from above. Then came the difficult part: how to dump Cartwright in the right spot and then stage a rescue.

But Brooks had the answer: he rigged the harness of the parachute so that the rider could release the towline by yanking on a rope, which Cartwright did at the opportune moment, thereby releasing himself into a slow descent during which, using his SAS training, he guided himself into a gentle turn ending in a splash-down a few feet from The Shark's stern.

He hit the release button on his harness and, leaving the 'chute to float, swam over to the sportfisherman. Without asking for permission, he clambered on board, giving The Shark's three occupants—Selim, Hosni and Ahmad—no choice but to extend their hospitality to the uninvited guest while he waited to be picked up. Fishing the abandoned parasail out of the ocean took a good fifteen minutes, time enough for Cartwright to look around Jabal's boat.

Then Lonsdale and his team arrived with a case of softdrinks and beer, which they broke out among much laughter and horseplay, thanking their friends' "rescuers" over and over. They stumbled about the sportfisherman and, playing the oafish holidaymakers, took pictures of everything and everybody in sight.

During dinner back at the apartment they compared notes.

Gal was very much on his guard. "These guys on The Shark do not sound like friendlies."

"Would *you* be if a bunch of drunks invaded *your* boat?" Lonsdale retorted, misunderstanding Gal's use of the word friendlies.

"I guess not."

"Well, then."

Gal was fidgeting. "There's something strange about them." He dismissed his own paranoia. "But you know me, I'm always suspicious of Arabs."

"What makes you think they're Arabs?"

"Hosni is—for sure. The name is Egyptian or Arab."

Lonsdale glared at his friend and partner, but Gal persisted. "What about this fellow Major?"

"Speaks pretty damned good French with a French-Canadian accent and knows Montreal well." Lonsdale was glad to give something for Gal to chew on.

"Maybe he's an Algerian or Moroccan," Gal kept at it, "and that would make him an Arab, too"

"The one that sure as hell isn't one is the owner—this fellow Jabal."

"He's pure Jamaican." This from Brooks.

"But a Muslim." Gal would not let go.

"And so are the Rastafarians." Lonsdale was getting fed up. "Let's talk about the boat itself."

"Nicely built, fast and well maintained," was Brooks' evaluation. "She'll do twenty-five knots if push came to shove and I dare say she's faster than La Pintada in any event."

"What makes you say that?"

"Look at her lines, man, then look at La Pintada. One's a purebread racehorse, the other a cow."

CHAPTER FORTY

Monday morning, September 10

Lonsdale woke up to his inner voice's insistent whisper: *The Shark is faster than La Pintada*, it kept repeating.

At first he was unable to work out the subconscious message, but fifteen minutes into his daily jog along the beach he twigged: The way to capture Martin was to let him leave Cayman in La Pintada, then race after him in The Shark and make a citizen's arrest on the high seas outside Caymanian territorial waters. Captain Andersen, by law in charge of the yacht, was bound to assist in the arrest of a suspected murderer and fugitive from justice.

But how to get on board?

Easy—by feigning illness and asking if there were someone on La Pintada who could help.

And then?

Captain Andersen could be persuaded to head for Guantanamo Bay where Martin would be arrested, charged and flown back to the U.S. to face trial, a plan to which not even Gal—forever cautious about breaking the law—could object.

But what if Gal were right about The Shark's owner and his guests?

Money would not buy their cooperation and Lonsdale and his group would have to take over the Jamaican's boat by force. The legal consequences could be substantial.

After a quick shower, he called Dr. Massimo Giugliani, the head of the UN Mosquito Research Unit in Grand Cayman, and made an appointment to see him at ten.

"I want to hire your helicopter and its pilot for aerial photography," he said to the affable Italian. "Do you think you could accommodate such a request?"

"That depends." They were sipping espresso that Giugliani had just finished brewing.

"On what?"

"When, and how much?"

"Spoken like a true Florentine." Lonsdale smiled. Before visiting the Unit he had gained background information on the doctor from Brooks.

"Ah, so you know all about me."

"Dr. G., you're considered to be a remarkable character by the people who live here. Daredevil pilot, social lion, expert on wine, epicure, tyrant."

Giugliani was taken aback. "Tyrant?"

"Benevolent tyrant. They say it's thanks to you and your strong will that this Unit is still functioning, having survived several budget cuts. You are considered the heart and soul of this operation. You drive yourself hard and you expect those who work with you to do the same."

"You're too kind, Mr. Lonsdale." The doctor made a deprecating gesture and finished his coffee. "Let's get back to business."

They drove to the airport where Giugliani showed Lonsdale the Unit's helicopter, an old Huey modified to suit local needs.

"At first, we used to spray with a fixed wing aircraft."

"Which you flew yourself, I'm told."

"Correct." Giugliani was pleased to see Lonsdale had done his homework. "But as we got the little beasties' habitat contained, with help, of course, from the developers who continue to build on land reclaimed from the marshes, we found that high-speed sweeps over large surfaces were no longer required."

"So you bought a helicopter and fitted it with tanks, a pump and spraying nozzles, I see."

"Don't forget the pontoons."

"Which you fly yourself."

"Yes, I do."

"How often?"

"Oh, about once a week in the offseason—more often in September when the little creatures are laying their eggs."

"I saw you doing a flight yesterday, so I presume you're not expecting to go up again much before mid-week."

"Not before the end of the week. I'm just about out of spray."

Lonsdale gave a nod of understanding. "Tight budget, eh?"

The Italian laughed. "You can say that again."

Lonsdale decided to take the plunge. "I presume that with your spray tanks empty you could accommodate, in addition to the pilot, a passenger up front and perhaps two in the back."

"I would think so."

Lonsdale went for broke. "Here's the deal. I want you gassed up and ready to fly starting tomorrow morning at eight, on one hour's notice. I can't tell you how many of us there will be going with you, but figure there'd be me and one or two cameramen. I'll pay you a thousand dollars a day for standing by from eight in the morning until six at night, and five hundred dollars an hour for flying us."

"For how many days do you want me to stand by?"

"Not more than two—maybe three."

Giugliani smiled. "It's a deal, but you've got to pay me two thousand dollars in advance, nonrefundable."

"Agreed." They shook hands and Lonsdale gave the Italian two thousand dollars in cash.

"Here's my card and three telephone numbers. Remember, I can't fly after eight pm I hope that's not a problem."

"I shouldn't think so."

Giugliani dropped Lonsdale off at the apartment in time for lunch. No sooner had he and Gal sat down to eat than the telephone rang. It was Stirling. "Edwards visited the Butterfield Bank building this morning. He saw the manager for about an hour, then used a computer-equipped office, I assume to clear his e-mail."

"And to organize the package which he is to hand over to Martin on Monday, Tuesday or Wednesday," remarked Lonsdale.

"You think it's money, don't you?" This from Stirling. "I wonder how much?"

"North of eighty U.S.." Lonsdale didn't have to guess—he had seen an extract of Martin's bank account that clearly showed the periodic cash withdrawals the Canadian had effected during the last few months.

"What do you want me to do now?"

"Come home and have lunch."

Lonsdale hung up. He did not expect Martin to meet Davis before midafternoon.

Stirling arrived within the half-hour, followed by Cartwright who had been tailing Martin since daybreak. "Your friend Martin had breakfast, then went for a walk along the beach," he reported between bites of a ham and cheese sandwich.

Lonsdale was disappointed. "That's it?"

"Yup. He's back on board La Pintada. Brooks' dive boat is anchored near him. He reports Martin is in clear sight on deck, sunbathing."

"And the rest of the crew?"

"Going about their chores. They're setting up to serve lunch."

Lonsdale looked at Gal. "In the lap of luxury," he muttered more to himself than anyone else. "My guess is we're stuck here for the next three-four days without much happening."

"Bloody boring." Stirling finished his beer.

"There's one possible bit of excitement," Carthwright cut in. "Brooks told me over the walkie-talkie that he thinks we're not the only ones watching La Pintada."

Lonsdale's arm, holding the can of iced tea from which he was about to take a sip, froze in midair.

"Who else is?"

"The people on The Shark. Brooks says there's always someone on deck watching what Martin's up to."

"You guys sure?"

Cartwright shrugged. "Who knows?"

"I'm telling you," Gal said. "It's the Arabs."

"But why?" Lonsdale said more to himself than anyone else.

He had his answer sooner than he expected; his computer began to blink. "You have mail" it insisted—two e-mails from Langley. The first read: Latest message received by Target noon September 10, Monday reads as follows: quote, Achieved breakthrough. Have perfected vaccine against nv CJD. Suggest board meeting soonest. Signed Moscovitch unquote. Message originated Budapest law firm Baker Mackenzie sent to James Gray, VP Sales, Kyoto Veterinarian Pharmaceuticals, c/o Panama International Trust. Forwarded to Target by Eduardo Samos, CEO. End.

The second message sent chills up Lonsdale's spine and jolted him into what he described as his state of "red alert." The full name of the female mechanic on board La Pintada was Layla Bouchiki-Floren, with whose antecedents and political leanings Lonsdale was only too familiar. Gal's instincts had been dead on.

Moscovitch's partner, the Iraqi-trained Esad Delic, was also a Muslim, and like Layla, probably a fundamentalist. Delic must have found out somehow that it was Martin who owned half of Phylaxos, and Saddam's people were now trying to gain control of the company—perhaps by acquiring Martin's share.

Lonsdale swallowed nervously. These people did not "buy out"—they took what they wanted and killed whoever got in their way.

The reason for Layla Bouchiki's presence on board La Pintada became clear: She was the Iraqis' Trojan Horse.

Martin's days were numbered.

But what about The Shark? What was its role in the kabal?

Lonsdale was about to consult Gal, but Cartwright, who had been monitoring Edwards' calls in the next room, stuck his head through the door.

"Martin just called Edwards. Wants to meet him between three and three thirty. He said something about following the same routine as always, this time in the washroom off the lobby of the Holiday Inn."

Lonsdale looked at his watch. It showed one twelve pm

He had less than two hours to sort out his priorities and take whatever action he deemed to be necessary.

Monday noon, September 10

Mike Martin was at peace with the world: For once, everything was going his way.

He drew himself up in his chair on La Pintada's afterdeck, took a sip of his beer and looked at his watch—one thirty pm He had over an hour before his meeting with that crooked son of a bitch Edwards. It never occurred to him that he—heartless, selfish, scheming and murdering—was by far the bigger crook.

Mike had been elated at the news from Moscovitch. The discovery of the long-awaited vaccine would solve most of his problems. Assuming the damned thing would pass clinical trials within twelve months, it could be test-marketed by the end of the following year and sold in large commercial quantities the year after. Humankind would be safe from Creutzfeldt-Jakob's disease, and the Brits and the French could go back to breeding cattle to their heart's content.

And Phylaxos would become an enterprise profitable beyond belief.

He took a stab at estimating how much his million-plus dollar investment might be worth and figured he could sell his half of Phylaxos "as is" for about ten times what he had paid for it. Not that he intended to do so just yet. When its vaccine would hit the market the company's worth would skyrocket to at least a hundred million dollars.

There's many a slip twixt cup and lip he reminded himself as he tried to figure out how to get around the problem of having someone representing his interests attend the board meeting Moscovitch was requesting. Phylaxos was at a crucial stage of its development and the directors were likely to be asked to make important strategic decisions. A mistake now would set the company back years; in fact, it might cause it to lose its competitive advantage and its market share with it.

Was there anyone on the Board qualified enough to make such decisions? Moscovitch? A young scientist with no business experience. Delic? A totally unknown entity.

Mike sighed and got up. Time to get cleaned up for his meeting, and to decide what to do about his bent banker's larcenous intentions.

He had two choices: stay away and do nothing, or stop Edwards right now before he involved anyone else. Mike was comfortable with his estimate that there was enough gold and money on board La Pintada to last him a year and a half, barring unforeseen emergencies—a bit tight, should he have to wait eighteen full months to get the price he wanted for his Phylaxos shares. To be on the safe side before going to alternative number two, he needed to lay his hands on the couple of hundred thousand dollars Edwards was supposedly going to deliver at their meeting.

He adjusted the showerhead. He wanted to feel the strong spray of lukewarm water on his body after a couple of hours in the sun. He liked the cleaning sensation of the flow washing away the mixture of soap and suntan oil coating his skin. He laughed out loud as he watched the oily water drain; it seemed his problems were draining away with it. The decision about what to do with Edwards would not be made by him, but by Edwards himself.

If the banker stopped stealing, Mike would not move against him. If, however, the Welshman were to persist in his attempts at extortion, he would kill him.

* * * * *

Martin's first impression of Cayman's Holiday Inn was that the place needed refurbishing big time. Of course he didn't know that the building, erected in the early seventies, had never recovered from the decade of neglect in the eighties when the island's economy imploded as a result of a series of bank failures during which ten percent of the workforce lost its jobs, and the hotel's occupancy rate plunged.

Mike searched through the drab lobby, past the reception desk with its cracked formica top and peeling wallpaper behind it, and guests lounging about on shabby plastic furniture.

He turned right.

In the lounge he slid into one of the booths and ordered a soft drink. None of the dozen or so guests present displayed the slightest interest in him, nor could he spot anyone who looked out of place. He left his newspaper and drink on the table, strolled over to the cashier, paid his bill, then made a beeline for the men's room door opposite.

No one followed.

He extracted an "OUT OF ORDER" sign from his satchel, affixed it to the stall furthest from the door, then returned to the lounge to finish his drink.

At ten past three he entered the washroom again and saw Edwards' feet under the stall door.

"Stripes, are you there?" he called out softly as he put on his surgical gloves and locked the door behind him.

"I am," came the whispered answer. "What are your instructions?"

Mike slid a receipt for two hundred thousand dollars under the partition and watched a large manila envelope slither at him from Edwards' side. He ripped it open; it contained sixteen thick, letter-sized envelopes and a thin one.

He opened the thin one—he could hear that Edwards was getting ready to leave.

"I'll call you in fifteen minutes," he said quietly, in a voice devoid of emotion. The envelope in his hand held only one sheet of paper: A copy of the photograph Edwards had given him the last time. There was a message crudely pasted to its back "SOP FROM NOW ON: 20% OFF."

Mike checked the other envelopes. Each contained ten thousand dollars. The Welshman was proposing, as a standard operating procedure, to charge him a twenty percent delivery fee for bringing him his own money.

Martin sighed. Edwards had just signed his own death warrant.

Monday afternoon, September 10

"Martin's meeting with Edwards was very short—less than ten minutes," Brooks reported on his return from the Holiday Inn where he had been playing waiter at the hotel's lounge. "I got there a few minutes after two and convinced my friend, Larry the bartender, to let me take a turn at serving on tables."

"What did you tell him?"

"That I was trying out for a movie you were shooting here and that you were going to give me a walk-on role as a waiter."

"What's the catch?" Lonsdale knew how Brooks operated.

"I promised I'd bring you around later tonight to meet him." Brooks' grin stretched from ear to ear. "He expects to be hired as an extra."

"Let me hear the details." Lonsdale, infected by Brooks, was grinning, too.

"Martin came in around two thirty, ordered a soft drink, dawdled over it for about half an hour during which time he visited the men's room once." Brooks explained how he, and Dilbert, who was sitting in the hotel's lobby, kept a constant eye on Martin and Edwards.

"Dilbert saw Edwards come in with a manila envelope under his arm at three on the dot. He went straight to the men's room. I saw Martin follow him at three ten. Edwards came out at three eighteen and Martin at three twenty-one. Edwards didn't have the envelope when he left."

"And Martin?"

"He had a satchel hanging from his shoulder and must have stuck the money in it while in the toilet."

"So it is your opinion that Edwards delivered Martin's money to him as planned?"

"Yes."

"Did you follow them?"

"Martin and Edwards? Of course." Brooks bit into an apple. "Martin ducked into the Ramada Inn to make two local telephone calls, then visited the jewelry store in the hotel, after which the steward took him back to La Pintada."

"And Edwards?"

"Hightailed it back to his wife at the Hyatt."

It took Lonsdale some time to digest that. "He was in a hurry, was he?"

"Seemed to be."

Lonsdale turned to Gal.

"It's obvious. He was rushing home to take Martin's call, which we intercepted, and in which Martin asked Edwards to have breakfast with him at The Wharf tomorrow at eight." Gal's analysis seemed reasonable.

Lonsdale turned to Gal. "What time did you say Martin called Edwards?"

"At three thirty-five, more or less."

Lonsdale shook his head: The meeting did not make sense. Martin had his money and could now leave Cayman if he so wished, without having to resurface for more cash any time soon. Why did he want to see Edwards again the next day? *To kill him of course, you bloody fool* his inner voice said. Lonsdale shook his head again: No, that would be out of character. At breakfast Martin would give Edwards detailed instructions on where to shift the portfolio so that Edwards could no longer rip Martin off.

But why bother with a meeting with all its attendant risks? Why not arrange everything by e-mail, as in the past?

And didn't Brooks say Martin made *two* local calls? Other than Edwards whom else would Martin telephone on the island?

The more Lonsdale thought about the situation the louder his inner voice grew. *Tomorrow's the day, tomorrow's the end of the caper.*

He took a deep breath. "It's imperative we snatch Martin from his yacht, if at all possible when he has cleared Cayman territorial waters. Since I expect that La Pintada will leave Cayman tomorrow and since I don't propose to get caught with my pants down, here's what we'll do during the next twenty-four hours."

Gal started to protest, but Lonsdale silenced him with a brusque hand veto.

"Brooks, Dilbert and Reuven will keep The Shark and La Pintada under constant visual surveillance during the night, which means they'll have to stay on board Brooks' boat—the one with the cabin on it—and take turns at sleeping. Stirling and Cartwright will relieve them tomorrow morning at nine."

"That's pretty uncomfortable," Brooks objected.

"But necessary," Lonsdale cut him off sharply. He was going to add "Besides, that's what you get paid the big bucks for," but now was not the time for that type of a remark: He had to keep the men's morale high.

Nobody said a word.

"Cartwright will stay here for the time being to monitor communications and coordinate the movement of team members. Stirling will take up position at the Ramada Inn so that he can be put on Martin's tail should he decide to go somewhere during the night."

"What about Edwards?" Gal inquired.

"Good point, Reuven," Lonsdale conceded. "Instead of setting up at the Ramada Inn, Stirling will be at the Hyatt and keep an eye on our banker for us."

"What if he's already gone out?"

"We don't give a damn about what he does before he goes to bed tonight provided he doesn't go near Martin. And he's bound to come back to the hotel to sleep. You all have walkie-talkies and you know the phone number here. Use your brains and keep each other posted about developments on a regular basis."

"What do we do for firearms?" Stirling asked.

"I have a Walther PPK and a shotgun," Brooks volunteered.

Lonsdale spoke with authority. "I'll take the Walther and you keep the shotgun. Cartwright can pick it up after this meeting and bring it back to me here."

"And you?" Gal wanted to know the complete picture.

"I'm going to see Giugliani, the pilot, and put him on red alert. I want him to be ready to get me in the air any time after eight tomorrow morning."

"And in the meantime?"

"I'll stay here with Cartwright and go through the details of a number of scenarios I have in mind for tomorrow."

"You're convinced then that La Pintada will sail tomorrow?"

Lonsdale considered Gal's question with eyes closed for a full twenty seconds before answering. "Reuven, there's no sense in Martin hanging around here any longer. He's got his money and as soon as he's through meeting Edwards tomorrow morning, he'll be wanting to cut and run, and head for a safe haven—Costa Rica, Aruba, Cuba... who knows? A place where he could melt into the woodwork, and lay low while his Phylaxos shares increase in value to the point where he would be a very, very wealthy man."

"And then?"

"The shares he owns are bearer shares. It wouldn't be difficult to put them in play when he deems it worthwhile to do so."

"You mean sell them."

Lonsdale nodded. "But not if we catch him before he disappears," he added, and went into the other room.

Monday evening, September 10

At six Mike appeared on deck.

"I have a dinner date," he told his captain. "At seven I want Mani to run me over to the Ramada Inn. He can ferry me back around midnight."

"Or later." Andersen was happy his boss had a date—the first he'd been on since the New Zealander became his employee.

Mike winked. "I'll call you on the ship to shore when I'm ready to come back."

"What about tomorrow?"

"As I told you earlier, it's time to move on. This island is just too boring."

"Then we'll leave tomorrow as discussed?"

Mike nodded. "If the light's right between seven and eight I'd like to snap some pictures of Seven Mile Beach from seaward," he forced himself to sound very laid back, very casual, "then head for Cuba's Isle of Pines"

"They now call it *La Isla de la Juventud*," Andersen reminded Martin. "Today, youth rules Cuba."

"Quite—the Isle of Youth." Mike smiled. "Very appropriate and a couple of hundred miles northwest of here."

"A ten-hour sail."

Mike pretended to be thinking matters over. "If we left at eight we'd get there by six, wouldn't you say?"

"Six thirty at the latest—before sunset."

"That would be great. Shall we, then?"

"Leave at eight in the morning? Your wish, sir, is my command. I shall so inform your loyal crew." Andersen gave a mock bow that made Mike laugh, easing the tension within him.

He had prepared himself for what he had to accomplish that evening with meticulous care, reviewing half a dozen scenarios in detail, discarding all but the simplest. Then he selected one of the cigar-shaped, remote-controlled explosive devices he had bought in Panama, extracted it from its airtight Tueros wrapper, broke out a couple of batteries from a virgin pack, and tested them for full charge.

He fetched the remote and inserted a battery. Then he unscrewed the top of the explosive device, thereby separating the trigger from the detonator. He popped the second battery into the trigger mechanism, and armed it by twisting its top counterclockwise. The tiny green indicator light at the side of the mechanism winked on. He wrapped a small piece of duct tape around the top to conceal the light and to ensure the top would not get twisted back accidentally into the off position, and activated the remote by inserting and turning a small key in the hole provided for this purpose. This switched on the green stand-by light of the remote. Holding the trigger mechanism to his ear, he pressed the red "fire" button on the remote and heard a dry click.

The combo was working perfectly.

He disarmed the remote and screwed the detonator back in place.

In his bathroom, he aligned two tie-sills, three inches apart, on a piece of cardboard and, using fast-bonding, all-purpose glue, stuck them to the cylindrical explosive device.

At a quarter to seven, satisfied that the glue held, he threaded the thin end of each tie-sill through the eye at its other end, then adjusted the straps so they formed a cradle around the cylinder by which it could be hung.

At seven, satisfied with his handiwork, he placed his creation into his satchel with the tenderest of care and went on deck.

From the Ramada Inn Mike took a taxi to The Wharf. Lesley was already at the bar, chatting with Clemens, The Wharf's owner. She made the introductions and Mike ordered champagne. Clemens shared a glass with them then led the couple to the gazebo where they were served the best crayfish dinner Mike ever remembered eating.

Although he had steeled himself against what he had foreseen would be a difficult conversation, he was not ready for the flood of memories Lesley's innocent questions about his background triggered. To cover up, he began to speak about an imaginary family in which the wife had died a tragic death, and two teenaged children were being brought up by a thoughtful and caring father who—alas—was forced to be away from home on business too often.

Since his grief was genuine, he spoke with great sincerity, which impressed the recently divorced Lesley who also had teenaged children to care for.

When Mike ordered coffee at the end of their meal Lesley excused herself. Mike sent his waiter in search of a good cigar and reached into the satchel lying at his feet. He extracted the explosive device and affixed it to the release handle of one of the clips holding the table top in place. He was in the process of tightening the tie-sills when Lesley arrived.

"What on earth are you doing under the table?"

"Looking for a little package I seem to have misplaced." Mike produced a small box that he handed to Lesley with a flourish. "I brought you a memento of our meeting," he added with self-deprecating modesty.

It was an exquisite set of crafted gold earrings, which Mike had purchased at the Ramada Inn Shopping Arcade that afternoon for the very purpose of justifying, if need be, his rummaging around under the table.

Lesley was touched.

"Where shall we go now?" Mike asked.

"How about a turn on the dance floor at the Wreck of the Seven Sails?"

"Where's that?"

"At the Holiday Inn."

Mike paid the bill and they went dancing, but his heart was not in it. He kept worrying about the device. Had he managed to place it in a position most likely to inflict the maximum damage to his traitorous banker's genitalia?

But what if the waiters decided to change tabletops?

What if Edwards did not turn up?

Had this gamble been worth taking?

Try as he would, he couldn't concentrate on the present.

Lesley soon picked up on the negative vibes and, a few minutes before midnight, suggested they call it a day. "I'm a working girl after all," she observed with a smile, "and I have to be in the store early."

Mike protested, but she would have none of it, afraid that if she yielded she would also yield to temptation and ask that he spend the night with her. "Let's not spoil the very nice time we had together by overcomplicating things. Maybe when you come back some day you'll look me up again." Relieved, he walked her to the parking lot where she gave him a light kiss before getting into her car. "Look after yourself and don't forget to call when you come by here again."

Mike was in his cabin by one am and glad of it. He still had lots to do before going to bed.

He was not the only one up late that night.

Lonsdale had spent an hour with Giugliani at dinnertime, setting things up for the next morning. During his drive back home he had developed a splitting headache that, he knew from past experience, was a harbinger either of coming down with a cold or having to risk his life in the line of duty.

But what duty?

A private citizen, and an entrepreneur no longer in the employ of either a national government or a group of governments, he was responsible for his actions only to himself and to his partner. Why the pressure to place himself at risk? What reason was there for constant self-inflicted stress? He and Gal were calling the shots and they could disengage any time they felt that going the distance was too rough.

The news Cartwright gave him when he arrived at the apartment only increased his apprehension.

Apparently, Martin had gone out on a date and was dining at The Wharf.

"And Edwards?"

"Having dinner at his hotel and being watched by one of the men from The Shark."

"WHAT?"

"Gal saw a man leaving The Shark and told Stirling to follow him. Stirling, who checked in with me at seven thirty, says the bugger's been sitting in the Hyatt parking lot since dusk."

That did it for Lonsdale; the coincidences had become too pointed. There was no choice—it was time to call Jim Morton.

Monday, midnight, September 10

Though the hour was late, Lonsdale knew Morton never went to bed before midnight, so he called Morton's home in Chevy Chase.

The answering machine clicked on. Morton was unavailable.

Lonsdale took a deep breath and dialed the special number of the CIA's Counter-terrorism Division. He asked for the Liquor Merchant, Morton's *sobriquet*.

"Who wants him?" asked a hostile voice.

"Snowman. Tell him this is a Code A1A call."

"Please hold."

After a pause the voice was back. "He will call you back within the half-hour. What's your number?"

"It's an open line," Lonsdale said, gave his number and hung up, mystified. From the rapidity of the reply he deduced that Morton was in the office. What was important enough to keep him at Langley—at midnight on a Monday?

Morton returned the call within fifteen minutes. "I know where you are. Go to police headquarters right now and ask for the highest-ranking officer on duty. He'll have already received instructions."

"What name do I use?"

"My code name." Morton hung up.

At Police Headquarters, located in George Town's tallest building, The Glass House, as the Cayman Government Administration Building is known, a young policeman led Lonsdale to the governor's office where an obviously annoyed functionary was waiting for him.

"I am Major Mackenzie, the Governor's aide." The man's tone was barely civil. "What is your name?"

"The Liquor Merchant."

Mackenzie acknowledged the information with a wry smile. "I am instructed to arrange for a call on our scrambler phone to a number in the United States which you possess."

Lonsdale nodded and was led to a small, well-ventilated cubicle with a table and two armchairs, just off the Governor's private office. Mackenzie picked up the red telephone on the table, inserted a key then turned to Lonsdale. "May I have the number?"

Morton was on the line within seconds.

"What can I do for you, my friend?" The scrambler distorted his voice almost beyond recognition.

It took Lonsdale fifteen minutes to brief Morton on the Martin case and to outline his concerns about Layla Bouchiki-Floren. "I am also worried about the presence here of three men on board a sportfisherman called The Shark."

"I have the e-mail you sent after you attempted to contact me earlier. We're trying to get detailed information on them, but it'll take time. All three seem to have passports that are legitimate, at least at first blush."

Lonsdale looked at his watch: He had sent the request for information less than an hour ago. Why was Morton—busy in the extreme (why else would he be in the office past midnight?)—giving top priority to his informal query? Sure, they were friends, but work always came before everything else. Lonsdale's antennae were up and twitching; all was far from well in Morton's kingdom.

"As you must suspect," Morton continued, sounding harassed, "I have been monitoring the information requests you've made during these past few months. With what you have told me now I have a clearer picture of your situation."

"You then understand why I had to call you."

"I assume to pressure me into giving you information on the men on board The Shark before your precious pigeon, Mr. Martin, flies the coop."

"Dead on. So how about it?"

"I'll do my best, but we might not be able to help you at all with anything during the next week or so, unless it involves Islamic fundamentalists."

"My situation very well might."

"That's the reason I returned your call."

"Should I know more?" Lonsdale's antennae were quiverring.

"Our information indicates that something very big is going to happen in mid-September probably involving Al Qaeda cells. I presume Osama bin Laden's name is well-known at NATO."

"It is, but my information is probably out of date." Lonsdale was cursing under his breath. Morton was not being especially helpful. "Do you think my situation down here might involve Al Qaeda as well?"

"Hard to say. Looks to me like a pure Saddam play. He may be after the nv Creutzfeldt Jakobs contaminated virus and its vaccine, because he's got a thing for biological weapons of mass destruction." Morton sounded quite sure of himself. "My guess is Bouchiki-Floren will try to steal Martin's Phylaxos shares. By the way, she's an expert safecracker."

"And the boys aboard The Shark?"

"Probably a backup team, but just as likely a coincidence. Even though…Who knows?"

Lonsdale thanked Morton, said goodnight and hung up shaken to the core.

His friend and colleague for over twenty-five years knew full well that Lonsdale did not believe in coincidences—ever.

So Morton was covering up something, but what, for God's sake?

CHAPTER FORTY-ONE

Tuesday dawn, September 11

Selim was aware La Pintada would be leaving Cayman at eight in the morning because Layla had briefed him about Martin's timetable.

Selim also knew that the meeting with Edwards had been a success; Layla had confirmed, after peeking into Martin's safe, that the money in it had increased by about a hundred and fifty thousand dollars.

This had simplified Selim's life a great deal; he could move against Martin at any time without having to snatch Edwards.

The initial plan had been simple: Allow La Pintada to sail for Cuba and chase after her a quarter of an hour later. Since The Shark was capable of five knots more than La Pintada's maximum speed of twenty, Selim figured he'd catch her in about an hour. By then both yachts would be outside Cayman territorial waters where he could either trick Martin into allowing him to board or force the issue with help from Layla and Mani.

On further reflection, however, he modified his plan because he did not like the odds. Martin, his captain and Mrs. Andersen made three, Layla and Mani only two. Since someone had to man the bridge at all times, Selim could foresee complications, so he opted, instead, to sneak on board La Pintada under cover of darkness with the help of his two accomplices already on the vessel.

At a quarter to five, Selim and Hosni set out in The Shark's painter to cross the hundred yards of water separating the two yachts, but the trip took longer than expected because they were rowing with oar blades wrapped in burlap to deaden the noise. Mani, who was expecting them at five, was forced to spend a quarter hour squatting on La Pintada's swimming platform, gaff at the ready, to fend off Selim's little boat before it bumped the yacht and woke everyone.

Sitting in the bow of the painter, and scanning his surroundings with a nervous eye, Selim cursed Hosni under his breath for rowing too slowly, the moon for ducking in and out of the clouds at the most inopportune moments, and the wind that kept increasing in strength as dawn approached, thereby making the hard-working Hosni's life even more miserable.

They got within gaffing distance by a quarter past five. Selim caught the shaft deftly with his right hand and threw his gunny sack containing his running shoes, sweater, pistol and other gear to Mani. Then he pulled the painter alongside the swimming platform, and stepped on board La Pintada. His bare left foot made no sound on the wet wood. With his right he kicked the painter back toward The Shark, allowing Hosni to row away without fear of hitting the bigger boat.

With teeth chattering, but without uttering a word, Selim followed Mani to the starboard companionway leading to the guest staterooms below. He was shown into the largest of the three rooms, located dead amidships, equidistant from the crew's quarters fore and the master stateroom aft.

Selim took off his windbreaker, pulled on a sweater and exchanged his soaking wet slacks for dry ones. He hung his wet clothes in the bathroom, locked the door, got into the empty bathtub and placed the gunnysack under his head.

He looked at his watch. It showed a few minutes past six am. He had almost two hours to get warm and dry and rested—perhaps even to sleep.

It was a moment to be savored. Three more hours and he would have Martin in his power. After that, in quick succession, he would lay his hands on Martin's money and the Phylaxos shares.

Ah, Phylaxos! The last communication from Delic by coded e-mail indicated that the batch of contaminated glue destined for Iraq was scheduled to reach Baghdad before the fifteenth of the month, and that—victory at last—Moscovith had found a way to manufacture a vaccine to neutralize the new disease Selim and his colleagues were about to unleash upon the Jews and the Crusaders.

May Allah be praised, no need to fear for the safety of Selim's brethren worldwide—the true believers would be spared.

In his reply to Delic he instructed the Bosnian to proceed at speed with the testing and subsequent production in commercial quantities of the vaccine, promising to wire whatever money Phylaxos needed for this purpose within seventy-two hours—it would be Martin's money, of course.

Selim concurred with Behna that the owner of La Pintada was none other than the CEO of Plasmalab, believed to be dead but, in fact, very much alive, masquerading as a man with a similar name. His disappearance would go unnoticed since, as far as the world was concerned, he no longer existed anyway. Therefore, Selim felt he could safely scuttle La Pintada with Martin on board as soon as The Shark caught up with them. Then he, Mani and Layla would join Hosni and Jabal on board the sportfisherman and head for Jamaica.

From Jamaica Mani and Layla would work their way to Cuba and from there to wherever the Cause needed them. Selim and Hosni would return to Panama.

This left the Andersens. They would have to be killed, of course. Collateral damage was unavoidable in times of war.

Footsteps above his head woke him with a start. By the light streaming through the tiny porthole his watch showed seven thirty. His ninety-minute nap had refreshed him and made him fit again for action.

The bathtub began to vibrate; Captain Andersen must be getting ready to head out. The noise of the engines increased and Selim felt the vessel move forward as it came up on its anchor. Then a soft easing and La Pintada began to move northeast—*shoreward*. This panicked Selim, but he forced himself to reason with logic: Martin must be taking a last look at the famous Seven Mile Beach before leaving Cayman.

He stepped out of the tub, put on socks and shoes, took off his sweater, slipped on his windbreaker and stuck his thirty-two caliber Beretta in his pocket.

Through the lone porthole to starboard he could see the buildings on the beach pass by one after the other. Then the yacht slowed and went into a lazy turn southward, proving that his guess had been right: La Pintada would hug the beach until it reached George Town Harbor then head out to sea.

Selim unlocked the bathroom door and went into the adjoining stateroom, which occupied the entire width of La Pintada amidships, with portholes to starboard as well as to port.

The vessel was slowing down as she approached the inlet where The Wharf Restaurant was located. She began a turn westward and when her bow pointed due north again Selim heard the engines increase their revolutions.

He breathed a great sigh of relief—Layla's information had been right on the money, as always.

The time, by his watch, was seven minutes past eight.

Tuesday early morning, September 11

Lonsdale was dreaming. He was snuggled into Adys' welcoming arms in the huge luxury bed in their Washington apartment. With her take-charge mouth she was muzzling the nape of his neck hungrily.

He awoke to find Cartwright tapping his upper left shoulder with the telephone. "Gal wants to talk to you. It's six thirty."

Gal sounded exhausted. "As agreed, Brooks, Dilbert and I slept on board Brooks' cabin cruiser. We took turns at watching. At a quarter to five I detected movement on board The Shark through my night-vision goggles. Two men got into their little boat—you know which one I mean."

"The Shark's painter," Lonsdale blurted. The adrenaline invading his body made it difficult to speak.

"That's it, the painter. They rowed over to La Pintada. Took them close to half an hour. I don't know why."

"Was there a wind? Were the seas rough?"

"No. Actually the sea was calm, but the wind was beginning to pick up."

Lonsdale's brain switched to field-action mode. "They must have wrapped their oar blades in rags to cut down the noise."

"You may be right. The one rowing seemed to be struggling a lot on the way there and back."

"They came back?" Lonsdale found that hard to believe.

"Just one of them—the slimmer one. The other stayed."

Lonsdale started issuing orders without delay. "Get in touch with Stirling at the Ramada Inn and tell him you'll pick him up at Brooks' dive shop within the quarter hour. You'll take him back to Brooks' cabin cruiser where you are all to stand by until you hear from me on the walkie-talkie."

"For how long?"

"Until after eight anyway."

"And then?"

"Hold on Reuven," Lonsdale snapped. He had a thousand things on his mind. "Cartwright will go over to the Hyatt to babysit Edwards until the bastard leaves for his breakfast meeting with Martin at The Wharf. He is to follow him and watch what the two do together and for how long." Lonsdale glanced at Cartwright who nodded.

Lonsdale looked at his watch and turned back to the phone. "I'll stay here until seven, then pick up Giugliani and take him to the helicopter."

"Which means that our communication center will be unmanned from seven fifteen onward," Gal, who was a very experienced field commander, did not like the arrangement.

"All the team will be together except for me."

"And Cartwright."

"Who will join me at the helicopter as soon as the Edwards-Martin meeting is over. To avoid confusion we'll use three walkie-talkies. You'll be Capo, I'll be Tony, and Cartwright—our floater—will be Sport. Is that understood?" Beside him, Cartwright nodded again.

"I'm Capo, you're Tony and Cartwright is Sport," Gal repeated from his end.

"I want everybody to check in on the circuit on the quarter-hour."

"First check-in at seven fifteen and every fifteen minutes thereafter." Gal wanted things crystal clear.

"Correct. Final point. We now have a golden opportunity to take over The Shark without difficulty since we have numerical superiority."

"Three of us on Brooks' boat—"

"Plus Dilbert."

"I wasn't going to use him," Gal objected.

"He can drive the boat."

"That he can," Gal acquiesced.

"Right. Get ready then to board The Shark when I give the word."

Lonsdale hung up.

By the seven thirty check-in everyone was on station, and Gal reported that La Pintada was heading shoreward.

This surprised Lonsdale. "Say again?"

"I repeat—heading shoreward. No, wait, she's turning south."

"What about The Shark?"

"No movement."

"Her engines?"

"Not running."

At a quarter-to-eight Cartwright reported he was following Edwards on his way to The Wharf.

At eight sharp Cartwright confirmed that Edwards had arrived at the restaurant and was being shown to his table. Gal cut in to advise that The Shark had started its engines.

"Where's La Pintada?" Lonsdale wanted to know.

"Just coming to the Wharf's inlet."

"Is Martin still on board?"

"Yes, I can see him clearly on deck. He's taking photos."

"Not getting ready to meet Edwards?"

"No, La Pintada is beginning to turn away from the shore."

"Say again?"

"Repeat, away from the shore. I can hear the engine revs being increased."

Lonsdale made a split second decision that was to save his life later in the day. "Board The Shark without delay and confirm takeover ASAP. Hurry before she starts chasing La Pintada."

* * * * *

By eight am Mike, who had appeared on deck half an hour earlier with camera in hand, had taken a couple of dozen pictures of the landscape with trembling hands as he fought his nerves.

Through the powerful telephoto lens of his camera trained on The Wharf's gazebo he could clearly see Edwards, already at their table, lifting his head to look straight into the camera.

Mike swallowed hard and resisted the urge to snap the picture. Instead, he tried to estimate the distance from his target—less than two hundred meters for sure, well within range. He turned toward his captain standing at the upper pilothouse controls half a dozen steps away. "Let's go," he ordered. Andersen began to swing La Pintada around and pushed the throttles forward to increase the vessel's speed.

Mike, who had armed the remote detonator before coming on deck, gingerly felt for the fire button on the device now in his windbreaker's pocket, and pressed it. Then he walked over to Andersen. "We should have a beautiful day for our sail," he said, pretending to be scanning the horizon ahead, while counting backward from twenty: The detonator on the explosive device at The Wharf had a twenty-second delay built into it.

"Another boring day in Paradise," Andersen chuckled.

The sound of the explosion—not much more than a very loud bang—wafted across the water to La Pintada just as Andersen brought the yacht to its cruising speed.

"What the hell was that?" They both spun around, Mike feigning surprise. A pall of smoke hung over The Wharf, where people were running around willy-nilly. Andersen grabbed his binoculars and Mike his camera.

Through the telephoto lens Mike could see the scene in detail. The gazebo had disappeared, and so had Edwards.

"Must have been a propane gas tank," Andersen muttered and turned to face for'ard. "They're a big, bloody danger."

Tuesday morning, September 11

Cartwright was on the walkie-talkie. "This is Sport. There's been an explosion at The Wharf. Edwards might be dead."

Lonsdale was so shocked he had difficulty marshalling his thoughts. "This is Tony. Where's Mike?"

"This is Sport. He never showed. Must be on board his boat."

"Can you see the boat?"

"She's heading out to sea."

"This is Tony, Sport. Join me at the chopper as soon as you can."

"This is Sport. On my way."

"Tony here. What's your status, Capo?"

"Capo reporting. Our target has its engines running, but has not weighed anchor. We're on our way over there now."

"Capo, this is Tony. Where's Mike?"

"Capo here. Last time I saw him he was on deck, standing next to his captain. His boat is moving at, I would guess, top speed."

"What about the night visitor, Capo?"

"Never returned to his boat."

Lonsdale looked at his watch. The time was ten minutes past eight. He turned to Giugliani some distance away. The Italian was in the midst of his walk-around, checking that his helicopter's major visible features were functional. "My assistant is on his way here," Lonsdale shouted. "Do you think we'll be able to get airborne within fifteen minutes?"

"Should be no problem." Giugliani got into the 'copter.

By the time Cartwright appeared, the pilot had completed his pre-flight check and filed his flight plan with the control tower: a half-hour sweep up and down Seven Mile Beach.

"Capo reports he has control of The Shark," Cartwright yelled into Lonsdale's ear. He took his place behind Giugliani and fastened his seat belt. "Wants to know what you want him to do."

Lonsdale climbed into the seat beside the pilot and whipped out his walkie-talkie. "Capo, this is Tony. Do you read?"

"Barely. There's a lot of background noise."

"It's the chopper. Start following Martin, I repeat, start following Martin." Lonsdale screamed, "Acknowledge!"

"I am to follow Martin."

Lonsdale could barely make out the words. "I roger that," he shouted. "We're taking off." He turned to Giugliani and gave the pilot the thumbs up. Then he put on the mike-earphone combo Giugliani handed him and, after turning off his walkie-talkie, put it in his pocket.

They took off at about the same time American Airlines Flight 11, piloted by Mohamed Atta, slammed into the South Tower of the World Trade Center, two thousand kilometers to the north.

*****

Layla rapped four times—one long, two short and one long, then whispered, "It's Layla." Selim opened the door.

She slid into the room. "Martin is in the pilothouse with the Captain. Mrs. Andersen is in the galley, getting ready to serve breakfast. Mani is helping her."

Selim looked at his watch. "I estimate we're about five miles north of the Cayman Islands."

Layla nodded. "Probably. We've been under way for forty minutes. That's time enough to cover ten miles or even more."

"Do you have a weapon?"

"Mani and I each have Berettas. And you?"

Selim showed her his own Beretta. "All right then. You and Mani seize Mrs. Andersen and bring her here. After that, Mani is to get Martin and bring him here, too. I'll take it from there."

"When do we start?"

Selim looked at his watch. "At eight forty-five. Let's synchronize. It will be eight forty on my mark."

Layla left to fetch Mani.

At a quarter to nine on the dot Mani and Layla entered the galley. Cathy Andersen was readying the breakfast tray she had prepared for Mike Martin.

"Let me help you with that." Mani stepped up to the counter next to her. Layla did the same on the other side.

"Look," Layla cried out in disgust and pointed into the sink. "We have cockroaches."

Cathy Andersen turned her back to Mani who slapped a chloroform-soaked cloth on her nose and mouth and held it there until the woman lost consciousness. He and Layla then carried her down to Selim's stateroom where her wrists were manacled behind her back and her mouth taped.

For good measure, Selim locked her in the bathroom.

At nine am Mani appeared in the pilothouse. "Excuse me, Mr. Martin," he said to Mike who was chatting with the captain. "Mrs. Andersen needs your opinion about what to do with the pictures in the main guest stateroom which seem to have fallen off the walls when we got underway this morning."

"Did they break?"

"I'm afraid so—most of them."

Mike left with Mani.

"Tell Mrs. Andersen to hurry up with my breakfast," Andersen called after them. "I'm starving."

Mani fiddled with the stateroom door before entering to give Selim time to hide in the bathroom and Layla to take up her position. When Mike entered he found Layla standing to port of the large bed, her pistol leveled at his face. "Raise your hands slowly," she commanded, "then stand still."

Mike, flabbergasted, obeyed. Mani threw a black hood over his head then, using flex-cuffs, manacled his wrists together in front of him.

"What the hell do you think you're doing," Mike shouted and took a step toward Layla.

Mani tapped him in the solar plexus. "Sit down Mr. Martin, *please.*"

Mike, in shock and somewhat winded, collapsed into an armchair.

Selim came out of the bathroom and sat on the bed opposite Mike.

"Layla, please join Captain Andersen and keep an eye on him. Mani will follow you shortly."

"Who the bloody hell are you?" bellowed Mike. "And what are you doing on my yacht?"

"Keep your voice down, Mr. Martin, unless you want me to hit you again," Mani ordered.

Selim cut in. "That's enough, Mani. Go see how Layla is faring." He turned to Mike. "I have looked forward for a long time to meeting you," he told the stunned Canadian. "Please sit up and take a couple of deep breaths. You'll feel more comfortable that way."

Mike was terrified. He could not get over Mani and Layla being in cahoots with the man facing him who had materialized on his yacht out of nowhere. Summoning all the courage he could muster he put on a show of strength. "Who are you and what do you want?" he barked.

Selim smiled. "Take it easy, Mr. Martin, and don't rush me. We have plenty of time since we're not due on the Isle of Youth until after six this evening."

"So your accomplices have told you of my plans."

"They've told me a great deal more."

"Such as?"

"That you're wealthy, clever, a fugitive from justice, probably a murderer and that the world thinks that you're dead."

Mike was speechless. "What's your name anyway?" he asked, playing for time.

"Call me Med."

"What's that short for?" Mike was no fool.

"Mohammed if you must know."

Mike blanched: He was beginning to put two and two together. This man was no ordinary bandit, no common criminal. "Let me ask again. What do you want?"

Selim shook his head in disapproval. "Why be in a hurry to hear the bad news? Why not enjoy the day to the best of your ability?"

"How can I possibly do that in the situation I'm in?"

"I see you don't deny my allegations," Selim continued in a conversational tone. "Therefore, I assume that I must have figured accurately."

"About what? That I am a murderer?" Mike thought about Keller and Edwards and couldn't stop himself from laughing out loud; he was near hysterical. He'd been so busy worrying about the authorities that he hadn't bothered to check out his own entourage in depth.

But, then, he had relied on Behna for that. Behna: another Arab-sounding name. And Mani—was he an Arab, too? Mike was beginning to realize that he may have surrounded himself with a group of Islamic radicals by pure accident.

Selim was about to reply when Layla burst through the door. "Come quickly; there's a helicopter following us."

Selim bounced out of the room, locked the door, sprinted up the companionway and up the steps to the upper steering station. He saw that the chopper—as far as he could tell a pontoon-equipped Huey—was closing fast. Both the pilot's and the copilot's faces were already discernible. Selim looked for markings and armament. There seemed to be none of the latter; as for the former, they stood out larger than life: UN Mosquito Research Unit GCA, in bold, high-visibility, yellow letters.

What in hell's name was going on? Why was the chopper this far from land?

The aircraft was almost on top of them. As it began to descend Selim realized it intended to land on La Pintada.

He screamed for Mani. "Come out here and cover me."

In the pilothouse, Layla drew her pistol and held it to the captain's head. "Easy does it Mr. Andersen. Hold steady on your course and pay no attention to what's going on around you."

Disoriented, the New Zealander assumed the chopper was attempting to land a party of hijackers. He started evasive maneuvers, steering hard to port, then to starboard, attempting to give the helicopter the slip.

Layla cocked her pistol. "One more move like that and you're dead." Andersen turned to face Layla and froze. The look of implacable hatred in her eyes shook him to the core. He realized he must be dealing with some kind of a fanatic and that he had two choices: obey, or die.

He chose to obey.

As soon as Mike heard Selim lock the door from the outside he tore off the hood covering his head and engaged the safety latch on the cabin's door. Then he unlocked the bathroom and went in search of some sharp object with which to cut the flex-cuffs manacling his wrists together. He tripped and almost fell over the semiconscious, terrified wife of his captain.

Cautioning her to keep quiet he removed the tape from her mouth. "Are you able to stand?"

She nodded. "I could if my hands weren't tied behind my back."

"Where can I find a knife or scissors?"

"Bottom drawer under the sink. I keep my sewing kit in this bathroom."

Mike had her scissors out in no time flat, and set her free. She reciprocated.

"Is there another way out of here besides going through the cabin?"

She nodded. "The panel behind the tub swings down to give access to the engine room and the escape hatch."

It was obvious what she meant. Above the tub, about three inches from the ceiling, there were four hexagonal holes in the wall.

"Where is the key to open the panel?"

"Under the sink, next to the life vests and emergency pack."

Mike folded the panel down and was about to climb into the space behind it when a mighty blow struck La Pintada from above, making it buck, throwing Mike and Cathy to the ground.

No sooner had they picked themselves up than they heard small arms fire from topside.

"How can I get back to my cabin quickest without going on deck?" Mike wanted to get to his shotguns as fast as he could.

"Across the engine room. With the key you're holding we can open the emergency panel in the bulkhead separating the engine room from the aft companionway."

"Where's the panel located?"

"Between the two generators."

"And where do I come out?"

"At the foot of the aft companionway, directly opposite your cabin door." Mike dashed back to the cabin and shouted for Cathy to follow him.

"We'll push whatever furniture we can against the door."

Cathy stopped him. "You can't. It's bolted down."

They ran back to the bathroom and climbed over the panel just as Layla shot out the lock of the guest stateroom door.

Tuesday morning (cont'd)

After takeoff Lonsdale asked Giugliani to head toward the northern tip of Grand Cayman.

"My idea is to continue straight out to sea in a northerly direction then turn left, describe a lazy circle, head toward land and fly along the beach at an altitude of a hundred feet, about two hundred feet seaward."

Giugliani laughed. "We can do that as long as we don't venture too far from dry land."

"Why not? We're pontoon-equipped."

"I'm superstitious I guess."

"What model of Huey is this anyway?"

"A Bell UH-1B."

"Then it has a range of about two hundred and eighty miles and a maximum speed of about a hundred and forty mph, if I remember correctly. We can risk a ten minute jaunt over the water."

"The max speed of this specimen is only one hundred and twenty."

"Because of the pontoons."

Giugliani looked at Lonsdale with renewed interest. "Have you ever flown one? You seem to know a hell of a lot about them."

Lonsdale shook his head. "Never piloted one, but flew *in* many."

"Where?"

Lonsdale did not like answering questions about his past. "South America," he said, in a tone that clearly indicated "no further questions."

They were over the sea, north of the island: It was time to start searching the waters below for a sign of La Pintada.

She was not difficult to spot from their altitude, sailing northward about four miles dead ahead. Lonsdale turned to the pilot and pointed. "That's La Pintada, a friend's yacht. I'd love to take a closer look."

Giugliani obliged: Within a couple of minutes they were almost on top of her.

"Look, you could land the chopper on the roof of her afterdeck."

The pilot shook his head. "It would be a bit tight, even if she were stationary; at sea I'd say it would be impossible."

"Even if your life depended on it?" Lonsdale gave the Italian a mischievous smile.

Giugliani smiled back, but he was no longer sure of himself. He could not decide whether Lonsdale was kidding or being serious. "In such situations almost nothing is impossible," he replied.

Lonsdale took his pistol from his pocket.

"Dr. Giugliani," he said, "I'm afraid I have to tell you that, although your life sure does not depend on it, mine might." He leveled the weapon at the pilot. "I would very much appreciate your trying to get close enough to that damned roof so I can jump onto it from one of your pontoons. Don't misunderstand. I don't intend to use my gun on you." He put the weapon away. "It's purely for self-defense."

Giugliani was white as a sheet.

"What on earth do you mean, Jesus Christ?"

"I work for the Canadian Passport Office." Lonsdale thrust a copy of Svoboda's letter at the disconcerted man. "Down there on that yacht," he continued, "there's a man by the name of Michael Martin, traveling on a false Canadian passport. He is a fugitive from justice and a suspect in a Florida murder case. Somehow I need to apprehend him on the high seas—outside Cayman territorial waters."

Giugliani was hovering above La Pintada, scanning Svoboda's letter.

"This is most unusual, most unusual." The blood had returned to his face. "Are you telling me you want to make a citizen's arrest on the high seas after boarding a vessel out of the blue all by yourself? Or will your assistant be going with you? I assume he also works for the Canadian government?"

"He works for CSIS," Lonsdale lied. "The Canadian Security Intelligence Service. But no, he won't be coming with me."

The intrigue and excitement was almost too much for Giugliani. "Aren't you afraid to try this thing by yourself? What happens if this fellow kills you and has you thrown overboard? The law would be on his side. He could claim you were attempting to hijack his yacht."

"His captain and the rest of the crew would side with me," Lonsdale continued to lie.

The Italian made up his mind. "I might as well give it one try. If I fail we'll head home and I'll let you explain to the Royal Cayman Islands Police what you were doing with a loaded gun on board my machine."

"Fair enough. By the way, doctor, there is a twenty thousand dollar reward for bringing this man in. We can split it fifty-fifty."

That did the trick. The pilot knew he was holding all the cards. Lonsdale couldn't fly the chopper; and once they were back on the island Giugliani's status and reputation in Cayman guaranteed that his word would always be preferred over the American's. So why not take the gamble?

They shook hands on it and Lonsdale placed his binoculars and camera on the floor then handed his pistol to Cartwright. Next, bellowing at the top of his voice, he explained to the SAS man what he intended to do.

"We'll try a high-speed approach," the pilot interrupted. "I'll come in fast from starboard, low over the water—about ten feet—and go up a little to skim over the yacht. You'll have to jump at the right moment."

Lonsdale edged back next to Cartwright. "Since Giugliani is sitting in the port seat, the chopper will shield him from gunfire. I'll climb out on the port pontoon during our approach. Should anyone fire at us, shoot back, but try not to kill Martin."

Giugliani looked around and Lonsdale gave him the thumbs up. Cartwright lay down facing starboard, his arms extended, ready to give covering fire. Lonsdale waited for the pilot to finish positioning himself for his approach. When Giugliani banked the chopper toward La Pintada, he began to inch his way onto the pontoon.

It seemed to Lonsdale the chopper would hit the swells at any moment as it sank toward the waves. La Pintada loomed ever larger. They were over the vessel now and it rose toward them on a swell. Lonsdale rolled off the pontoon and onto the roof of La Pintada's saloon just as Mani opened fire from the upper steering station.

Cartwright fired back. One of his shots hit Mani who dropped his Beretta. It slid along the roof and clattered onto the afterdeck. Giugliani watched Lonsdale slither down the steps leading from the roof to the afterdeck, then banked away.

Lonsdale picked up Mani's pistol and raced down the aft companionway just as Cathy and Mike emerged into the space at the foot of it.

Mike tore open the door to his cabin and the three of them tumbled in. Lonsdale locked the door, then spun around, weapon raised. Mike, whom Lonsdale recognized as soon as he laid eyes on him, was unlocking the cabinet holding the shotgun and ammunition. Cathy, whom Lonsdale had identified by the process of elimination as being Mrs. Andersen (because she was *not* Layla Bouchiki), was helping him.

Lonsdale checked Mani's weapon—a Beretta. It had four shots left in the magazine and one up the spout. Before he could say or do anything someone knocked on the cabin door. It wouldn't give. A shot rang out and the door's lock shattered. The door, which opened outward, swung open as Lonsdale fired three shots through it. The last hit Layla in the lung, missing her heart by inches. She collapsed in a heap at the foot of the companionway.

Lonsdale retrieved her weapon—it had five bullets left in it.

"Mrs. Andersen," he said to Cathy, "I work for the Canadian authorities. Your employer, Michael Martin, is a fugitive from justice, wanted for murder in the U.S. Your mechanic, Layla Bouchiki-Floren is an Islamic radical, hell-bent on stealing your employer's money. She is in cahoots with Mani the steward, who is also an Islamic fundamentalist. There may be a third terrorist on board as well."

"You're right, there is." Mike was pulling the shotguns off their racks. "He was just beginning to interrogate me when the helicopter arrived."

"Step away from the shotguns, Mike," Lonsdale commanded. "Cathy, pick them up and bring them over to me with some ammo."

Cathy hesitated. Lonsdale leveled his pistol at her. "DO IT—NOW." Dazed, confused and terrified, she obeyed.

Layla could be heard moaning in the companionway: She was losing blood fast. In fact, she was dying.

Lonsdale was loading the shotguns when Selim's voice came over the intercom. "Layla to the bridge on the double. Layla to the bridge."

With the loaded shotguns under his arm Lonsdale went over to Layla who had somehow managed to pull herself up into a sitting position, her back to the stairs. Semi-delirious, she was babbling something in Arabic that Lonsdale did not understand. Her mouth was bubbling bloody froth. Opening her eyes wide, she looked into his, and began to whisper in English with fierce urgency driven by such intense hatred that Lonsdale recoiled. "The soldiers of Allah will triumph over the infidels. You shall see. Thy blood shall be tainted by animal blood and thy vomit shall mingle with that of millions of others like thee."

"What on earth are you talking about?" Lonsdale asked, leaning over her.

"Phylaxos, the secret weapon of mass destruction." She grabbed his hand and squeezed it so hard it hurt.

It was her final act.

Tuesday morning (cont'd)

With numerical superiority and surprise on their side Gal's team had no difficulty gaining control of The Shark.

A few minutes after eight, Dilbert steered Brooks' cabin cruiser over to the sportsfisherman. Stirling and Brooks, each carrying a case of beer, hopped on board Jabal's vessel. They were followed by Gal with a duffel bag slung over his shoulder.

Jabal and Hosni, who were securing their gear below in preparation for leaving, were faced with a *fait accompli* when they rushed back on deck: Gal was at the helm, the SAS men by the fishing chair, opening bottles of beer.

Brooks and Stirling, playing the drunken boors, began to sing "Waltzing Matilda" to drown out Hosni's angry protestations. When they came to the second chorus Stirling grabbed Hosni and Brooks Jabal. Gal pulled the shotgun from his duffel bag and trained it on the two struggling prisoners-to-be.

The melee was over in minutes, with Jabal and Hosni securely tied up and locked into The Shark's stateroom.

Under his direction, Brook's colleagues got The Shark ready to chase after La Pintada. Once they were underway Gal and Stirling searched the vessel, Mossad-style, that is to say inch by inch. Their efforts yielded Selim's fully-charged satellite telephone in the "on" position, two shotguns, an Uzi submachine gun (hidden in the head), plenty of ammunition and three cellular telephones with their memories intact.

At half-past eight they met in the pilothouse to check the workings of their newfound weapons and to plot the course they would take to catch up with La Pintada. Then they reported in by walkie-talkie.

They were ready to go and fully armed when, a quarter hour later, Lonsdale ordered them to chase after Martin's yacht.

They estimated they were five miles north of Grand Cayman, clipping along at twenty-five knots when, around nine fifteen they spotted the Mosquito Research Unit's helicopter making for them.

"Capo, this is Sport. Do you read?"

Gal pressed the walkie-talkie to his ear so hard it almost hurt. "This is Capo. I read you with difficulty—too much background noise."

"I have you visual Capo. Slow down. When, in two minutes, we start hovering over you, throttle back and I'll throw my gear down, aiming for the deck. Fish it out if I miss. Once you're done I'll jump into the sea and climb on board. Acknowledge."

Giugliani brought the helicopter down to less than twenty feet above the sportsfisherman. Cartwright's clothes, wrapped around his pistol and Lonsdale's binoculars, hit the vessel's afterdeck dead center; Cartwright himself splashed down about ten feet from the boat.

While toweling off he brought his listeners up-to-date on what happened at La Pintada and at The Wharf. "I can't be sure, but I think Edwards is dead."

"Who do you think is behind that?" Stirling asked.

"Martin is the most likely candidate."

"But how? He was on board his yacht, in plain sight of everyone."

Gal shrugged. "Remote controlled explosive, set off by radio from La Pintada's deck."

Silence, then: "What about Lonsdale?" Brooks asked.

"When I looked at La Pintada last he had disappeared below decks," Cartwright replied.

"Which means that, sooner or later, he'll have to fight three fundamentalists: the steward, the mechanic and the man who calls himself Sam Major, according to the passport we found here"

"And Martin," Brooks added in a low voice as he worked The Shark's helm and throttles to coax maximum performance out of the engines.

"I believe I wounded the steward." Cartwright went on, "He

dropped his gun and grabbed his shoulder just before we pulled away."

"Where's the chopper headed?"

"He's been ordered back to base. All aircraft in the vicinity have."

"How come?"

"Haven't you guys heard? Two commercial jetliners have crashed into the towers of the World Trade Center. Terrorism is suspected. All aircraft flying toward, in and around the North American Continent have been ordered to land immediately at the nearest airport."

"It's the fucking Arabs again," whispered Gal, his right cheek twitching. "I knew they'd try again after they failed the first time."

"When was that?"

"In 1997, if memory serves me right. When they tried to blow up the World Trade Center with a truck bomb in the parking garage."

"But those guys were caught."

Gal was shaking his head like a wounded animal and banging his fist on the control console. "I told them they would, I goddamn well told them over and over again."

"Told whom?"

The Israeli did not seem to hear the question: He just stood there like a stunned bull. Then he straightened his shoulders and turned to Brooks.

"How long do you figure before we catch up with La Pintada?"

"I estimate we've covered about eighteen miles since we started the chase three quarters of an hour ago. La Pintada has a forty-five minute head start—she left at eight sharp. Let's assume she's been underway for an hour and a half. At her speed that means thirty nautical miles. I calculate we're twelve miles behind her."

"And?" snapped Gal. He was raging mad and thirsting for revenge.

"We're going five knots faster than La Pintada." Brooks turned to Gal, his face expressionless. "If all goes well, we'll catch her in a couple of hours, provided..."

"Provided what, dammit?"

"We don't lose time having to look for her. We need that chopper to direct us to her in the straightest possible line."

Gal's eyes were blazing. "Hold the course we've chosen and push the engines as far as you dare. Turn on the radio real loud and get as much info on what's going on in the world as possible. Give me fifteen minutes in absolute privacy with those bastards below and I guarantee we'll have our chopper to guide us to Lonsdale."

Gal knew exactly what to do next, because he had been there before.

As a young man in Israel he had had frequent contact with all kinds of Arabs: Jordanian, Palestinian, Saudi, Syrian, Algerian—the lot. He knew from experience gained in the army and in the Mossad that one could not get anywhere with radicalized Arab Muslims unless one showed the same disregard for human life and civilized behavior as the Arab did. One had to be totally focused on physical violence—a difficult proposition for a liberal and educated Jew.

In the cabin Gal stepped over to Hosni, lying on his side in the port v-berth, ankles tied with rope, wrists manacled behind his back. A heavy-gauge fishing line drawn taut led from the flex-cuffs to the rope. Hosni was hog-tied like a steer.

The Arab looked up at Gal and spat at him. Gal smiled and wiped the spittle off his face. He turned to Jabal in the starboard berth, also shackled. "Showtime," he said to the Jamaican, sounding friendly, and broke the man's nose with a powerful punch, delivered with expert precision. Spitting blood, Jabal screamed, his eyes already beginning to swell closed. Gal grabbed him by the hair and yanked him out of his berth.

Jabal landed on his face, and screamed again. Gal cut the fishing line with the heavy scaling knife he had picked up in the galley and grabbed the flex-cuffs, pulling them upward, thereby forcing Jabal to stand up and back toward the cabin door behind the Israeli.

Gal kept pulling until Jabal's two arms were stretched high enough behind him to allow Gal to slip the flex-cuffs over one of two clothes hooks jutting from the cabin door.

The pain in Jabal's shoulder muscles, which had begun to tear, was almost unbearable. He tried to ease it by standing on his toes.

"What's the name of the man you guys rowed over to La Pintada during the night?"

No answer.

Gal pushed down on Jabal's shoulder.

"Sam Major," Jabal screamed.

Gal gave Jabal another push. "That's the name on his passport—a forgery. I want his real name."

"Ask him," said Jabal spitting blood toward Hosni who was watching, terrified. "It's his uncle."

"I'm asking you," observed the Israeli and tweaked his prisoner's broken nose. Jabal screamed again and fought hard not to lose his balance.

"I swear to Allah, I do not know."

"You said Allah, not God. Why?"

"Because I am a true believer."

"Of Islam?"

"Of Islam."

"Who are you working for?"

"Myself. I rent out my fishing boat for sports fishing."

Gal slapped the man. "I ask again, for whom are you working?"

Jabal was only semiconscious. The pain was pushing him into shock.

"His uncle." A nod toward Hosni.

"And who is his uncle working for?" Gal tapped Jabal's nose again.

A scream, but no answer.

Gal kicked Jabal's feet from under him, dislocating his shoulders.

He turned to Hosni. "Your uncle, who's he working for?" he asked in Arabic.

Hosni's eyes widened in shocked surprise, but he said nothing.

With a lightening fast blow Gal broke the Arab's nose. Hosni groaned in agony, but did not speak.

"You saw what I did to your comrade and I'm not even angry at him," Gal continued in Arabic. "I gave him a break because he is only a poor, misguided Jamaican, not one of the inner circle. But you, Hosni, are, I suspect, one of those dedicated infidel-hating sons of Islam with whom nobody can reason. Where were you trained, in Afghanistan or Palestine?" Gal tweaked Hosni's broken nose. Although scared out of his wits and in great pain, Hosni refused to cooperate: He said absolutely nothing.

"Come on, Hosni," Gal said almost kindly. "From your looks

and attitude I can tell that you are Algerian. Consequently, your uncle must be Algerian, too. What are you: preacher or combatant? You must have attended finishing school in one of the terrorist training camps. Am I right?" With a swift flick of the knife that he had picked up in the galley, Gal nicked the stern-faced Arab's neck deeply enough to make him bleed, but not enough to sever an artery.

That did it. "Afghanistan, Yehudi swine!" Hosni screamed at Gal at the top of his voice. "As Allah is my witness, I and my comrades shall not rest until we have wiped your filthy kind off the face of this planet!"

"Spoken like a true fighter, but of what? Hamas? Hezbollah? Islamic Jihad? Or Al Qaeda? Give your friends Bin Laden and Al Zawahiri my regards when you meet them in hell—as you will shortly." He turned away from the terror-stricken Arab and pulled Jabal off the hook. The barely conscious Jamaican collapsed at his feet. Gal stepped over him and left the cabin, locking the door from the outside.

He felt no remorse whatsoever for having behaved like a barbarian, an enraged animal, a throwback to prehistoric times. "An eye for an eye," he kept muttering in Hebrew, "an eye for an eye." He extracted a faded photograph from his wallet and kissed it: the picture of a happy, smiling young girl in her early teens—his kid sister—taken three days before she burned to death in a car bombing in Haifa, on her way home from school thirty years earlier.

Back in the saloon he immediately called Jim Morton on the satellite telephone at the emergency number Lonsdale had given him.

Tuesday midmorning, September 11

"The only way we can survive until help comes is by splitting up and making them waste time while they try to round us up," Lonsdale told Cathy and Martin. They were huddled on the bed in Mike's cabin.

"Why not stay here?" Mike sounded doubtful.

"Because this place only has one exit, which means that if we stay we're trapped. Coming after us one by one will take time and one of us might get a lucky break."

"What about my husband?"

"Last time I saw him he was on the bridge, at the controls, surrounded by the terrorists."

"One of whom is now dead." Mike turned on Lonsdale, eyes blazing. "Why the hell should I do what you tell me? I remember you now. You were at Fred Keller's trial, on Hauser's defense team. Who are you anyway, some sort of policeman?"

"I guess you can call me that. I work for the Canadian Passport Office on a contract basis from time to time." Lonsdale picked up his weapons and stood up. "We're out of time. When Layla doesn't show they'll come looking."

Mike was amazed. "You know her name?"

"Mr. Martin, I know all about you and your crew, but almost nothing about your stowaway."

"At least give me a shotgun," Mike begged.

Lonsdale removed two shells from one of the weapons and gave it to Martin. "You have one shot, so use it wisely. Make sure you don't shoot one of us. As for you," Lonsdale handed Cathy the other shotgun, "hide somewhere and give yourself up a couple of hours from now, but before you do, throw your shotgun overboard."

"Are you sure help will come?" The woman was working hard at conquering her fear.

"It's only a matter of time. The helicopter that brought me here has gone for help, but it will take at least two hours for help to get here."

Lonsdale left through the opening to the engine room, where he hid behind one of the airducts, Layla's pistol at the ready in his hand, Mani's pistol stuck into his belt.

In the pilothouse, Selim was doing his best to keep an eye on Andersen while attending to Mani's wound. He was in desperate need of another pair of hands.

"Layla, report to the bridge immediately," he repeated over the intercom, wondering what was keeping her. He had dispatched her to check on their prisoners locked in the main guest stateroom. But that had been some time ago.

Selim kept glancing at Andersen. The man seemed to be cooperating, checking their course, making steering corrections and fiddling with the throttles. From where Selim knelt he could not see that, in fact, the captain kept reducing La Pintada's speed gradually. He had worked out that help, which the Mosquito Research Unit's helicopter must by now have summoned, could only come from the closest inhabited island: Grand Cayman.

For a while he had even considered altering course toward the Caymans, but remembering the merciless hatred in Layla's eyes, had thought better of it.

Selim continued working on Mani's wound, dousing it with sulfa powder then bandaging it.

Still no Layla.

Something must have happened to her.

"Do you have the strength to steer?" he asked Mani.

"Yes," the steward whispered.

"I can't leave you my weapon so I'll have to tie up the captain before going to look for Layla." He secured Andersen's wrists behind his back, and tied him to a handgrip on the control console, then helped the unarmed Mani into the helmsman's chair and went to look for Layla.

Discovering her lifeless body at the bottom of the rear companionway shook Selim to the core.

How could his simple, well-prepared plan go so wrong so fast, perhaps even beyond redemption? Or was it still possible to get his scheme of acquiring Martin's Phylaxos shares back on track?

He stepped over the woman's body, cautiously opened the master stateroom's door and stepped inside, gun at the ready.

Empty.

There was no one in the cabin, or in the bathroom adjoining it. The gun rack was open, the shotguns and some of the ammo gone. His prisoners were not only free, but armed as well: in possession of the shotguns and Layla's pistol, and the weapon Mani had dropped.

Selim's anger rose as his preoccupation increased.

How could an armed, experienced, well-trained veteran of Layla's caliber allow herself to be overpowered by two unarmed amateurs?

Stupidity... crass, careless stupidity.

Selim was beside himself with rage. Frustrated in the extreme, he picked up the box of cigars on top of the night table and hurled it across the room against the mirror above the vanity. The mirror shattered.

By a box of cigars that was supposed to weigh almost nothing?

He went to investigate. The box of Tueros had split open, its contents of cigars, each in its individual tube, scattered. He picked one up. It felt heavy. He unscrewed the top, slid the cigar out, peeled off the aluminum foil wrapper and found himself looking at something very familiar: an explosive device filled with plastique, manufactured by the thousands in the Czechoslovak Socialist Republic.

Selim was forced to consider the possibility that Mike Martin could not be considered an amateur any more. To go chasing after him and Cathy alone would be foolhardy and could jeopardize the mission even more.

No. The smart thing to do was to adopt a defensive mode and await The Shark's arrival.

He separated the five explosive devices from the real cigars, put them in his pocket then went to join Mani in the pilothouse to help search the horizon for The Shark.

The time was ten o'clock in the morning.

CHAPTER FORTY-TWO

Tuesday, midmorning (cont'd)

Selim found Mani glued to the radio, beside himself with excitement. "What a coup! The soldiers of Allah are winning. Death to the U.S.A.!" His voice was hoarse from shouting. "Al Qaeda's fighters have struck a great blow against the American Satan. They are in the process of destroying the twin towers of Jewish evil at the World Trade Center in New York, and are bombing the Pentagon."

"Have you taken leave of your senses?" Selim was flabbergasted. "What are you babbling about? What's happening?"

Instead of answering, Mani turned up the volume and, for the next three quarters of an hour, they listened, mesmerized, to short wave broadcasts describing the events of the hellish attack.

At ten fifty Mani spotted a helicopter on the horizon aft of La Pintada. It seemed to be flying toward them, but then it turned away, much to the dismay of Captain Andersen who was suffering from severe fatigue brought on by the heat and great physical discomfort. Tied to the control console, he could not stand up or sit down and had, therefore, to remain on his knees when not squatting.

The appearance of the helicopter galvanized Selim into action.

The moment for The Shark to have appeared on the horizon was well past. He tried to raise the sportsfisherman by radio, but failed.

He could wait no longer: Mani was fading fast from loss of blood and the heat.

"Mrs. Andersen, your husband is in bad shape," he announced over the intercom system. "Let me tell you—and I know you can hear me—how bad. He has been forced to kneel or squat for the last two hours and he has terrible cramps in his legs. He is getting dehydrated and is very, very thirsty. His wrists are bleeding and his hands are swollen because of lack of circulation. In fact, they have started to turn blue. I'm afraid that, in this heat, gangrene might set in pretty soon unless you give yourself up and I cut him loose."

Hiding behind the air conditioning duct behind the port generator, Lonsdale checked his watch: ten fifty-seven. The Shark was due to appear on the horizon within the quarter hour and would catch up with La Pintada thirty minutes later. Her appearance would embolden the terrorists because Selim could not know that those on board her were no longer friend, but foe.

The time for Lonsdale to act was now—before Cathy Andersen abandoned her hiding place, before her husband's hands turned black, before Mike Martin was murdered without having been brought to justice.

He took off his sneakers and retraced his steps to Mike's cabin. Instead of entering, however, he sneaked up the companionway to the saloon. He crossed it on the run and dove under the dining-room table.

No sooner had he taken cover than he saw, through the legs of the chairs around the table, Cathy Andersen and Mike Martin tiptoe into the dining room. They had not taken his advice to split up.

Londale called out to them in a whisper and they dropped to the floor beside him.

"Mani and his leader are in the pilothouse with your husband, but I want to check on that. To divert their attention, Cathy will have to pretend that she's giving herself up. That's when we'll attack them."

Lonsdale crawled forward into the passage connecting the dining room to the galley, flattened himself against the steps leading from there to the pilothouse and, using Cathy's silver-coated sunglasses for a mirror, cautiously peeked into the room. Though the reflected image was not clear he could make out the bandaged Mani in the helmsman's chair with Andersen kneeling to his right and the third terrorist standing to Mani's left.

"Cathy, go to the afterdeck," Lonsdale commanded, "climb the ladder, work your way forward to the upper steering station, then start down into the pilothouse, calling out as loud as you can that you're giving yourself up. When we hear your shouts, Mike and I will rush the pilothouse—I from the galley side and Mike from the other. I'll take out the leader and Mike will shoot Mani. Is that clear?"

Cathy and Mike nodded.

Lonsdale took the shotgun from Cathy and gave her a gentle push. She started aft through the saloon. Mike followed her. To get into position he needed to work his way forward along the portside deck.

Lonsdale transferred the three bullets left in Mani's pistol to Layla's Beretta and stuck it in his belt. When Cathy began shouting, Lonsdale leapt to the top of the starboard stairs and dropped to his knee, ready to fire, but Cathy had by then come between Selim and him. He couldn't get a clear shot. At the same instant, Mike dashed into the pilothouse from portside.

Selim, whose reflexes were like those of a cat, shot Martin in the stomach, causing him to squeeze his shotgun's trigger. The blast mortally wounded Captain Andersen, who was crouching to the right of the unarmed Mani. Selim drew Cathy toward him as a shield against Lonsdale's fire and took aim. Cathy gave the Arab a shove and his shot hit Lonsdale above the left hip, only grazing the bone. The intense sear of pain made Lonsdale drop his shotgun. Selim was struggling with Cathy, trying to push her away. Lonsdale, his left side a flaming wall of agony, was blindly groping for his weapon when he heard Mani shout, "Look, look, The Shark."

Selim propelled Cathy away who stumbled toward her dying husband and fell. Selim kicked at Lonsdale's shotgun, which went sailing into the dining room. Lonsdale tried for the pistol in his belt, but he was too late. Selim was on top of him, his automatic's barrel pointing at Lonsdale inches from his head.

"You move a muscle and I kill you," Selim yelled.

Lonsdale raised his hands in surrender.

Selim stepped back. "Stand up slowly, the both of you, and hold your hands out." Lonsdale and Cathy obeyed and Mani tied their wrists with flex-cuffs.

Although he held himself in tight check, Selim was seething at being caught unaware. Where had the gunman come from? When did he board La Pintada? Did he drop down from the chopper—and if so, how come Mani had not spotted him?

"Lock the man up in your cabin," Selim commanded Mani. "The woman stays here." Mani pocketed Lonsdale's pistol and led him through the starboard passageway to the crew's quarters where he shoved him into a tiny cabin with no portholes. Lonsdale fell and briefly lost consciousness from the pain that engulfed him when his injured hip hit the floor.

He came to a few minutes later and fumbled around in the darkness until he found the light switch. He tried the cabin door.

Locked.

He unzipped his blood-soaked windbreaker gingerely and discovered that Mani had failed to search him. His walkie-talkie was still in his pocket.

He looked at his watch: eleven thirty.

Although every movement created its new agony, Lonsdale somehow managed to coax his walkie-talkie out of his windbreaker onto the lower bunk and switched it on.

"Capo, this is Tony. Do you read?"

CHAPTER FORTY-THREE

<u>Tuesday midday, September 11</u>

From his days with the Mossad Gal knew that getting hold of Jim Morton would be very difficult, given the stress under which he imagined the CIA's Counter-terrorism Division must be operating as a result of the chaos of the day.

He was right.

When the Duty Officer answered his call to the emergency number Lonsdale had given him he did his best to impart sufficient pertinent information to excite Morton's interest to the point where he would take Gal's call.

"Tell Jim Morton that the Snowman's friend is calling and that the Snowman has been captured by Al Qaeda terrorists whose whereabouts I know."

"Hold the line."

The Duty Officer was back in thirty seconds. "Where can we contact you?"

"You can't. Tell Morton I'll call again in exactly five minutes and to take the call."

"That's too soon."

"This is a Grade Red Emergency," Gal shouted. "I may not be able to contact you much later."

"Hold." A fifteen second pause. "Call back in fifteen minutes."

Gal did not get to speak to Morton before a quarter past ten. It then took ten minutes to bring Morton up to speed about Mike Martin, the whereabouts of The Shark and La Pintada, the shoot-out between Cartwright and the terrorists on board Martin's yacht, and the role the Mosquito Research Unit's helicopter had played in the chase.

"I need that same helicopter to show us the quickest way to La Pintada. I want to get to her before the Snowman has to handle the consequences solo."

Morton had other pressing priorities. "I want the telephones you captured, including the one you're talking on, so we can download the information they contain. I also want to speak with the stowaway."

"You mean Sam Major."

"His real name is Mourad Haouari, an Algerian."

"I knew it!" Gal exclaimed with deep satisfaction.

"But he goes under the *nom de guerre* of Selim," Morton continued, irritated by the interruption. "When do you expect to catch La Pintada?"

"If you can organize the chopper for us, by eleven thirty."

"Call me back in fifteen minutes."

Gal's next conversation with Morton at ten fifty-five was brief.

"For the record, what is your social security number?"

Gal told him.

"What are the initials of your first and last name?"

Gal told him.

"I now have adequate personal data to assign a code name for you, but for this operation only. Do you have any preference?"

"To avoid confusion use Capo."

"Capo it is," Morton confirmed and gave Gal a dedicated telephone number to call. "Now listen," Morton went on, "the chopper you requested is on its way and should reach you in ten minutes. It will guide you to your target and assist you in whatever way possible. When you reach your target do your best to achieve the following objectives: one, the capture, alive, of Selim; two, the capture, alive, of the steward and the female mechanic on board; three, the capture, alive or dead, of Michael Martin; four, the takeover of the target vessel; five, the rescue of the Snowman."

"In that order!?" To Gal, Lonsdale should have headed the list.

"Affirmative. I am sure the Snowman himself would have it no other way."

"Is that all?" Gal asked. He felt bitter, betrayed.

"No. In five minutes, that is to say, at 11:00 hours, a VTOL experimental aircraft, the Osprey, will take off from Guantanamo Bay with a platoon of SEALS and a four-man medical team. It is capable of vertical and horizontal flight and will be over La Pintada at 12:30 hours. It will assist you in attaining your objectives under the direction of Captain Philip Koenig."

"I hear you clearly." Gal was still smoldering. He was getting shafted and Lonsdale abandoned.

Morton sensed his anger. "Capo, I know how you feel. Remember, the Snowman is my friend, too, but, under the circumstances, I have no choice. It's war here. One final thing: I need those telephones badly, so be sure to give them to Captain Koenig immediately."

"Understood." Gal saw the helicopter appear on the horizon. There was an awful lot to do in very little time.

On board the helicopter Giugliani turned to his passenger, Major Ross Mackenzie, the Governor's aide, who, after taking Morton's call that morning, volunteered to accompany the Italian.

"That's The Shark." The pilot pointed downward and began his descent. "And *that*," he went on, indicating a yacht about five miles ahead of them, "is La Pintada. At this rate The Shark will catch her in less than half an hour."

Giugliani took a reading on La Pintada then fed the vectoring information to Mackenzie who leaned out of the chopper, bullhorn in hand. "Your target is heading north at 280 degrees," he called out to Gal. "Steer 260 degrees, repeat 260 degrees, and you'll catch her in less than thirty minutes. Switch to the 39.3 frequency on your radio and acknowledge."

"This is Capo in charge of The Shark," Gal replied on the indicated frequency. "Confirming I will steer two-six-zero degrees to intercept La Pintada at approximately 11:30 hours."

"This is the Research Helipilot. Will now return to base for fuel and return at intercept time, which is 11:30 hours."

Less than five minutes after Brooks brought The Shark's bow onto the indicated heading La Pintada appeared on the horizon. By eleven twenty the two vessels were only about a mile apart, and Gal, who kept switching back and forth between the radio frequency of the helicopter and the one used for general maritime communications, was receiving regular contact requests in Arabic from La Pintada, requests which, of course, he ignored.

At eleven twenty-five Gal switched on his walkie-talkie.

At eleven twenty-eight it squawked into life.

"Capo, this is Tony. Do you read?"

"This is Capo. I read you five-by-five."

"What is your position?"

"Approximately one half mile astern of La Pintada. And you?"

"I am disarmed and handcuffed and being held in the port forward cabin in the crew's quarters. There are six people on board: the terrorist leader, armed with a pistol; the wounded steward Mani, steering the yacht, also armed with a pistol; the captain's wife, Cathy, who is unarmed and manacled, probably on deck with the two terrorists. The captain has been shot and is dying—he's lying on the floor of the pilothouse. The female terrorist is dead. Mike Martin has been shot in the stomach and is also lying on the pilothouse floor. I am wounded. As best I can make out the bullet is lodged in the flesh just above the left hipbone, which is chipped. I'm not bleeding too much and I don't think any vital organs have been hit."

"Are you in pain?"

"Yes, but tolerable. I'm worried about Martin, though. He could die on us."

"Hang on, old friend. We'll storm the boat very soon."

"Be advised the terrorists also have two shotguns and spare ammunition. For all I know they may have—"

The rest of Lonsdale's words were drowned out by a high-pitched screeching sound from The Shark's engine room. Smoke began to billow from below.

Brooks disengaged the engine from the drive shaft and the screeching faded then stopped.

"The shaft bearing must have seized," he reported to Gal. "We may have lost our means of propulsion. I'm going below to investigate."

"Tony, this is Capo. Do you read?"

"Five-by-five."

"I acknowledge six on board, with one dying, one dead, two wounded, and two healthy, two pistols and two shotguns with ammo, possibly other weapons. Be advised we're having sudden engine trouble and must wait for the arrival of the helicopter to assist."

"What is its ETA?"

Gal looked skywards. "I can make him out. He should be above us within minutes."

"This is Tony. I'm switching off to save battery power. Will stand by every quarter hour and I suggest you do the same."

"I roger that, Tony. Next contact is at eleven forty-five. Be advised there's an amphibious VTOL hybrid aircraft on its way with a medical team and a platoon of SEALS on board. Their ETA is 12:30 hours. Hang in there; we're coming to get you. Capo out."

Tuesday afternoon, September 11

Through his binoculars Selim saw The Shark lose headway and stop in the water a few hundred yards from La Pintada. Then the helicopter came up on the sportsfisherman. Selim was amazed to see that, instead of opening fire with the Uzi, Hosni allowed the chopper to descend unharmed within feet of the vessel's afterdeck. Two men got into the painter that then left the sportsfisherman. The chopper followed it and lowered a length of rope the end of which the men in the painter took back to The Shark.

That's when Selim realized there were not two, but at least three men on board.

He made a desperate effort to raise The Shark again, this time in English. "This is La Pintada calling The Shark. I have wounded people on board and urgently need assistance. Please acknowledge."

Nothing.

Selim went at it again as he watched the men attach the rope to

The Shark's pulpit. "This is La Pintada. I need assistance. I have wounded on board."

The men finished attaching the rope then dashed aft and disappeared from view.

The chopper began to tow The Shark toward La Pintada.

All of a sudden Selim understood: Hosni and Jabal must have been overpowered, but by by whom? Police? Hijackers? Pirates? CIA, or worse: Israeli agents?

Merciful Allah, he'd never thought about *that* possibility. Maybe the man Mani trussed up and took below the man who had tried to shoot him was CIA—or, Allah forbid—Mossad.

And Selim had never interrogated him!

"Get the prisoner back on deck," he screamed at Mani then picked up the microphone again. "This is Selim, a Jihadist leader. I order the men on board The Shark to stop all hostile activities against La Pintada and to release my two comrades from captivity. Unless you obey my instructions I shall start executing the hostages I have on board."

He repeated the message in Arabic.

No answer from The Shark.

The helicopter began to bank away from La Pintada. The Shark followed.

Mani reappeared with the prisoner who seemed to be in great pain.

"We have no time for civilities," Selim told him. "Get on the radio and tell your men on The Shark to leave us alone, otherwise I'll start shooting."

"I have no idea what you're talking about."

"Like hell you don't. Do as I say or I'll shoot the woman." Selim cocked his pistol and pointed it at Cathy Andersen who was sitting on the deck, her back against the control console, stroking her dead husband's head in her lap. In shock, she was quite out of it.

Her sobs were heart-wrenching.

Lonsdale took the microphone from Selim. "Capo this is Tony. Do you read?"

"Go ahead, Tony."

"I'm in the pilothouse with two terrorists. One of them has a gun to the head of the captain's wife and is threatening to shoot her unless you do what he says." He handed the mike back to Selim.

"This is Selim, Capo. Why are you being towed by the helicopter?"

"Engine trouble."

"Where are my comrades?"

"Below deck."

"Are they hurt?"

"Not badly."

"Get them on deck. I want to talk to them."

Selim watched The Shark follow the helicopter in a lazy turn a couple of hundred yards off the starboard beam. When the sportsfisherman's bow was once again pointed toward La Pintada the chopper slowed.

"Selim, this is Capo. I have your comrades on deck."

"Let me talk to Hosni."

"This is Capo, Selim. Understand this clearly. You have two hostages and so do I. I know that your Norwegian mechanic is dead, as is the captain. The owner of La Pintada, Michael Martin, is seriously wounded and will die unless he gets immediate medical attention. Your associate, the steward, is also wounded. I propose you allow one of my people, a qualified paramedic, to attend to the wounded on board La Pintada. In exchange, let the woman go." Lonsdale was marveling at Gal's craftiness. He sounded so genuine that only someone who knew that help was on its way would realize Gal was only playing for time.

"You mean swap the woman for one of your men?"

"Yes—a paramedic."

"Let me speak with Hosni."

"OK."

Selim was deeply troubled. How did Capo know what was happening on board La Pintada? He lowered his pistol and spoke a few sentences under his breath to Mani in Arabic then picked up the microphone again. "Very well. Your conditions are acceptable. We shall continue our negotiations after the wounded are treated."

"Capo here, Selim. Before I put Hosni on, tell me how you propose we handle the exchange."

"Have the helicopter tow The Shark within a hundred meters of

La Pintada, her bow facing away from me. I will then back up. When we're within ten meters or so of each other you will put your paramedic and Hosni in your little lifeboat and attach a rope to it. The paramedic will row over to La Pintada and attach the boat to our swimming platform. After he and Hosni have climbed on board, the captain's wife will get into the boat and you will pull her over to The Shark."

"I thought we were doing a one-for-one swap."

"I've changed my mind. Your paramedic sounds too dangerous. By the way, he is to come over dressed only in his bathing suit."

"How about bandages, drugs and suchlike?"

"We have all that on board."

"I'm OK with everything you propose except Hosni. The swap has to be one for one."

Selim looked across to The Shark—she and the helicopter were getting too close for comfort.

"Capo, tell the helicopter to back away."

"Do you agree to deal one-for-one or not?" Gal's voice was sharp.

"I do." Selim gave in with a shrug. He had a hidden agenda anyway. "While Mani and Capo are maneuvering their boats into position I want to have a chat with you," he said to Lonsdale. "Sit down over there," he pointed to the settee along the port wall of the pilothouse, "and you," he waved at Cathy with his pistol, "sit beside him."

Cathy did so.

Lonsdale lowered himself into a sitting position with some difficulty and stole a glance at his watch—ten past twelve. The Osprey's ETA was in twenty minutes, if all went according to plan. He needed to play for time. "What do you want to talk about?" he asked Selim who was standing in front of him next to the groaning, semiconscious Mike Martin lying more or less where he had fallen when he got shot.

"What's your name?"

"Call me Lonsdale."

"Why did you come after me?"

"I didn't. I was after him." Lonsdale nodded toward Martin.

"Are you a policeman, Mr. Lonsdale?"

"Sort of. I work for the Canadian Passport Office."

"As a special agent?"

Lonsdale decided to strive for the upper hand. "No more questions. I need medical attention, not interrogation."

"It's on its way—as you heard."

"And after?"

"After what?"

Lonsdale gave Selim a withering look. "What are you going to do with us after the paramedic has finished? Take us to Cuba?"

"Maybe," Selim shrugged. "That depends on what Castro's attitude toward us will be now that we've shown what we're capable of."

"Who's 'us'?"

"Never mind."

"Are you one of the leaders?"

"In Central America, yes."

"What do you mean by showing what you're capable of?"

Selim struck his forehead with the palm of his hand. "I forgot. You're not aware of what happened in New York this morning, are you?"

Seeing the blank expression on Lonsdale's face Selim launched into a glowing account of the plane hijacking and the destruction of the Twin Towers. Lonsdale wanted him to go on talking as long as possible. Every minute that passed brought the Osprey nearer.

The squawk of the radiotelephone silenced Selim. "This is Capo. We're ready for the exchange."

Selim grabbed his prisoner's flex-cuff and jerked him to his feet. Lonsdale almost passed out from the pain. The terrorist then dragged him to the port side of the control console and tied him to the same handgrip to which Andersen was attached.

"If he tries anything funny, shoot him," he commanded Mani. "I'm going to the afterdeck. How do I communicate with you?"

Mani handed him one of a pair of walkie-talkies. "This is what we use to give the helmsman instructions from the foredeck about how to steer during a docking maneuver," he explained.

Selim took it, tested it, then grabbed Cathy by the arm and took her aft.

The time was twelve twenty.

Lonsdale was in a daze, stunned by the events in New York City, furious because he could do nothing to help—not Andersen, lying beside him, dead; not the people of New York, buried under tons of rubble; not those who would be killed by the wave of bioterrorism about to engulf the world. He continued to rage, not only against his own impotence, but also against his superiors' inaction in spite of his department's warnings that arming and financing the mujahedeen in Afghanistan back in the eighties would inexorably lead to a dangerous expansion of the Islamic Fundamentalist Movement.

What irony. In the name of God (Allah, Adona, call Him what you will), enlightened twenty-first century man was being forced into a medieval Holy War in which, as usual, both sides would claim Divine support and, therefore, argue that *their* cause was the just one.

And which side's cause is just? Lonsdale asked himself as he drifted into unconsciousness. "The side of freedom," he mumbled and passed out.

Tuesday afternoon, September 11 (cont'd)

Selim marched the handcuffed Cathy to the aft companionway where he tied her to the railing. Peeking out from behind the wet bar to port of the door leading to the afterdeck, Selim saw that The Shark's painter was being deployed with a man wearing a bathing suit and sneakers in it.

He turned on his walkie-talkie. "Back up some more, The Shark's too far," he told Mani in Arabic.

Mani reversed and La Pintada began moving toward The Shark. "Tell Capo to start the exchange procedure," Selim commanded. The man in the painter bent over his oars. "Keep backing up," Selim told Mani. The distance between the two yachts was now about thirty meters.

"Capo says he wants to see the woman," Mani reported.

"Tell him she'll show when the paramedic climbs on board La Pintada."

"Capo says that unless he sees the woman right away he'll abort."

"Tell him to give me thirty seconds." Selim cut Cathy loose from the railing and ordered her to show herself in the doorway.

The helicopter, which had been hovering just ahead of The Shark, began to pull the sportsfisherman away from La Pintada.

"Capo says we're getting too close. He wants the woman on deck before he'll let us approach any closer." Mani reported.

"Tell him I'll send her out in exactly two minutes and tell him to tell the paramedic to get ready to climb on board La Pintada as soon as he can."

With rope he had put in his pocket for this purpose, Selim hobbled Cathy so she could take only small steps. He extracted two explosive devices from his pocket, set their delays at one minute by twisting their tops counterclockwise as far as they would go and taped one of the devices to the back of Cathy's left thigh under her skirt, the other to her right. Then he taped her mouth shut.

"Start walking toward the swimming platform and stop when you get to the steps leading down to it," he ordered. "I'll be right behind you with my gun in your back, so don't get any ideas." Using her as a shield, Selim walked to the edge of the afterdeck.

"Tell Capo," Selim instructed Mani, "that we're going to back up some more. His man is to tie The Shark's painter to the swimming platform and let the woman climb into the boat. He is then to climb onto the swimming platform and proceed to the afterdeck with hands in the air. There I'll tell him what to do next."

Selim could hear Gal transmitting these instructions to Stirling in the painter via the bullhorn.

La Pintada backed up slowly.

Selim reached down and twisted the top of the device taped to Cathy's left thigh clockwise, thereby arming it. He did the same with the other. Then he instructed Mani to put the boat into neutral.

"Get into the little boat as fast as you can," he commanded Cathy. "Your life depends on being quick."

Cathy hobbled down the stairs and scrambled into the painter. Stirling swung on board La Pintada and untied the painter.

Selim spoke into the walkie-talkie. "Full speed ahead." Then he turned to his prisoner. "Keep your hands above your head and precede me through the saloon. When you come to the dining room table, stop and turn around slowly."

Selim was handcuffing Stirling's wrists behind his back in the dining area when the explosive devices went off. By that time, La Pintada was about fifty meters from The Shark. She suffered little damage.

Stirling was devastated. A glance out a porthole was enough to confirm his worst fears. The Shark had been blown up and his comrades with it.

Selim pushed Stirling into the cabin that had previously held Lonsdale and locked him in. Then he rushed back to the pilothouse to assess the situation.

About a hundred meters aft of La Pintada The Shark was aflame and settling in the water. Selim could imagine the sea pouring into her through the holes created by the explosion. It was a question of when rather than whether she'd go under. And when she went she'd take the helicopter with her: The aircraft, resting on its pontoons, its two occupants struggling to get out of their seats, was still attached to her by the towrope.

Selim put down his binoculars and looked around the pilothouse.

Lonsdale was lying on top of Andersen's body, feverish and fidgeting, begging for water and calling out in pain every time he moved. To Selim he seemed a coward—a wretch who posed no threat to anyone.

Martin was doubled up where he had fallen, groaning and cursing in semi-delirium. He wouldn't survive much beyond the time The Shark sank, which, Selim estimated, would happen within the half hour.

Mani, resting in the helmsman's armchair, was not in good shape either. The loss of blood, the heat, the excitement of the past thirty minutes, the pain and the effort to keep up with Selim's instructions had exhausted him. It was only the adrenaline created by the excitement of victory that was keeping him going.

Selim fetched him a couple of Tylenols and a large glass of cold water.

"Take it easy *habibi*, we're on our way to win. Give me a few minutes to figure out what needs to be done and then I'll spell you. Meanwhile, turn this boat toward Jamaica and put her on autopilot. After that we'll move these moaning, groaning sons of bitches out of here so you can get some rest."

The time was thirty-nine minutes past noon.

Tuesday afternoon (cont'd)

The devices strapped to Cathy's thighs exploded as Brooks and Cartwright were helping her to get on board. Both were killed instantly, as was Cathy. Hosni, who had also been on deck, was blown into the water; unhurt except for a mild concussion.

The Shark's afterdeck looked as if a giant can opener had cut it open at its center: her fishing chairs blown away, her engine below now damaged beyond repair. Smoke and flames were everywhere. Water was pouring into the hull through a hole under the engine mounting.

The force of the explosion was such that it caused the helicopter towing The Shark to buck forward, but, since it was restrained by the towrope, instead of rising, it was forced into a dive. First the aircraft's rotors hit the water, then the pontoons. However, the chopper had been no more than five meters above the sea when disaster struck; its occupants would survive.

Gal, at the helm when the explosion ripped through the vessel, had been near enough to feel the blast, but far enough not to be killed by it. Stunned for a few moments, he recovered quickly and grabbed the radiotelephone. To his surprise, it was still working.

He switched to the emergency channel. "Mayday, mayday, this is The Shark sportsfisherman about thirty nautical miles dead north of Grand Cayman. I'm on fire caused by an explosion. Over."

"Shark, this is the Osprey," a reassuring voice boomed at Gal. "I have you visual. Go to frequency 39.9 and recontact."

"Osprey, this is Capo. We have been attacked and destroyed by a group of terrorists on board La Pintada. Over."

Gal could not believe his eyes. La Pintada had turned around and seemed to be heading directly toward him. Was she coming back to lend assistance or to finish them off?

He soon had his answer: Halfway through her turn La Pintada veered off and headed south.

"This is the King." Gal understood he was talking to Captain Koenig. "I am aware of your mission. We will land our people in your immediate vicinity within five minutes. Hold out until then."

Gal saw the Osprey above him slow down, then, as she rotated her engine nacelles from horizontal to vertical, stop in midair—an incredible sight. The aircraft descended to a few feet above sea level. Its contingent of SEALS completed the launching of their Avon rubber dinghies in seconds. One team plucked Gal and Morton's precious telephones from The Shark moments before she sank, the other rescued Giugliani and the injured Major Mackenzie from the helicopter.

On its way back to the Osprey the first team fished Hosni out of the water. He had been lucky: Gal had brought him on deck to speak with Selim and had manacled his hands in front of him, so he was able to keep himself from drowning.

Jabal could not be found.

The entire operation took less than twenty minutes.

With its rescued passengers safely on board and under medical care, the Osprey lifted off, giving the astonished Selim, watching through his binoculars on board La Pintada six miles away, the impression that he was home free.

At twenty thousand feet the Osprey leveled out for its pre-arranged rendez-vous with a refueling tanker from the Pensacola Naval Base that was waiting for it it just off Swan Island.

After taking on board about four tons of aviation fuel—enough for five hours flight—the aircraft set off to chase down La Pintada, launching its team of SEALS once more, this time to free Stirling and Lonsdale and to capture Martin, Mani and Selim.

* * * * *

Stirling, who never went anywhere on "business" without his SAS survival kit, had made extensive preparations prior to embarking on his mission to rescue Lonsdale.

From the kit, which he kept in his duffle bag with the rest of his gear, he selected three items: a flexible diamond-studded wire saw that looked like a piece of shiny string; a small scalpel; and a length of thin rope that was, in fact, almost pure *plastique* explosive.

He made an incision in the heel of his left sneaker, inserted the scalpel and partially sealed the hole with Krazy Glue. He used surgical adhesive from The Shark's first aid box to fasten his BIC lighter to his inner thigh next to his genitalia.

With the drawstring of his boxer-style bathing suit he drew the wire saw into the channel provided for the drawstring itself. When the end of the wire saw reached halfway around the waist, he made a hole in the channel and pulled some of the wire saw and drawstring out. He detached the wire saw from the drawstring and tied the explosive rope to the drawstring. Then he pulled the rope through the channel until its end appeared at the front of the bathing suit.

He tied the ends of the explosive rope and the wire saw into a bow at the back, put on his bathing suit, tightened this improvised belt and tied the rope and the wire into a bow, this time, at the front.

Then, as instructed, he rowed over to La Pintada.

His gamble to smuggle his 'tools' on board Martin's yacht paid off. In the confusion caused by the explosion Selim had neglected to search him.

No sooner had he been locked into the cabin than Stirling had gotten down to work.

Since his hands were manacled behind his back he undid the rear bow on his 'belt,' let his bathing suit fall and stepped out of it. Having extracted the wire saw, he looped it around the flex-cuffs and, holding the saw between index finger and thumb of each hand, began the laborious task of cutting through the flex-cuffs.

This took fifteen minutes.

He rummaged around the cabin and found a T-shirt, a windbreaker and a pair of jeans that he put on. Next he pulled the scalpel out of its hiding place and cut a three-inch piece off the explosive cord, which he stuffed into the cabin door's keyhole, except for a half inch fuse that he lit with his lighter.

The lock blew and Stirling was out the door in a flash, scalpel at the ready. His luck held. The roar of the departing Osprey's engines had drowned out the noise of the explosion.

Stirling tiptoed into the dining room and crawled under the table. His hand encountered a hard object: the Beretta Lonsdale had emptied and discarded prior to attacking the pilothouse.

He checked the weapon: no bullets, but useful for bluffing.

He was contemplating his next move when two men, carrying a

third, struggled down the stairs from the pilothouse and dumped their cargo into the forward port corner of the room.

It was the semi-delirious Michael Martin, his hand clutching his middle, a mass of blood.

Stirling watched him for a few seconds trying to determine the gravity of his condition. He was about to crawl aft into the saloon, but before he could get started Lonsdale appeared, with an Arab holding a gun to his back. He was hurting; his captor knew and reveled in it. He kept punching Lonsdale in his wounded left side, making him grunt with pain.

After counting to ten Stirling crawled over to the opening leading from the dining-room into the saloon just in time to see the Arab disappear down the aft companionway.

What next?

Stirling decided to head in the opposite direction, toward the door leading to the starboard deck.

He was outside on the deck in seconds moving aft as fast as he could. When he reached the afterdeck he worked his way around the corner, and, on his belly, crawled to the opening leading to the aft companionway area. There he found Lonsdale with his hands behind his back, manacled to the companionway railing. He was about to go to his aid when he saw Selim emerge from below and give Lonsdale a contemptuous jab in the side.

"I'll leave you here to moan and groan for the time being," Stirling heard Selim say, "and to contemplate your handiwork," he pointed to Layla's body. "When I'm good and ready, I'll come and fetch you and we'll continue our little chat." For good measure Selim kicked Lonsdale in the side. Lonsdale fainted.

Selim then went forward to the pilothouse.

Stirling cut Lonsdale loose and revived him with water from the wet bar.

"Martin is in pitiful shape," Lonsdale managed to mutter, massaging his swollen hands and wrists. "Unless we do something about him he'll die soon."

"Why haven't the men on the Osprey rushed La Pintada?"

"I guess the aircraft had to refuel; it's at least five hundred miles from here to GITMO."

"How's your wound?"

"I think infection has begun to set in, but it doesn't hurt that much."

Stirling was surprised. "How come? You sounded in agony when Selim marched you down here."

Lonsdale managed a feeble grin. "Don't you remember your training days? Always act more fragile in front of your captors than you really are."

Stirling grinned back in relief. "I'll start a fire in the saloon that will bring Selim and Mani running. We'll jump them when they get here."

Lonsdale shook his head. "First we need to get hold of some weapons. I see all you have is a scalpel."

"I've also got this, but it's empty." Stirling shoved Lonsdale the Beretta. "I found it under the dining-room table."

"Let me see if I can find some bullets."

Lonsdale climbed down to Layla's stiffening body and searched her. Sure enough, there was a spare clip for the Beretta in her windbreaker's pocket. He entered Martin's cabin, curious about why Selim had visited it a few minutes before. His answer lay on the top of the dresser: a half-empty pack of batteries. Selim needed power for some kind of electronic equipment: a watch? a computer? a camera?

Lonsdale grabbed a bunch of shotgun shells, joined Stirling in the saloon and gave him a few shells and the spare clip for the Beretta. "Selim is up to no good. He's got some kind of electronic gizmo for which he just fetched some batteries from Martin's cabin."

Stirling was in the process of placing whatever was left of the explosive cord under the pillows of the saloon's sofa. "Marvelous stuff this," he observed. "It acts as a fuse when deployed as a single strand, but knead it together into a bit of a mass and it becomes a powerful explosive." He was going to light the end of the cord hanging out from under the pillow, but Lonsdale stopped him.

"We still need some sort of a weapon for me."

"How do you propose to acquire one?"

"When Selim and Mani smell the fire they will probably come running, as you suggest, and leave their shotguns in the pilothouse. We can double back there after you've set the fire and grab the guns."

Stirling lit the fuse. Then they worked their way for'ard on their fours along the starboard deck and hid in the space leading from the dining room to the galley.

Lonsdale, whose wound had, in fact, begun to throb painfully, started to feel weak and thirsty, but willed himself to go on.

Within minutes they could smell smoke.

So could Selim.

CHAPTER FORTY-FOUR

Tuesday afternoon (cont'd)

Selim saw thick black smoke billowing from the far end of the saloon—the furniture was in flames. "Quick, the fire extinguisher," he yelled to Mani and sprinted aft. Mani followed, clutching his shoulder.

In two bounds Stirling was in the pilothouse. He grabbed the shotguns lying on the couch and checked them. One was empty, the other fully loaded. He threw the empty one to Lonsdale, who inserted three shells and then returned to the space leading to the galley, positioning himself at the top of the forward companionway. From that vantage point he could control access from the lower deck to the upper deck, entry from the starboard deck to the pilothouse and attack from abaft through the saloon and the dining room.

Meanwhile Stirling established himself to port of the helmsman's chair where he could cover the three access points to the pilothouse: the steps from the portside deck, the steps from the galley and the steps from the upper steering station.

Selim saw at a glance that only the pillows were on fire. He let Mani combat the flames and, once the thick smoke cleared, went to check on Lonsdale. The cut flex-cuffs lying on the floor told him all he needed to know. The paramedic, who must have somehow managed to get out of the cabin, had set Lonsdale free.

But how, damn it—how? From the moment Lonsdale had appeared, as if out of nowhere, Selim had begun to panic. How could both he and Mani have missed him jumping from the chopper?

Never mind—Lonsdale had no weapon.

Then it dawned on Selim that he had been suckered. The fire had been a ruse to get him out of the pilothouse. While he and Mani were putting out the flames, Lonsdale and his comrade must have doubled back on the outside and were now in possession of Mike Martin's shotguns.

So be it then: a fight to the finish, without mercy!

When Selim and Mani were dragging the unconscious Mike Martin into the dining room, something that looked like a small camera had fallen out of the Canadian's pocket. After a closer look Selim had recognized it for what it was: a remote control trigger.

He had re-examined the explosive devices remaining in his pocket and discovered that two of the three could be detonated at a distance.

There and then he had made up his mind: If all else failed, he and Mani would take to the life rafts and blow La Pintada up from afar, if possible with the inevitable enemy boarding party on board. In preparation, he had armed and placed one of the remotely operable devices in the drawer of the chart table situated on the portside of the pilothouse. He now placed the other in the drawer of the vanity in Martin's master stateroom.

Selim took the remote out of his pocket and turned it on. Then he called out to Mani in Arabic. "The infidels are in the pilothouse and have our shotguns. Go to the upper steering station; there's a fire ax there. Take it and work your way forward to the windows of the pilothouse on the starboard side. I'll be doing the same on the port side. On my signal, smash one of the side windows with the ax. Our enemies—there are two of them—will turn and open fire on you. I'll jump down the stairs leading from the upper steering station into the pilothouse and shoot them while they have their backs to me."

The voice in Lonsdale's head was apprehensive. *You don't know what's happening on deck*, it kept repeating, which made him very nervous because it was dead right. Though he and Stirling controlled the nerve center of the vessel they were vulnerable from the outside.

Lonsdale heard a thump above his head, then another. He stepped outside, looked around and seeing no one, rushed forward. There was a crash and a tinkling of glass, followed by a shotgun blast and small arms fire. He looked up: Mani was squatting on the pilothouse cover, holding on to the handle of a very large ax with its head embedded in one of the pilothouse's windows.

Lonsdale raised his shotgun and fired. Mani let go and rolled off the cover, landing at Lonsdale's feet with a thud.

Lonsdale fired again, blowing Mani's face away.

Spattered with blood, his wound throbbing, Lonsdale took the dead Arab's pistol then retreated into the space from which he had just stepped out and came face to face with Selim who was in the process of reloading his Beretta at the top of the stairs.

Lonsdale pulled the trigger a third time. The blast caught Selim's left thigh, shredding it. He dropped his pistol and tumbled down the stairs after it.

Stepping aside, Lonsdale kicked the pistol away, threw down the empty shotgun and aimed Mani's gun at his adversary's head.

"Move a muscle and I'll kill you," he mimicked.

The terrorist's face distorted into a grotesque grin. "You mean we'll kill each other."

"Not bloody likely."

Lonsdale stepped closer, his finger on the trigger.

"That's close enough," Selim screamed. "I have my finger on a remote detonator in my pocket. You shoot me and my dying reflex will be to press down. That will blow you, me and this boat into a million pieces." He withdrew his hand from his pocket and showed Lonsdale the remote. "Now drop your gun."

"I will do no such thing," Lonsdale screamed back. "First, I don't believe you; second, you're not the only one who's willing to die for a cause. Give up and at least save yourself. My rescuers will be here soon."

"What rescuers?" Selim was getting weak from the loss of blood and had difficulty concentrating.

"The aircraft you saw landing near The Shark it will be back in minutes. It's just gone to refuel."

"Where?"

Lonsdale pointed upward with his thumb. "With a tanker circling above us."

Selim looked up into the sky through the door and Lonsdale shot him between the eyes.

The dying terrorist pressed down on the trigger, but nothing happened. He had forgotten or not known about the twenty-second delay built into the explosive device.

Nor did Lonsdale, but he had to take the gamble.

He raced into the dining room, and dragged Martin toward the forward exit. He got as far as the starboard deck railing when first the device in the pilothouse and, three seconds later, the one in Martin's cabin went off.

Because the first explosion originated on the port side of the pilothouse, at a level about five feet above his head, and because the walls of the pilothouse and the passageway deflected the force of the blast, neither Martin nor Lonsdale was maimed by it. The second explosion was, of course, too far to wound. However, it did punch a hole in La Pintada's hull, just below the waterline, and demolished the partition between the Master Stateroom and the engine room running from the aft companionway to the starboard side of the hull.

At once, La Pintada's stem started to settle as the sea flooded the Master Stateroom. From there, the water spilled into the engine room and the vessel began to list to starboard. Lonsdale tried to pull Martin for'ard, but the going became very tough as the yacht's bow lifted.

From the corner of his eye Lonsdale saw the Osprey touch down and start deploying its contingent. Beyond pain, he pushed and clawed his way to the foredeck, dragging Martin after him, and propped him against the port anchor capstan.

Next, Lonsdale slithered and skipped back into the pilothouse to check on Stirling.

The SAS man was dead. The blast had ripped him apart.

The backward tilt of the hull was, by now, quite steep and Lonsdale had to fight hard to make headway. In agony, he managed to reach Martin again.

Blood was everywhere—some of it Lonsdale's, some of it Martin's.

The list to starboard increased and Lonsdale could see the sea rising toward the gunwale. He also noticed shark fins in the water: the blood and noise had attracted the vicious predators lusting for the opportunity to get at their bleeding victims.

One of them tried to reach Lonsdale, but couldn't; the gunwale was not under water yet.

Then something gave within the hull and La Pintada lurched to starboard some more. The bow rose and Lonsdale had to hang on to the capstan with all his might while jamming Martin against the anchor chain to stop him from sliding away.

The bow settled and the water rose: The sea began to wash over the gunwale.

There was a burst of machinegun fire somewhere behind Lonsdale and he saw one of the sharks start to trail blood.

Then something hit Lonsdale on the head from behind and he let go of the capstan, of Martin, of life itself and he sank into an abyss of pain.

The nurse was very pretty—a dead ringer for Adys. Lonsdale tired to tell her that he loved her, but his mouth was full of broken glass and he couldn't make a sound without hurting himself. Then the pain stopped because somebody had taken a huge weight off his left side; in fact, it seemed as if his entire body had become weightless.

He opened his eyes and found that he could see, but before he could focus he fell asleep.

He awoke again after many hours of deep, drug-induced sleep and found himself in a hospital bed. Adys was sitting beside him, stroking his hand, weeping.

"Welcome back sweetheart," she murmured, and kissed him. "I love you. I was so frightened."

"I love you, too," he whispered. "Forgive me for having given you such a scare again. Where am I?"

"At JFK Memorial Hospital in Palm Beach."

"What day is it?"

"Thursday, my darling."

Adys pressed the bell and a doctor appeared, accompanied by a nurse.

"Good evening, Colonel," he said to Lonsdale. "How are you feeling?"

"My left side is terribly sore and I ache all over. I'm thirsty, woozy and tired. Other than that, just dandy."

"We removed a bullet from above your left hipbone. The bone was chipped, but the damage was minor. It will heal. We've checked for fractures and injuries elsewhere, but found none. You were lucky; the bullet hit no vital organs."

"How long will I take to recover?"

"I'd say four to six weeks depending on the physical shape you're in."

"Can I go home tomorrow?"

"Tomorrow no, that's out of the question."

Lonsdale turned to Adys. "Where is Reuven?"

"He's been pacing back and forth outside your door, waiting all this time for you to wake up."

Lonsdale sighed with relief; he had no idea of who had died, who survived, who was wounded or who got away.

"Could I see him now?"

The doctor nodded. "Just for a few minutes."

Gal's visit was charged with emotion. The almost euphoric relief both men had felt when they saw each other was profound, but muted by Gal's account of how Cathy, Cartwright and Brooks had been murdered.

"We were damned lucky," Gal whispered and squeezed his wounded friend's arm with great emotion. Though a man of deep and powerful feelings, he found it difficult to verbalize affection.

"What about Martin?"

"The sheriff's office is holding him in the prison hospital. He lost a lot of blood and infection set in, but he's expected to make a full recovery."

"Has he said anything about Phylaxos?"

"On the advice of his attorney he's not talking."

"What about his wife?"

"I've notified Jackson, the Toronto lawyer, about us capturing Martin alive."

"Barely."

"You said it. The operative word is 'barely.'" Pensive, Gal was nodding his head. "It was a close call."

"A very close call, far too close." Lonsdale turned away, crying freely.

* * * * *

EPILOGUE

Robert Lonsdale, formerly Bernard Lands, was discharged twelve days after having been admitted, a Sunday. He flew back to Washington with Adys in an Agency plane Morton had graciously placed at their disposal.

Home at last, they feasted on his favorite Sunday evening snack: smoked salmon with onions, lemon wedges and capers served on toasted Montreal-style bagels slathered with cream cheese.

They were watching the sunset from their terrace and having coffee when the telephone rang.

"How do you feel, sport?" It was Jim Morton.

"Getting better fast. Thanks for the bus ride up."

"Hey, just call me Jim Greyhound. You busy?"

"At the moment?"

"No. Six weeks from now. What do you think?"

"Well, we're just finishing our coffee. Would you like to join us?"

Morton was there in ten minutes.

"Jim, I don't know how to thank you for saving my life yet again," Lonsdale told his old friend after they had shaken hands. "I owe you...."

"You mean that?"

"Absolutely, I do. How can I help you?"

Morton took a sip from the cup of coffee Adys had handed him.

"Robert, I'm in deep trouble. As director of the Agency's Counterterrorism Division I am being held responsible for not providing advance notice of what Al Qaeda was planning for September 11. The White House needs a scapegoat, and I may very well end up being sacrificed."

"Jesus! That's totally unfair, I remember all the occasions when you stuck your neck way out to protest the Administration's policy favoring the Agency's training and arming the Afghani Mujaheddeen." Lonsdale was upset and sounded it. "You always said the fundamentalists were fanatics who, in the end, would spin out of control and attempt to terrorize the West into submission.

"You warned the Wise Men about Al Qaeda as far back as the mid-nineties if I remember correctly," he continued, punching the air with his index finger for emphasis. "What more do they want from you now that they're been exposed publicly for the fools that they are?"

In spite of his anger, Lonsdale was hardly surprised. He had so often, during his career with the massive bureaucracy that was the Agency, witnessed how the large institution reacted when, as a result of the monumental incompetence of its politically appointed leaders, it failed to achieve what it was being tasked to accomplish.

Morton nodded. "You're right, Robert, but, just now, nobody listens to reason at the office. The pressure is intense. I've been managing on less than a couple of hours' sleep since September 11. We're desperately short of well-trained, experienced, multilingual field officers."

"What are you trying to tell me, Jim?" Lonsdale was becoming more and more apprehensive. This was not the effusive and self-confident Jim Morton he was used to.

Morton gave him a bitter smile. "Look, I obviously can't make you do anything against your will—and, of course, Adys also has a thing or two to say now—but I do need to have you back at the Agency again and soon, dammit."

Lonsdale was floored.

"Come on Jim, after you've pensioned off so many like me ten years ago and replaced us with cameras, spy planes and other kinds of whiz-bang machinery? No way! I wouldn't want to go through all the backstabbing again in addition to having to risk my neck in the field."

Morton's face flushed red. "I admit we've made mistakes, Robert, lots of 'em in retrospect, but before the shit hit the fan, we figured we'd be able to run the ship the way the White House wanted. Didn't work out. Now we've run out of time. We need men like you again—trained, experienced, with proven loyalty—to come back to Langley NOW. I don't want to beg, but I have no choice. I'm asking you, as a personal favor, to help us out for at least the next six months."

Lonsdale looked at Adys then back at his old friend and shook his head. "No sale, Jim. Look at me. I'm really too old for all of this. Besides, I've paid my dues. I have a business to run. I can't start up again now."

Morton closed his eyes and said nothing for a while. He looked suddenly old and bone weary. What he said next upset Lonsdale even more.

"Well, I wish that was all there was to be concerned about. I hate like hell to lay this on you so soon after what's happened, but after we fished Hosni out of the sea, we subjected him to intensive interrogation. After a few days he told us that Selim's people in Hungary were on the verge of shipping contaminated surgical glue to Iraq for bottling and distribution throughout the West. We asked our British friends to send a contingent of SAS men to Budapest from Banja Luka in Bosnia, to grab it before it was too late."

"Well, that's close enough. Piece of cake. Less than four hundred kilometers from the Hungarian capital, as the crow flies."

"As you say," Morton nodded glumly, "as the crow flies. They were to take possession of the contaminated glue and the vaccine Moscovitch was developing, and to persuade Moscovitch to return to Canada for his own safety. Robert, the mission failed."

"Say again?" Lonsdale was suddenly keenly alert.

"The glue, the vaccine and Moscovitch have all disappeared."

Lonsdale was stunned into silence.

Morton poured himself another cup of coffee and went on, hands ever so slightly trembling. "We don't have a single senior, experienced Hungarian-speaking agent in all of Europe," he continued, sounding discouraged in the extreme. "We did ask the local authorities to help, but I'm afraid our evaluation of them is that they are pretty inept."

Morton stood up and faced Lonsdale. "Robert, we need you to locate the Phylaxos virus before Saddam Hussein gets hold of it and tens of thousands more people die as a consequence. Believe me, the new virus is very much a potential weapon of mass destruction."

So there it was, all laid out in the open. The Agency, which had shunted him aside after almost three decades of faithful service during which he had been manipulated, humiliated, betrayed and lied to countless times, was now pulling him back in, baiting the hook with the fate of his good friend Jim Morton in exchange for Lonsdale's services for God only knows how long!

"No wonder we've all become so cynical," Lonsdale raged. "There is no safe haven, no respite, nowhere to turn, without getting hurt." But they sure do know their own, he conceded to himself silently. *Save Morton, save Western civilization—together we can do it, just come back in.*

In a pig's eye!

He turned to the woman he had come to love and trust so completely, so quickly, and whom he had already betrayed twice by exposing himself to extreme danger.

She shrugged, sighed and then nodded.

"I know what you are thinking *querido,* but life goes on. The privilege of deciding where and when to measure up is not always given to us. You must confront—we must confront together—our duties and responsibilities as they are thrust upon us. *Eso es la vida, mi amor. Eso es la vida.*"